PADDY DOYLE'S HAT

By

January Jones

Published by New Generation Publishing in 2017

Copyright © January Jones 2017

First Edition

The author asserts the moral right under the Copyright, Designs and Patents Act 1988 to be identified as the author of this work.

All Rights reserved. No part of this publication may be reproduced, stored in a retrieval system or transmitted, in any form or by any means without the prior consent of the author, nor be otherwise circulated in any form of binding or cover other than that in which it is published and without a similar condition being imposed on the subsequent purchaser.

www.newgeneration-publishing.com

 New Generation Publishing

Introduction

Year 10 History Project

for Mr. Briggs

Family Politics - a study of how an ordinary family was affected by events between the First and Second World Wars

By

Maria Sutton

The project is based on letters, newspaper cuttings, etc. from my Great Grandmother's memory box

> Very good Maria, if a bit brief.
> B+ Well researched
> It would be interesting to know how
> the facts in these documents coincide
> with what really happened

'Grandad, you promised that if you were still alive when I was eighteen, you would explain all those letters and things that Grandma gave me for my project.'

The old man stubbed his cigarette out into bowl of hyacinths on the table by the side of his chair and looked quizzically at Maria. 'And what letters and things would those be?'

She had been expecting the old man to be difficult. She reached into the hold-all resting against her chair and pulled out a battered, school folder. 'You remember. Years ago. Grandma gave me a box of old papers for my Year Ten history project. There was a big family row. You were furious with her when she said that they weren't important any more. They were just a load of old junk that great grandma had kept under her bed:

Granny said that the letters and newspaper clippings were all history now. You tried to take them back, but I wouldn't give them up. Then you wouldn't let her tell me what they were really about. In the end you said you would, when I was old enough.'

'And you think you're old enough now?' the old man demanded in a voice that was only just teasing.

'I'm eighteen; I'm old enough to vote, to get married and fight in a war.'

'Eighteen,' he echoed, half closing his eyes, as he looked out of the window across the garden. For a moment he forgot her and was caught up in nostalgia, which is all old men have left. *What is eighteen years? Less than a quarter of a lifetime* he thought, then added aloud, 'perhaps I'll wait until you're a little bit older.'

'Grandad, you promised.' Maria was very fond of the cantankerous old man, but he did make her cross sometimes.

'Ask your Grandmother.' He muttered and began to shuffle around, looking for his tobacco pouch to roll himself another cigarette.

A sadness tinged the young girl's voice, the old man

sometimes forgot that his wife had been dead for more than three years. 'Grandad, you know I can't. I asked her before she died, but she wouldn't say. She said I had to ask you. Dad knows, but he won't say; you know what he's like. Mum would tell me, but she doesn't know the story. Do you want to take the secret with you to your grave?'

'What a nosy little girl you are,' he muttered. 'It might be better if I did. You might not like what you hear.'

'Grandad,' she shouted. Infuriated with him, she thrust the green cardboard folder onto his lap. 'Tell me, or I won't bring you anymore tobacco in. I'm not supposed to anyway, the doctor's told you to stop smoking.'

'All right, all ready, my life,' he said, pretending to give into the threat. He had already made up his mind to tell the story. After all, what did it matter now? It was only to prolong his granddaughter's suspense a little longer that he drew out a cigarette paper from its packet and slowly sprinkled a thin line of tobacco along the valley. Having rolled it, he raised it uncertainly to his lips to seal it and tried several times to light it. Peering at her from under his shaggy eyebrows, he asked. 'Light my cigarette for me, there's a pet. I'm too old to stop now.'

Maria took the old fashioned cigarette lighter out of his gnarled fist, his fingers weren't strong enough anymore to quickly flick the wheel on the top. She flicked once, twice, it sparked but didn't light the wick sticking from the top of the old cartridge case. 'Why don't you get a new one?' she demanded. 'This old thing keeps breaking my nails.'

'Oh, it'll see me out,' he replied.

She tried again, and again and eventually it spluttered into flame. He took the lighter from her and let it play over the cigarette end, while he drew hard. The effort of taking deep breaths sent him into a spasm of coughing, but the tobacco in the narrow rickety roll began to smoulder.

'Pass me my reading glasses,' he said, nodding towards the table.

Maria picked a pair up and went to hand them to him

'No not those, they're my television glasses. The ones

near the paper.'

Having been given the right glasses and fitted the old fashioned spectacles over his nose, he began to study the folder. 'I'm glad to see you that you got a good grade for this,' he mused looking at the *B+ Well Researched* scrawled on the front cover.

Slowly his shaking hand opened the folder and he looked at the first page. He chuckled quietly. There was a picture of him as he was sixty years ago. Dark and brooding eyes peered out suspiciously from under the brim of an old black beret, resentful of whoever was taking his photograph. He couldn't remember any more who it was. Probably his dad, he thought, with the little Box Brownie they had for years.

'I wonder what happened to that hat?' he mused.

'Knowing Granny, she probably threw it away,' Maria said. 'You know what she was like.'

He nodded and turned the page, but in his heart he knew that she would never have thrown that hat away. It was in the bottom of a drawer somewhere. He'd look it out when he got home. He sighed and glanced around him, *if he ever got home*.

On the next page there was a letter pasted, above the spidery writing of a fourteen-year-old. An odd place to start, he thought, but, it was her project.

Chapter 1

Dear Alice,

It's been that sort of week. On Friday, the washing I did for Mrs. Weeks was hanging out to dry and the line broke. I did most of it again, but there was some mud on a pair of her drawers. She wouldn't pay and said she wouldn't use me again and we're so broke.

On Tuesday we had some terrible news down our street, Florrie Higgin's youngest boy Maurice was knocked down by a bus and killed. Cathy Fuller's husband works at the bus garage, and she told me that it went right over his back. The awful thing was that he was stuck between the wheels and they couldn't get him out. They say he drowned in a puddle in the gutter while they were trying. The funeral was on Wednesday. Young Jack was very upset and has been having nightmares ever since. The boys had all been out together only the day before.

It was Saturday young Tommy went up to Ally Pally with Maurice Higgins. I made him take Jack with him to keep him out of my way while I did some house work. Jack came back in tears. He wouldn't say what the trouble was, but Tommy said they'd been told off by some old woman for messing around by her tent. I gave them both a right belting.

I'm doing three mornings for Mrs. Weitzmann now, a Jewish woman up on the Hill and the money comes in right handy. Tom's still off work. Poor man, its driving him mad, he's out first thing in the morning and some days doesn't come in 'til it's dark. He's gone back down to Jepson's at Enfield Lock again. He was talking to somebody yesterday who said that there was vacancy for a lathe operator there. He left at four this morning so he could be near the front of the queue. I suppose I must be getting down hearted too, but I don't expect he'll get it.

To put the kibosh on it all, our Sue broke out in spots yesterday. I think she's got the Chicken Pox which is all I need. I'm just grateful that the others have already had it.

I've told her not to, but Sue's started scratching her spots like mad. The real reason I wrote was to see if you've any of the camomile cream left that you had for Mabel. If you have, can you bring it with you when you come.

See you Thursday

Your loving sister Aggie

Seen from the top of the hill, the charging horses looked like a bunch of whippets racing across a green meadow. They were so far away that the runners had already pulled up when the cheer of the crowd, along the white wooden rails, drifted up to the four boys leaning on the stone balustrade of the Palace promenade. 'That was the last race, and we missed it.' Maurice Higgins said pointing an accusing finger at Tommy Sutton. 'All because of you, we wasted thruppence on bus fares.'

'I couldn't help it,' Tommy shouted back in his own defence feeling the same sense of anti-climax. 'Ollie Dodds was drinking with his mates in the White Swan 'til nearly three. He was as drunk as a rat. I had to grab the steering wheel twice and we only just got back to the yard in one piece. Anyway I don't know what you're complaining about, it was my thruppence that paid for the bus.'

'I'm going to have to walk home aren't I? We might as well start now; I don't suppose you're going to pay our fares back.'

'You're damned right I'm not, I only had sixpence to start with.'

Acky Ackfield stepped between them with a laugh. 'Pack it in you two. Look on the bright side. Tom's mum gave him tuppence for young Jack and, at least, we managed to get him up here without paying. Come on let's go down, there's still plenty going on down by the race track. You never know, some lucky punter might have dropped some money and not bothered to pick it up. I once found a shilling after one of these meetings. Anyway everything's cheap now. All the gypos will be packing up and trying to get rid of any stuff they've got left. You can get three ice creams for a penny sometimes and you never know, we might get a free ride on the roundabout before they pack it up.

Encouraged by Acky's cheerful enthusiasm, the three older boys gave a loud cheer and began to run down the hill leaving Jack to keep up as best he could. Not wanting to be left behind and get lost in the crowd, Jack wailed and let his legs whirl faster and faster to try and keep pace, until he was out of control. With an even higher pitched scream, he tripped, and rolled in a tangle to the bottom. His damaged pride rather than any injury made him want to cry, but his brother and friends had not even noticed his fall enough to laugh. They were already moving off, looking for a place to slide under the fence.

With the last race over, nobody cared about the little knot of boys appearing among the tents of the show ground, like moles from their hole in the ground. Or perhaps more like foxes as they went scavenging through the debris left by the race goers. Every cigarette packet they saw they pounced on, certain that one would accidentally have a fag left in it.

'Two,' yelled Acky, exultantly holding up a crushed packet of Capstans. 'Anybody got any matches?'

Tommy rooted in his pocket. 'A bloke left a box on the counter in the Gillespie yesterday. I snaffled them when no one was looking.'

With the practised ease of the habitual smoker Acky lit a cigarette, took a deep drag and passed it onto Tommy. Tommy did the same and handed it to Maurice. 'Give us a puff,' Jack demanded. The other boys ignored him. 'Give us a puff or I'll tell.'

Everyone knew that it was an idle threat. Jack idolised his brother. He lied for him, stole for him. He did whatever was asked by his brother, but even threatening to tell tales was worth a clip round the ear and the threat of a lot worse if he ever did open his mouth. Jack knew it was necessary for Tommy to prove how tough he was and he took the blow stoically. He escaped anything worse when the attention of the three older boys was caught by a noisy group coming away from a fortune teller's tent.

In the centre of the little crowd, they recognised George Harris. They rushed forward to the front of his group in the hope of being noticed themselves. George used to play professional football for The Orient and might have played for the Spurs if he hadn't damaged his knee in accident at work a couple of years ago. He was only a few years older than them, but he was the man they all wanted to be. He didn't live in their street anymore, but his married sister Gladys did and the boys knew him fairly well. Not only was he their hero, they knew that on a good day, he could be relied on for a couple of coppers.

George was a brewery drayman by trade, but hadn't worked at it for ages, not since the stack of barrels fell on him. Mrs. Sutton said that it was no more than he deserved and that all the Harrises were a bad lot. Gladys was no better than she should be and George had the taste for the good life far beyond his station. He gambled, and hung around with loose women. The boys had heard it said that he was mixed up with the Alexandra Park racecourse gang and did a little debt collecting for a local bookie. It was often said that he was going to come to a bad end. The boys, who fed on a diet of George Raft and Edward G Robinson, loved him for it.

Even Acky, who was a Communist, looked up to him. Acky's mother was dead, so when he wasn't at school or working for his father on the coal round, he did and thought much as he liked. He said that George was a working class hero, an anarchist setting out to overturn capitalist society. Acky was the intellectual of the group. It was not the sort of thing you could say down at the YCL branch, where he was nicknamed 'Little Lenin' even though, privately, Acky thought that with his glasses he looked more like his other hero, Trotsky.

Most of the rest of Wilmott Street looked on Gentleman George Harris as a thoroughly bad lot and the boys were forbidden to talk to him, by their mothers. That only made him more of a hero to them. George had a car and lots of money. He often brought sweets or pennies for the kids down the street. They would return the favour by watching his car and collecting betting slips from the men hanging around the place when he was busy elsewhere. He could be very generous.

His aura of danger was attractive to all sorts of

people. In the group hanging about the mouth of the fortune teller's tent waiting for him, was the son of the Sutton's doctor and a number of other bright young things from Tottenham, rebelling against their bourgeois lives by slumming it with the local rough.

'Hello George,' cried Tommy, standing firm and making the crowd of George's followers flow around him.

'Piss off kid.' George scowled and slouched by.

Phyllis Bainbridge, whose dad ran the Gillespie Arms Public House in Seven Sisters Road, where Tommy got the matches, was hanging on his arm, making sure that none of the other girls got close. She knew the boys as well. Though she was older than them. They had grown up together and most of their fathers owed her's money from time to time. 'He's had a bad day with the gee gees.' she shouted out with a laugh, 'and the gypsy's just told him that she can't see an end to his bad luck.'

'Shut up,' George snarled and shook his arm violently to try to dislodge her.

Phyllis, who used the stage name of Geraldine De'Beauvoir when she sang with two other girls in a group called the Berkeley Nightingales, laughed in the high pitch, affected way, which she thought an actress should. George knew some big names and being seen with him could be good for her career. She didn't let go.

As the group following George and Phyllis swirled away past Tommy, a young girl at the edge of George's bunch wasn't looking where she was going and walked into him. She wouldn't step aside to go round him and Tommy didn't move. They stood face to face. She wasn't intimidated by his angry stare. 'Oh go away, little boy, like George told you,' she said accentuating her middle class accent as a sort of sneer. She didn't recognise him, but he knew Katherine Hartwell from junior school. She was in the year below him, though she wasn't much younger. Her dad had started a little engineering business down in Northumberland Park when they were in the infants and as soon as he'd made a little money, he made sure that she moved to a better school.

Tom could cope with being snubbed by George. George had a reputation to keep up. He was a hard man who was expected to walk over anybody who wasn't quick enough to get out of his way and Tommy played the game. But Tommy had a reputation to build too and couldn't be seen to take lip from any girl. No tart putting on airs was going to make him step aside. Certainly not this one, whose posh accent had been bought with the blood and sweat of people like his old man. It was about time she got taught the real cost of things.

Acky recognised her too, he'd been in her class, though she pretended that she didn't know him either. He knew that old Tom Sutton had been nearly crippled in an accident at Hartwell's and could read what Tommy was thinking by the fire in his eyes. He was sure that Tommy was going to hit her and so leapt between them. 'Let's have our fortune told,' he exclaimed, catching hold of Tommy's right arm as if trying to drag him towards the booth. 'I'll be leaving school in a couple of weeks. The old witch might be able to tell us where to get a job.'

'What do you want ask the gypsy for?' Maurice sneered. 'We all know that you're going to be a coal man like your dad.'

'I might not be,' Acky protested. 'I'd like to be a motor mechanic and build racing cars.'

Maurice snorted. 'You don't need to be a bleedin' fortune teller to see what our lives are goin' to be. You're going' to be a coal man Acky, my dad'll get me onto the railways and Tom'll finish up on the dole like his old man.'

In his new anger with Maurice, Tom forgot about Katherine Hartwell and she was swept away by her crowd. 'I'll tell you where I'm goin' Mo,' he snapped 'I'm goin' to the top, but let's ask the gypsy to tell your future. She can see if I'm going to smack you in the mouth,'. Walking to the door of the fortune teller's tent he thrust his head in. 'Lady tell us our fortunes for thruppence?'

A walnut face looked up from polishing her crystal ball with her head scarf. 'sixpence.' The old crone's toothless mouth snapped like a turtles. Her short stem pipe wavered, but didn't fall.

'We've only got thruppence,' Tommy persisted.

'Then live in darkness. Piss off.'

With a face like thunder, Tommy reappeared before the others. 'No gypo's going to tell me to piss off,' he snarled. 'If she's so bloody good at telling the future, let's see if she expects this.' He pulled the box of matches from his pocket.

'You're not going to burn her tent down are you?' Maurice demanded in horror.

'I might do.' Tommy snarled, 'Keep your eyes peeled.' Leaving his friends to make sure that no one was coming, Tommy ducked around the side of the tent and dropped to his knees. Acky followed, Maurice kept watch and Jack hovered behind him. His head swung from the fairground to his brother, in agitation, while he muttered, 'Don't do it Tom, please don't do it.'

'Shut up or she'll hear you' Maurice snapped, 'he's not going to burn her down. We're just going to teach her a lesson. Tom took the last cigarette from the packet, lit it and drew heavily. He handed it to Acky who did the same before handing it to Maurice who passed it back to Tom. Then, like a snake, he dropped on his stomach and wriggled under the tent's brailings. Without making a sound or a flutter, he reached out and dropped the cigarette end into the frayed fringe of the gypsy's long skirt and slipped away.

It took about a minute before there was a scream and torrent of oaths from inside the tent.

With a matching shriek of laughter, the boys dashed out into the open, in front of the tent, and danced like demons, waiting for her to come out. In a fury, the old Gypsy woman leapt from her chair and let her crystal ball fall onto the soft, trodden ground. She had suffered a life of persecution and knew instantly what had happened, but was too old to give chase. She stood at the door of the booth, screaming abuse after them. 'You little bastards,' she shrieked. The hem of her skirt was still smouldering. 'If I get my hands on you I'll rip out your eyes. I'll tear out your tongues and feed them to the crows.'

Waiting for the last of the punters to finish the last of the rides, one of the fair-ground roustabouts was leaning against the merry-go-round. He was dreaming that he would never again have the back breaking task of tearing the ride down and loading it onto a wagon, only to build it up again the next day, in a new place. He was jerked back to consciousness by the old woman's cries. 'You evil sons of bitches, you warts from a toad's arse, you want flogging, you do, you little savages.'

Jack saw the dark man with a pigtail and a gold earring come back from where ever his dreams had taken him. He straightened and began to sidle towards them, slowly, like a cat stalking sparrows.

Tommy, Acky and Maurice were too busy baiting the old woman to notice him. They were prancing like demented clowns, pulling faces and thumbing their noses at the old woman's fury. Thinking that they were safe and out of reach of her anger, they laughed at her and the storm of useless abuse she hurled at them.

Jack shouted a warning. The other boys froze, caught between their pleasure and the danger from the man sliding around the corner of the tent. They seemed to be the only people standing still against the seething back drop of the departing crowds. The gypsy man knew he had been seen and stopped. He bent slightly as if he were a coiled spring. He wondered if he were close enough to make it worth a charge. Tommy, Acky and Maurice eyed him warily, ready to flee, but not afraid. They were certain they could out run the man.

Suddenly Jack saw that the gypsy wasn't watching the boys anymore and he forgot the danger from the roustabout. The man only had eyes for the old woman. She was still, and now silent, looking away into the far distance. Her left hand stretched up to the sky and her right, with a single bony finger outstretched, pointed at her tormentors. Her face was white beneath its coat of grime and her eyes blazed like black stars. Jack had seen people have seizures at the pictures and thought she was going to die. Glancing towards the fairground man, Jack saw that his eyes were locked onto the fortune teller's face. His expression showed a look of horror. He was seeing something his grandmother had told him about. Some nearly forgotten spirit was laying its hand on the old fortune teller so that all the future opened up to her in horrific certainty. She could no longer choose, but had to tell what she could see. The roustabout moved back, he did not want those eyes to fall on him. He didn't want to know what tomorrow held. Jack felt the same fear knotting up his insides. Something dreadful was going to happen and he didn't want it happen to him.

In a hoarse voice, hardly above a whisper, the old woman began to cry. 'I see blood. I see bloody murder. You'll all die. You, you scum pot,' She pointed at Maurice. 'I can see you lying face down in a sea of blood and no one will save you from drowning.' Shakily the pointing finger moved along to wave at Tommy. 'Murderer,' she whispered. Then the shaky finger waivered between him and Acky and she said. 'You two toads will die together, hand in hand, cuddling like girls, in a ditch and even your mothers will deny your names. All of you, I curse you all to a bloody death.'

The roustabout made a hurried sign of the cross and kissed his thumb before he turned away.

Jack could see that the gypsy man was just as frightened as he was, but Jack didn't understand why. 'No,' he cried out, his dread for Tommy finally swamping his fear for himself. He rushed forward to catch the old fortune teller by her sleeve and drag her hand down to stop her pointing. 'Don't hurt them.'

Her eyes flashed again, but seeing the small boy's terrified face looking up, she calmed. She pinched his cheek and chuckled like a witch. 'Too late for them, deary, the words is spoken,' she chuckled evilly, 'but don't you worry my little worm. You're only cursed to be a man and marry an ugly woman.' Dismissing him with a flick of her hand, she tapped her pipe on the heel of her boot, turned away and went back into her tent.

Jack snivelled all the way home and the others sneered at his tears, but it was a very quiet group of boys who walked back to Tottenham.

Chapter 2

Dear Mr. Harrington

I am writing this letter on behalf of my son Tommy Sutton, who you sacked on Thursday. He is a good boy, strong and a hard worker. If you look at his record you will see you had no trouble with him before.

The way that men are means that he couldn't put his side of the story properly, but I thought that you should know that Mr. Dobbs, who I'm told you have properly sacked, was drunk and out. Tommy was only driving the lorry because there was another delivery to make. Tommy knew he wasn't supposed to drive and wouldn't have done if it hadn't meant letting down the customers. It's not the first time this has happened, Tommy's had to bring Dobbs home before, but there was never any trouble before.

As you know the accident wasn't serious and no one was hurt and the police aren't pressing charges so I wonder if you could reconsider your decision and give Tommy another chance. He did only have the interest of the brewery at heart.

He has promised that nothing like this will ever happen again.

Yours obediently

Aggie Sutton (Mrs.)

'Be a good sport, Tommy, lad,' Ollie Dodd's wheedling tone set Tommy's teeth on edge, he wasn't in the mood for the drunken old fool's nonsense this morning. 'Go an' see if Bowler's about in the yard.'

'He's not about,' Tommy snapped. The shift foreman had been in the office when he clocked in and he hadn't come out yet. 'Bung whatever you're going to nick on the back of the lorry and don't mess about. Let's get on the road. I'm going out with me mates tonight to meet some girls and I don't want to be late because of you.'

Grinning sheepishly, Ollie glanced around to make sure no-one was watching, then sidled across to the stack of boxes of bottled beer against the wall. With the power of a life time of lifting, he swung two crates off the top of the stack and onto the back of their truck. Then, taking Tommy at his word, he hurried, as fast as his great bulk would allow, round to the driver's side. The lorry lurched as he pulled himself up into the cab. Starting the engine, he crashed it into gear, then hurried through the yard and out into the High Road traffic before anyone thought to stop them and double check their load.

Their first stop was the Spread Eagle at Bruce Grove. Frank Sackville was a good publican. He looked after his customers by looking after his beer. He knew all the tricks that dray men got up to. He was known as 'Snap' to the brewery workers because of the way he only left one door unlocked at any time and firmly shut the bolt as soon as he was finished. Frank always kept his cellar flap firmly locked on delivery days.

Ollie swore as he climbed down from the cab. It was always the same at the Spread Eagle, delay, delay, delay and they wouldn't even get a drink out of the old skinflint either. He rattled the saloon bar door to let Frank know they were there and then they kicked their heels on the pavement for five minutes waiting for him to appear. Eventually the split door in the pavement at their feet slowly opened like the gate to Hell and the publican's sharp little face poked out.

'You go easy today,' Frank demanded, 'that mild you bought last week never settled after the shaking up you gave it. I'm not paying for that, I tell you, you can take it back.'

'Come off it Guvnor, we never shake up nothing, do we Tommy?' Ollie declared. Tommy didn't reply, he began rolling kegs to the edge of the dray and tipping them off onto the hessian bumper laid on the pavement. With practised ease Ollie trapped each falling barrel under his foot like a football player. Then, as soon as Tommy had jumped from the lorry and on, down into the cellar, he flipped a loop of his rope around each in turn and pushed it over the edge and let it slide underground.

'There we are guvnor,' said Ollie, when they'd finished, touching his cap with his index finger. 'No one could have put 'em down gentler than that, like thistle down it was and I've picked up that barrel of mild you said was off.'

Frank Sackville grunted and went on with his task of checking the bottles in the cases to make sure no one had slipped in an empty one with the bottle top replaced. Eventually he stood up and accepted the stub of pencil that Ollie pulled from behind his ear and signed the delivery slip.

He thrust them both back, forcibly flapping at Ollie as he ushered him towards the ladder. The fat old dray man stood his ground. 'Not a barrel shaken, Mr. Sackville, not a case dropped, and we worked like greased lightning.' he said. 'Not a break, even though we was dying of thirst.'

Again Frank Sackville grunted, but this time he rooted through his pocket and thrust a begrudged sixpence into the drayman's hand. It was worth that much to avoid having the barrel's deliberately shaken and bottles broken.

'Bloody sixpence,' Ollie snarled as he thrust the coin into his pocket. It was against his religion to make a delivery without stealing something, but all he had managed to snaffle at the Spread Eagle was a bottle of stout. He didn't even like stout, but he wasn't going to let it go to waste. With practised ease he twisted off the cap with one hand. As he slipped the lorry into gear, he tipped the contents down his throat in one huge gulp. Replacing the cap, he dropped the bottle into the crate behind his seat. It would get lost among the breakages or slipped into some other crate to make it look full.

The next stop was the Red Lion on the boundary. Gordon Postlethwaite, the publican, was a piss head and on his way out with liver failure. His great red face glowed with welcoming delight when Ollie arrived. It was only ten o'clock and the pub wasn't open yet, but Gordon and his good lady were already two thirds of the way through a bottle of gin. With Ollie to accompany him, he moved into the saloon bar and onto bitter. The two of them left Tommy to unload the delivery into the cellar.

After his first pint, Ollie stuck his head out. 'How many cases of light ale on the list?' he demanded in a low voice.

Tommy looked at the invoice, 'ten.'

'Give him eight. And give him that barrel of mild we picked up at the Spread Eagle. I'll fill up a barrel with swill at the Swan and take that back.' Ollie took the delivery board with him, for Gordon to sign, as he returned for another couple of pints.

Tommy knew better than to ask why Ollie turned off their route and headed down into the Industrial Estate by the river. There was only one pub down there and there was nothing on the delivery docket for the White Swan. The first time it happened he had asked why. Ollie wasn't a violent man, but he grabbed Tommy by the lapels of his jacket and dragged him up close to his face so that Tommy's toes danced to touch the ground. 'Keep your nose out of things that ain't none of your business and you won't get it broke.' he snarled.

Now it happened so often that Tommy no longer even thought about it. Ollie would park up in the disused entrance of a derelict factory at the back of the pub with the lorry pulled back well out of sight. He was too idle to do it himself, so told Tommy to unload whatever he had managed to steal during the round, then wait for him in the cab. As soon as he was sure that Tommy was busy, Ollie slid away and crept in through the pub's back door.

A few cases of beer and the odd barrel don't take long to unload. Normally Tommy would settle down with a newspaper he'd picked up somewhere along the way. Today Tommy was thinking about Dottie Savage and his evening out with the lads. He began to chafe at the delay when Ollie didn't return. As he thought about some-one else taking Dottie home and kissing her in the alleyway behind her house, his anger rose. He decided to ignore Ollie Dobb's order to stay outside and wait. Jumping down from the cab, he walked through the empty yard and followed Ollie into the pub to see if he could hurry up the drunken old sod.

It was nearly five o'clock in the afternoon and the pub doors were firmly locked to the public, but in a corner of the bar, not visible from the street, a group of about ten men were drinking as though the licensing laws didn't exist and playing cards with no thought for the laws on gambling.

'You're after having company Reggie.' The landlord, standing behind the bar wiping glasses, saw Tommy first and growled a warning in a deep Irish accent.

'Who're you?' a fat man with a camel hair coat draped over his shoulders demanded as Tommy appeared at the door into the bar. A table turned over with a crash as the men behind it leapt to their feet. Bottles and glasses smashed to the ground, spilling their contents everywhere. An ugly, little, scar faced, man who had been watching out of the front window, suddenly had a cut throat razor in his hand and the eyes of the whole group were fixed on him in hard dangerous stares.

Tommy's mouth dropped open in fright and, try as he would, he couldn't make any words come out.

'You stupid little bleeder, I told you to stay outside.' Ollie shouted, with slurred difficulty, he pulled himself upright from where he'd been hanging on the bar. Struggling with his uncooperative limbs to stop them knocking over the pint and scotch in front of him. 'It's OK

Mr. Green, he's with me, he's the boy off my lorry.' Drunk as he was, he had sense enough to be frightened by the reaction Tommy's unexpected appearance had caused. He was afraid that he would be blamed for the trouble. 'I told him to unload some stuff for Mick and to wait in the lorry for me. I'll give him a right belting when I get him outside.'

'You couldn't whip cream.' a voice sneered from a corner. There was a general snigger and the tension slid away.

Tommy couldn't see the speaker in the smoky shadows, but immediately recognised the laughing voice from among the crowd standing around Reggie Green's table.

'Hello George,' Tommy said, running his fingers through his hair, relieved to find an ally among the hostile crew. 'I was looking for old fat guts. Didn't expect to see you here. I've not seen you since the races at Ally Pally, that was months ago now. Your luck changed yet?'

George frowned and tried to recall their last meeting, it was a long while ago. He remembered and laughed. Stepping out of the group and beyond the broken glasses and spilled drink, he came into the light. 'No, not really,' he said, 'but I can't complain. After all it don't do no good. Things have been better, but then again, things have been worse. How about you? Doing better than Maurice, I'll bet.'

'You heard what happened to him then.' Tommy felt a twinge of guilt, this was the first time that he had thought about his late friend for two or three days. Everyone had said he would get over it in the end, but it had taken a long while.

'Yeh, I heard he got run over by a number twenty-nine. How unlucky's that; twenty-nines are always late. Not a nice way to go through, but the way I heard it, the old gypsy had put the sign on him.'

'Tommy slowly shook his head to dust off his memories. He noticed how the tale of bloody violence had caught everyone's attention and the room had become perfectly still. 'Not nice at all.' Tommy tried to speak lightly with a sneer in his voice, the way that George would. They almost pulled his arms off before he died, but they couldn't keep his head out of the water. They say that he coughed up so much blood that it looked like he was drowning in it, just like the old witch said. I suppose almost anything's better than Maurice's luck, though I sometimes wonder after I've spent all day with fat guts.'

'Who you calling fat guts?' Ollie demanded angrily. He gave away the support from the bar and lurched towards where Tommy stood in the doorway, intent on smacking him round the ear. He didn't make it. His rubber legs tangled in a bar stool and he pitched forward onto his face.

Everyone in the room laughed at his drunken efforts to get up again. The emergency was over. If George Harris spoke for the boy, they accepted that Tommy was no threat and as Ollie was no more entertainment, they turned away to pick up the cards and finish their business. Mick quickly moved in with a tray of fresh drinks and kicked the broken glass out of the way under the settle. As soon as he was forgotten, Ollie gave up the task of trying to rise and lay down onto the floor to sleep. Tommy was nonplussed. Forgotten by the bookmaker's men, he didn't know what to do.

A few minutes later, it was George who put him out of his misery. When Reggie Green finished giving him his instructions for the evening's meeting at Haringey dog track and looked for his next man, George broke out of the pack of those still waiting to be briefed. He came across to where Tommy was still standing at the door.

'You want to look after him,' George said, indicating Ollie's prostrate figure with the toe of his shoe. 'If he keeps on drinking like this, my boss is going to get fed up with him. One day he's going to make a real mistake; he's going to miss making a drop with somebody's betting slip and that somebody's going to win. No slip, no money. That somebody will be very angry with your mate. That sort of mistake is likely to get a person killed.'

'He's no mate of mine,' Tommy snapped as he kicked out at the snoring heap. 'He's a drunken pig, greedy and mean. I've only been working with him for a couple of months and already I've thought I might do it me self.'

George laughed his easy laugh and gave Tommy a playful punch which nearly knocked him over. A thought occurred to him. After checking the betting slips he had taken from Ollie's satchel and slipping them safely under his hat, he dragged a big roll of pound notes from his pocket and pealed a couple off. 'Give these to Ollie when he sobers up. If you give 'em to him now, they might fall out of his pocket when you drag him back to the truck.' George gave another guffaw as he stuffed the money into Tommy's pocket, then with a big wink turned back to join the crowd by the bar.

Being abandoned by George and being sure that there was no way that Ollie would be able to drive the lorry back to the depot, Tommy turned to Murphy for help. 'Help me drag him into the lorry, mister and we'll get back to the depot.'

'I'm after thinking that the man's in no state to drive,' said Murphy stating the obvious, but making no effort to help.

'I'll do it; I've done it before.' Tommy neglected to mention that the only time he had driven the lorry before, it was only up and down the yard. 'All I want is a hand getting him into the cab.'

George was keeping a watchful eye on Tommy and saw his problem. He broke away from the conversation with the ferret faced man who had pulled the razor when Tom had first entered. 'I'll give you a hand.' he said. Catching hold of Ollie's collar and, ignoring the protest of his flapping arms and muddled curses, he dragged him towards the door.

Tommy was impressed by George's power. Six months of brewery work had developed his own neck to the thickness of a woman's thigh and given him shoulders which were his mother's despair, but he couldn't easily have moved the fat man. It wasn't until it came to the final shove, to pour the unconscious dray man onto the floor of the lorry cab that George needed any assistance.

As Tommy started the engine and searched for reverse, George wandered round to the driver's side. 'You manage?' he asked. 'You could always leave him 'ere and walk back.'

'Not a good idea George,' Tommy answered. 'We're not supposed to be 'ere. You wouldn't want anyone asking questions now would you?'

George nodded. 'I'll drive it up to the High Road.'

After another ear splitting grating, Tommy found the gear he was looking for. 'No problem George, I can manage.' he shouted out of the window. The lorry shot backwards out of the alley where Ollie had left it and demolished Murphy's gate post. Having started, Tommy wasn't stopping for anything. He smashed the gear lever forward into first and leap-frogged away. Glancing back at George in his mirror, Tommy snatched a quick wave, before grabbing the wheel again to drag the lorry off the pavement.

George pushed his hat up with his forefinger in salute. He watched Tommy to the corner and then, with a shrug, he returned to the bar. It was none of his business now. From the back yard of the pub he heard Tommy roar up the street in too low a gear and then the savage grating as he searched for another.

Chapter 3

Dear Mrs. Weitzmann

I'm sorry, I shan't be coming to your house after this week. I was perfectly happy with you and you have always treated me and mine fairly, but a Jewish gentleman has insisted that I come and work for him. He is offering a shilling a week more and with things being the way they are, I don't feel that I can refuse and therefore give a weeks notice. I'm sorry if this causes you any inconvenience

Agnes Sutton (Mrs.)

'Sue,' Aggie Sutton, yelled from the kitchen. 'It's nearly five o'clock.'

'Oh, Mum, I got plenty of time,' Sue whined back.

'No you haven't. It's getting foggy. It'll be dark early tonight and you know what Mrs Weitzmann's like. She'll give you what for if you're not there to let them in and put the lights on when they get back from schul and you know there's always something she's not got from the shops. She'll expect you to go and get it for her.'

'Oh Mum,' Sue whined, 'do I 'ave to go. It's foggy and I don't wanna go on me own.'

'Yes, you do have to go, if you didn't want to do it you should have said so at the beginning. Now people are relying on you.' Aggie was adamant, she knew that if her daughter started messing the Weitzmanns about, it wouldn't just be Sue they got rid of, they'd dump the whole family and she'd lose her little bit of cleaning. On the other hand, it was going to be a nasty night and she didn't really want Sue walking back on her own in the fog. 'Someone will go with you.'

There was a clatter in the scullery and the back door slammed. 'Tommy,' his mother cried.

'He's gone,' Sue complained.

'Damn the boy,' Aggie muttered under her breath, then shouted, 'Jack.'

'Ah, Mum,' Jack protested, furious with his brother for slamming the door behind him and stopping Jack from escaping too. 'I've only just got in from work. Let Dad or Tommy do it.'

'You know full well that Tommy's run off and I'm not having your dad going out in this fog with his chest. You don't want your sister going up there on her own do you?' Without waiting for a reply, she ranted on. 'Now you put your coat on and don't give me any more of your lip or you'll be feeling the weight of my hand, big as you are. You're going to the Weitzmann's with your sister while she does the Shabbat work and that's final. It won't take long. I'll have something hot ready for you when you get back'

It was a foul evening that was turning into an evil night. It was certain that by the time the Weitzmanns got back from the synagogue and Sue and Jack could leave, it would be really unpleasant.

The rabbi and the cantor obviously didn't relish a walk home on a foggy evening either and the service was over promptly. Jack hardly had time to light the fire and stoke up the boiler before Mr Weitzmann was rattling his walking stick up the steps to let the goyim know that they were home. That was not work, it was merely an old man having a little difficulty climbing the steps. No sooner were the Weitzmanns in than the Suttons were out of the basement door in their rush to get home, but they hadn't reached the top of the basement steps when the front door flew open above them and little, fat Mrs. Weitzmann came bustling back out onto the top step, her arms whirling like windmills as she did when she was agitated.

'Susan, my dear,' she cried. 'you must save my life. Isn't it bad enough that it is foggy enough to keep a mensch from schule, but there isn't bread in the house. I know I bought matzos only yesterday and it's gone, stolen. Be a precious, run to the shop and buy me a box already.'

'Mrs. Weitzmann,' Sue protested, 'It's Shabbat, everywhere will be closed. I'll not get Matzos now.'

Mrs. Weitzmann moved a little further down the steps and lowered her voice conspiratorially. 'My dear, I'm told there's a little Greek shop near Seven Sisters, he vill still be open. It seems that he stocks a few kosher items, for emergency; for those times when someone steals an honest woman's bread.'

'Yes, I know it,' Sue said icily, 'it's just round the corner from where we live.'

'Mrs. Weitzmann beamed, 'see, no problem.' she chucked her under the chin and thrust some money into Sue's hand. 'Be quick my child, we shall be eating soon.'

Mr. Contaninounou was still open and he did have unleavened bread, but having bought some, Sue was torn between the thought of her mother's nice warm kitchen a few hundred yards away and the fat tip she would get back at the top of Stamford Hill. 'Jack,' she began in her wheedling voice,' the fog's getting thicker and I can feel my cough coming on.' She coughed a couple of times to prove her point. 'Be a dear and take Mrs Weitzmann's bread back for her. She's a bit of a dragon, but she's quite generous really. There'll be a good tip for you and you can keep it all.'

Jack sucked the air through his teeth, tasting the sulphur of the coal smoke in the fog. It was a foul night and he'd sooner go home. He had to get up early in the morning, but if he didn't take the bread, then Sue would have to and he would have to go with her anyway and she'd keep the money. He thought of Tommy's new motor bike. *One day I'll have one just as good if not better. In any case, a little bit more money always came in handy.* Giving in, he said 'OK, I'll take it.'

Jack walked as quickly as he could, hand outstretched, eyes bulging to pick out any landmark and ears straining to catch any noise. You think you know the way, but you keep bumping into trees, or tripping off the kerb or falling over people's walls.

Fog deadens sound, but Jack clearly heard a scream in the blackness ahead of him and somebody shouting, 'Filthy Jew bitch.' Instinctively he rushed forward and burst in upon the noise. The small figure of a woman, all wrapped around a little boy, was hunched up on the floor, hard against a burnt brick wall. Her white face seemed to be made only of wide brown eyes full of terror and an open mouth which screamed endlessly. Two giant shadows towered over them, shouting abuse and threatening them with raised fists. At the instant Jack realised what he was looking at, one of the men lashed out and he saw a swinging boot crash into the girl's shoulder so that she shrieked even louder with the pain. On a clear night, the two Fascist Blackshirts would have been easier to see under the gas lights and Jack would probably have slid up a side street before he got near. He had had run-ins with Mosley's

Pitfield mob before, when he's gone out chalking with Acky and there were scores to be settled between Shoreditch and South Tottenham.

Colliding with them in the fog like this, there was no time for choices. 'Oi,' Jack yelled and charged forward. He didn't have time to think of the odds. Not only was it two to one, but they were both big, fully grown men.

The first man swung round to see who was attacking and turned into Jack's punch. It was an exquisitely timed blow. Jack felt the man's nose break as his swinging fist hit him in the face, or it could be that he felt his knuckles break, the pain in his hand was excruciating. Reacting as quickly as Jack had done, the second Blackshirt turned to face him. 'Fucking Jew lover,' he bellowed and grabbed his cap off his head to swipe it across Jack's face.

Jack tried to parry the blow and at the same time lashed out with his foot. He was aiming for the man's balls, but suddenly seemed to have gone blind. The swinging boot only caught the Blackshirt on the knee. It was good enough. Letting out streams of anti-Semitic filth the two men ran off.

The girl continued to scream and the little boy, wrapped in her arms, cried loudly. Jack couldn't think of anything to say. He just stood there swaying, watching the pools of black blood on the pavement run in little rivers towards the gutter and wondering where it was coming from. Suddenly there were more people swirling all about him in the mist, bearded men with long ringlets, big black hats and long, shiny black coats. Then they were hitting him too, kicking him, driving him down onto the ground.

Above their angry shouts, the girl screamed again. The blows stopped. Out of the darkness, a voice said, 'My sister says you saved her life. We beg your pardon. What we have done is unforgivable and on Shabbat as well. We are forever in your debt.'

Jack said nothing, his legs buckled and he crashed to the floor, unconscious.

Waking rushed in on him and ran away again, like playing 'It'. He vaguely remembered being half carried, half dragged through the streets. He was bumped up some steps and people began shouting in words he couldn't understand. Then he was laid down on a bed or sofa in a dark room. All the time there were people talking, shouting, crying and he couldn't be bothered to fight to be heard above them.

Later, when there was pause in the constant babble that bounced around the room and swamped his mind, he called out 'Where am I'.

'You are in the house of Israel Rabinovitz,' a young man answered from somewhere out beyond his hand's reach.

'Why is it so dark?' Jack asked, 'can't you put the light on?'.

'You have been cut,' the young man paused to measure his next word; 'badly. You have a cloth across your face to try to stop the bleeding. I have a friend who is a nurse, I have sent for her, she is not far away. She will be here soon.'

'Where are the matzos?' Jack demanded, memory was washing back and he recalled why he had been out on such a foul night.

'What,' the young voice sounded incredulous as though he thought he was dealing with delirium. 'What matzos?'

Jack tried to rise, but strong hands held him back. 'I work for the Weitzmann's as a Shabbat goy. Mrs. Weitzmann sent me and my sister to fetch the bread. I was bringing it back when I ran into the Blackshirts. She gave me the money and there'll be hell to pay if I don't get the bread back. It could cost us all our jobs.'

There was a deep muttering in the room and then an older man spoke, though he obviously wasn't talking to Jack. 'Moses, my boy, get bread from your mother's kitchen and take it to the Weitzmann's at once. The Sabbath is not broken in a case like this. Tell Lazar Weitzmann what has happened. There is no fault with this boy.'

'Miriam,' the older man's voice continued, 'you go

to the front steps with a lamp so that the woman your brother sent for can find us in this filthy air.

'Oh Papa, can't I stay inside with him?' a girl demanded.

'After all he has done for you and your cousin, it is the least you can do for him. Do not argue. Stand at the gate with a light until the woman comes. You owe this boy a great debt.'

'Don't worry, Papa, we shall pay it in full, I promise.'

Jack heard her footsteps leave the room and was quite sad, she had a sweet voice and he would have liked to have seen what she looked like. There was a moments silence and then an older woman's voice asked, 'Oi vei, and what did she mean by that, do you suppose?' There was no answer.

Thoughts about the room and the people in it drifted away from the forefront of his mind as the pain in his face began to seep into his eyes, ears and mouth. It felt as if it were on fire and he couldn't bite back the groan from his throat or stem the tears burning his cheeks. He was terrified that he was blind and wanted to drag the cloth from his face to test whether he could see, but his hands were trembling so much he had no control over them.

Suddenly the light of the room burst in on him as the cloth was pulled away. He hadn't heard anyone come in and now he was staring up into this beautiful woman's face. She had staggeringly blue eyes, blonde hair cut short into a modern bob, and was wearing bright red lipstick. She looked like a film star or an angel. As she pressed his cheek and the pain stabbed him in the eye, she proved she wasn't an angel. He yelled at her in protest and she laughed. 'I thought you Tottenham boys were as hard as nails.' Her laughing mouth glistened with perfect white teeth. This was not either of the women who he had heard before.

'Your hands are cold,' Jack lied, but the tears cut channels through the blood on his face.

'Moses,' The girl looked back over her shoulder to

the tall, sallow faced youth hovering behind her, 'is there any gin in the house?'

The lanky youth shrugged and turned his palms to the sky. 'Who knows what there is in this house, Peggy, I will ask.'

In a scurrying of silk from outside the door a plump elderly woman rushed in without the question being asked. 'Gin, in my house. God forbid,' she shouted and then added more quietly, 'but who knows what there might be in the medicine chest. I will look.'

Before Peggy had finished unpacking gut, needle and swabs from her Gladstone bag, a half empty bottle of Booths appeared beside them on the table.

'Oi vie,' the older woman rolled her eyes to heaven as the young girl splashed the clear spirit over her hands and then proceeded to swab the boy's face with it.

'You're lucky comrade,' Peggy said, 'The fascist pig had obviously just bought a new cap. The razor in the peak wasn't rusty. It's a nice clean cut, forehead and cheek, but it has missed the eye.' The nurse spoke with calm detachment. 'You'll have a nasty scar when I've finished. It'll make you look like a Prussian, but you'll be as right as nine pence in a few days. Just let me stitch this up and Moses will walk you home. I'll come and see you one-day next week, when I get off duty, to make sure the cut is healing and take the stitches out.'

'My name's Jack Sutton,' he told her, 'what's yours?'

'I'm Margaret Watkins, I'm a nurse at the North Middlesex hospital,' she replied. 'My friends call me Peggy. In the name of the Party, I would like to thank you for the blow you struck against Fascism.'

Chapter 4

Dear Alice

Thank you so much for the little parcel Mabel left with us when she called on Sunday. She's such a big girl now that I hardly recognised her when she knocked on the door. Now she has this position in Finchley, it's nice to think that we might see a bit more of her. A special thank you for the honey, Mabel says you look after the bees yourself. You are turning into a proper little country woman.

Things are very much the same here. We hang on as best we can. Tom has been doing a bit of casual work for Mr. Ackfield in the coal yard across the road. Young Tommy is still working at the brewery, but he hates it so much that every night he comes in, I think he will have told them to stick it. If he didn't need to keep up the instalments on his motor bike, I'm sure he would have done it weeks ago. As if that wasn't enough our Jack's been in trouble again, this time with the police. It seems there was some trouble down the Green when the Blackshirts started speaking. A fight started and Jack got arrested. The police let him go with a warning because he's so young and he looks so bad with that cut already on his face, but his name was in the Herald. I was almost too ashamed to cut the piece out and put it in my shoe box.

Lucky he works for the Co-op and they're very understanding about these things, it would have got him the sack from a lot of places. Even so they took him off his round for a few days and made him work in the yard because he looked so dreadful and they didn't want him frightening the customers. I told him to go to the doctors to have the cut seen to, but he says we can't afford it and the nurse who stitched him up is going to come down in a couple of days and take them out for nothing. Oh, Alice, I'm afraid that he's going to be horribly scarred.

Tom blames me for Jack's temper and young Bill Ackfield for getting him mixed up in politics, but your Uncle Bill says, and I don't dare tell Tom, that Jack's mixed up with a bunch of Communists up on Stamford Hill and its them who are leading him on.

Anyway, we must soldier on and I hope the vests and knickers I sent back with Mabel will do a turn for little Shirley, I held on to them when Sue had finished with them because I knew they'd do a turn some time. I hope you and the family are keeping well and that we'll see you before too long.

Your ever loving sister

Aggie

Tottenham Herald

LOCAL YOUTH ARRESTED

Last Friday a meeting of the British Union of Fascists was addressed by Charles Hartnell, the prospective BUF candidate for Tottenham at Tottenham Green. During Mr. Hartwell's address, a group of young rowdies tried to disrupt the meeting by shouting and throwing eggs.

The police made a number of arrests including Harry Hawkins, an unemployed railway worker from Graham Road, Hackney and Jack Sutton, a milkman, from Wilmott Street, South Tottenham. Both were bound over, on their own recognances for a period of six months.

The 4.10 from Cambridge to Liverpool Street pulled up the grade out of Tottenham Station and filled the streets below with smoke and steam. As Peggy Watkins turned into Wilmott Street, it was as though she had walked into a sheet hanging on a washing line. She held her hand in front of her face to try to shield it from the smuts and smells and stood still until she could see where she was going again.

Without realising it, the people in the street at the foot of the embankment, also closed their eyes and stopped talking until the puffing engine reached the Lea level and the driver could close the throttle. Then they took up their conversation at the word it had reached minutes before. They did it without thought, they did it twenty or thirty times a day, every day and it was second nature to them.

'Mucking trains,' Tommy muttered, still not daring to swear within earshot of his mother's house, and he took the old rag he'd been using to polish the exhaust of his motor bike and brushed a few imagined smuts off the petrol tank of his beloved Triumph. Jack who had been sitting astride the machine, twisting the throttle and day dreaming about taking Peggy for a spin through country lanes, suddenly stood up on the foot rests. There she was. She had just turned the top corner into the street. He would have recognised her anywhere. He was lucky Tommy was looking the other way and didn't notice him blush.

At the same moment and from the other end of the road, a brand new beige Humber emerged from the gloom and pulled into the kerb. Wilmott Street held its breath a little while longer. The car's appearance threw the residents out of their stride; they weren't used to brand new motor cars. A new attractive young female in the street was one thing, but this car was something else again. The men leaning against the wall of number seven did not restart their argument about the attractions of the stranger. They watched the light brown coupe cut through the swirling grey smoke still lingering between the little brick houses. They stood as still as the lamp posts, but their suspicious eyes followed the unknown vehicle down the street.

Its quiet arrival surprised the knot of men outside the entrance to Ackfield's coal yard. Their heads had been close, in private conversation, watching the girl. They snapped apart and their eyes switched guiltily towards it as if they thought it could read their minds.

Mrs Shaunessy remained leaning against her door post. She had been grateful to be drawn away from donkeying her doorstep to gossip, but she stopped listening to the list of little Lucy's latest ailments. Mabel Potter only chattered on about her daughter out of habit, not caring that her neighbour wasn't listening any more. Their eyes were fixed on the beautiful car, watching hungrily to see who climbed out. Even Mrs Botterell lingered on her front step. She didn't mix with her neighbours much and didn't go in for idle gossip, but she didn't push open her front door after she had turned the key. Louis, who had been shuffling along behind carrying the shopping was caught in the no man's land of his front path. He scurried to the door step and then back to the gate. He was aware of the tension in the air. This unreal stillness in the street bothered him. 'What's going on? What's going on?' he asked anxiously of no-one in particular and nobody answered him.

The car door opened and a tall, handsome man, expensively dressed and with his black hair slicked down, slid out and looked around. His swivelling eye took in the two groups of men, stopped for a moment on the gossiping women and then swept over the rest of the street. Apparently satisfied, he reached back into the car and pulled a camel-hair overcoat and a cream Trilby off the back seat. Draping the coat around his shoulders and pulling the hat low over his eyes, he repeated the surveillance of the scene.

The women had given up any pretence at conversation and stood with folded arms frankly admiring him, windows were beginning to open and heads pop out. 'You look gorgeous George,' young Tilly Prentice called from her bedroom window, one of the other girls, further along, let out a long low wolf whistle in imitation of some of those she had received in her time. George Harris smiled, gave his moustache a brush with his knuckle and pulled the brim of his hat half an inch lower. His narrowed eyes took in the pretty woman standing beyond the crowd, she wasn't smiling, didn't seem so impressed, but to Hell with her, everyone else was.

Doors were opening on every side and people were pouring out into their little front gardens. Like a wave, children came rushing past their parents, leaping over walls and gates to be first in the street to greet their hero.

'George, George, Gentleman George,' they chanted and cheered as they converged around him. The big man reached in his trouser pocket and drew out a handful of half pennies and pennies which he tossed onto the pavement in front of them. It turned their charge into a scrum as they fought to grab a coin. Louis Botterell danced at his garden gate desperately wanting to join the melee. The gate was closed against him, but he pleaded with his mother 'Can I go, mother, please, please, please?'

'No, Louis,' she snapped gruffly, 'it's common to fight in the street like that, come in doors at once.' She had noticed that he had wet himself in his excitement.

Jack watched Bill Ackfield and one or two of the other older boys, dive in and quickly elbow their way to where the brightest coins were, but he could also see the look of scorn on Peggy's face. There weren't enough pennies in the world to make him risk her turning that look on him.

'Golly,' Archie Cross cried. He had his fingers full of pennies and now surfaced to look more closely at the car. It was slashed across its sides with chrome which glowed in the late afternoon sunshine. The machine, resting on its white walled tyres, was like something out of a film. 'It's brilliant George, what is it?'

'It's just a car.' George said with a shrug, the way that George Raft might.

'How fast does it go,' Acky demanded as he freed himself from the knot of smaller children still fighting on the pavement in case there were any money left. He whistled as he ran his hand over the mudguard with its great silver headlight.

'Get your mucky paws off,' George snapped, raising his fist threateningly. 'It goes fast enough. If there's a scratch on it when I get back, I'll break someone's arm. On the other hand, if someone wants to clean the muck from the trains off it, there might be some sweets in it for them.

George Harris turned away and strolled through the children, leaving them arguing in his wake, over the pennies or who was going to clean the car. He was certain that there wouldn't be a mark on his beautiful new car when he came back from his sister's.

Conscious of the eyes on him, he swaggered along for a few yards. Then he stopped performing for the admiring women and his eyes became firmly fixed on the four men standing on the pavement ahead of him. The one who had been leaning against the lamp post was now standing up straight and the one who had had his back to him when he arrived had turned to watch him with the others. Each of them had a look of undisguised hostility on his face.

'What you doing down our street George Harris, your kind's not welcome here.' said the short red faced man who had turned to face him and now stood at the front of the little group.

George stopped an arm's length in front of them. 'I walk where I like Bill. I don't ask permission from nobody. It don't matter to me if I'm welcome or not, if someone tries to get in my way, I walk over them.'

'You won't walk over four of us,' growled Sammy Gutter.

'Won't I?' George laughed derisively. 'Look at yourselves, you're old men, I won't even notice the bump. Face it, you've had your day. It's time for us young ones to have our turn.'

The tension crackled like electricity. The women watching silently from their houses could feel it. It wasn't a joke anymore. Even the children temporarily lost interest in the shiny new motor car, watching to see if a fight was going to break out. If it did, they would take sides, shout and cat call. The boys would all have shouted for George, but they knew it would be silly to declare their choice before a fight, because if he walked on by, the old men would box their ears to try to teach them loyalty.

It was a fairly even match, George Harris, was in his early twenties, big and fit. He was a man who knew how to look after himself. He dressed like a toff, but everyone knew that underneath the sharp suit, he was as hard as the cobble stones. Three of the older men, facing him, lived in the street. They were known to be ill tempered and argumentative, with all the softness worn out of them by lives of poverty and want. They would as soon fight as not and weren't going to back down easily. George watched Tommy and Jack's Uncle Bill, he was the leader and what happened depended upon him. He was no harder than the others, but he hated George Harris personally. He hated him for being rich, for being young, for being blatantly unprincipled. Most of all he hated him because he was the hero down the street. All their lives Bill and his like had struggled against the injustices of the world. They had fought the Germans and stupid officers, grappled with poverty and bloodsucking bosses and landlords. They had nothing but endless defeats from all their fights and this clown had it all for the taking. By being successful, he had betrayed them and Bill could never forgive him.

'Turn's right,' sneered Frank Smith, the thin weasel faced man who had been leaning against the lamp post moved to the edge of the group, 'music hall turn. You look like Max Miller dressed up like that.'

George Harris stood eyeing the angry men, silently cursing his own stupidity. He knew them of old and shouldn't have antagonised them. He knew they would fight because fighting was all they knew. It was all anyone knew down Wilmott Street and it just needed the spark to set them off. Not that he wasn't a scrapper himself. In the normal course of events, he would have gone for them and backed himself to win, it was just that the suit was new and he didn't want to get it dirty or torn before Phyllis had seen it.

The options open to him raced through his head. There was a set of brass knuckles in his coat pocket, but with it casually draped over his shoulders, he wasn't sure that he could slip them on before the blows started raining down on him and any quick movement now would certainly bring the first punch. On the other hand, he couldn't turn around and walk away; he had a reputation to think of.

There was a movement in the corner of his eye and George saw another figure leap over a garden hedge and move purposefully across the road to stand behind him. He didn't dare turn away to gauge this new threat, but slowly his hand began to creep out from under his overcoat.

'What you want our Tommy?' Bill demanded looking over George's shoulder to where the newcomer had stopped. By where he stood, Uncle Bill knew which side he was on. 'This ain't none of your fight. Stay out of it.'

Tommy Sutton flicked away the end of his cigarette and moved a little closer to George's shoulder. 'I didn't see no-one pick up sides. It seems to me that it's anybody's fight.'

'Your dad's not going to be pleased if you take his part against us.'

'I'm a big boy now Uncle Bill, I choose where I stand and I don't ask me dad's permission anymore.'

George risked a glance over his shoulder to check who the new arrival was and relaxed when he saw Tommy Sutton. 'Long time no see, Tom,' he said, without taking his eyes off the men who barred his way. 'I'm on me way to see our Gladys before I pop in on Phyllis. I'll be in the Gillespie later if you've got time for a drink?'

'Always got time for a drink with you George, I probably owe you one. Lead on. I don't think there's any problem here anymore.'

George laughed. 'You could be right. There's racing at Ally Pally this evening, Me and Phyllis is going up there to meet some blokes I know. Fancy coming?'

'Why not,' Tommy mused. He hadn't been up the

Palace for ages, not since Maurice Higgins died and that was a long while ago. 'I've not been up there for years,' he exaggerated, 'and there's not much happening down here. Mind you, I've got no money. I can't even buy you that drink.'

'That's OK,' George nodded at the gleaming motor bike in the Sutton's front garden. 'I can see I'm not the only one who's got a new toy. I'll sub you for a few quid. You can let me have it back later.'

The four old men saw the balance of power swing against them. They had taken enough beatings over the years on matters of principle not to waste their time getting another, just for the sake of it and so, begrudgingly, they moved aside. As George passed Bill Duncan, he half turned and drove his fist like a piston into the old man's stomach, sending him sprawling into the road. 'If I'm like Max Miller, why aren't you laughing Bill? Lost your sense of humour?' He demanded, spitting the words at the old man in fury before he walked on. Tommy winced at the power of the low blow. Anger flared, he stepped forward, then, like a match in a wind, it quickly disappeared. 'You asked for it Uncle Bill,' he said looking at his uncle lying among the horse shit in the gutter and panting for air. 'When you tell me dad what happened, tell him that too.'

'And tell him that there's always some fascist to give it out.' Peggy shouted from the back of the crowd 'Come the revolution and scum like you will get what they deserve.'

Everybody gawped at the newcomer.

'Mind your own business darling,' Tommy snapped, 'I think you're in the wrong street.'

'Don't you darling me. or I'll kick you in the crutch so hard that your balls will come out of your head like another pair of ears.'

The watching women were impressed and called out an 'oooh' to mock the two men.

'Don't argue with the silly tart,' George snarled, 'belt her.'

Looking over the hedge from his seat on the motor bike, Jack watched the two people in the world he cared for most, crash head on. A sense of panic bubbled up inside him, he wanted to step between them, make them friends, but couldn't move. In the end all he could do was call lamely, 'it's all right Tom, she's with me'.

Tommy turned on his brother in fury. 'Oh, this is the nurse is it? I should have guessed, they've all got mouths the size of the Holborn Tram Tunnel. If you take my advice Jacky boy, you'll get Loopy Lou to take those stitches out, he may be rough, but he'll be softer than her.' Then Tommy laughed, but there was no humour in his voice.

'Watch what you're saying, Tom, she's my friend.' Jack shouted back. He felt tears burning in his eyes, but he chose his side too. He leapt over the hedge to angrily face his brother on the pavement.

'Then you should choose your friends more carefully.'

'That goes for us all,' Jack snapped back. The two of them stood eye to blazing eye.

Tommy let his heavier body sway forward and Jack couldn't resist his strength, he had to back away. 'You better start watching your lip, little brother, a mouth like that could get you razored just as easy as being a hero.' Tommy pushed his brother across the pavement and turned away. Without looking back at him, he said, 'you're right George, it seems we do all have new toys'.

He bent down and picked up the battered old cap from where it lay on the paving stones and threw it to his uncle. 'Come the revolution and the same people will get the cake as 'ave got it now. I'm going to get my slice while I can.'

'We're picking sides for a new game, young Tom,' Uncle Bill growled. 'And if you want to be on the winning side, you'd better stay away from the likes of George Harris.'

Part of Jack wanted to laugh. The four old men looked like the Four Stooges. He wanted to believe that they were a comedy team and it was all a laugh. Tommy had laughed at his uncle tumbling over in the road and the other three scrambling back out of the range of another blow. He was used to being pushed around by Tommy, but today it was different. Somehow Jack couldn't laugh. He was burning up inside with fury, but wasn't sure who he was angry with. He shouted at Peggy.

'What did you do that for? It's none of your business. You should have stayed out of it.'

Jack's anger seemed to pass Peggy by. She spoke to him quietly, like a school teacher to a child. 'It's Party business Jack. Stick with me and I'll show you how every time some little thug starts knocking down old men in the street, just for standing up for the rights of workers, the comrades must fight back. You were there when comrade Pollitt told us about this bloke Hitler in Germany, Mosely's the same and so is George Harris. We fight them all, we fight all fascists.'

'She's right Jack, it's all for the cause.' Bill had climbed to his feet now and was picking the lumps of horse manure off his worn and patched trousers. 'and our brothers are the comrades from the Party.'

Acky pushed his way out of the scrum of children to join Jack. 'Here,' he said, sliding four pennies into Jack's hand. 'It's money for old rope.'

'Stuff the money Acky. I don't want nothing from George Harris.'

Acky shrugged when Jack turned fiercely on him, almost as though he thought it was his fault, he was used to the Suttons' temper and it didn't bother him anymore. Acky felt that despite his being a comrade, Bill had it coming. Jack's Uncle Bill had a big mouth and it was only a matter of time before somebody shut it for him with their fist. It was a shame it had to be like this. George Harris was just that bit too old to ever have been a friend, but he was almost a neighbour. He didn't say that to Jack. 'George didn't need to hit him like that.' he admitted.

'Tommy shouldn't 'ave let 'im.' Jack snapped

angrily. He looked at the pennies in his hand which Acky had gathered off the pavement and, letting his hurt flow into them, threw them with all his might over the roof of Acky's house up onto the railway.

Acky looked at the gleaming coins in his own hand, there were sweets, fish and chips, or a trip to the pictures there. Resignedly he spat into the palm of his hand and sent them spinning after their compatriots.

'Who's Loopy Lou?' Peggy asked, when she finally let herself be led up the front path of number twenty-four.

Jack had a quick look up the street. 'Louis Botterell; he gone now, but he was the fat moonfaced bloke dancing up and down at his gate. He's the local loony. He lives with his mum down in the end house. They say he likes little boys, but because he can't get any, he makes do with looking after animals. He keeps picking up stray cats and dogs and tries to sew up their cuts and mend their broken legs. There's no harm in him really, but when he has one of his turns, he's been known to hurt them so bad that they die. His mother tries to keep him out of trouble, but my Mum reckons that it's only a matter of time before they put him away.'

'I noticed him,' Peggy said. 'Mongol boys don't normally live that long. Somebody should do something.'

'Oh, Peggy, stay out of it. What's there to do? Loopy's a simple soul. If the authorities got involved, they'd only lock him up in Colney Hatch. That would mean they had to put his mother away as well. He doesn't mean any harm and nobody down this street would shop him for the sake of an odd old dog or two.'

Peggy reached out and gently traced the livid line across his forehead and cheek. 'Your thinking's like your face, a mess, but we'll see what can be done about both of them.'

Jack reached up and held her soft hand against his cheek. It was cool against the still inflamed flesh. Even though they were standing on the front door step, with an impetuous gesture, he pulled her hand across slightly so that it rested against his lips. He didn't want her to move her hand, but she firmly insisted. To his amazement it was only to replace it with her lips.

It was just a little peck, but in that instant Jack too changed in the eyes of Wilmott Street.

Chapter 5

Respected Comrade Robertson,

I send this letter as an addendum to my monthly report of July on branch matters and personnel and forward it to you through the usual confidential channels.

I feel I should draw your attention to some of the actions of Comrade Rabinovitz. He is beginning to show some evidence of a divided loyalty in his approach to the Party's position with regard to Anti-fascism which might be regarded as leftist. Comrade Sutton revealed to me that Rabinovitz has lately become involved in a Jewish defence organisation in the East End of London. Rabinovitz's involvement with this Jewish Defence League seems, at present, consistent with the position laid down in the Daily Worker and explained at branch meetings. Rabinovitz has spoken at Branch committee meetings, of the strongly anti fascist nature of the organisation and says that it recruits from a broad spectrum of the Jewish community. He feels that such an organisation, using the concept of the United Front, and if led by active Party men could form a nucleus from which a Red Militia might be formed.

I have also attended a secret meeting in East London where Cmde Rabinovitz has spoken. When he has spoken of armed uprising, it was not in the cause of the Worker's Dictatorship, but in the narrow cause of Jewish self interest. On both occasions his speeches have quoted Trotsky. He has not mentioned the heretic revisionist's name in my hearing, but the use of such a source for quotes when better examples can be found in the work of Cmde Stalin or Lenin, must be suspect. The support of violence not sanctioned by the Party and the use of such leftist deviationist terms show a pattern of thought which, I feel I should inform you about. They could, eventually, lead him to question the Party line.

I have not discussed my concerns with Cmde Sutton, rather I have encouraged him in his association with Rabinovitz as I feel it is the best way of keeping the Party informed of any departure to the Party Line.

I have formed an intimate relationship with Cmde Sutton. I cannot deny that this is not unpleasant for me, but I feel it is also beneficial to the Party's interest and I shall allow it to progress as it will.

Using our closeness, I shall endeavour to advance his education in the line of right thought and avoid his being contaminated with the deviationism of the Rabinovitz clique. I hope you will inform me of any specific area of information I should pursue and of any action that you think would be advantageous

Comrade M. Watkins

'Acky,' Jack yelled as he raced across the street. 'Lend us your bike'

'Do what?' Acky demanded.

'Lend us y' bike for the weekend,' Jack repeated. 'Go on, be a sport.'

'Get lost, I'm using it.'

'Don't mess about Acky, this is important. You never use your bike at the weekend, you always use the horse and cart.'

'Well I'm using it this weekend, so y' can go whistle.'

'Oh come on Acky,' Jack dropped into his most wheedling tone. 'You know you don't really need it. Lend us it. I'll make it worth your while.'

'Forget it, Jackie, I'm going up to the YCL camp up at Broxbourne. I put my name down at the last YCL branch meeting.'

'You can't. That's where I want to go. You said you were going out with your old man to see your auntie and you couldn't go. Ah come on Acky, I promised Moses that I'd go.'

Since the razor attack, Jack had grown quite close to Moses Rabinovitz. Moses had adopted him as his sort of lieutenant and they worked together a lot. Moses would often pop in to their house after they'd been out selling the Daily Worker or chalking slogans on pavements and walls. His mother thought he was an odd man and was uncomfortable having her employer's son in her house, acting as her equal, particularly as she felt that his own father would not have approved. But she did her best and hid her feelings and tried to treat him as kindly as any of Jack's friends.

Jack's dad couldn't stand his politics, he'd sit and talk socially enough while the chat was about Spurs or what Middlesex were doing pre-season, but if ever the conversation drifted towards unemployment, the Labour Party, or what was wrong with the world, Mr. Sutton would grunt, knock out his pipe and stomp out of the room. He got enough of that from Jack.

'Well it looks like Moses will have to do without you,' Acky said callously.

'But you wouldn't go without me would you?' Jack demanded.

'Well,' said Acky defensively, then, taking a deep breath added. 'All right then, if you don't go then I won't.'

'You're a good mate, Acky,' Jack said with relief. 'So you're not going?'

'No.'

'Well if you're not going can I lend your bike? Peggy said that if I could find one, I could cycle up there with her on Saturday morning and come back Sunday night. It's all organised, I've got George Turrell to do me round on Saturday.'

'You bastard. So that's what it's all about is it? You randy little sod? Well hard cheese, I've got me own plans. You're not the only one that can get a girl. I'm going with Muriel. We're all riding up together.'

'Oh no, not Muriel Potts,' Jack protest, 'you know what she's like, for a small port and lemon, she's anybody's.'

'Yes,' Acky leered, 'and with a bit of luck, this weekend she's mine. Anyway what do you want my bike for? Why don't you borrow Tommy's? He doesn't use it anymore.'

'He sold it when he bought the motor bike.' Jack grabbed the spindly Plane tree which stood in the street outside Acky's house and banged his head against it. 'There must be somebody with a bike I can lend.'

'Loopy Lou's got bike and he never rides it. His Mum won't let him.' Acky pointed out with a half laugh. 'Give him a kiss and he'll lend it.'

Jack sucked air through his teeth. 'I wonder if he'd do it for a bag of sweets.'

'He might, but I wouldn't let his Mum see you asking. You know what she's like.'

Thrusting his hands deep in his pocket Jack

contemplated the situation. His Uncle Bill would certainly lend him his if he asked, but if he turned up on that squeaky old bone shaker, everybody would laugh at him. This weekend was far too important; he couldn't risk Peggy laughing. Whichever way he looked at the problem, it had to be Loopy's bike. It was nearly new, bright red, with drop handle bars and a racing saddle. There was nothing for it, it was going to be Loopy's bike.

'You've no chance,' Acky laughed when Jack told him his decision. 'You'll never get past the old dragon.'

'No problem,' Jack said determinedly. 'I can get past her easily and speak to him. Loopy's got no idea what's going on. We can tell him anything. And I'll buy him some sweets. I'll give them to him on Monday, when we bring the bike back.'

'Where did this 'we' come from all of a sudden?'

'Oh go on Acky, we can sneak down the railway embankment on Friday night and borrow it out of their coach house. We can hide it in your yard until Saturday morning and then we'll put it back Sunday night. They won't even miss it.'

'You hope,' Acky commented dryly.

'Anyway, we're comrades and they're the bourgeoisie. We're liberating it for the use of the proletariat,' said Jack. 'All property is theft.'

'Yeh,' Acky gave in as he usually did and with a laugh they exchanged clenched fist salutes.

***

Though Jack seldom rode a bicycle or took any regular exercise away from work, he had no trouble in keeping up with the leading group of cyclists as they streamed out of White Hart Lane onto the Cambridge Road. His present milk round, which took him up Stamford Hill and through Clapton, was a killer. Old Len Barnes, who had the round about three years ago had literally dropped dead behind his milk float and George Turrell who had the round last, had to move onto lighter duties in the yard because he couldn't cope with the Hill anymore. After only a couple of months Jack had legs like Oak branches, a back of iron and shoulders like a spiv's jacket. It was only his backside which was soft and before they had gone five miles, he was beginning to wish he'd borrowed Loopy's mother's bike which had a saddle like an armchair. It was as they were coming to the Halfway House pub, one or two of the less dedicated showed that they were suffering too. They began calling to each other about the chance of a quick break in loud voices so that the leaders could hear.

Jack realised that to be a leader in the Party, one had always to be at the front. Moses, like a bean stick on an old 'sit up and beg' machine which was even older than Uncle Bill's, was driving his pedals round like a maniac in an effort to keep up with Frank who was puffing and blowing as he fought not to be left behind, while Peggy was red in the face in her effort to keep with them and ahead of Doreen. None of them allowed themselves a backward glance or listened to the weak.

Jack and a few of the others could have sailed on ahead of their leaders, but there was a silent barrier across the road which kept them in their place. From time to time he would ease up alongside Peggy and exchange a smile. One of them would say something silly about the weather or how near the end they were and then he would ease off and fall back into place behind her rear wheel.

He was not unhappy there. He could watch her tight little bottom rolling on the saddle and dream erotic dreams. She was wearing black cycling shorts, a red short sleeved shirt and her hair was tied up with a red scarf. As she became hotter, her sweat soaked clothes clung more tightly to her, accentuating the curves of her body and revealing more about her underwear than she might have wished.

The delights of the view could not prevent Jack's joy as they eventually turned off the road and bumped down the track to the field where their tents were already pitched beside the river. For the last four or five miles his backside and thighs had been so sore that he had been standing on his pedals to avoid any contact with the saddle. He wasn't alone, as the group tumble through the gate, they threw their bikes onto the ground and staggered round like stick men trying to restore the circulation to their bodies and then crying bitterly as the pain engulfed them from the waist down.

'Comrades,' Moses called them to order. 'Comrades Peggy Watkins, Frank Mitchell and myself have divided you up into groups. Comrade Peggy will lead the girls group which will be called La Passionaria, Comrade Frank will lead you six. With a nervous flick of his hand indicated the knot to his right. You will be known as the Stalin group; I will lead the other five in the Georgi Dimitrov group.' Acky caught Jack's eye and winked, they were both in Moses' group. Frank was a boring old fart with no sense of fun and Moses was a lot easier to live with.

'I have drawn up a rota of duties for each group.' Frank took up the control of the meeting. 'Each group will carry out the first item on their list immediately, then we will break for a meeting on the political situation in Germany which will be led by Comrade Moses.'

'Oh, no,' Acky protested, 'It must be gone one, I'm starving, let's eat our sandwiches first.'

'Yeh,' one of the Stalinists agreed, 'and I'm knackered after that bike ride. Let's have a rest. We could go for a swim.'

Everyone looked at the cool clear inviting water of the river less than twenty yards from where the tents were pitched and there was a murmur of agreement.

'Comrades,' Moses protested,' we are not just here to enjoy ourselves. We are here to sharpen our assessment of the current political situation. Our fight against the Blackshirts is only part of the great international struggle. Which is itself part of the struggle of the proletariat against the forces of capitalism. The meetings must come first, enjoying ourselves is secondary, no; enjoying ourselves is nowhere.' Moses was beginning to shout and the group around him shuffled uneasily.

'I think we should vote.' Acky stuck to his guns.

Jack knew exactly what he wanted to vote for. The river looked so inviting and the thought of soaking his sore buttocks and aching legs in the cold water was almost sexual. He made the mistake of glancing at Peggy. Her full, red lips pursed slightly as she caught his attention. He sighed and thought of the first time he had really kissed them. In his mother's back kitchen as Peggy was washing blood from his face after removing the stitches. He expected an experience a little like kissing his mother, he expected her lips to be soft, warm and damp. They had been hard and hot, they had clamped themselves to him like a hungry limpet and not let go until they were satisfied. Blood was running from his mouth where she had bitten him in her passion. He wondered if she were thinking the same, her eyes were deeper, cooler than the river and he couldn't tell. Her firm look made his stomach knot. She would want him to vote for the meeting and he put his hand up as required to ensure that the will of the leadership carried the day.

It was late afternoon when they finally broke free of their chains and were able to race across to the river bank and fling themselves into the water. Jack liked swimming, but loitered at the back of the group. Peggy was still in her tent, she said that she had to finish writing up the report on the meeting before she allowed herself to relax and he wanted to be near her. Also his legs were so sore after the towel whipping he had received from those he voted against, he didn't want to risk any more punishment.

When Peggy finally slipped out her tent and ran across the field to the river's edge, Jack had abandoned his guard duty outside the tent and ran for the water's edge. He and Acky were in the middle of a water-weed fight with the others when she finally strolled onto the bank. They had climbed onto a little boat, tied up to the opposite bank, where the sun still shone. They were kicking and pushing the rest away to hold onto their prize. In order to claim a place in the sun, the boys in the water were ripping up handfuls of weed and throwing it at Jack and Acky while the girls nearer the bank cheered them on.

The sight of Peggy in her tight knitted swim suit, with her bouncing breasts looking to escape at any moment from their folds, brought Jack to an excitement which he couldn't conceal from the rest. They howled in derision. As much to quench the blazing fire in his face as the embarrassment in his trunks, he hurled himself off the boat into the water to swim as far and as deep as he could.

Peggy laughed with the others, but with the elegance of a kingfisher, dived into the river towards him. As he surfaced, she was alongside him. She squirted a mouth full of water at him to further cool him down. It was an eloquent statement to the watchers who recognised it as saying that the two of them were now together. The rain of water weed couldn't wipe the smile of smug satisfaction of his face as he swam ashore in Peggy's wake.

'Can I come to your tent later?' he asked, as he reached back to pull Peggy up onto the bank. Suddenly he felt full of confidence and daring.

'Perhaps,' she replied, but her eyes smiled and he was sure she meant yes.

The evening dragged on interminably through camp fire songs and speeches, but at last the fire began to burn down and no one wanted to go and find more wood. They began to remember the cycle ride which had brought them into the country and realise how tired they were.

'Coming to bed?' Acky enquired thoughtlessly as he picked up his blanket from the ground where he had been sitting.

'No, not yet,' Jack stammered. 'I'm not sleepy. I'll think I'll sit by the fire for a while.' It was time for him to test his knowledge of women.

Acky realised that his friend was about to embark on a tremendous adventure. He envied him, was frightened for him, but knew he could be no help to him. After an exaggerated yawn, he gave Jack a playful punch on the shoulder and hurried away to the Dimitrov's tent.

When they finally broke from the passionate

embrace, Peggy pushed him away. Jack's brain was on fire and his body was demanding a satisfaction that he didn't really know how to satisfy. He made a grab for her to pull her back into his arms and in some way search for a release.

'No,' she commanded in a harsh whisper.

'But you said,' he protested.

'I said you could come to my tent, perhaps. I never said anything else. There was no promise'

'But, I thought.' Jack said lamely. He didn't understand and felt totally rejected. He felt as if she was treating him as a boy and he couldn't find a word to say in his own defence. Tears of fury and frustration were making his eyes burn, He could feel the muscles in his arms knotting up and he beat his fists against his own chest to stop from hitting her.

'Don't do that,' Peggy demanded. She swept her arms around him and pinned his arms to his sides. 'You don't understand.'

He struggled to break her grip, but she wouldn't let go. The scent of her body, hot, clean and musky, filled his mind and he wanted her more than he had ever wanted anything and could feel a rage growing inside. 'Let me go,' he pleaded, 'please.'

She shook her head, Jack felt the movement of her breasts held tight against him and it was unbearable.

Uncontrollable tears were coursing down his cheeks. 'Peggy, please let me go. I don't want to hurt you.' Jack was becoming aware of a new self, a dark powerful stranger inside him, who was threatening to break free of the old, easy going boy. He was frightened. He knew what he wanted and if this stranger promised that Peggy would be his, then there would be no restraining him.

'Oh don't be silly, Jack,' she replied. 'I'll let you go when you promise to behave.'

Speaking quietly, so as not to frighten her in the same way that he was afraid, he said. 'Peggy, every morning I lift nearly fifty crates of milk onto my float, two at a time, and then push it to the top of the Hill. I can make you let go, but it would hurt you and I don't want to do that. Don't make me, please.'

What he said was true. She could feel the hard muscles rippling under his shirt. She could feel the power in his body. She could feel the man she had released in him.

With a carefree toss of her head she let go, but moved quickly back towards the end of the tent and temporarily out of his reach. She knew what she had done and realised that there was no escape from the force she had awakened. Truth to tell, the thought of his vigorous young body making love to her was exciting. The thought of opening the door for him to taste the forbidden fruit for the first time with her, and she had no doubt that it would be for the first time, was bringing a hot glow into the depths of her body which the woman did not want to resist.

But she was a leader, she told herself, what she wanted could only be secondary to the best interests of the Party. Giving in to her own passions had to be logical and controlled.

'Jack, this is ridiculous,' she said, trying to regain control of the situation, but in a voice she felt was no longer convincing. 'How old are you?'

Unwilling Jack dragged his mind back from the tension that had set his whole body in a spasm. It wasn't just between his legs, the muscles in his arms ached and his chest had clamped his lungs in a vice and wouldn't let him breath. 'I'm eighteen,' he whispered, his voice grating low and foreign.

'Liar,' Peggy trilled in false gaiety, 'you're seventeen and I'm twenty-four, an old woman.'

'I'll soon be eighteen, anyway age isn't important,' he snarled, 'all that's important is that we love each other.'

Peggy risked reaching out to gently run her finger down the white, puckered scar which divided his left eyebrow in two. It gave a hard edge to his boyish good looks and it fascinated her. 'Jack,' she said gently, 'it isn't like that. I like you, I like you a lot. You are very special to me, but I don't love you.'

Jack caught hold of her hand, too roughly at first and she winced as he crushed it. Instantly he eased his grip and moved down to kiss her fingers and make it better. Speaking with a quiet intensity, he said. 'Peggy, I don't care if you love me. I love my mother, I love my sister, I love you as a comrade, but what I feel for you at the moment is so strong that I don't have a word for it. It's a feeling unlike anything I've ever had before. Whatever it is, it has to be enough for the two of us.

Peggy's free hand softly touched the back of his neck and her fingers twisted the ends of his hair distractedly. 'This is mad,' she whispered. 'What would the others say?'

Jack jerked his head upright and stared angrily into her deep, deep blue eyes. 'You don't care what they think. I've heard you say a hundred times, that you believe in free love; that you'll take any man who catches your fancy.'

'Oh, yes,' she agreed with a sigh and swayed forward to let her lips brush his. In her heart she had given in to the powerful physical attraction and had surrendered to him. She freely acknowledged a weakness in her character. Her desire for a man would sometimes tempt her out of the company of the comrades. She told herself that she would work on this weakness, but not now. Now, she could not wait for him to take possession of her. 'And what makes you think that you have caught my fancy?' she teased, but there was no more resistance in her voice.

To test his claim on her, he slid his arm around her back and drew her close to him. She didn't resist, rather she inclined her face towards his and, half closing her eyes, ran the tip of her tongue over her lips. Unable to resist, he kissed her as hard as he could. Her cry of protest was swallowed up in his hungry mouth, she struggled, beat his chest with the heel of her hand to try to escape his suffocating grip. All that he had claimed for his body was true and there was no way she could break out of his fierce embrace. She stopped trying and let her hungry mouth kiss him back savagely, sinking her teeth in his lip. When he opened his mouth in protest, she forced her tongue into his throat as a prisoner to fortune, if he wished to hurt her back.

As one hand let go its iron grip to hold her breast, suddenly, she thrust herself backwards, away from him. He made a grab for her, to recapture his power, but she knocked his hands away. She had her own imperative now. Kneeling in front of him she caught the edge of her shirt and pulled it up, over her head. Jack stopped, wide eyed, mouth hanging open as Peggy reached awkwardly up her own back and unclipped her bra.

A groan of amazement and desire mixed with horror escaped Jack's lips. The sight of her soft rounded breasts capped with hard pink nipples washed away the last of his self-control. There was no controlling him now. He flung himself at Peggy, clumsily grabbing at her full rounded body.

'Gently,' she commanded. 'You're not lifting crates of milk now.'

As if he were finally convinced that his treasure was not going to be snatched from him at the last moment, he became still and let his hands rest under the hot silky globes.

'Better,' she whispered, laughing softly, then, placing her hands over his, she drew them up to cup her hard pointed nipples and pressed. 'Even better,' she sighed. Leaving his hands to complete their investigation, she caught the waist band of her trousers to wriggle her hips free of her tight black shorts and tighter, white knickers. Kneeling on the crumpled clothes, she raised herself level with him, to reveal herself fully to him.

Of course Jack had had glimpses of his mother and sister without their clothes, but he had never really seen a woman blatantly naked, kneeling before him, like a present, unwrapped and waiting to be played with. Lost, he gazed down at her flat white stomach and the small clump of dark down climbing up from between her legs.

He gave up trying to think, to plan and let himself go. When he wasn't sure what was wanted, he was content to let Peggy guide him. She drew a hand down from her breast, pressing slowly firmly to her body, to ripple of each slight curve, to leave it, at last, tangled amongst her pubic hair.

Jack was terrified, he heart was pounding, sweat poured across his forehead and flooded his eyes so that he couldn't see her naked body any more. He desperately wanted to wipe the sweat away, but he was too frightened to move. He was powerless. Even if he had wanted, he could not have stopped her hands from unbuckling his belt, unbuttoning his flies and pulling his trousers down. She reached between his legs and gently caressed him and suddenly it all became very clear, very simple.

***

When Jack woke next morning, he found himself alone under the blankets. He fought to focus his eyes and thoughts. When he realised that Peggy was missing, the attractive warmth of the bed disappeared and he sat up with a start. Peggy was curled up at the end of the tent. Still naked, she sat still, her knees drawn up under her chin as she hugged herself into a tight ball. Jack had the feeling that she had been like that for a long while, watching him. 'Are you all right?' he asked anxiously.

'No,' she muttered, 'no, I'm not all right.'

'What's the matter?' Jack demanded. A horrible thought had occurred to him, one that he knew he should have thought before.

'You are,' she said 'I think you are dangerous, little boy.'

'You're not going to have a baby are you?' he demanded, blurting out his fear.

She dismissed the question with a jerk of her hand and an indignant snort. 'don't worry about things like that. I'm a nurse and such things are easily organised. No, I'm afraid that I could come to care for you, if I'm not careful.

It was Jack's turn to snort. He snuggled back under the blanket and muttered. 'In that case I'm quite safe, you've never been careful in your life. Remember the time down our street when you called George Harris a Fascist. If I'd not been there, you'd have got your teeth broken.'

'I remember,' she whispered, 'I remember.'

Chapter 6

Dear Alice,

Sorry about the delay in answering your last letter. This is my second or third attempt to write it and put it into a fair hand. It's a shame to have missed you at Nan's on Saturday, but I had to do an extra mornings cleaning at the Jew's house. They were having a do on Sunday for Mrs. R's cousin from Germany, so not working on Shabbat didn't extend to the skivvy and, like you know, you can't say 'no'.

I know I shouldn't really complain, but if you can't moan to your sister who can you moan to. Nothing changes much in our house since I saw you last, which is a good thing and a bad thing.

The good things are that we are all well. Tommy and Jack are both still working and our Sue will be leaving school in a little while with every chance of a job at the Co-op store in the High Street. My sciatica has been quite good recently, which is probably due to the warm weather. Even though Tom can't find any regular work, we're doing all right for money at the moment.

But the atmosphere in the house is dreadful. I'm expected to find a Shabbat Goy every Friday evening to do any work that needs doing up at the Jew's house. I like to send one of the boys, because the rotten old boiler up there is always going out over night and Sue's not very good at lighting it. Jack would volunteer, but Saturday is the busy day on his round. That's good in one way because, he's getting too chummy by half with the Rabinovitz boy for my liking. I think that's where he gets most of his hot headed ideas about equality, revolutions, Russia and the like and that's causing endless rows with his dad.

Tom does it occasionally, to help out, but he's not happy up there and would rather one of the others went. Tommy won't go any more; he says he's too busy, so that just leaves Sue and me.

I don't like to try to force Tommy, because he seems to be getting in with a better set now days. He tells me nothing of course, but I've been told that he's been seen around with Charles Hartwell's crowd. That's the son of Sam Hartwell of Hartwell Engineering. They say that Charlie Hartwell's going into politics and is going to be important one day. I've told Tommy that he should think about coming off the lorries and going into the office. He's a clever boy, he could have had a scholarship, and should start doing something about getting on.

I'm sorry to go on so, but I feel the need to have a good natter to get these things off me chest, so do you fancy going shopping up the Green on Thursday? I'm running short of all sorts of things. And you know what its like having two women in a house, I desperately need to get some you know whats before the weekend. If you can make it, I'll see you in Lyons about ten o'clock.

Hope to see you Thursday

Your loving sister Aggie

'Tommy,' the old Italian barber's smile was broad and genuine. 'I didn't think to see you so early.'

'No, Joe, I'm running ahead of time. Frank Sackville, the publican of the Spread Eagle down Bruce Grove is off on holiday this week and his brother in law is running the place. He's right slap dash, not like old Snap. I was in and out in no time.'

'It's good.' Mr. Ferucciano flashed his golden teeth again. 'You got time for a haircut?'

Tommy ran his fingers through his lank black hair, 'No, I don't think so. I want to get on.'

'It's on the house.'

Tommy smiled, he liked the open hearted little man. He was a rotten gambler, but his haircuts weren't bad. 'No, thanks, Joe. Perhaps I'll pop in later in the week.'

'Don't leave it too long, it's getting very long at the back. People will be taking you for a signorina.' He shrugged his shoulders. 'Ah well, something for the weekend then.' With a wink, he went to the drawer by the till where he kept a stock of contraceptives and from the hiding place under this secret store, brought out a wad of betting slips. 'Not so many this week,' he said, apologetically.

Tommy nodded. With a quick glance towards the door to make sure they weren't observed, he tucked them into the lining of his cap.

The drive down into the industrial estate and the reverse into the bricked up gateway at the back of the White Swan had a new routine to it now. It was Tommy who tucked the brewery dray out of sight and looked around to make sure the coast was clear. 'Stay there and wait for me,' he ordered Cyril Tupper. 'I won't be long. Cyril was a big, open faced lad, who had been given to Tommy as a mate when he was promoted to take over Ollie Dodd's round. He wasn't very bright, but he was strong and willing.

'Yes, Mr. Sutton,' Cyril said, his gaping smile was full of crooked teeth. Tom smiled back, but his eyes narrowed and the corner of his mouth curled slightly, making his expression cold. The lumbering lad didn't notice. He was quite content to stand and wait to be told what to do, in fact, Tommy noticed that he became agitated if he had to make a decision for himself. He didn't think he would have the trouble with Cyril that Ollie used to have with him, but he didn't take any chances. Tommy unloaded any stolen stuff himself and delivered it into the yard, so young Cyril had no reason to wander about.

'Stay in the cab, and don't get out until I come back. Do you understand?'

'Yes, Mr. Sutton.'

Tommy went to slam the door shut when he had an idea. 'Can you read, Cyril?'

'Oh yes Mr. Sutton.'

'Well read this then, it'll improve your mind.' He pulled a newspaper out of his coat pocket and thrust it into the boy's hand. 'I'll ask you questions when I get back.' Tommy had started the habit of pinching a copy of the Daily Worker off the stack Jack left on the hall stand. They were dumped on the front step to deliver by some mystery van driver who appeared out of the dark, unfailing every morning. Jack hid them under a box on his milk float and delivered them when he was out on his round. He or one of his mates would try to sell the rest at Seven Sisters in the evening, after work. No one seemed to count the number of papers delivered and Jack never said that he missed one. It wasn't much of a paper, Tom thought, but it was free and it always had the runners and riders of the day's races on the back. 'And one more thing,' he said.

'Yes Mr. Sutton.'

'Stop calling me Mr. Sutton.' Tom had quite liked the novelty of being called by his surname name, at first. It gave him a sense of importance. Like when Ollie had tried to make him call him 'mister'. Now, at the end of a long day, he was fed up with it. 'Call me Tommy.'

'Yes, Mr. Sutton.'

Tommy scowled, but cut his losses and turned

towards the dilapidated pub. The depression had certainly left its mark in this part of Tottenham, Tommy thought, looking around him, derelict factories, broken walls, piles of rubbish. The only person to be seen was a down and out, with nowhere to go, leaning on a lamp post on the corner. Tommy stared at the man for a moment, then shrugged his shoulders and turned away. He had hated his mother's interference at the time, but he supposed that he was lucky to have been given his job back after he crashed the lorry. He told himself that if he had lost his job, he wouldn't have given up like that bloke had. Tommy had things to do, places to see and there was no way he was going to be a loser.

The gate post he had knocked down on the trip with Ollie Dodds when he'd first driven the lorry, was still lying across the path. He jumped over it with a smile. It was funny how far the world had moved on in a few short months.

As he walked through the pub's kitchen, Tom gave a long low whistle to give a warning that he was on his way. He was becoming used to the conventions of the criminal world. He'd long ago found out that it was sensible not to walk into the saloon bar of the White Swan unannounced. Things went on in there which it was better that he didn't know about.

'Afternoon, Slippers,' Tom said cheerily, as he delivered the betting slips and money he had collected on his round, to Sam Daventry. He was called 'slippers', not because he took the betting slips, but because of his feet. He had terrible bunions and wore carpet slippers nearly all the time. Slippers was Reggie Green's book man, a qualified accountant, though he looked for all the world like a Co-op tally clerk, with his thin pasty face, receding hair and thick glasses. He was as bent as a nine bob note. He'd done time in Pentonville. George said that he'd been caught for getting too involved in a couple of Jewish stock takes, the burning down of factories for insurance purposes.

As soon as he had finished checking in, the constant pressure of the knot of men waiting around Slippers eased

Tommy out to the edge of the crowd. He still didn't know anybody to talk to, except for George, and he seemed busy. Reggie Green liked to keep his runners fairly sweet and there was always a drink at the bar for those who wanted it. Tommy dithered, he didn't really want another drink, but it was the way to get accepted. He looked around at the noisy bunch of hard faced men. 'sod it,' he thought, 'they'll all be here again next time. I'll stop for a drink then.'

'Tommy, you got a minute?' George's voice rang out across the bar catching Tommy before he could make good his escape.

'Sure George, what d'you want?' Tommy asked as he turned back.

'I'm looking for a favour.'

'Anything for you George, you know that.' Tommy raised his hand to catch Michael Murphy's eye. 'What you drinking?'

'Nothing for me, kid. You have one though.

Mick had turned up at his shoulder and Tommy felt that he had to have something. 'Pint of Mild, Michael.'

'What you doing Friday night?' George asked when Tommy had his drink.

Tommy thought for a few minutes. 'Not a lot.' he admitted. 'I'm a bit skint at the moment.'

'Good, good.' George leant close to Tommy's ear. I've got a little job on. I need to get a few of the lads together to do some stewarding for a meeting over at Ilford. You interested? Pays a fiver for a couple of hours' work.'

'Yeh, count me in,' said Tommy enthusiastically. 'God knows, I can certainly do with the dosh. I've already missed one payment on me bike. A couple more and they'll come and take it back'

'Good, we'll turn up there mob handed. I thought we could meet up at the Wheatsheaf first. D'you know it?'

Tommy shook his head.

'Little pub on the corner of Walthamstow High Road, near the station.'

Tommy nodded uncertainly; it wasn't a

Charrington's house 'I know where you mean. It's not one of ours though, and I've never been in there.'

'No, none of us have. That's the point; it means that no-one'll know us.'

Tommy nodded again. He didn't ask why it was a good idea that they weren't known.

'Oh, one last thing,' George tossed at him, just as he was leaving. 'You got a black shirt or jumper?'

'No,' Tommy admitted, not appreciating the question at first and then, as it sank in, he demanded. 'What sort of meeting is this George?'

'You know, Tom,' George grinned 'political. It seems that Charlie Hartwell wants to go into parliament. He's speaking for the British Union of Fascists. You know what these meetings can be like. He wants some muscle in the hall, just in case your brother or any of his mates turn up and try and spoil the party.'

'You're joking?'

George put his oak branch of an arm around Tommy's shoulder to reassure him. 'No one will know. It's miles away. Believe me, I've done loads of them before, there'll be twenty old farts there, Charlie Hartwell and us. There'll be no trouble. It'll be money for old rope, believe me.'

'I don't know George; I really don't know.'

George pulled his arm away. 'You're not getting soft are you Tommy lad?' George demanded with a hard edge to his voice. The implication was clear. There was no place for softness in the gang.

'Me? Soft? Never, you know me better than that. I quite like the old punch ups. It's not that. But a Fascist meeting, cor bloody Hell, George, if anyone found out down our street that I'd been wearing a black shirt, there'd be fucking murder.'

***

'Doing anything exciting tonight, Jack?' Tommy asked casually, as he reached across the red check oil-cloth covering breakfast table, for the jam.

Jack yawned and rubbed his face. He'd been arrested again last night for causing an affray on a picket line at a clothing factory in Stepney. The owner had locked out all his workers when they had demanded a rise in wages. He'd been let off with another caution, but the police waited until all the fuss had died down before releasing him. They hadn't let him out of the cells till nearly two in the morning. It was gone three before he finally got to bed. He couldn't really take in his brother's question. He was too busy trying to pour tea into a cup rather than over the table to think about what he was supposed to be doing.

'I don't know. What day is it?'

'Friday.'

'It, isn't,' he muttered. 'I was sure it was Thursday. Oh God, I've got to go to work. What time is it?'

'Half past six.'

'Oh you're joking,' Jack groaned. He snatched Tommy's slice of bread and jam out his hand and jumped up from the table. 'I can't afford to be late again.'

Tommy made no attempt to defend his breakfast. 'Can you remember what you're doing tonight?' he repeated.

'I don't know,' Jack replied, grabbing his jacket off the back of the door. 'I think that Moses Rabinovitz said that he wants me to meet a couple of people he knows. Then there's a Fascist meeting up Ilford. I should go there, but Peggy's on nights this week and Acky says he's going down the Palais. I don't fancy going on me own. I'll probably go and see Moses; Why?'

'Oh no reason, I was thinking I might go down the Palais me self. I wondered if you wanted to go.'

'No, no thanks Tom,' Jack muttered. 'A nice thought. Another day perhaps.'

'Yer, yer, another day,' Tom agreed. His heart leapt. He'd dreaded the thought that Jack would have been at the Fascist meeting. If he'd have seen him there, it would have torn it good and proper. He knew that Mum would have come around in the end, but Jack would never have spoken to him again and his old man would have taken Jack's side in this, even though he never did in anything else. It was doubly good that Jack's tart wasn't going to be there either. It might just be the doddle that George said.

Agnes Sutton stood to one side to allow Jack to rush for the door. 'I think that you should both spend more time in doors,' she said. 'You're both burning the candle at both ends and you'll make yourselves ill if you're not careful.'

'Oh, Mum, don't be stupid. I haven't got time to sit around. The revolution's coming and I want to be there. It's for the cause.'

'Don't you speak to your mother like that,' Tom yelled at his son. 'I demand some respect in my house.'

'It's not your house; it's Isaac Prendergast's house, this house and hundreds of others. It's social fascists like you who prop up the system by paying exorbitant rents without protest. You're the landlord's lackey.'

'Don't you come in here with your half-baked left wing ideas. I'm nobody's fascist and I'm nobody's lackey. I like to pay my way.'

'How can you pay your way when you can't even get a job?'

That was a low blow and Tom couldn't answer. He flung his pipe into the corner and stormed out into the garden, slamming the door behind him. The sound of echoing crockery filled the resulting silence.

'You shouldn't say things like that to your father. He does his best to find work and you're happy enough to live here.' Agnes shouted at him, twisting her apron in her fists, in agitation.

Jack hadn't meant to say what he had said, the words came out wrong. He respected his father and wanted him to take his place in the class struggle, where he belonged. Flushed with anger and unable to bring himself to say sorry, he stormed out the front door.

Though he hadn't deliberately engineered the row between Jack and their father, Tommy did nothing to calm the situation. He had been worrying how to get the parcel he picked up from Eddie Bainbridge out of the house. He took advantage of all the yelling and slamming doors to race upstairs. He grabbed the brown paper package out of the bottom of his wardrobe and with it discretely hidden under his jacket, ran for the front door. Once the black shirt was safely out of the house and stuffed into one of the panniers on the back of the bike, he breathed a sigh of relief and set off for work with a lighter heart.

***

It wasn't just Tommy who felt uneasy about wearing a black shirt. He was late. George was in the chair and Pete Armstrong and Wally Cook were already well down their second pints and speaking loudly when he arrived at the Wheatsheaf. 'Thought you'd bottled out,' Pete said morosely.

Tommy didn't answer, but was thankful for the glass of beer that George placed in front of him. He raised it in grateful salute and ignored the fact that it was cloudy. 'Just us four?' he asked dourly.

George glanced up at the clock. 'Looks like it,' he muttered. 'Chalky said he was in. Now I'm not sure. We'll give him another few minutes.'

Tommy stared reflectively at the dregs of the beer in his glass. He wished that he had as much guts as Chalky White. He was likely to get a good punching for his principles, but it might be worth it. He wrenched his mind back from such soft thoughts. What did he care what anyone else thought? He was on his own and he'd make it any way he could. 'Give us another, Landlord,' he snapped, pushing his empty glass across the bar, 'and see if you can find something where I can see the bottom of the glass.'

'You saying my beer's cloudy?' the man behind the bar demanded truculently.

'Who knows,' Tommy snapped back, staring him straight in the eyes. 'The glass is so fucking dirty, who can see the beer.'

The landlord could see the anger burning in Tommy's eyes. He glanced nervously at the rest of the group. They were all strangers, but anyone could see that they were hard men. It was obvious that you didn't mind trouble, if you walked into a strange pub in that part of London, wearing a black shirt. 'Sorry mate,' he muttered, 'new barrel, probably hasn't settled yet. Have another on the house.' The publican took a new glass from above the counter and polished it on his apron before filling it generously.

Tommy didn't even acknowledge his victory. He sank the pint in a single gulp. 'Come on,' he said to George, 'Sod Chalky, if we're going to do this, lets it get it over with.'

The others nodded in agreement. 'I'll tell you something for nothing, Georgie,' Pete muttered through clenched teeth as they pulled away from the bar. 'We go back a long way, you and me, and you know I've always been a straight up villain. I know now why the others that you used before didn't come back. I ain't in for this sort of thing and you shouldn't 'ave asked me. I ain't going to back out on you this time Georgie, but I ain't never going to dress up as a Fascist again. Not for nothing, not for nobody, so don't waste your energy punching me 'ead.'

There was a dribble of a crowd around the entrance to the hall when George's big Humber pulled into the car park at the back of Ilford Town Hall and Tommy pulled his bike up alongside him. Tommy, Pete and Wally slunk into the hall behind George and while he went to report to Charlie Hartwell, they slid down to the end of the room. Trying to be invisible, they huddled in a little disconsolate knot in the shadows of a huge Union Flag, which draped across the stage, where the speaker's dais was.

'Well if it isn't Tommy Sutton.' A woman's voice, close behind him, made Tommy jump. Spinning round, he came face to face with Katherine Hartwell. 'Do you remember me?'

Tommy remembered her. He remembered every time he'd seen her since that time, at Alexandra Palace, the week that Maurice died. She was strikingly pretty and it seemed to him that each time he saw her, she looked better. He was amazed that she not only remembered him, but knew his name. 'Hi,' he murmured, attempting to hide his confusion and embarrassment. 'Surprise.'

What on earth are you doing here?' She demanded. 'I was told that your politics were more red than black.'

'Who told you that?'

It was her turn to be a little taken aback. 'No one special, I just heard it around.'

'Was it the same no one who told you my name?' he asked.

'It might have been,' she replied with a arch little smile, 'I really can't remember. But you haven't answered my question, what are you doing here?'

Tommy liked this girl more and more. There was laughter in her voice and a smile in her eyes, which made him relax. He felt he could speak with an honesty that he would never have allowed himself with anyone else except, perhaps, his brother. 'I'm making a fool of myself and wishing I was somewhere else.' Tommy said. 'What about you?'

Katherine recognized the self-deprecation and responded with a little half smile. The girls all said that Tommy Sutton was good looking, but perhaps he wasn't the boorish fool, which she had always been led to believe, by friends who knew him better. 'Yes,' she agreed, 'I'd rather be somewhere else as well, but the family demands. You know how it is.'

He laughed quietly. 'Yes,' he said, 'my family demands that you are not seen in a black shirt at a BUF meeting. George promised that there wouldn't be any one here who could possibly recognize me, but you're the second person I've seen who knows me.'

'Well at least I haven't that problem. Charlie says that it is good public relations for a political figure to have a good woman beside him. As he doesn't have a good woman of his own, I've been delegated to serve. The loving sister, full of good works and patriotic fervor.' Her eyes stopped laughing as she spoke and there was no avoiding the bitterness in her voice.

Tommy nodded in agreement. 'I'm liking this less and less. Let's see what we can do about cutting the old nonsense short. I've got an idea.' He leaned a little closer. 'From what I remember, your brother's no great hero.'

Katherine gave a snort. 'I'm a better man than he is. He has the back bone of a jelly fish.'

'Yes, that's what I remember.' Tommy said. 'Now, if you sidle up to him and say that there are half a dozen or so Bolshie hard liners in the hall. He knows the type, the ones with knuckle dusters on their fists and razor blades in their caps. Say you've been warned that they intend to cause trouble. Tell him he's not to worry, because if a fight breaks out, me and a couple of the others are under orders to get him and you out of the back door.'

Katherine smiled nervously, 'there aren't, are there?'

Tommy grinned broadly, 'would I lie to you, lady. Now go and do your bit. I'll go and talk to one of my mates. He doesn't like this any more than I do. Then I'll go and get George stoked up.'

'I think we might have a problem here George,' Tommy said quietly sidling up behind him and trying to stay as much in the shadows as possible. 'My brother Jack said that some of his crowd are going to be here tonight. I know some of this lot by sight, Jack's pointed them out. round and about. They're Bolshies for sure. There must be three or four of 'em in the hall and there's going to be more outside. If they're here mob handed like this, it must mean trouble.' Tommy didn't actually recognize any of the audience, but there were two other men in their working overalls already in their seats and a couple of hatchet faced women, who looked the part. Any way it didn't matter, he was only interested in putting the idea in George's mind. And he knew Gentleman George well enough by now, to know how to plant the doubts in a place where he would take notice. 'If I was you, I'd think about moving me car out of the car park. Both you and it are too well known, even out here. When we throw them out of the hall, they'll try and smash it up for sure.'

'Just let the bastards try,' George snarled and he smashed his right fist into his left palm. 'We'll see what gets smashed.' Like a tiger, he began to prowl up and down the central aisle, eyeing each new member of the audience who came in, with deep suspicion. Taking a decision, he called out to Pete, 'you're in charge for a minute, I'm going to move me car round the Johnny Horner.'

Pete nodded that he had heard and his face showed that he didn't like it. 'I wish I was round the bleedin' corner,' he said and then added. 'I've had enough of this. I'm off.'

'I'm with you,' Tommy muttered grimly, 'but I'm not keen to get me head punched in by George. 'I've got a plan to finish this. Are you in?'

Pete smiled grimly, 'I'm in.'

Tommy nodded, 'when the trouble starts give me darkness and a riot.'

Charlie Hartwell was a good speaker. His powerful voice boomed through the ornate room and filled every corner without the need for microphones. 'Fellow citizens,' he began. 'Brother Englishmen,' and then remembering that women had the vote added 'And English ladies. I am here to unashamedly appeal to your patriotism. There is a deadly peril stalking across Europe out of the East. Russian Bolshevism is…'

'Lies,' a young man, in slacks and a blazer, totally unknown to Tommy, leapt to his feet and began to shout. He was red faced with passion. 'It is Germany which is the threat.'

'Get him,' Pete growled to Wally. 'And punch his lights out before you throw him in the street. I don't want him in any state to cause more trouble.'

'Right Pete,' said Wally, unenthusiastically and he lunged over the rest of the audience in the row to grab the young demonstrator. People close to the young man sprang to their feet and tried to get more than a fists length from the impending action.

'Down with the Fascists,' one of the hatchet faced women cried from another part of the hall. 'Long live Soviet Russia, Long live Stalin.'

Pete made a grab for her, then an attractive blonde at the back of the hall began to chant, 'Down with the Fascists.'

'Oh shit,' Tommy muttered. He recognized Peggy Watkins at once.

'Get her Tommy,' George chose that moment to walk back into the hall, 'and give her a right beating. She's had it coming.

Tommy shrank back into the gloom and looked towards the back door. It was Pete who turned the lights out and saved him. Tommy merely tipped over a cupboard to increase the confusion; then threw a chair though a windows to give the sense of an attack from outside. Women started to scream and men shout, chairs were overturned and the audience began to fight among itself in an effort to reach the doors.

Tommy had his route to the front of the stage mapped out before the lights went out and quickly hurried to where Charlie Hartwell was shouting out into the darkness for light and for no one to panic.

Tommy crashed through the tumbled chairs, flinging one up onto the stage where it struck the prospective candidate on the knees. 'Come on Charlie,' He said catching him by the shoulder. 'George said to get you out of here. He said one or two of the Bolshie's have got razors in their caps.' He didn't give him time to argue, even if he had intended to. He pushed him off the stage and bundled him towards the back door. As Charlie stumbled out in front of him, Tommy reached out and caught Katherine's hand. With a conspiratorial squeeze, he pulled her after him, down the steps and out into the night.

Pete was already there. 'You go with Charlie and Katherine,' he said pushing them towards the big black Austin. It took of an effort of will to send any one else with Katherine, but he didn't see Pete Armstrong as a possible rival and he wasn't going to leave his motor bike behind. 'I'll follow you on my bike.'

With George in the lead, the little convoy roared away into the night at top speed. It slowed momentarily as a police car raced past in the opposite direction with its bell clattering and then raced back towards the safety of North London. As they reached The Angel, Edmonton, and stopped at the lights, Tommy allowed himself to pull up alongside the car. Katherine was looking out. He pulled his goggles up onto the top of his head and winked. She smiled.

The lights turned to green and the Austin moved away, rapidly. Tommy let out his clutch, intending to stay alongside but his front wheel hit the metal strip marking the center of the road. The next thing he knew, he was lying in a heap, with the Triumph sliding away across to the other pavement.

He staggered to his feet and watched the retreating car disappear without the driver giving him more than a departing glance in the mirror. 'Bastard' he mouthed and raised his arm in a Fascist salute, then impetuously changed it into a clenched fist.

He didn't know that Katherine had seen his tumble and yelled for her brother to stop. Charlie didn't listen, the soldiers of the right must expect to fall in the service of their leaders. Looking back through the rear window, she saw Tommy on his feet in the road.

When he saw her white, anxious face watching him, his straight arm crooked and his fist clenched into the Communist salute. She laughed. He didn't look too badly hurt and was still defiant against her brother's stupid ideas.

He saw her smile. The sore hip which made him limp across to his fallen machine, was nothing. He didn't even mind the scrape on the petrol tank, the dented mudguard or the bent foot rest. He sang *The Internationale* as he chugged home like a true son of the revolution. Jack would be proud of him.

Chapter 7

Dear Alice,

Just a brief note to ask if you saw the local paper? Jack says that this was Tommy's doing. It seems he teamed up with Jack's lot and shut down the Fascist meeting. His dad hasn't said anything, but I think he's really proud of him. I cut the piece out and will show you when I see you.

Love Aggie

TOTTENHAM HERALD

RED RIOT WRECKS B.U.F. MEETING

A meeting of the British Union of Fascists was ended when a number of Communist agitators disrupted a meeting addressed by Mr. Charles Horville at Ilford Town Hall on Wednesday evening. Mr. Horville was attempting to lay Mr. Oswald Moseley's policies before the electorate before the Bolshevik rabble forced the early close of the meeting. Mr. Horville was unable to deliver his message of hope to the nation, but a transcript of his speech is printed on page seven of this newspaper. The Editor of the Gazette will not let an anarchist minority disrupt the freedom of speech which is the right of every true

Englishman.

'Coming to the match this afternoon' Acky's words were more of a statement than a question. He knew that he'd have a battle to persuade Jack, but he was determined. 'Well,' Jack said defensively. 'I've only just got in from work. I rushed round special to get back early, but I don't think I've got time. Peggy said that there's an Aid Spain rally at Battersea today. She wants me to go to make up the numbers. I've got a pile of 'Workers' on the hall-stand which won't sell themselves and I said to the committee that I'd start looking for a hall for our Aid Spain Dance.'

'Look, Jack, you know I'm as much for the Party as the next comrade,' Acky said with true passion, 'but we're playing Bradford. It's a key game and we'll slaughter them. You've got to be there. If we're going to get back into the First Division, us supporters can't abandon the team now, just when they really need us. It's disloyal, the Party wouldn't want that.'

'No,' Jack admitted grudgingly, 'It's just that, well.' He let the sentence peter out with the crucial point unsaid.

'Yeh, I know, Peggy said,' Acky growled and gave an irritable kick at a clump of grass growing out of the pavement. Then an idea suddenly struck him and he beamed. 'I know, we'll take a dozen or so Workers with us and sell 'em outside afterwards. If we win they'll be gone in ten minutes. And if we lose. 'He shrugged elegantly. If the lost, then they might just as well stay down White Hart Lane trying to sell papers. And we could put a couple of lumps of chalk in our pockets and do some chalking down the High Road on the way. Think of the crowds that'll see them. That'll earn us a few points.'

Jack smiled and Acky could see that he was weakening. He knew that Jack wanted to go and sensed that he had nearly worn Jack's resistance into holes.

Building on his advantage, he said 'We could come back via Tottenham Hale and have a look at that hall that Alf told us about down there. It might be good for the dance. Go on, it'll be great.' Scenting victory, Acky threw down his final card. 'We could take Tommy with us and we could ask my dad and have a whip round for yours. It'll be just like the old days.'

'It's not just going to the match.' Jack still struggled with his conscience. 'What about the 'Workers'? I'm down to sell them for a couple of hours this afternoon.'

'No problem,' Acky countered, not prepared to be defeated in his plan. 'Ask Skinny Wheeler to do it for you. He's a Gunner's supporter and they're away at Wolves today. You can offer to do one for him next time Arsenal's at home and we're away. Perfect. Without giving Jack time to think of any more reasons, he said, 'I'll go and ask my dad, you go and ask your lot. Whatever happens, call for me about one, OK?'

'OK,' Jack agreed morosely already feeling guilty at having given in. To rely on comrade Wheeler went against the grain. He was a man Jack saw as a possible rival. Skinny was two or three years older than him and was a fairly recent recruit to their YCL branch. He had an enthusiasm for Party business, which Peggy was always holding up to Jack as a shining example. Jack could have disliked the man intensely, if he put his mind to it. Though he had to admit that he would have been even more jealous if Harry Skinner wasn't built like a six foot bean stick, with teeth down to his chin. Skinny had supported The Orient before he joined the YCL, but felt that the Gunner's red made them a more proletarian team. Peggy had smiled at that and made a snide remark about those who draped themselves in blue.

Jack had indignantly protested that Tottenham Hotspurs didn't play in blue They were the Lillywhites, he said proudly and Peggy had laughed at him again. Sometimes she treated him like a boy, to put him down. 'That's even worse,' she chided, 'white is the colour of the counter revolutionaries.'

Peggy's jokes always had a strand of barbed wire running through them and Jack had briefly thought about changing teams as well. He rejected the idea almost at once.

He had always been a Spurs supporter; the family had always been for Tottenham. His dad used to take him and Tommy to the match when they were small and they would stand on boxes behind the Park Lane goal with the rest of Wilmott Street.

Jack loved Peggy more than anything, but if she'd made an issue of his supporting the Lillywhites, he would have to stop going altogether. That would have been like going into exile. He could never have sold his soul and gone to Highbury; that would have been treason. Except, of course, when The Spurs were away and there wasn't much else to do.'

'Cheer up,' Acky said, giving his friend a punch, 'It'll be worth it, it'll be a great game.'

'OK. I'll come,' Jack nodded, 'It might be a good opportunity to have a talk with our Tommy away from the house. There's a couple of things that need sorting out.' It seemed to him that there might be another advantage of going that he'd rather Peggy didn't know about. Acky had obviously heard the rumours about Tommy being at the Fascist meeting and now would think that Jack wanted to talk to him about that. Jack knew his friend wouldn't want to see another row in the Sutton house, particularly one that was likely to come to blows. It would be a good cover for his real need to see Tommy somewhere quiet.

'I think it's a wonderful idea for you all to go to football together.' Aggie Sutton beamed and, looking Tommy straight in the eyes, added, 'and your dad won't mind you paying for him. Hasn't he paid for you both often enough in the past.'

The thought of domestic peace breaking out galvanised Aggie into a flurry of action. Dinner would have to be on the table early so she wanted something quick. 'Run down to the butchers for me, Sue, and get two pound of beef sausages.' she ordered, rummaging under the sink to make sure she had enough potatoes.

'Oh Mum, do I 'ave to,' Sue whined. 'This'll be me last Saturday off before I start work. Can't one of the boys go.'

'Do as you're told.' Aggie drove her out of the kitchen with a flapping apron. 'and don't you dare stop and talk to anyone on the way. I want you back in five minutes.'

'Football, yuk,' Sue grimaced at her brothers as she went out of the back door. 'Who wants to go and see a lot of grown men chase a ball around.'

Planning the meal as if it were a special banquet, Aggie thought she would get one of Tom's cabbages out of the garden and she had some stale bread, she might have time to make a bread and butter pudding for afters.

Aggie was pink with pleasure as she stood back from the three men eating around the kitchen table. In her delight, she dragged their old scarves out of the bottom drawer and found the rattle they always used to take when they were boys.

'Oh Mum,' Jack started to complain, 'we're not kids any more, you don't expect us to wear those old scarves like...' Jack caught his brother's eye and glanced across at his father. The old man's knuckles were white as he hung onto his knife and fork, fighting with himself not to spoil his wife's pleasure by arguing at the dinner table again. Jack caught the mood, he coughed and then applied himself to almost scraping the pattern off his plate as he finished his pudding, not saying another word until he complimented his mother on her cooking. As he left he took the Tottenham scarf off the hall stand without a murmur and tucked as much inside his jacket as he could. His only consolation was that Peggy was unlikely to see him. Everybody at the hospital wanted to go to the match and she had swapped her free Saturday so that she could go to the BUF meeting at Ilford. He was sure no-one would swap back.

After the game, Tommy, Jack and Acky entered the Gillespie as if they were the conquering heroes. They had their arms around each other's shoulders, their scarves were wrapped around their arms like banners. 'Up the Spurs,' Tommy bellowed to the startled occupants of the Public Bar and Jack whirled the rattle so that it sounded like a hail storm on a tin roof.

They had not got down to much chalking and what they had was more in favour of their team than supporting the cause of the left. Len Ackfield had been so elated by the game and the result that he bought all the 'Workers' off the lads and had the good grace to wait until their backs were turned before he binned them. Even so it had taken an age to walk up the High Road. The pub doors had been open for five or ten minutes by the time they arrived

'Hold your noise lads, you're not at the match now,' Eddie Bainbridge complained, but there was no venom in his protest. He would have given a lot to have gone himself. To know the local team had had a victory gave him considerable pleasure, but he was the landlord, and he would have order in his bar.

'I'll get 'em in.' Tommy shouted over his shoulder to the crowd bustling to get in behind. He danced to the bar. 'You should have been there Eddie, it was magic. Morrison scored four before half time.'

'The chance would be a fine thing. I'd get a right load of complaints if I wasn't open on time because I went to watch football on a Saturday afternoon,' Eddie grumbled. 'What do you want to drink?'

'Oh the usual for the old 'uns,' he said nodding to his father and Len Ackfield. 'I'll have a pint of bitter. What about you Jacky boy?' he called across to his brother. Jack had pulled old Mrs Grimble, Acky's maternal grandmother, out of her corner seat and was pretending to dance with her.

'Champagne,' Jack called back. 'Nothing but the best for the proletariat.'

'Champagne, be buggered, you'll drink ordinary and like it,' Tom laughed.

Before they had finished their first round, a steady trickle of people coming in after the match was beginning to pack both bars of the Gillespie. The few women in the crowd were given the seats and the men of Wilmott Street commandeered the corner by the dart board. There was a festival atmosphere in the pub, constant laughter and loud talk about first division football.

It was Bill Duncan who brought the first cloud over the day. 'What you drinking Uncle Bill?' Tommy called out, seeing his uncle walk through the door.

Bill Duncan didn't have any sons to buy him a ticket to the match and had the hump with the world. 'I don't drink with Fascists,' he snapped.

In the crush, Tommy was packed tight to his brother and Jack felt his body go rigid next to him and sensed the eruption of anger that was about to burst. 'Tommy ain't no Fascist, Uncle Bill, you know that,' he said quickly, before his brother had the chance to respond.

'Then what was he doing at that meeting in Ilford the other night?' Bill Duncan demanded belligerently. The old man's loud accusation had broken into the conversations of the groups close about and a rippling silence lapped across the room.

'I'll tell you what I was doing there.'

The cold fury in Tommy's voice was chilling to his brother's soul. He pushed himself into the narrowing gap between the two men keeping his hands clamped around his brother's wrists to stop him raising his fists. 'Keep your voice down, Uncle Bill,' Jack hissed. 'We're not supposed to say, but Tommy was there because I asked him. He was a sort of agent provocateur for the United Front. He went to break up the meeting. Did a good job too.'

Uncle Bill believed him. He deflated like a balloon. 'Oh,' he spluttered, shuffling about uncomfortably, 'sorry Tommy; didn't know; no one said; should have known better; sorry.'

Tommy seemed equally embarrassed, muttering that it was all right and Uncle Bill shouldn't mention it again. He quickly moved away to buy his uncle the drink he had offered earlier.

Old Tom said nothing, but Jack was aware of his dark eyes staring at him and then at Tommy. Even when Jack shuffled away to help his brother at the bar, he could feel his father's eyes fixed on his back.

'Thanks, Jack lad,' Tommy murmured as they stood together waiting to be served. 'Saved my bacon there. It could have got nasty.'

Jack sniffed. 'From what I heard, you did so much damage, you might just as well have been on our side.'

'Bloody Hell where did you hear that?' Tommy demanded. He was afraid that if George Harris heard the same thing, then there could be real trouble. George didn't like the idea of being double crossed. Then Tommy remembered, 'Oh, your doll was there, wasn't she, I suppose she told you.'

'Yeh, but don't worry. I lied to her as well. And now you owe me a favour.'

'What?'

'We can't talk here,' Jack said. 'When we finished, we'll go for a walk down by the river.'

'OK,' Tommy agreed, curious to find out what was on his brother's mind. 'If it was about Wednesday night, don't worry. I was conned into it.' He said, but he didn't think it was the BUF meeting that Jack was thinking about. He spoke to try and get a clue what Jack was driving at. 'I went through with it for George and for the money. I won't be doing it again.'

'I believe you,' Jack said in a tone which suggested that he didn't, 'but that's not what I need to see you about. We'll talk about it later.'

Like the arrival of the king, George Harris strode into the bar and stood surveying his loyal, and not so loyal, subjects packed into the public bar. It was a warm evening and the atmosphere in the Gillespie was already beginning to steam up the windows, but George was impeccably dressed. He wore his camel hair overcoat draped over his sharply tailored suit, a beige fedora was pulled down over his eyes and he held kid leather gloves in his hand. Phyllis was draped over his arm like one more fashion accessory.

George no longer drank in the public bar, he had claimed the Private bar as his territory and though there was a door into it directly from the street, he always came in this way.

Pete Armstong and Charlie Williams pushed their way towards the back room, making a path for George to stroll along.

He caught Tommy's eye and Tommy raised his hand above the intervening heads in a smiling salute that he didn't feel. If George heard the story about him being a stool pigeon for the Reds at the BUF meeting, there might be trouble. On the other hand, the fact that Chalky White was still in favour and hadn't had his face rearranged in retribution for not turning up at all, was a good sign.

George returned his wave. He had no qualms about being identified with the Blackshirts and shouted above the general din. 'Charlie Hartwell sends his thanks for pulling him out of the firing line on Wednesday.' He then added, for Jack's benefit, 'Bloody Bolshie's, I knew I should have smashed that woman's face, down Wilmott Street, when I had the chance.'

Jack moved to fight his way through the crowd to get at George Harris and try his luck, but it was Tommy's turn to grab his brother and reinforce his father's fist, which was knotted up in the folds of his Jacket tail. 'Easy our Jack,' his father muttered. 'Don't ruin a good day. This ain't the time or the place.'

'When is the time?' Jack demanded angrily. 'There's another war coming, Dad. There's no point in sticking your head under the table and pretending you're looking for your matches. The bullies have to be faced.'

'You youngsters, you're still wet behind the ears.' He snapped losing the battle with his temper. With a power that was surprising in an old man, Tom Sutton pushed his hand round and up so that his son was forced to turn and face him. 'You think you know it all. You don't know nothing. You talk about war like it's a game of football. Let me tell you that I've seen war. I've seen things that I could never tell you or your mother about because you would never believe me. I hope you never have to sit under a table in your own shit because you're too scared to move, when your best mate's head has just been chopped off by shrapnel and is still talking on the floor.'

Old Tom suddenly lost the taste for his beer. 'Bloody sons,' he cursed. It was a long while since the nightmare of the Somme had forced its way out into the daylight. He turned on his heel and began to force his way through the crowd that was shouting like frightened men, and pressing in on him, so that he could get out into the air.

Tottenham had been the recruiting ground of the Middlesex Regiment in World War One, and nearly half the men over forty, standing in that bar had served with them in France. They all looked hard at their own sons, understanding what Tom Sutton was saying as he crashed through them towards the street.

'I think we'd better go,' muttered Tommy. 'You said you needed to talk to me.'

As the evening drew in, it began to get a little colder. Tommy and Jack walked in silence, shoulders hunched and hands thrust deep into their trouser pockets. The silence between them wasn't a wall, it was more of a card table. Each struggled with his thoughts, getting them in order and waiting the moment to begin, for his own best advantage.

They were standing on the towpath of the canal lobbing stones at a floating bottle when Tommy began. 'You know there was nothing political about me going to that meeting. I went as a favour to George.'

Jack threw his next stone with more venom, it struck the bottle which shattered and disappeared. 'It's your business, Tom, but when the revolution does come, and it won't be long, you'll have to work out who your real friends are.'

'You're fooling yourself Jack,' Tommy replied. 'There ain't going to be no revolution. And the only people who are going to count are the ones with money. I intend to be a rich man when I die.'

Jack lobbed another stone into the water and reflectively watched it ripples run outwards until they finally reached the bank. 'The old gypsy said that you and Acky were going to die together in a ditch, but she didn't say you were going to be poor, I suppose. Anyway,' Jack took a deep breath, 'that's why we're here. I want to put some money your way.'

'Go on,' said Tommy suspiciously, 'What sort of money? How much?'

'That's up to you,' said Jack. 'I represent a group of people who want to buy some merchandise and they think you would have the contacts to get it for them.'

'Oh, yeh,' Tommy said with a mocking little laugh, 'and what do they want a couple of boxes of Frenchies?'

'They want to buy some guns.'

'Guns?' Tommy echoed the word in horror. The look on his brother's face assured him that this wasn't a joke. 'Bloody Hell, Jack, what are you getting yourself into?'

'Tommy, do me a favour,' Jack said 'You don't want to know who wants them or what they want them for. Don't ask any questions and I'll ask no questions about where they come from. What I need to know is, will you try and get them for me. The people I represent aren't rich, but I'm sure there would be something in the deal for you.'

For the first time that Jack could remember, Tommy was speechless. He stood, holding his brother's shoulders so tightly that he left a cluster of five bruises on his arm. Tommy was shaking his head, trying to rock his ideas into a coherent order

Afraid that his brother's next words would be 'no', Jack pulled back out of his grip. 'Don't say anything now,' he said. 'Think about it. If you can get them, tell me what's on offer and the price. I need to know your answer fairly quickly.'

Tommy whistled low. 'The revolution's that close is it?'

***

The White Swan was even more of a dive on non-race days. There were never more than three or four people drinking in any of the bars. Not enough to cover the tattered seats or block the sight of the dirty faded and peeling Lincrusta wall paper which covered the walls and ceiling with the same uniform brown.

When Tommy walked into the saloon bar on Sunday lunch time Mick Murphy was openly surprised and thought that Gentleman George's young mate must be bringing bad news. 'What's the matter? What brings you in here at this time?' he demanded, nerves making his Irish brogue even stronger. 'You know there's no-one about.'

'Guilty conscience Mick?' Tommy asked with a smile. 'Don't get agitated, I've just dropped in for a chat. You know, while it's quiet.'

'Are you buying a drink or what?' Mick demanded still on the defensive.

'Yes, all right, anything in a bottle. Remember, I know what your cellar's like. And get one for yourself,' he added.

'I will,' Mick said softening slightly, 'I'll have a whisky.' He reached under the bar and pulled out an unlabelled bottle. 'Will you have one, it's me own special Irish, friends from the old days bring it over for me.'

Tommy raised the tumbler of amber liquid to the landlord in salute. 'It's about the old days, I wanted to talk to you. Do you keep in touch with any of your old I.R.A. mates?'

'I.R.A.?' Mick queried, new suspicions flooding in. 'I don't know any of that lot.'

'Come off it,' Tommy countered, 'If we worked our way down this bottle, you'd be singing rebel songs, before we were below the shoulder and by the time we'd reached the bottom of the label, you'd be telling me about the bold Feinnian men and how you blew up the post office and how you shot the Black and Tan.'

'That was a long time ago and we never blew up the post office. I was young then. None of us is active any more. Everyone is like me, running a pub and talking about the old days.'

'That's a shame,' Tommy said with a sigh and drained his glass. 'I know somebody who's looking to buy some merchandise. If you knew anyone willing to sell, we might all make ourselves a few bob.'

'And what merchandise would that be?' Michael asked, refilling Tommy's glass. He was happy now. He understood what was going on. This meeting was about money.

Tommy looked around just to be sure that no one had moved into earshot. 'Shooters,' he muttered.

'Guns,' Mick Murphy was surprised and suspicious. He sold a little bit of gelignite from time to time, but there wasn't much of a market for firearms among his clientele. 'Did George tell you to come and see me?'

Tommy had been keeping out of George's way as much as he could since the fight at Ilford. He wasn't sure what mood he was in or if he held anyone to blame, but there was no harm in letting Murphy think he was involved. 'no names, Mick, you should know better.' he said.

Murphy nodded, 'what are you looking for?'

Tommy ran his hand through his hair as he thought. 'Rifles, pistols, machine guns, get me a price for whatever you can, the guys I represent are out to start a war.'

Chapter 8

Honoured Sir,

As my message is of the utmost delicacy I will avoid using any names. Your interest in our cause has been passed on to me by a mutual friend. He will tell you my name as the one who handed him this envelope and vouch for me in lieu of any signature on the letter. He does not know what I have written.

I am told that you are a man upon whom no one walks, but you will know that your people are being trampled underfoot the length and breadth of Stepney. Our fathers have told us, as their fathers told them, that one does not defy the goyim as it only makes him worse. The news coming out of Germany says that he can get no worse and now is the time to make a stand.

As yet we can not stand in Germany, but we can raise ourselves up in the East End of London. I can put men on the street to ensure that there is no pogrom in the Whitechapel, but all I can give them are sticks and stones. You can put guns into their hands, so that when the Fascists come, there will be a reckoning. I know where these guns can be bought and there would be an irony to make even the rabbi's smile if your money should buy them from such cut throats and thieves.

Any reply you send would be more joyously received if it were written on five pound notes.

Locheim

The Jewish Defence League.

With a burst of fiery smoke from the funnel and a blast on its whistle, the train jerked out of the station heading on its way to the East. Four men in black were left behind, standing on the deserted platform. It was the late afternoon of a miserable damp and dismal Saturday, with more rain threatening. It could have been Siberia if the sign above their heads hadn't said 'Do not cross the lines here'. It seemed that everyone who lived in the place was indoors and there wasn't another soul to be seen. Even the signal box was empty and the level crossing gates had been left raised over the pot holed road which ran down onto the marshes by the Thames. It was a good job that it was late and the few people who worked in the area on a Friday had gone home. There was no one about to see that the four men who had climbed from the train were most out of keeping with their surroundings.

Mordecai Leibnitz scanned the horizon in all directions as he hurried from the platform onto the road. He felt the weight of the money in his inside pocket, like mill stones, threatening to drag him down into the mud. He had the good sense to dress in old clothes and boots for this trip into the depths of the country. Certain that each of the mean little cottages around the church, housed brigands and thieves wanting to steal the treasure, his eyes blinked constantly in the strong light. He peered through his pebble lenses in a ceaseless search for an ambush, not knowing what he would do if it came. But he was a man with a mission, which would not allow for too much caution and he hurried his comrades on.

Solomon Epstein, even though he was a tailor, only had the one suit and the one pair of shoes. They hardly kept out the weather in the Whitechapel Road. Here, on the track churned up by the week day passage of endless lorries and heavy wagons running down to the factories on the bank of the river, they leaked like his mother's roof. He leapt from dry spot to dry, as if dancing a Hora, but the high points were too far apart and his feet were wet before he had gone twenty yards. Still, he snapped at Mordecai's heels, chivvying him to go even faster. He wanted to run to get to the meeting place, in a passion to see his dreams realised before the coming of the stars, but his need to make the contact was balanced by wanting to stay close to the money.

Like the other two, Moses's eyes were fixed on the horizon. His father was rich; his eyes had not been ruined by pouring over the Talmud by candle light or sewing in the gloom. He could see that they were alone and he wondered nervously, where were the people they had come to meet. He was even taller and thinner than Solomon, but with the same stoop, pale complexion and the lank locks of black hair hanging from his temples. Less interested in the money, he hurried after the other two, anxious to take the first step towards Zion in Stepney. He knew in his heart that everything would be all right, he trusted Jack, but was anxious to find his friend, to put the minds of all the others at rest.

These three, who raced ahead, were pale, spindly men with bright eyes; dreamers chasing their dream. The fourth man, plodding determinedly in the rear, was short and stocky. His bespoke overcoat was an expensive tailored Crombie, like the gangsters wore on the movies. His face carried the unmistakable signatures of the boxing ring, a flattened nose, puffy cheeks and eyebrows crazed with scar tissue. His gaze was controlled and searching. He spent as much time looking over his shoulder as he did ahead, but it was still he, who saw Tommy and Jack first.

They were parked on the top of the embankment which ran along the river side as some sort of flood defence. Jack was sitting astride the motor bike and Tommy leaning casually against the side car. It gave them a good view of the surrounding country and of the four men struggling along the road towards them.

'It is always the way with the goyim, that they sit on the high ground with the sun behind them.' Solomon said bitterly. 'They think that if a man has to look up to them and shield his eyes, then they must be the equal of God.

'The day is coming when we, by the grace of God, will take the high place. Then they will know what it is to be scorned. We will need no one but God and our own right hand,' Mordecai replied.

'These are our friends,' Moses protested, 'Jack is a comrade and takes risks for us. Thomas is his brother.'

Solomon cleared his throat and spat. 'They take their risks for money.'

'No, not Jack, he is a Party man and he is my friend. We are all in the League together' Moses caught Solomon by the sleeve and pulled him round to argue the point, but the boxer knocked his hand away and pushed them both on, up the slope.

'This is no time for arguing,' he snarled. 'There is business to be done.'

Moses and Jack gave each other a half smile of welcome and stood aside to let the rest of the group sweep past them and gather together by the motor cycle. They stood a little way off, watching the transaction, but not involved. They had done their part.

'Have you got the merchandise?' the boxer demanded without any formalities.

Tommy frowned, apart from Moses, he didn't know these men. He recognised Mordecai and Solomon as typical of most of the East End Jews he had ever met, but this man who pushed himself to the front and acted so arrogantly was more like the men from the White Swan, who hung around with George Harris.

Tommy was instantly afraid of him, He looked dangerous. He was a professional and not at all like these other dreamers who called themselves revolutionaries. He was too hard, too mean, to be a member of any so called 'Jewish Defence League'. 'Who are you?' Tommy demanded.

'They call me Sammy, but who I am doesn't matter. More, you should ask who sent me.' the boxer growled.

'Well then, who sent you?' Tommy demanded nervously.

'I am Jack Spot's man.' Sammy said. 'You know that name?'

Tommy nodded. Anyone who had any dealings with the betting rings in London knew the name of the notorious East End gangster.

'Jack has put up some of the money to buy this merchandise and asked me to come and see that no one take advantage of his young friends. He would not look kindly on any schyster who tries to cheat them.'

'No one's going to cheat any one.' Jack broke in. He didn't like the little man either, nor did he like the way his brother was reacting to him. There was an edge to Tommy that he'd not seen before. Tommy must know that this wasn't just about money, even though Jack had never spelled it out. He knew it was about the cause. 'We bought the rifles at twenty-five pounds each and we've got six of them. Ex-army Lee-Enfields, the pistols are forty pounds each, there are three Webley's and a German Luger. The ammunition is ten bullets for a pound and we've got two hundred rounds. That's two hundred and ninety pounds all together; that's what it cost us. We agreed another fifty pounds for Tommy's expenses. It seemed fair.'

'Show me,' demanded the boxer.

Jack opened the canopy of the motor cycle side car which Tommy had borrowed form one of his work mates and bolted onto his machine. He drew the black steel and burnished wood of a First World War service rifle from it hiding place in the centre of a roll of carpet. He passed it to the squat little man, who handled it awkwardly before passing it on to Mordecai. Mordecai held it with outstretched arms as if he had been passed a scroll of scripture. Impatiently, Solomon took it from him. he held it to his shoulder with casual familiarity and peered through the sights, lining up a distant chimney as if it were Mosely himself standing on the sky line.

'Do they work?' Sammy demanded.

The question took Tommy aback. 'I don't know. The man who sold them to me said they did. Invest two shillings and try it out.'

Solomon worked the bolt of the rifle expertly, he held it up towards the sky and peered along the barrel. He shook his head. Jack had picked up a few words of Yiddish when he worked as a shabbat goy and recognised something which sounded like 'schmutt'. He didn't think much of it.

Sammy took the rifle from Solomon and handed it back to Tommy. 'I have a better idea. I'll invest two shillings and you try it out.

'OK,' said Tommy and with a swagger, he walked to the side-car to choose a bullet from the jumbled mass, rattling around in a biscuit tin. He knew nothing about guns, but wasn't going to admit it to the jumped up little Jew. He chose one of the longer bullets from the burnished muddle. He had no idea if it was a 303, but it seemed more likely to fit the rifle than the others. He'd never fired a gun in his life, but he had seen rifles being fired on the pictures and knew that you loaded them from the top. It took him nearly a minute of pulling and pushing at the bolt before he could draw it back and reveal the breech. Sliding the bullet in and closing the chamber, he raised the rifle to his shoulder and took aim at the chimney across the river which Solomon had been sighting, a few moments before. He was amazed how heavy the rifle was, it kept drooping towards the muddy water. He remembered the picture of his father with a gun like this slung across his shoulder as if it had been an umbrella. To think that the old man, so thin and broken down by injury, had spent years of his life, day in and day out, running through the Flander's mud, firing guns like this and killing Germans.

Gently he squeezed the trigger. With a roar the rifle fired and kicked. Tommy was flung backwards and finished sprawling in the mud in front of the motor cycle. 'Oh, my sodding shoulder,' he yelled, 'I've broken it.'

Sammy picked up the undamaged rifle from where it lay. 'OK,' he said with a laugh, 'so they're covered in shit, but they work. So Mordecai, give the gonniff his gelt.'

Still blinking like an owl caught out in the morning

sun, Mordecai reached deep into his top coat, turning the lining inside out. With the experience of a life time behind a sewing machine, he bit through the cotton and brought out the cloth covered package he had sewn into his clothes. Nervously he handed it across to Tommy.

'Count it,' Sammy ordered, as Tommy went to slip it into his pocket, seemingly more concerned about his damaged shoulder than what was in the package.

'I trust you,' Tommy replied with a cold laugh.

Jack looked at him closely and his muscles tensed. He knew his brother well enough to know that he was nervous and could feel that something was wrong.

'Sammy, there are only nine guns here,' cried Solomon who had started to root around in the side car. 'One of the hand guns is missing.'

Like Tom Mix, the cowboy, Tommy grabbed for his pocket. His bruised shoulder didn't slow him now and his hand came up holding the fourth revolver. 'It's not missing. I've just borrowed it for a while.'

'Tommy, what the Hell are you playing at,' Jack cried, leaping towards his brother. 'The guns are paid for, give it back.'

Tommy shook his head and pushed Jack to one side. 'No little brother, not yet. It's a dangerous game we're playing here. If they've got all the guns and we've got all the money, who's to say it will be allowed to stay that way? This little baby is insurance to make sure we don't get any trouble in leaving. How do you know they don't mean to have the guns and the money and leave us floating in the river?'

Jack moved even more quickly than Tommy had, when he drew the pistol. His hand shot out, catching his brother unaware and snatched the pistol out of his grasp. 'Because they are my friends, that's how' he shouted, waving the gun under his brother's nose. 'Don't be stupid Tom, we can't fight the Fascists with ten guns, and Mordecai won't get his revolution with two hundred bullets. You're the only person we know who can get us guns and ammunition. None of us are going to kill you or steal your money. I hope you can be so sure of the rest of your friends.'

The danger of the moment had brought Jack out in a sweat. His hands were shaking, but his mind was crystal clear. 'Moses, give Tommy your train ticket.' he ordered his friend 'Them four can go back to town on the train. We'll take the guns back on the bike.'

'I give the orders here,' Sammy snapped, 'I go with the guns.'

'Not any more, you don't,' 'Moses argued, 'stay with this lot and keep them out of trouble. Do as Jack says.'

'You can't take the bike, I've only lent that side car from Sid Pratchett,' Tommy began to protest. 'You don't know how to ride it with a side car fixed to it.'

'Of course I do. I've ridden your bike loads of times when you've not been about and it can't be so different with a side car.' Jack snapped. 'Any way we have the guns and we can do as we like. Give me the goggles.' To prove his point Jack snatched the goggles from his brother and strode over to the bike. Tossing the pistol into the side car with the others, he climbed astride. With a single kick of the starter and a little tweak of the throttle, the big Triumph roared into life. 'Come on Moses,' he shouted above the noise of the engine, 'let's get out of here just in case some body heard that shot and comes to investigate.'

Moses leapt onto the pillion and caught Jack tight about the waist. Jack pulled the side car canopy shut, lowered the goggles and opened the throttle. The engine revved up into a deafening roar and as he let the clutch lever out with a jerk, the back wheel spun wildly. It sent a cascade of mud and stones over the four left standing on the top of the dike as it lurched down towards the road.

'If anything happens to that bike, Jack, I'll bloody kill you. Sodding gun or not,' Tommy yelled after the retreating machine, but it was already too far down the track for either Jack or Moses to hear. Tommy felt very vulnerable, alone with the three young Jews. The wad of money weighed as heavily on him as it had on Mordecai. He hoped that Jack had been right about their needing him.

Thrusting his hands deep into his pockets and pretending to ignore his unwelcome companions, he followed the motor cycle's wheel tracks back towards the station. Luckily the Jews were anxious about the sun dipping into the west. It was Shabbat and they should not be here. The women would be dousing the candles with the wine and breaking Havdalah bread. They had broken the Sabbath, there would be many more than three stars in the sky before they reached their homes.

About an hour later Jack turned off the main road and eased the bike into the kerb in a quiet side street alongside Victoria Park. Looking around to ensure they were unobserved, he nervously pulled the shielding roll of carpet a little higher in the cockpit of the side car, to be sure that their cargo was totally hidden. Then, pulling the goggles up off his eyes, he turned to Moses. 'Have you thought where we're going to hide this stuff?' he enquired.

'Mordecai, has arranged a safe place.' Moses assured him and then slapped his forehead with the heel of his hand. 'But he didn't tell me where it was.' he added gloomily,

'Oh, no, where does he live?' Jack demanded, beginning to panic. He hadn't a licence to ride a motor bike. What if the police saw him, they were sure to stop him. 'We'll 'ave to go round to his house.'

Moses threw up his hands in horror at the thought. 'He lives in lodgings off Leman Street. We daren't go there. His landlady spies on him all the time. Anyway it is just round the corner from the police station.'

'Well we can't leave them in the sidecar, Tom will park it in the front garden of our house until he takes it back.' Jack hesitated and then said quietly 'and I'm not sure we can trust him.'

Moses pulled at his hair locks in despair. Then he had an idea. 'God willing, my father and mother are going out this evening, they have been invited to the Clerkenwell Road Cohens. We can put them in the coal cellar until tomorrow when Mordecai can come with his handcart and collect them.

Chapter 9

To the editor of the Daily Mail

Sir,

I have served my country for fifty years, both in France and on the sub-continent. Having recently returned to England, to retire to Broadstairs, I am appalled at the condition that I find the country in. Immediate action is called for to rid the streets of the plague of wastrels and ruffians that one sees everywhere. Mr Moseley is right in his diagnosis of the dangers posed by the unholy alliance between Judaism and the Bolshevik scourge seeping out of Russia. One only has to look to Germany and to Mr. Hitler to see the model for the way we should proceed. I wholeheartedly commend your newspaper on the courageous stand it is taking in fighting the lily-livered leftists who are bringing this country to ruin.

    Lieut. Colonel A.R. Peterson - Davies [retired] 'a patriot'
October 1936

'Do you remember where my house is?' Moses demanded, leaning forward to shout in Jack's ear, when they pulled up the traffic lights at Mare Street. Jack had been trying to stick to the side streets of the East End and Moses thought that they were both lost.

'Of course,' Jack shouted back, 'I've been there often enough'.

'Are you sure, it's the right house,' Moses insisted. 'You know we can't afford to take any chances'

'Bloody Hell, Moses,' Jack cursed, he knew how his companion felt. He was nervous too. Who wouldn't be, transporting an arsenal through the streets of London in broad daylight? 'It's just at the back of Clapton Ponds. It's only about a quarter of a mile off my round.' As he was shouting back to his passenger, he was waiting at the traffic lights waiting to pull out onto the main road which led over Stamford Hill. He proved his point by indicating he was turning right

As the lights turned green, a policeman strolled round the corner by Jack's shoulder. Jack let the clutch out with a bang and stalled the engine. In a panic he stamped on the kick starter. The engine fired immediately and he was able to slam the machine into gear to pull away before the constable could show any more than a passing interest.

When, at long last they turned into the wide road of big Victorian four storied houses where the Rabinovitzs' lived, Moses shouted, 'stop here.' The engine died and the deep silence returned to the road. In the gathering evening gloom, lights were coming on in houses on either side as families settled down for the night. The street seemed empty and there was no-one about. 'Let's push the bike down from here,' said Moses.

Jack felt that every illuminated window contained a pair of eyes, spying on them, anxious to know what criminal cargo was in the side-car being pushed along the road by the two men who were almost running. He was thinking that some of the houses down this road had telephones and at that very moment somebody might be calling the police to report their suspicious behaviour. *If a police car pulled into the road now,* he thought, *I'll abandon the motor bike and the guns and try to get away down one of the little alleys running between the houses.* No cars arrived, no-one came out of any of the houses and finally he let the Triumph roll to rest against the curb.

'I'll shoot in and find the key for the coal cellar and you start unloading the guns into the basement area.' Moses ordered. 'Be quick and be quiet. There's bound to be someone peeping from behind their curtains. I can think up a story later'.

Though the light was fading into evening, there were no lights showing in the house or those on either side. The terrace reached up into the darkening sky like a cliff. Jack had never realised before how big these houses were before. Taking a few of the rifles out of the bundle, he slipped them deep into the side car. With the rest, he crept up the front path, holding the bundle tight against his chest. The end of the carpet rested against his face so that he could just see over the top. All he could see were the entrance steps, climbing up to the main front door.

Jack thought of the first time he came to the house. All he saw on that occasion were men's legs in strange black silk stockings, their owners resting before the final effort of carrying him up into the house. They held him face down, close to the stone treads unaware of his brief drift into consciousness. He could still picture the growing puddle of blood dripping past his eyes as the men in black held him off the ground.

His mother must have scrubbed the steps recently, he thought, as they shone dully in the street's gas lights, which were just beginning to assert themselves along the pavement edge. Some other skivvy would have washed his blood away on the first occasion. For no clear reason, he thought of the bloody pool Maurice Higgins drowned in.

Adjusting his grip on the carpet to better conceal a rifle barrel which had ridden up and seemed to shine like a beacon despite the poorness of the light, he ducked down the small steps at the side of the entrance stairs, into the basement area, away from the big front door, still gaping open after Moses had rushed in.

'Vot d'you vont?' The deep voice with the unmistakable Polish accent boomed down from overhead. 'Vot you doing down there?'

Jack nearly jumped out of his skin. The carpet roll slid through his arms and the butt of a rifle crunched down on his toe. With a desperate lunge he wrapped his arms around the bundle to stop it spilling its contents for the world to see. 'Mr. Rabinovitz,' he exclaimed. 'I didn't know you were here.'

'This is number 123 Graham Street; it is my house. Who else would you expect to see, the Tzar?'

'No one, no one sir,' Jack's words came tumbling out, tripping over each other and he knew he looked as guilty as sin. He could feel the blush flooding up from his collar and turning his face into beetroot. He hoped the darkening shadows of the basement area were deep enough to hide them. 'I just didn't expect to see you. Moses said that you and Mrs Rabinovitz were out.'

'If the stranger upstairs kept himself half as informed about his parent's business as he does about that gang of crooks in Moscow, he would know that his mother is ill and we are in.' Mr. Rabinovitz adjusted his spectacles and leant further over the balustrade so that he could see the figure in the basement area more clearly. Though it was beginning to get dark, the figure standing below him in the gloom holding a roll of old carpet looked vaguely familiar. 'Do I know you boy?'

'Yes sir, it's me, Jack Sutton, my mother cleans for you. I do jobs for you on Shabbat. I deliver milk in this area now.'

'Shabbat goy? Milk man? Isn't it a little late to be delivering milk? Already there are stars in the sky. Anyway we don't have a milk man' The old man was becoming suspicious once more and took a step down from the front porch.

'No, I don't deliver here. I deliver down the road.' With the inspiration born of panic, lies flowed from Jack's lips like the Thames in flood. 'Moses and I have been to a meeting in the East End, Stepney, near Stepney. We saw some carpet lying in the road, someone had thrown it out. We have my brother's motor bike. I thought it might do for my sister's scullery.'

'A motor bike for your sister's scullery?' Mr Rabinovitz queried, bemused by the flood of explanation.

'No, the carpet, Sir.'

'So why is it my basement area?' Rabinovitz was not a suspicious man by nature, but all of this had a smell which even he could tell was not Kosher.

'We've got to get the motor bike back to Tottenham. I'm not really supposed to have it. Moses said I could leave the carpet in your coal hole and pick it up tomorrow when I finished my round.'

'So then you can put it in your own coal hole? Is this a good way to treat carpet?' Despite his protest, Israel Rabinovitz 's suspicions were allayed and he came no further down the steps.

'We so rarely have coal nowadays that Dad knocked our coal bunker down and uses the space for some chickens. I'll put it in the shed at home.'

The old man nodded, it was a good thing to be reminded of the poor, he told himself, otherwise a man might become too proud.

A light came on somewhere in the house and in the moment before the curtains were drawn it shone down onto the upturned face. Mr. Rabinovitz did not notice the dull gleam of a rifle barrel sticking out from the carpet again. He saw the dead white line running down the boy's face. 'Now I can see that mark on your face and I properly remember you, boy, 'he said. 'I remember why your good mother works for us and that my family is in your debt? You are the one who saved my jewel from the wild animals in black. '

The kindly old man saw what a struggle it was for

the boy to hold up a small roll of carpet and guessed at how the Sutton family was getting by at the moment. 'You are a good boy. Hold on, my son, I'll give you a hand with the carpet.'

'No,' Jack squeaked in alarm. 'I'm only waiting for Moses to come with the key and open the door. And the carpet's in a bit of a mess, you don't want to get your clothes dirty.'

Israel looked down at his best suit, he had been ready to leave for the Cohen's house when his wife, God bless her, had decided to have a headache. What did business mean to her? What did it matter if he lost his best customer? Perhaps she would like being as poor as the Suttons. But the boy was right, the carpet was very dirty. 'Throw that piece of carpet away.' He said with an expansive gesture of his hand, 'I'm sure that in this place, Mrs Rabinovitz can find a better piece.'

Jack could feel the panic rising again. His stomach was in a knot, it only required Mr. Rabinovitz to come one pace further down the front steps and he would either have to run away or be sick. The flood of lies had dried up and he couldn't think of another word to say. He was saved by Miriam walking out onto the entrance behind her father.

'What's going on father,' she demanded. 'Moses is tearing the kitchen apart looking for the key to the basement.

'The milk man, not our milk man but your brother's friend the milk man, the man who saved your honour, wants to store a piece of carpet in our coal cellar, but we are going to throw it out into the street and find him a better piece for his sister.'

'The man who what?' She demanded and peered down over the low stone balustrade. She recognised him immediately. She gasped, stumbled and nearly fell.

'Are you all right child?' Mr. Rabinovitz demanded lunging towards her so that she shouldn't tumble down the steps.

'Yes, father, don't fuss. I stumbled. I'm fine.' *God,*

she cried silently *why did you have to make me trip, did you have to show him I am such a gornischt*. As she looked down at the eyes, wide with fear, gazing up from the white face, she realised that he had no concern for her afflictions.

Even though his face was as pale as a winding sheet, the razor scar above his eye was whiter still. She could remember every detail of their meeting in the fog. What he wore, the feel of his hands, the scent of his body. She realised that he hadn't even recognise her, but then why should he. He had only that glimpse of her face in the fog and it was a long while ago. Her brother had casually mentioned that he had been up in the attic once, but she had not seen him.

Perhaps one day, when he walked without fear, her face might come back to him. She sniffed in self-deprecation, who was she fooling, a nice looking boy like that would not have eyes for a schnorrer like her. Even so, she tried not to limp from her bruised foot, as she walked to the top of the steps.

'Is the piece of carpet important?' she enquired. Her eyes were big and brown, but narrowed in shrewd suspicion; she marked that it did look very heavy. She knew things about her brother's activities which were still shielded from her father. Moses did not normally worry over the front door keys. He normally came and went up the back stairs and she was sure that there was more to this than they were being told.

'Oh yes,' Jack said with a fervour that no second hand carpet could ever warrant. 'I only want to store it until tomorrow. If your father kindly finds me a better piece, I will be most grateful, but I should be even more grateful if I might leave this piece here, now. I haven't got anywhere else to put it. I'll take it away as soon as I can. I have to go' he hesitated, trying to think of one more plausible lie which would buy them time, 'I have got to go to a meeting'

'Another meeting?' Mr. Rabinovitz raised his eyebrows, 'these young people seem to spend their lives at meetings. They think they can change the world in a day, which even God, bless his name, took six to make. Is the stranger who lives in my house going to the same meeting?'

Jack looked to Miriam in a desperate search for explanation.

'My father means my brother Moses. He thinks that his son has turned his back on him because he has turned his back on his studies. He was to have been a rabbi.'

'Son? What are you talking about girl?' Israel Rabinovitz broke in, 'You know I have no son. I have an ingrate, a great student who could have been a great teacher. And what does he do with his talent? I'll tell you what he does with his talent, he does nothing. He does worse than nothing, he organises other men to do nothing. He organises the unemployed wastrels to stand around and calls those who are in honest work out on strike to ruin honest businessmen. It is him who should be thrown into the street, not a piece of carpet.' He threw up his hands in despair, 'but your mother says that I must be charitable to strangers.'

'I don't know if he's going to the meeting, sir. He's a busy man, he may have other things to do. Important people who he has to see urgently.' Jack looked up at Miriam, his dark fiery eyes stared deep into hers. She read the unspoken demand that she acknowledged her debt to him and help him now.

Miriam nodded and turned to her father. 'The carpet, Papa, do you want to throw it into the road now? You know it will lay there for days. It will lower the tone of the house. Let the man take it away tomorrow or we can throw it out on Wednesday when the dustman comes.'

Israel Rabinovitz gave a tug at the fringe of his tallit, hanging from beneath his waistcoat, in the unconscious gesture he used when he had made a decision. 'If your brother, this man who lives in my attic, who I do not know, can find the key, then we will store the milkman's carpet until Wednesday.' He gave an affectionate tug at his daughter's cheek. 'If only all the children in this house were so thoughtful.' he said and went in doors.

'Thank you,' Jack sighed with relief, 'It's …'

Miriam held up her hand. 'Don't tell me. I don't want to know what foolishness my brother has got himself into this time.' She corrected herself and smiled that crooked little smile she had. 'It's better that I don't know. Tell me something else. Tell me what beautiful eyes I have.'

'Pardon?' Jack demanded.

'Nothing, a Jewish joke, you wouldn't understand. Would you like a cup of tea?'

'Yes please,' Jack replied. He felt as if he had sweated a gallon in the last ten minutes and his throat was parched. 'I'd love a cup of tea.'

The tea arrived before the key, but Jack still had time to finish unloading the sidecar, putting the rest of the guns and ammunition out of sight under a laurel bush. Miriam brought two cups and a few biscuits on a tray. 'Moses is working his way up the house. He has reached the first floor. He has only one more to go. Put your carpet down and drink your tea.'

Jack carefully propped the roll of carpet into a dark corner and joined the young Jewess, sitting on the bottom step. 'I put milk and sugar in, I hope that's right.'

He nodded, 'beautiful,' he said and sipped the dark beige liquid in the tiny tea cup then smiled. He liked this girl, so she wasn't much to look at but she had a sense of humour which put him at his ease. 'You're very kind.'

'Yes,' she nodded, secretly watching him drink; knowing that he would not guess what she thought was so beautiful. 'So very beautiful.'

The tone of her voice told Jack that she wasn't talking about tea and he looked up quickly to find her staring at him. Embarrassed, she said the first thing that came into her head. 'The scar is not so bad.'

Jack ran his finger along the mark across his face and remembered that it was because of her he got it. 'No,' he said, 'it's healed up nicely. It's just enough to make me look tough.'

'It doesn't make you look tough,' she protested, 'it makes the corner of your mouth turn up as if you're smiling,' and then blushed at her boldness.

'I have it,' Moses yelled triumphantly from the door above them and then realising that what they were doing was supposed to be secret and dangerous, repeated in a whisper. 'I have the key; I have found it.'

Chapter 10

Dearest Comrade.

I have sent you a messenger in the name of the Party because I can not come myself. Sufficient to say it is my duty to go to another place which I can not mention for a reason no one must know.

Plans have been made for a party and I must have new clothes. As I can not go myself, you, my dearest friend and closest comrade in arms, must go for me.

I have material which must be made into a coat immediately. It must be delivered to the tailor today for him to cut the cloth. He will sew all night and it will be ready in the afternoon. You will need to collect it immediately it is finished and bring it away.

It is the Sabbath and it would provoke questions if your guide did the work. You must push the cart and ask no questions. Then there will be nothing you can tell, if pressed.

Do not fret about your own plans for Sunday, they will not be compromised. You will be close by.

Salud.

All the men in the Sutton household signalled their return with the same two tone whistle. Most of the time, Agnes could recognise which of them had come in through the door. So when Jack returned from work in the middle of Saturday afternoon she called 'You have a visitor,' without coming out of the kitchen. 'She's in the parlour.'

A woman and in the front room; Jack was curious. He caught a slight hint of awe in his mother's voice, so it wasn't a relative or friend. It obviously wasn't Peggy, Mrs Sutton never missed an opportunity to point out that she was no better than she ought to be. She would never have received that respect and would have had to make do with waiting in the kitchen. 'Who is it?' he called back, oblivious to the fact that the person could clearly hear his question and any answer nor did he hurry to hang his leather money satchel on the hall stand or take off his striped apron.

When he stuck his head around the front room door, he was amazed. Sitting bolt upright in one of the best chairs, hands folded demurely in her lap, was Miriam Rabinovitz. She always looked pale, but sitting primly in the curtained gloom, she had a ghost like quality. 'Miriam,' he exclaimed. 'What are you doing here?' He glanced at the clock on the mantle-piece which showed just after three. 'It's still Shabbat.'

She was so angry to have been forced to face such embarrassment that she was no longer embarrassed. 'Don't tell me,' she exclaimed, raising her hands in her characteristic gesture of resignation. 'I had to walk all the way.'

'Surely catching a bus can't be work,' Jack said.

'You don't think its work, I don't think its work, but you try telling my mother. If anyone had seen me standing at a bus stop on Shabbat, my life would be a misery for weeks. My good for nothing brother, the one who cares nothing for the Sabbath, nothing for the Law; he doesn't care a fig for the family good name, he could catch a bus, but he's too busy to bring you a letter.'

'Letter?' Jack demanded.

'Of course a letter, do you think I should walk all this way, just to see the colour of your eyes.' As she spoke she blushed because she would have walked for ever, to see anything of him.

As he took the brown manila envelope, Jack had a horrible feeling in his stomach. This had to be important. The strangeness of this Jewish girl leaving her world to enter his, gave him a sense of impending disaster which made him feel sick. The last time he could remember feeling like that was like the time when Tommy set fire to the gypsy's skirt. As she handed the envelope over, Miriam's eyes burned with a similar sense of horror. This was just like her brother, but then it was not like her brother at all.

Jack turned it over and over, as if the plain cover might give him a clue as to the contents in the end it was Miriam who could not stand the not knowing. 'Well, are you going to open it? Or do you expect me to take it back?'

'Why couldn't he bring it himself? Is he all right?'

'He says that he has been called to an important emergency meeting at some one's house, somewhere. He said that you would know the name, if he said it, but of course, as you know my brother, you know he couldn't say it. He says he does not want to go, but says he has to. It is for all the London branch secretaries; something about tomorrow's big anti-fascist demonstration and he had to be there. He says it would cause talk amongst the comrades if he were not there. He says this business is secret, it is not to be spoken of and it isn't to be put into a letter.'

'So what's in the letter then?'

'How would I know, it's something too secret even to tell his sister. His sister, who lies for him and hides his every sin from her parents. It seems that she is not to be trusted.'

The moment could be put off no longer. He tore the envelope open and pulled out a single sheet of paper with Moses's immaculate writing covering half of one side. He read it and frowned. 'The whole thing's nonsense,' he complained and waved it under her nose. 'All he wants is for me to get him a new suit. It doesn't say anything about a meeting.' He paused suspiciously. 'How did you know about the meeting, Moses said that it was a secret.'

'Secret,' Miriam sniffed derisively. 'A man roars out of the night on a motor cycle last night and wakes the whole street. He then tells Moses about this meeting at Piratin's house without checking that there was anyone standing behind the door. He was lucky that it was me and not my mother.'

'If you know so much, what's this letter all about?'

Miriam turned up the palms of her hands. 'All I know is that we have to go my house and pick up a package out of the coal cellar. Then I need a Shabbat goy to take it to Shadwell. It seems that I cannot take it because one, it is heavy and two, we must pass through Whitechapel and it would excite comment for me to work on the holy day. Similarly, I cannot give you the address, because it must not be written down and I cannot tell you because you might forget or you would have to ask someone the way and that too would cause comment. So I am your guide and we both have to waste our time walking to Whitechapel.'

Jack rubbed his hand over his face nervously, he's never asked Moses what had happened to the guns, he had a horrible feeling that at least one of them was still in Graham Street. It would explain the secrecy and the need not to attract attention. 'You don't know what's in the package, I suppose?' he asked.

Miriam shrugged, 'I know my brother and this has the smell of pork about it all. It is too much to hope that it is cloth to make a coat. He should look so smart.'

Jack nodded. 'Shall we go now?' he asked and then, as they passed out into the hall shouted. 'I've got to go out again, mum. I'll probably be back late.'

Agnes appeared, flushed, at the kitchen door. 'What about your tea?' she demanded.

'Sorry, Mum, something came up. I'll get something while I'm out.'

'There's enough for two,' Mrs. Sutton persisted, but when Miriam blushed and looked away in embarrassment, she realised what she'd said. 'I'm sorry, nothing's Kosher.'

'That's all right Mrs. Sutton. A cup of tea would be very nice. No milk, thank you.'

'We haven't got time,' Jack protested. 'It's take us ages to get there. I'll buy you a cup later, if we get time.'

'I'm sorry, Mrs. Sutton,' Miriam murmured as she allowed Jack to shepherd her towards the door.

'Don't worry about it dear. I know what these men of mine are like. After all I've lived with them long enough.' Then addressing Jack demanded, 'and what shall I tell anyone if they ask where you've gone?'

'Tell them I've gone out.'

'What if the nurse comes round asking for you?'

Jack paused. There was a branch meeting that evening. Peggy might very well come looking for him when he didn't turn up. He knew Moses well enough to be certain that this trip up to the East End was one of his hair brained schemes. Jack was also certain that it wasn't Party business and it would be better that Peggy didn't know about it. That would avoid the need to lie about it later. 'I didn't say where I was going.' As he was pulling the door shut behind him, he stopped and looked his mother straight in the eyes. 'And if anyone asks, anyone at all; I was on my own.'

There was now a bolt of cloth in the coal cellar where he had left the carpet. Dark grey fustian, made even darker by the coal dust. Before attempting to lift it out into the light, Jack confirmed his dark suspicion by running his hand across the end. He felt the cold polished wood of a rifle butt nestled among the folds.

Jack felt physically sick. If he took a single rifle into the East End on the day before Moseley marched through Whitechapel and delivered it to a Jewish tailor he had no doubt that he was setting his hand to murder. He chewed his fist in an agony of doubt. If he didn't deliver the gun, then no one would be killed and he would not have blood on his hands.

'Well,' Miriam demanded, 'is there a package or is there not a package.'

Jack sighed deeply. He thought of Moses's sister curled up on the pavement, screaming in terror as she tried to shield her cousin from the fascist boots. If he didn't take the gun then no fascists would get killed, but how many children and young girls would be kicked or raped. How many Jews would be die in England? There would be even more blood on his hands, innocent blood.

'There's a package,' he whispered quietly.

'Well bring it out quickly and let us get away from here before one of the neighbours strains a neck from peeping around the window sashes.' Miriam commanded shrilly. Then, when she saw his white face and frightened eyes, and the way he cradled the roll of cloth carefully out into the basement area, she whispered, 'Oi vei.' The battered old piece of carpet she remembered being delivered so suspiciously, was now a roll of cheap grey cloth. She had the same horrible certainty about her brother's action. She wanted to scream to God to pour vengeance on his head that he could not even be there to run his own dangers, but heaped them on the shoulders of this man she worshipped 'Do not tell me what is in the package,' she said hoarsely. 'I do not want to know.' and she pulled her shawl up over head to cover her face as she might if he were carrying a dead child. 'I suppose it is too late to leave it where it lay?' she asked in hopeless desperation.

He didn't answer and she nodded her understanding. 'Mordecai Levy, my brother's friend and another lunatic has left his hand cart behind the side gate. And I had to ask why do we need a cart for a roll of cloth.' she said, mocking her own stupidity. Accepting the reality of the moment, she led the way up the steps towards the road. 'It would look better if you could carry it to cart. Turn left up the road. I will follow you at a proper distance.'

Jack laid the bundle on the hand cart and wheeled it into the front garden. He took a moment to marshal his courage and collect his thoughts. 'Where are we going?' he asked.

'We are going to Shadwell,' she replied, 'near to the docks.'

'It must be over three miles to Shadwell,' he said, 'can you walk that far?'

Miriam silently screamed with pain. He had noticed her limp and she had been so careful to hide it. 'I have one leg a little shorted than the other,' she snorted. 'That is not to be a cripple. Do not worry about me. I can walk as far as you.'

'You realise that your brother is mad,' Jack muttered. 'There's no way I'd let my sister go down there, even with an escort.'

Miriam threw her arms upwards and out. 'At last we have something we can agree upon. So let us go.'

At first the only sound was the rattle of the iron hooped wheels of the hand cart on the cobbles, the steady tread of Jack's boots and the uneven chatter of Miriam's shoes bringing up the rear. At first the streets were empty, there wasn't a soul to worry them. By the time they had reached Hackney and begun to move amongst gentiles, the slow whirl of people on the pavements brought a different sense of security. There was traffic on the road. There were other hand carts, horse drawn vehicles, bikes and the occasional lorry or car. People standing talking or hurrying along all had their own business and did not waste a glance on the bolt of cloth trundling past.

Away from the eyes of the Orthodox, Miriam moved up alongside him to talk and even add her weight to the handles on any up slope. She put her fear in her apron pocket and let herself enjoy as much of Jack's company as he would allow her.

Sometimes it was hard for her to smile, like when he was talking about the Peggy woman, and he spoke about her a lot. Miriam had seen her, spoken to her and did not think she was so wonderful, but did not think it was wise to point out what a hard, insensitive bitch she was. She did not think

Jack would listen, he would get angry and would not talk to her at all. So if she found the chance she would direct his thoughts to his brother, his friends, his job, football, she even enjoyed him talking about the Party when it didn't involve that one.

He let her talk about Moses occasionally, but she could have told him about music and art, dinner parties, faith, love, but he didn't give her any chance. Any way she was content to be with him and to listen.

It took over two hours to walk to Wapping and twilight was on them by the time they entered the stettle beyond Bethnal Green. Shabbat was near enough over for the windows to be open and the women to be shaking their table clothes out. Old men were beginning to emerge out on the steps of shops and houses to watch the children play. There were now plenty of people to ask directions from, if you could speak Yiddish. Among her own, she kept her eyes on her shoes, apologised for her boldness in addressing them, but would they be so kind as to point the way. While the women clicked their tongues, the men took sly looks to see if she were pretty or not. No-one took too much notice of the goy with a bolt of cloth toiling on the Sabbath so that a poor tailor could work all night to meet the demands of his landlord.

There was a policeman standing on the corner of the Whitechapel Road. It seemed to Jack that he was staring at them as they trudged their tired way towards him. He didn't dare stop because he was certain they would be challenged. He launched himself out into the main road and brought curses from the drayman returning empty to the nearby brewery. Another constable, on the opposite corner, seemed to be waiting for him and the man leaning against a wall smoking a pipe must have been watching his every move. By the time they passed the house where Peter the Painter had made his last stand, Jack was so frightened that he could do little more than put one foot in front of the other. He was so exhausted, that in his mind, the clip clop of horses' hooves was transformed into the rattle of gunfire and the whistle of the train passing over their heads became the sound of a hundred police preparing to chase them.

When they finally rolled into Cable Street, his thoughts had so frightened him that he could hardly speak and hadn't the strength to bang on the street door of the stairs which led up to the tailor's shop.

Miriam could see that Jack was close to the end of his tether. She stepped forward and rapped with her knuckles. No one came. She knocked again. There was silence within the building. Finally, she knocked and kicked at the shabby door so that it rattled on its hinges and her clammer was answered by the creaking of the stair.

'Who is it?' a man's timid voice, speaking in Yiddish, enquired from within.

Miriam replied in the same language. 'We have a delivery for Solomon the Tailor.'

'Wait, wait,' the voice commanded in frightened tones, 'say nothing; wait, wait.' Locks slid back with a clatter and the door creak open an inch or two to reveal a single eye set in white skin, the same pale complexion as Miriam. 'No names,' whispered the voice, 'there's no knowing who is listening.'

'There's nobody here but us,' Miriam snapped. She was tired too and Jack's fear was transmitting itself to her. She wanted to be finished with all this and go home and this lunatic who kept her waiting needlessly in the street was making her angry. 'My brother.' The eye blinked fearfully. 'A man who has no name told us to bring this,' She waved vaguely at the cart and its load, now no more than a dark mound in the gloom of the evening.

The tailor opened the door and stood back. Jack recognised him from their meeting on the river bank and groaned. All this effort and danger, when he could have given him the gun then, if he'd known.

'Mazl tov,' Miriam said in ironic greeting.

'Mazl tov,' he replied, embarrassed to have his bad manners pointed out in such direct way. 'This way.'

'No way,' Miriam countered, 'we have brought it this

far, Shabbat is almost over, you can take any further. It is delivered and we are done with it.'

'No, no,' the man protested, 'that is not what was arranged. When I have done my part, I will put ...'; he hesitated, looking for a word which could be spoken aloud, 'put my rubbish in a sack and put that sack in my neighbour's dustbin.' He pointed at the rusty old can at the end of the little ally running between the buildings to the yard at the back. 'You must collect it at once and take it away.'

Miriam unwillingly translated what she had been told and then added in English. 'I think you have done enough, let the mad men who organised this, sweep up after themselves.'

'No,' Jack protested wearily. 'In for a penny. Tell him that I'll come and take it away.' He retained his hold on the cloth, 'and if I am to be Kosher, I should carry the cloth upstairs.

Solomon's English was as good as Miriam's Yiddish. He smiled nervously. 'Thank you comrade, but the sun is setting. I can do this last little bit on my own,' he whispered and risked a half clenched fist hidden at his hip. 'You can leave the cart in the alley if you want to. It will be safe enough and you may need it tomorrow.'

'No,' Jack said wearily. 'As I said, I'll see it to the end. I'll take it upstairs and then I have to walk Miriam home, so we might as well take it back with us. We only brought it for show. It means that I can come straight here tomorrow and she doesn't have to be involved anymore.

Miriam curled her lip and spat out something in Yiddish. Solomon blushed, but didn't explain. 'I shall be here tomorrow,' she said. 'You will need someone to watch your back.

Chapter 11

Dear Alice

Just a quick note to ask if you saw the newspaper or heard the radio about the trouble up in the East End on Sunday. Our Jack was there and right in the thick of things. His Dad doesn't normally approve of what Jack calls direct action, but this time I think he was actually proud of him, though he wouldn't tell him of course. I cut a piece out of one of the Daily Workers for my box to put in a scrap book one day when I've got the time.

Aggie

DAILY WORKER 5th. October 1936

Mosley said he would march his militaristic columns through the East End of London. The police said yes; the Home Secretary said yes; the Cabinet said yes; but the workers said NO! and NO it was. Well done, historic East End of London.

Solomon Epstein was forced to admit that he was the chosen one. God could not have spoken more clearly if he had written on the damp stained wall with a finger of fire.

'All right, already,' Solly cried out, not only to God, but to the crowd in the street outside, whose relentless chanting was rising in crescendo and beating in through his closed window. Neither gave any sign that they had heard him. He shrugged, if it was to be done then he had better be ready.

He tied off the thread and with practised ease, bit it through, freeing his needle from the jacket he was sewing. 'Thank you God for such good teeth,' he said to himself, 'but it would have been useful if You had blessed me with steady hands,' he added, as he dropped the needle onto the floor, 'especially today of all days.' Needles did not come cheap, but he had no time to search for it among the threads and swatches that littered the floor. Instead he let his eyes wander towards the street outside.

For five years now, no he was a liar, it had to be close to six, he had sat at his workbench and looked up occasionally to watch the world go by below his attic window. Never, in all that time, had there been a day like this. He gazed down at the narrow cobbled street as if he were looking at it for the first time. It was a dark canyon between brick warehouses, their walls blackened by the coal smoke that billowed out of a thousand chimneys pots all around him. The iron gantries bolted to the warehouses, used to drag sacks up from the street or drop tobacco down into waiting lorries, took their day of rest and lay back against the wall. He felt as if he were the only man in Stepney who was working. The doors were locked, the factory fires were out and their windows blind. On a normal Sunday afternoon there would be hardly a soul to be seen anywhere from the Tower of London to Shadwell. Today, the whole of East London seethed with noise and activity.

Shut your eyes and the noise was like a Cup Final or the King passing by in procession. Open your eyes and it was like a riot. People running this way and that as new rumour after new rumour swept through the crowd.

The tailor couldn't see him, but Jack stood in a doorway close by, at the top of a flight of steps, which ran up from the pavement to a house door. He braced himself against the iron post.

Someone came elbowing their way through the crowd shouting, 'Everyone to Aldgate, they're going that way.' He didn't move, nor did he change his position when another man came bellowing, 'They're coming this way. Everyone to the barricades.'

Jack, sick to his stomach, knew they were coming this way. His eyes were fixed on the top windows of the workshops opposite. One had just opened and he could see the pale faced man looking out. He leant back slightly seeking the support of the wall, but Miriam was pressed close against him, warm and comforting. He knew where she would be looking and so dragged his eyes back to the crowd. Two people staring into the air might attract attention.

From his lofty perch the tailor could just see the top of Royal Mint away to the West. The cheer from the crowds gathering in its shadow had been loud enough to drown out that of the crowd in his street. It was this noise that dragged him from his sewing and brought him back to the task in hand. Gently he lifted the unfinished jacket from the bench and let the afternoon sun bathe it in light. *It was a nice bit of schmatteh*, he thought, as he examined the tight even stitching on the newly cut lapels. It was a shame that he had been chosen, because he was a very good tailor. How he was going to be as an assassin was not so certain, but now was the time for him to find out.

'Solly,' God seemed to be saying, 'all your life I have been preparing you for this moment. If I had not made you a tailor, you would not be able to sit here, without any questions being asked, finishing Mr. Aaron Goldbloom's suit that he urgently needs for his nephew's wedding. If I had not made you Jewish, today would be the day you rested and you would have finished the coat yesterday. If I had not made the world so stupid that for a year of your life you lived as a soldier and that year was 1918 and you learned to shoot straight and kill men. If you didn't know Moses Rabinovitz, who is a member of the union, even though he cannot sew, and a member of the Party and if he didn't know a man whose brother was a gangster; if your work-room wasn't in Cable Street; if I had not made you poor so that your workshop is up five flights of stairs, under the roof. A successful man would have one on the ground floor; If...'

'Yes, Lord, I know already,' he said aloud and with a sigh. Solly hung the jacket on a hanger behind the door and covered it with a square of old sheet to keep the dust off. Turning back to his beloved sewing machine, he reached beneath it and dragged out the roll of shoddy, that the goy had brought, from under the stand. As he pulled the bolt of poor cloth out of its hiding place and lifted it up to lie on his cutting table, he handled it gently. Though he offered no prayers as he unrolled it, he used the same care as he might if he were unwrapping a scroll of the Torah.

'This is poor grade stuff,' he mused inconsequentially, as the material from the roll piled on the floor, burying his feet. With the last turn, the bundle clumped down onto the bare wooden bench and from the very centre of the cloth emerged the gun. The Lee-Enfield service rifle had journeyed a long way, to France, to Ireland, to Hackney and now it was back not so far from the river where it was made, waiting to be fired for the first time in anger.

Last night after the sun had set and Shabbat was ending, he came to his workshop to meet with the goy who had brought the gun. He told Zelda, his wife, that he had a rush order to complete. 'You work too hard,' she told him as she wrapped a scarf around his neck and kissed him good-bye. When she heard his footsteps disappearing down the tenement stairs, she raised her hands to heaven and begged God to provide more work for her man then, perhaps, they would be able to buy shoes for Gretel before the winter came and it would keep him out of the company of Communists, radicals and other rogues. She asked no questions, he often worked late and would sometimes not return home until the next day. His single, unshaded, light bulb burning into the early hours of the morning raised no eyebrows in Wapping.

When the gentile boy with the scar face had pushed his cart up to the workshop door, last night, no one looked twice. Tongues would have wagged questions asked if a Jew had trundled the hand cart through the streets of Whitechapel before the sun had set. As it was, they had acted as if it were no more than bolts of cloth to be made up into countless numbers of trousers.

The boy, Moses's friend, was obviously tired, he had struggled as he carried it to the bottom of the stairs and Solly had watched nervously in case anyone should notice how heavy a roll of cloth could be. Despite Solly's urgings that if he insisted on carrying the load, he should be quick and be quiet, even though there was no one else in the building. The boy had to rest on his way to the attic. Each time he turned a corner on the stair, he struck the wall with a deep thud that seemed to rock the street. Eventually Solly opened the door to his workshop. 'Over there,' he pointed to the darkest corner under his sewing machine. It was with a great sigh of relief from both of them that the cloth slid out of sight.

As he straightened up, the boy wiped the sweat from his eyes and smiled. His danger was done for the day and all that was left was to walk back to Clapton. 'Good luck Comrade,' the boy whispered and slipped away into the night.

Solly stood for an age; first listening to the retreating feet on the stairs, then to the sound of the hand cart bumping over the cobbles in the side alley and then to the noises of the night. Zelda would hope for his return home, but he knew she would not worry. She would send Gretel with tea and bread as soon as it was light. It was enough that the goy who brought the gun guessed what he was to do, his daughter must only find him sewing. She was too young to understand, so he had to prepare now. Perhaps he would have a chance to explain why he had done what he had done when she was older. Then she could tell her mother. Zelda was a child of the stettle who had learned from childhood that only looking at your shoes would save you from the blows of the gentiles. She would never understand the idea of fighting back. He sighed, murder was murder, however justified, and he would surely die too for acting as the arm of God. No-one who loved him would ever tell his story.

When Solly first carefully unwrapped the rifle he discovered that it was like its cover, in a poor state. This was not the gun that had been his constant companion for a year. This had not been fired since the war ended or cleaned since it was last fired. All its joints were stiff with rust and grime, but he had stripped it down and oiled it as in the days of old. How pleased his sergeant would have been with him. Now it lay gleaming in the autumn sunlight, ready for use. He took five cartridges from the little cardboard box that had snuggled inside the rifle's sling. They shone in the sunlight even more, paying him back for the effort of polishing each in turn, by looking like fingers of burnished gold as they stood in a row across the bench. One by one they winked out as he fed them into the breech to charge the magazine. With a deadly clunk, which echoed around the tiny workroom like the slamming of a door, he worked the bolt to bring the first bullet up into the breech. The loudness of the noise frightened him and he stood listening for a moment to hear any sound of footsteps on the bare boarded stairs. There was not a murmur, not a creak from within the building.

Laying the rifle aside, he carefully re rolled the bolt of material. He clicked his tongue angrily; what a schlemiel he was; he should have wrapped the rifle in sacking after he had cleaned it. Now he had stained the cloth with oil. So, it was only shoddy, but it would do a turn for somebody who could afford no better. He paused and thought. That was if anyone came after him to make it up.

    The job done and the cloth safely stored away, he looked around. The room reproached him for abandoning it. 'Have I not served you well? Am I not cool in summer, warm in winter? Do I not give you all the light of the sky?' The material he had cut for the Rabbi Helmann's new coat lay over the back of the chair, it shouted that he had promised faithfully that it would be finished by Tuesday. There was a tear in his eye as he stretched out a hand to feel the beauty of the cloth and beg its pardon. It was a sad thought that it would not be done in time, he doubted that the rabbi would understand either. At schul, the rabbi had said that when the Blackshirts came, the children of the faith should close their shutters and turn their minds to the teaching of The Law.

    'Ah well,' Solly sighed, 'it could be worse, the rabbi had paid him nothing on account and was always slow in settling what he owed.' He took off his glasses and carefully placed them on the shelf, he only needed them for fine, close work. He could easily manage without them to kill a man at four hundred yards.

    Walking to the window, he rubbed the mucky glass with a scrap of material he picked off the stool and looked out over the heads of the crowd towards the City. From his eyrie he could see the forest of banners milling around at the edge of the City, and the Blackshirts circling beneath them like crows, just waiting for the police to clear the way so that they could swoop down into the East End and pick its bones. The street below him was packed with people and, as he opened the window, the cries of the crowd came surging in. 'No Pasaran,' they roared. 'Death to the Fascists'.

    Even as he watched, a herd of horses galloped out of a side street to form a wall across the road. Though the smoke stained warehouses towered up four and five storeys high along each side of Cable Street, the riders, perched on top of their great steeds and with their high helmets steepling to the sky, seemed to cut out more light than the buildings.

'Charge,' came the bellowing cry from the sergeant at the front and with batons drawn, each policeman jabbed his spurs into the flanks of his mount to hurl himself at the mob ahead.

Solly watched in horror as the battering ram of cavalry crashed into the crowd. In the narrow street, there was no escape. Man after man was knocked sprawling to the ground and trampled under the flying hooves. Those that tried to run back, were beaten to their knees. As they fell, they were dragged away, either by the police or by rescuing friends. Solly still felt tears burning in his eyes, but now they were tears of anger. They were so brave in the face of such brutal force, but he was certain that they would be beaten in the end. The odds were too great against them. They had to break under such force and would be driven off and hunted down through the back streets of the docks. They would not think themselves beaten, they would lick their wounds and regroup for the next battle. He shrugged, what did he expect? Most of them did not live here, they were not of the faith, they were not neighbours or family. They fought on his doorstep out of principle and would not stay.

He wiped the tears away with the cuff of his shirt to clear his vision. He had seen young revolutionaries so many times before. Here today, tomorrow they would be fighting someone else's battle far away. Solly knew, from bitter experience, that it was the Blackshirts who stayed. They lived here. They jostled his wife off the pavement when she went shopping in the Whitechapel Road, they spat at his children when they made their way to school in Stepney Green. They threatened him with death when he went to the synagogue at Aldgate. They would not go away. Like him, they had nowhere else to go. They were also fighting for the land and so it was a battle to the death.

Solly had heard the news coming out of Germany. Each ship that tied up in the docks brought more refugees from the East. He had been down to Commercial Road where his grasp of Yiddish and German could be useful in helping the newcomers get papers, find lodgings and make contact with relatives who could offer sanctuary. These tired, frightened, confused waifs all came with the same story, but no one outside Stepney listened to them. One of the refugees brought news that struck close to home and had told him what happened to his own cousin Rueben Klein and his wife Rachel from Munich. An old lady who came from the next courtyard told him that they had been sent to Poland. To a new Ghetto, beyond another Pale. He didn't know if what she said was true. He could not check. He wrote, but the letters just kept coming back.

Solly cleared his pattern books from the window sill to give himself a clear line of fire. No-one was going to put his wife in a barbed wire cage or send his children away while he lived.

Nervously he opened the breech, checking again that it was loaded. Then, kneeling down at his bench, he fed the muzzle out into the air. He took aim at the pub sign at the corner of Leman Street He had stepped out the distance yesterday to set the sight. Adjusting it by a hair's breadth, he waited.

Again there was a clatter of hooves on the cobbles and the roar of the crowd rose to a scream of protest. Looking down, he saw the police coming again like the Cossacks from the old country. The barricade at the end of the street was giving way under the weight of charging police horses and the defenders were, once more, running for their lives before the plunging beasts.

With a sigh, he took his position, wrapped the rifle sling around his arm and slowly raised the barrel. Peering over the sights, he could make out the distant swirling banners of the Blackshirts above the heads of the fleeing crowd. They were on the move. It would only be a matter of minutes before the blue ranks of police opened a corridor that would let them slide down the street like an invasion of cockroaches.

Solly knew that the Fascist's cheer earlier had been for their leader arriving amongst them. He planned to march in triumphant procession at their head as they came in to conquer the East. Before The Leader could take his followers across the road and left up Leman Street, Solly meant to cut him down.

'They're on the move' one of the young reds in the street called to his comrades. Solly did not look down, the boy was only telling what he already knew.

He released the safety catch, and felt the steel trigger, cold against his sweating finger as he began to apply the pressure. 'Wait, wait,' he told himself.

In the street a whistle blew. Sweat was trickling into his eyes, but he dare not try to wipe it away. With a wry smile, he remembered that unusually for a Jew, he had never been good at waiting. In Flanders, on those dreadful days when they had been ordered to attack across the barbed wire and mud of no man's land, he would be struggling out of the trench before the officer could give the signal. Those assaults were dreadful, hundreds of his friends were cut down around him and every time he was so certain that he was going to be the next to die that he couldn't stand the delay. It was only the hands of his mates hanging onto the tail of his jacket which held him back until the whistles blew. Today was one of those even worse attack days when there was no need to run, you had to wait for the enemy to come to you.

He began to recite, from memory, the orders written in his little note-book. A black frock coat for the rabbi Helmann, with silk facing on the lapels and a fullness to hide his belly. A third pair of trousers for Hymie Strauss to go with the suit he hadn't paid for yet and if there was any material left, a pair of shorts for his son Jacob. On he went, through the list of jackets, trousers and waist-coats. He was quoting the details of Abraham Finsberg's bar mitzvah suit when a great cry stopped him. 'Get that lorry' a tall thin man with a huge moustache, standing on the pavement almost beneath his window was shouting and pointing towards a builder's yard. 'Tip it over across the street.'

Against the tide of running men, a group of boys

rushed towards the lunging police horses. As they reached the front of the crowd they rooted in their pockets and drew out handfuls of marbles. These toys, which they had struggled to win in mighty contests on street corners and in alleys, they now threw down as their contribution to the battle. Like hailstones they clattered away over the cobbles. The first horse plunged down onto its neck pitching its rider into the gutter. With a scream of fury those of the crowd closest to him fell on the policeman and pummelled him with their fists. Paying back in a small way the beatings they had received from boots and batons. Horses skidded, shied and the unstoppable advance whirled into chaos. Other policemen fell, but these leapt to their feet like Jack in a Boxes and fled to the rear in pursuit of their terrified mounts. Their colleagues fought to control their horses enough to run away.

From the windows of the houses between the warehouses, a rain of milk bottles, pots, pans and vegetables, began to hammer down on the invaders. Behind the cover of the artillery barrage, the lorry was dragged down the road and a score of sweating, straining men rocked it harder and harder until it slowly capsized at their feet. A roar like thunder swept down the narrow alleys

'They shall not pass,' yelled an urchin, who had quickly climbed on top of the barricade, shaking his fist at the sky. Peering down the rifle's barrel, Solly saw the Blackshirt's banners lift and straighten into line. For a moment they seemed to hesitate, not sure of their direction, then they moved away and Mosley led the Fascists retreat back into the City.

As Solly sat back heavily on the floor, a twinkle caught his eye. Gratefully, he laid the gun aside and picked up the needle lying under his sewing machine. *God is good*, he thought, *better a tailor than an avenging angel*.

In complete contrast to Solomon's recovery of his natural calm, the scene in the street below continued in frantic chaos. There wasn't a single policeman to be seen. Cable Street, Leman Street, Gardiner's Corner and down

Commercial Road belonged to the people. It was as though they had just stormed the Winter Palace and the revolution was under way. Every one in the crowd felt that they were comrades: in arms, in spirit and in politics. It was a glorious moment.

'Salud,' a complete stranger shouted at Jack to ensure he was heard above the roar of the crowd. Grinning like a drunk, he repeatedly punched at the air in an extravagant Communist salute.

'On to Madrid,' Jack yelled back with a feeling of utter relief, returning the clenched fist greeting and grinning broadly. His reprieve had reached him on the gallow's steps and he did not have to die, 'On to victory.'

'There's a celebration at Shoreditch tonight, 'another man bellowed close to his ear as he caught Jack around the shoulders in a comradely embrace.

'I shall be there Comrade,' Jack replied.

Using handshakes and embraces to lever himself along, Jack swam back through the crowd to the narrow alley alongside the tailors' workshop with Miriam doing her best to follow. It was a good job they had taken Mordecai's handcart with them yesterday or it would have surely disappeared to take a heroic place in one of the barricades which had turned the fascists back. The battered old bin had survived and the end of brown, hessian sack was silhouetted against the light from the back yard.

The terrors of yesterday were completely forgotten and there was a sense of joy as he pulled the heavy bag out of the dustbin. Jack felt a madness upon him, he had to fight the urge to pull out the gun and wave it above his head with a demand for the crowd to march on Parliament. Miriam silhouetted against the light at the end of the alleyway just had time to fix him for an instant with hard eyes before she was swept away.

Solomon's instructions had been definite and allowed no deviation. Whatever had happened, whether Mosley had been killed, whether the shot had even been fired, whichever way the victory, Jack's task was to retrieve the rifle. He had to take it to the river and throw it in to destroy all the evidence. But, Jack argued to himself, if the tailor could see the completeness of the victory down in the street, he would have allowed the glorious army of the proletariat to storm out of the East End. The City of London was only a quarter of a mile away and he could see the very heart of capitalism rising up above the roofs at the end of the street.

The regrouping of the mounted police at the end of street to form a bastion for the capitalist told Jack that revolutions are not won that easily and returned him to some form of sanity. 'The Cossacks' had been driven back and would not risk another charge, but they held the line at the Royal Mint and it would take more than one rifle and a few bullets to break through. Regretfully, he swung the sack onto his shoulder and trudged away from the battle field. He walked through the archway at the end of alley, across the yard at the back of Solomon's workshop and then out into Wapping where it was a normal Sunday.

Jack had not thought about access to the river, but as he emerged from the alley into the next street he looked right and left, to be faced with an unbroken façade of black warehouses. It was unnerving to pass from the middle of a victorious crowd into a deserted street where he could hear his own footsteps. Without the prop of comrades, fear once more churned his stomach. Stopping to consider his next move, he heard the loud lap of waves and, looking through another alleyway on the south side of the road, he saw a set of stone stairs leading down to the water. Glancing around to make sure he wasn't observed, Jack hurried through towards the river.

''Ere, what you want?' A watchman, standing in a little hut set into an alcove on a riverside wharf, demanded as Jack drew level with him.

Jack jumped in surprise. The sack slipped off his shoulder and clattered onto the stone flags of the dock. In quick witted desperation he asked, 'have you been up and seen what's going on in Cable Street?'

The old man pulled the stubby pipe from between his

gums so that he could shake his head. 'I ain't got nothing to do with Cable Street and you ain't got nothing to do with this dock, so clear off before I calls the law.'

'The people have taken over the streets. We've kicked the fascists out of the East End and given the Bobbies a bloody good hiding. There isn't a copper within a mile of here.'

The old watchman considered what he had just been told. 'That's as maybe, but they haven't taken over this street so it still ain't none of my business. Like I said, my job is to stop people going down onto the wharf without permission.'

Jack looked at the weather beaten old face showing a life time of toil; at his twisted hands that could no longer haul on ropes and twisted back which could no longer unload a ship like a human donkey. He didn't want him to risk his job, but he desperately needed his help. 'Of course it's got to do with you, Comrade, this is the day when the workers beat the bosses. This is the day of solidarity.' He raised his clenched fist above his head.

The watchman looked sideways at the intense young man with his hammer and sickle button-hole badge. He said nothing for a moment while he took a final pull from his pipe before knocking it out against his heel. 'I ain't solid with nobody,' he said. 'I does me job and minds me own business.' Without another word, he stepped out of the hut and locked the door behind him. He was paid to stop people taking sacks off the wharves. Nobody ever said nothing about bringing them on. Without a backward glance at the boy, he turned away and began his leisurely patrol of the dock.

Jack watched him walk away, uncertain for the moment where he was going, then, slinging the sack across his shoulders once more, he hurried in the opposite direction. Though there was no ship tied up alongside, there was no easy access to the water's edge. A double bank of lighters was tethered to wharf, waiting to move up stream on the mornings high tide.

Jack had no love of boats, not even when they were so closely tied to the land, but he wasn't sure how long he had before the watchman's return or if he would come back alone. He jumped onto the nearest barge and used it a springboard to launch himself onto of the one the outer boats.

He didn't know if the tide was on the flood or ebb, but the heavy slap of waves on the hulls of the lighters made him feel that no-one would hear the splash, if he flung the sack out into the river. He didn't doubt that it would sink, but even if it didn't, he felt that there was so much debris floating in the water that no-one would notice one more piece of rubbish.

With a final look around to make sure there were no witnesses, he drew the sack back and then hurled it out over the murky river.

The splash as it hit the water was louder than Jack had expected. He turned around guiltily, but still seemed to be alone. By the time he looked back at the muddy water, even the ripples had been mopped up by the waves and there was nothing left of their plot to kill Mosley. Jack sighed a deep sigh of relief. 'Good riddance,' he mouthed. If he never saw a rifle again in all his life, it would be too soon.

When he got back to Cable Street, the crowds were still there, but no longer rushing like wild horses. Most of them were now in groups, heads together trying to work out what had actually happened, and when they moved it was en masse, like the tide. There was no sign of Miriam by the entrance to the alley next to the entrance to Epstein the tailor's workshop. He walked in that direction and glanced down. The dustbin had gone to spend its final role on this day of days as a victory drum. A surge in the crowd swept him past in an instant and he had to fight to backtrack and look again. The tailor was in the dustbin's place, sitting on the ground, hunched back against the wall.

Where Jack stood out in the light of the street it was exhilarating. He had to brace himself against an iron bollard to resist the drive of the crowd. There was a buzz of excitement punctuated by cheers, singing, shaking hands all around him and down in the gloomy court, Solomon Epstein the tailor was crying.

'It's all right. The job's done. It's all over.' Jack had walked into the alley where he could speak quietly and still be heard.

The tailor looked up, held out his arms and wailed.

Not knowing why the tailor was so upset, Jack had a vague suspicion that it might be his fault. 'Don't worry Comrade,' he said,' the...' He hesitated and glanced over his shoulder back towards the crowded road. 'The thing is at the bottom of the river and no-one saw me. I have come back for Miriam; she is supposed to be waiting for me. She won't be able to cope in all this bedlam and you can't rely on Moses to look after her.'

Epstein began to nod his head with all the vigour of davening. 'Yes, yes, yes,' he repeated over and over again, as if in prayer, getting louder and more exited with each repetition. Finally, the tailor leapt to his feet and danced a few frantic steps. He caught Jack by the shoulders and shook him. Thrusting his thin, bearded, white face close, 'Yes,' he agreed, 'it is done and I can go home to my wife and my daughters. For me, the war is over.'

Jack finally began to understand what this conversation was about and became angry. 'No,' he shouted pulling himself free. 'No, the war's only just beginning. We've sent the Fascists running with their tails between their legs, this time, but now we have to do the same in Madrid. Then we will be able to drive them out of Rome and Berlin. You are a soldier, you're trained, you can lead us to take the fight on.'

'No, little brother no,' the tailor's tears had stopped and he was smiling. 'No, I have thrown my stone in punishment and retribution. For me the trial is over and I can go home.'

Jack wanted to hit him, to smash the smile from his stupid face. 'Don't be daft. You of all people must see. We're cheering like mad here, but this is nothing. If we can't stop them in Spain, then there is a real war coming. It will be a clash of civilisations, of economic systems, of social justice. And don't think for a moment that they'll let a Jewish tailor sit at home sewing bar mitzvah suits. They'll call you to the colours like they did last time and you'll have to fight then.'

Epstein the tailor's smile broadened, 'they will call me,' he said, 'and I will go and they will make me a cook or a clerk or a lorry driver or a radio operator and I shall sit quietly and earn more Schekels than I do now.

'You're a fool...' Jack began, but the tailor laid a finger on his mouth. 'No, little friend, I am close to being an old man. And now I have you to look after me and mine. It is your turn now. You have learned the weight of a rifle and now you must learn how to use it.'

Chapter 12

Dear Tommy,

Thank you for taking me roller skating last weekend, it was very jolly even though I have bruises in places I don't like to mention. Perhaps we can do it again with some of the others. I would dearly love to see Sally falling over and showing her legs to the world.

My cousin Angie is staying at our house for the week while she and her mother do some shopping in London. She really is a sporty girl and I'm sure that you would like her. From all I've told her about you, she already likes you.

She is getting a party together to go to Paris before Christmas to do some shopping there. She asked me if we would like to go.

I told her I wasn't sure how you were fixed at the moment, but I would ask. It would be great fun, I'm sure, but it is likely to be a touch expensive. Angie's fellow Claude Philips is paying for her. Naturally I wouldn't expect you to do the same for me, we're not that good friends are we?

I'm free on Thursday to go dancing, if you still want to. Hoping that you do, I'll meet you in the usual place at seven thirty unless I hear to the contrary.

Yours till the cows come home

Kitty

Tommy sensed danger in the air as he strolled into the Saloon bar of the White Swan. None of the card players acknowledged his entrance with a glance, but no-one laid a card down on the table. The drinkers at the bar didn't stop their conversation, and none of them gave him a nod to indicate they had seen him come in.

Normally Tommy would have had to elbow his way to the front of the knot of runners around Slippers, but today the crowd was no more substantial than the cigarette smoke hanging heavily in the bar and he was instantly at the front of the queue.

He knew he was in trouble, but he wasn't sure why. He glanced around and saw how alone he was, the normal jostling bickering crowd had moved away to join other knots of men in their various corners. None of them were looking at him. There was no point in making a run for the door and so he pulled off his cap and spilled his slips on the table in front of the book keeper.

With his practiced ease, Sam Daventry ran his hand lightly over them to fan them over the table top. Slipper's eyes were always cold, but now, as he looked up, there was a frost which made Tommy shiver. The book-man's glance merely skidded across Tommy's face, looking for someone in the crowd behind him.

Tommy would have turned to see who Slippers was looking at, but a hand caught him around the back of his neck to stop him moving and from the hidden world behind him another reached past him to place a broken glass on the table. The hand on his neck began to press. Tommy resisted, but the second hand had now caught his left arm and was twisting it up his back. Tommy tried to stand up straight, but hand on his neck was too strong. It was pressing him inexorably forward and down towards the broken glass.

Instinctively Tommy realized that only one man in the room was strong enough and tall enough to push him down like that. ''Ere George,' he screamed in panic stricken protest. 'What you doing? What's going on? I ain't done nothing. Honest I ain't.'

'What ain't you done?' George demanded, but the pressure on Tommy's neck didn't slacken.

'I ain't done nothing, George, I swear it. You know I wouldn't double cross you.' Tommy was screaming in terror, the tallest pinnacle of the broken glass was only inches from his left eye and he couldn't move to either side to hope to avoid it. It was Gentleman George himself who jerked Tommy's face a fraction to the side and smashed his head against the wooden table. All the betting slips danced in front of his eyes.

Tommy felt the glass brush his cheek. It was the thump of his head that rattled his teeth and made him think he was hurt.

'You're short of slips,' George snapped. 'This is the third time it's happened. It better not happen again Tommy. You know Mr. Green don't allow no one to skim off the green punters and run his own book.'

The pressure was released from Tommy's neck and he stood up straight. His jaw dropped open in amazement. There was a puddle of blood on the table in front of him which rippled as more dripped down from his. 'You've fucking cut me, George,' he said in disbelief, putting his hand up to his cheek to make sure that it was his blood. A wave of fury rose up inside him and the colour of blood seemed to wash over the whole room. Before he could stop himself or anyone else could move he smashed his fist straight into George's face.

George had been hit harder, a lot harder. You could hit Gentleman George with a brick and he wouldn't flinch, but he wasn't ready. He stepped back, tripped and crashed down on his back side. Everyone was watching now and two or three of the audience laughed. Up until now, it had only been business, now George was angry too and as he leapt up from the floor there was a knife in his hand.

There was not a thought in Tommy's head, but somehow he found himself holding the broken glass from the table. 'If you come for me George, I'll have your face, you bastard. I might be dead, but I swear, you won't be pretty no more.'

George wasn't prepared to take risks with his good looks. He knew he would get even later and let the point of the knife droop.

Feeling safe for the moment, Tommy turned to the corner where his long term safety lay. 'I didn't take any bets myself, Mr. Green. All I collected are on the table in front of Slippers. If there's some missing, then it's down to somebody else.'

Slippers had been shuffling through the slips of paper in front of him. 'It could be Ferucciano,' he admitted. 'It's mainly his stuff that's short; was last time too.'

Reggie nodded, that was likely. 'Shake hands you two,' he commanded. 'A misunderstanding; forget it; nothing personal. George you will call on Mr. Ferucciano and discuss the matter with him.'

With an involuntary gesture, Tommy ran his hand over his cheek and looked at the blood on it. He had no doubt the George had intended to cut him and was in no mood to shake hands.

'It's only a scratch Tom,' George chuckled, as he caught hold of his blood stained hand. 'You ain't going to be scarred like your brother. If I'd a done it with a chiv, you could have called yourself a hero. Come on, I'll get you a drink.'

Tommy's burning anger slowly cooled. The blood stopped running and, looking at himself in the mirror behind the bar, he could see that George was right. It was only a scratch.

'It's your own fault,' George said as he watched Tommy studying himself. 'You can't blame Reggie for getting suspicious. After all you have pocketed the odd bet in your time and the word is out that you're short of money.

'Short of money?' Tommy demanded defensively. 'Why should I be short of money?'

'You tell me,' said George, 'but I heard that you were trying to sell your bike. Knowing how much you love that machine, it can only mean you're really short of money.'

Tommy lifted his drink and drained the glass. 'If I sold my bike, I would be short of money, because I'd take my girl to Paris for a few days, but no one's got the money to buy it; so I won't be taking her to Paris; so I ain't short of money.'

'So that's what it's all about,' George laughed. 'It's always the way. Women will keep you poor. I should know.' He up ended his own glass in sympathy, but as he slammed it down on the bar, a strange expression came over his face. For minutes, he watched Tommy in the bar mirror almost as though he had never seen him before. 'Hmm,' he said reflectively, 'a thought occurs to me. You fussy how you make this money?'

'I'm not doing any more stewarding at Fascist meetings,' Tommy replied.

George snorted derisively. 'That's peanuts and we both know it. I'm talking real money here Tommy. I'm talking a couple of hundred quid here, maybe more.'

Tommy whistled. 'Two hundred pounds,' he echoed. He could really impress Charlotte with money like that. He could match anything that ponce Claude could do. And there was no knowing how impressed she might be, it would certainly be worth investing in a packet of Joe Ferucciano's frenchies for the trip to Paris. He didn't think she'd let him book a double room, but she might agree to him slipping in, in the night, if he could get two rooms close to each other. 'No, I don't think I'd be too fussy about how I earned it.'

George tapped the side of his nose and winked. 'Say no more, for the time being. I've got to talk to a couple of blokes. If they say you're in, you're in.'

'When will I know?'

'You going to that dance your brother's organised down Tottenham Hale tonight?' George asked.

'I thought I might,' Tommy said. 'I ain't got a ticket, but Jack'll let me in.'

'Don't worry about tickets, I've got loads. Phyllis is singing with the band and I said I'd get a crowd organised.

Charlie Hartwell can't go of course, wouldn't be done for your local Fascist to go to a Commie dance, but it's likely your woman will be there with some of her friends.'

'Yes, she told me she was going slumming; that why I thought that I'd drop in. Will you know about the money by then?'

George shrugged. 'I've got a job to do for Reggie this afternoon. I don't know how long it will take, but if I get time, I'll find out for you.'

***

George Harris walking into Ferucciano's Barber's Shop was like the turning out of the sun on that sunny Saturday. His huge shoulders blocked off half the shop window as he reached across and reversed the 'open' sign.

'Afternoon Joe,' he said amiably, as he slipped into one of the vacant chairs, 'give us the works.'

The man sitting with his son, on one of the seats along the wall, waiting his turn for a haircut didn't object to George jumping the queue. Instead he glanced at the clock and decided that, perhaps this wasn't a good time to get a short back and sides after all and left, pushing his unprotesting boy in front of him.

Joe knew he was in trouble; he could feel the tension in George Harris's neck as he wrapped a hot towel around it. He could see his hand gripping the arm of the chair like a vice as he began to apply the lather, liberally, to his chin. Gentleman George was goading him, daring him to cut his throat, betting that the little old Italian wouldn't have the courage, even though he knew what was going to happen next.

Knowing made Joe tremble as he stropped the razor, but as soon as he laid the blade on George's tanned skin, his hand was like a rock. A life time of shaving, drunk and sober, excited and in the depths of despair, allowed him to cope with fear. He knew that he could have cut George's throat, but he didn't nick him. When Joe handed him a towel at the end to wipe his chin while he brushed the last cut hair from George's collar, there wasn't a speck of red on it.

As he handed the towel back and turned to admire himself in the mirror, 'nice haircut, nice shave Joe,' he said and reached into his pocket.

'No, no Mr. Harris,' Joe protested, there was no 'Georgio' now. 'She's on the house, you know, always on the house for you.'

George withdrew his hand and the brass knuckles glinted for an instant as he smashed them into the little Italian's face. His nose split and burst like a ripe tomato. George tutted. 'That's very unprofessional, Joe,' he said quietly, 'you've got blood on my shirt. I think I'm going to have to find myself a new barber.' His left hand snapped up from its rest at his side and sank into the pit of the old man's stomach. He collapsed like a feather pillow and George's knee jerked up to catch him in the face. The barber went down on his back and George kicked him. He tried to get up and George knocked him down to kick him again.

When he no longer moved, no longer groaned to show he felt any blow, George stopped hitting him. He wandered to one of the basins, washed and dried the worst of the blood off his hands. Pausing for a moment in front of one of the mirrors to straighten his tie, he turned to leave. The unconscious hairdresser lay across his path, so he picked him up and tossing him out of the way; threw him through the glass partition which separated the salon from the waiting area.

As he walked towards the door, George nudged the till with his elbow and sent the draw pinging open. With a single sneering snatch, he cleared out the few notes and coins and stuffed Ferucciano's stock of contraceptives into his pocket. With a last glance in the mirror to draw down the brim of his hat he walked casually away.

Chapter 13

Dear Peggy and Jack

Just a quick note to say thanks for all your help at the warehouse at Lloyd Baker Street last weekend. Without your help we would never have organised the last shipment onto the boat for Bilbao. I know it's a bit of a cheek, but there is a freight wagon of clothing in the Somers Town siding at the moment and two vans of tinned vegetables coming down from the Nottingham Co-op sometime during the week, and I wondered if I could count on the South Tottenham Comrades for help to sort it out.

I'm expecting to be back at my mother's on the 13th., but there's a Labour Party meeting on the 14th. that I have to go to. I don't think I'll be able to make the dance, but I could try and pop in towards the end of things to try to drum up a few volunteers, if you think it would help.

If I do make it, I could also accept the donation on behalf of the Aid Spain Committee while I'm there, which might make a headline in the Herald. I don't know how much they're getting in, but I can tell you we need every penny we can get at the moment so go out, spread the word and shake the tins.

Keep it under your hats, but I had that meeting with Atlee and Bevin, I was hinting at. I think Atlee might go out to Spain to see for himself. If he goes, it's not possible that he could see the struggle of the Spanish people and not be moved. Let's hope for a change in Labour's position on non intervention.

I'll try and see you both on the 14th., if not, bring the take with you on Saturday. In the mean time, be kind to each other and remember that I love you both.

Salud. Ted

'What about the music?' Jack demanded, still smarting from Doreen's implied criticism of the way he was organising the refreshments. It wasn't his fault that there wasn't a drinks licence at the hall. He only suggested the place; Frank should have checked that out before he agreed to them booking it.

Peggy's blue eyes flashed a warning, but for once Jack wasn't looking at her and missed it.

'What about the music, Comrade?' Frank Mitchell repeated the words, truculently, pushing his florid face out over the table towards Jack. The committee room was so small that it brought them eye to eye.

Peggy coughed, but Jack was wrapped up in his idea and wouldn't back away. 'Oh come off it Frank, that band we had for the District YCL dance was rubbish, everybody said so, and you know it.'

There was an instant of silence before the explosion of anger that showed it to be fake. Frank leapt to his feet and began to pound the table with his fist. 'That band is made up of dedicated Party members. I'll have you know, some of that band have played in Russia.'

For the first time Jack sensed that he had gone too far in his outburst and looked to Peggy for support. Her eyes were staring hard at him, warning him of danger.

There was no comfort there, but he could see no way back. Like Frank, he rode his fear as if it were real anger. 'I don't care about that. I still say they're rubbish. I've been selling tickets to all my mates and they've been selling them to their mates. I've been selling tickets in all the pubs. Eddie Bainbridge, the landlord of the Gillespie Arms took a few. George Harris has bought a wad of fifty. People round here think a lot of George and even you know what he's like,' Jack was shouting too, but as he looked around the table from Peggy to Doreen, to Frank to Moses, he suddenly realised that they didn't know. None of them lived around here; none of them knew the lads down his street; the gang from Haringey dog track or the wreckers from Lorenko Road. Peggy was a nurse, Doreen a teacher, Frank a bus driver and Moses an intellectual. They didn't understand that if you put that sort of music on for people who had paid 6d. a ticket for a dance, there would be a riot. They would wreck the hall. Jack found his words running out, 'I tell you it's rubbish and what's worse its 1920's German rubbish. Nobody listens to that sort of music anymore.'

As Jack's anger burnt itself out, Frank exploded. 'Comrade Sutton,' he screamed, 'you're an unreconstructed revisionist. That band is made up of comrades dedicated to the cause. They are Party men through and through, who will play for the revolution just as I work for it and would die for it. Your Trotskyite attitude is a disgrace to the proletariat.' He took a deep breath and raised a clenched fist over the table. 'I demand that an emergency resolution is put before this committee. I demand that Comrade Sutton is ejected from membership of the organising committee of the Aid Spain Dance, forthwith, and a report be submitted to the next branch meeting of The Party with a recommendation that his membership is cancelled as of now.'

Moses's quiet voice slid into the stunned silence which followed Frank's outburst. 'Comrade Mitchell is right. Jack has overstepped the mark here. In normal events, his comments would be entered into the minutes for the necessary action, but.' The word *but* was like the valve being pulled out of an inner tube. Frank's hand dropped to his side and he flopped back into his chair as if the air had been let out of him. He knew he was beaten.

As if still considering the situation, Moses paused. He sucked, reflectively, on his teeth and stared at the ceiling, 'but, comrades, these are not normal events. Comrade Sutton was wrong to criticise a band which has The Party's endorsement, but what he said about the dance is true. This dance, in aid of the gallant people of Spain and our compatriots who are fighting and dying alongside them, has to achieve many things. It undoubtedly has to raise money for the cause, but more importantly it has to raise the people's awareness of the issues and the Party's lead in the struggle. Of necessity, we will wrap ourselves round with the banners of the Popular Front, we will invite Labour League of Youth to stand at the front of the platform, sell tickets to the ILP, look for a blessing from the church, but at the end of the day no-one must be in any doubt that we, the Communist Party of Great Britain organised this function and that it is due to us that it was a great success. When the report appears in the Tottenham Herald, I want the words 'Communist' and 'Triumph' to be in the headline. Do I make myself clear?'

'Yes Moses,' they all muttered.

Jack's face was like stone, but inside he rejoiced. He had won. Now it was no problem to end the awkward silence which followed. 'I'm sorry Frank, 'he said, 'I didn't mean to criticise the band like that. I was wrong in what I said. What I meant was that they're a marching band, they're the head of a protest rally band, but they're not a dance band. You have to listen to what's being played down the Palais to know what young people will buy tickets for.'

'Take your point Jack, take your point,' Frank said grudgingly. 'So what are we going to do for a band?'

'Well,' Moses said turning to Jack. 'You seem to be well ahead with your job of running the kitchen, and, though the hall's all booked and the deposit paid, Frank says he needs more time to spend on publicity, I think we can safely turn that over to you.'

'The one they used at the Co-op dance last month was quite good.' Jack said, already regretting his outburst. He didn't want to be responsible for the music as well, that would mean that he spent no time with Peggy. 'It was LLY too. My sister knows some body in the band's sister and I think I could get them,' he added, looking to seal the point. 'They made over ten pounds for Spanish Aid at that dance.'

'Oh no,' Moses stopped it there with a gesture of his hand. 'No, I don't think we want to go quite that far. I think you'll be able to find a YCL band that can play just as well. And we'll make over twenty pounds.

Doreen and Peggy clapped, but Peggy had a sly feeling at the back of her heart and wondered if being so deeply involved with Jack was such a good idea. He had come out of this little run in with Frank as the winner, but his political naiveté over all, could be a liability to someone determined to rise within the Party.

***

'All property is theft,' Jack declared to what he thought was an empty hall and he took a bottle of unlabelled light ale out of the crate hidden under a blanket by the back door. He knocked the top off against the bar. After raising the bottle towards the stage, to salute himself; he poured it down his throat. He'd worked bloody hard this last fortnight and if the dance was a success, then it was largely down to him. He'd earned this free beer.

'I'll drink to that.'

Jack swung around from the door looking out into the hall to see his brother, standing in the back entrance from the kitchen to the yard. 'What you doing coming in that way?' he demanded. 'What you doing coming in at all, I don't remember you buying a ticket?'

'Bloody cheek,' Tommy protested, 'don't forget I was the one what got you all this cheap booze.' He took a bottle out of a crate, half hidden, beside the tea urn. The label had turned to an illegible mush on the side. 'What's in here?'

Jack accepted that Tommy was right and he probably hadn't got any money for a ticket anyway. 'Can't be sure, old Bowler gave me a list of the damaged goods I could take, but I can't really work out what's what. I think those one's are stout, these are pale ale and those over there are crates of Bass. He indicated three innocuous piles of drying up cloths which were supposed to hide them. 'They were all left out in the brewery yard during a storm and the labels got washed off, or ruined. That's how we got 'em for nothing. It was cheaper to say they'd been dumped than run the cost of rebottling them. I also got two barrels of bitter and one of mild for almost nothing, they're hidden out the yard. I had to buy the spirits and the women's drinks, but I got them through Eddie Bainbridge, wholesale and I can take back anything that isn't opened. They're in the oven.' After he'd given Tommy the information, a thought occurred to him. 'Are you staying?'

Tommy slipped the top of a beer bottle with his thumb. 'Did you get any glasses?' he asked.

'A few, but mainly for the women, the blokes are going to have to drink out of the bottle or jam jars for draught. Are you staying?'

Tommy looked round the Free Trades Hall kitchen, which was acting the part as bar for the evening. 'I might, for a while. I saw George Harris earlier and he told me that Phyllis is making her debut as a solo artiste tonight. He said she was singing with your band. George said that he might turn up later with some of his crowd. I thought they might liven things up a bit and it might be worth a look in.'

'Oh,' said Jack knowingly, 'so that's it, you think Katherine Hartwell might turn up. God, I know it's a Popular Front do, but I didn't know we were inviting the bloody Fascists. I'll tell you for nothing, there'll be trouble if that brother of hers turns up.

'There won't be any trouble,' Tom said angrily. 'Anyway why would he want to come down this tin pot little hall, he's got better things to do.'

'Good,' Jack agreed, 'and so have you. If you're staying, you can make yourself useful. There's a couple of girls helping with the teas and orange juice, but if I'm going to get to dance with Peggy, I'll need somebody I can trust to help me with the booze.'

'Fair enough,' Tommy laughed. 'Free drinks for bar staff and their friends?'

'Free drink for bar staff and his friend and you can charge George and his mob double to make up for it.'

'What's the time?' Tommy asked. 'How long

before the doors open?'

'Dunno, there's a clock over the stage, but I don't think it's right,' Jack admitted. 'It's nearly dark so it must be getting on. See if Phyllis is back from her break, she'll have a watch.'

Tommy wandered to the door into the hall and leaned against the door post. There wasn't a hammer and sickle to be seen, but the red bunting which swamped the walls left no-one in any doubt about who had organised this dance. Even the band's music stands, empty for the moment on the stage, were draped in Moscow red. 'What's the band like?'

'It's OK,' Jack said defensively, 'they've been rehearsing all afternoon. They're getting better.'

Tommy grimaced, 'don't forget I've heard the Berkeley Nightingales sing and believe me, Phyllis is no song bird. If the rest of the band's not that good, it had better be loud.'

'Oh, it's not that bad. Hughie, the saxophone player is the brother of one of the girls Phyllis sings with. He's a bus conductor, but he's not bad. He's semi-professional and as he put the band together, is the sort of band leader. His mate is the double bass player, he's all right too. Now here's a surprise. Do you remember a kid from school called Dennis Hodges? He was in my class; his parents were Salvationists; they ran the Seven Sisters Citadel.'

Tommy shook his head.

'Yes you do, he was fat and wore glasses, we called him Porky. He used to play the Euphonium with the Salvation Army band for the meetings on Edmonton Green.

'No, sorry,' Tommy persisted.

'You'll recognise him when you see him. Well it seems he also plays a mean trumpet. Hughie says that he really is good. Trouble is that his parents don't approve of him playing modern music and the Salvation Army owns the trumpet. He has to sneak it out of the house when his mother's not looking. 'Jack began to point at each of the band stands in turn remembering who was there. 'Then there's a bloke I know from the YCL who plays the trombone and he's brought his girlfriend who plays the drums. They were playing some American swing this afternoon, but they said they'll stick to stuff that's good to dance to. Anyway, it is loud, and you can't hear too much of Phyllis.

His finger came to rest at the piano. 'I have got one problem though.'

'What's that?'

'Hughie wants a piano player, but I ask you, where does he think I can get a piano player this late on a Saturday?'

'What about the bloke that plays in the Wellington, he's good?'

'I've asked him. He said he doesn't play charity gigs.'

'You could have offered to pay him.'

'Tommy,' Jack protested, offended by the suggestion. 'He's not that good, and if I pay him then I'll have to pay the rest. Moses said he knew someone, but there's no sign of him. If he's not quick, Hughie's gonna have to play without a piano. I'm out to make a big profit on this shindig. Peggy's going to be proud of me.'

Tommy's low long whistle showed that he wasn't listening. 'Our Phyllis may not be able to sing, but who will care, dressed like that.'

Jack hurried to join his brother at the kitchen door. 'Wow,' he exclaimed.

Phyllis's midnight blue dress sparkled like a summer night full of stars. She had lovely figure and this dress, with its plunging neck line, did more than hint at the treasures which lay beneath. 'Do you like it boys?' she shrilled in her best Hollywood voice, and spun round so that the hem swirled up like the light studded canopy on a roundabout.

'It's stunning Phyllis, stunning,' Tommy replied. 'George had better watch out; any one would cheerfully kill him to get at you.'

Phyllis giggled. 'You boys are awful. And how

many times do I have to tell you that when I'm appearing professionally I'm called Geraldine De Beauvoir.'

'Sorry Geraldine,' Tommy laughed.

'You will be if you do it again.' she said only half joking then added 'I might have to have George kill you.'

There was a crash and an oath as Hughie arrived and kicked Porky's music stand off the stage. 'Have you got anything in for the band to drink?' he demanded seeing Tommy standing at the kitchen door with an open bottle in his hand. 'Me and Henry,' he nodded towards the man struggling to do a strip tease from an assortment of banjos while standing astride a huge bass. 'We drink pints.'

'Well hard luck,' Tommy replied, 'cos we don't have a licence.

'What's that then?' Hughie demanded, pointing at the bottle in his hand, 'Scotch mist.'

'Talking of 'scotch', I'll have mine with a whisky chaser,' Henry added.

'Fat chance,' said Jack. 'We've only got one bottle of whisky and we're going to raffle that, so you'll have to buy a ticket for your whisky chasers.'

'OK, make it two pints then,' Hughie said grudgingly.

'No pints, we ain't got no glasses.'

'If you've got no glasses, what you going to serve from those barrels which I saw falling off the back of that lorry, this afternoon?' Hughie demanded.

Jack flushed slightly, 'jam jars.' he admitted. He could have hired glasses from the Gillespie, but it would have really cost and Sue got him a half a dozen cases of returned jam jars from the grocery department on the understanding that he'd only have to pay for the ones that got broken.

'Jam jars?' Hughie and Henry howled. 'Gordon Bennett., I hadn't realised that it was going to be that sort of dance.' Despite his protest, Hughie knew the score, he played a dance like this most Saturdays, though he generally got paid. With a shrug of resignation, he reached into the old bag which carried his music, sandwiches and spare mutes and pulled out a battered pewter tankard. He'd given up on a beer glass years ago, they always got broken when the fight started. 'Here you are Jack, fill this up, there's a good lad. It's thirsty work playing the Sax.'

'I'm Tom, he's Jack,' Tommy grunted, but walked forward to collect the tankard.

'Do this one while you're at it Tom,' Henry added.

Before he could turn away with the two tankards, Porky beamed at him, 'well if you're doing the honours I'll have one too.' He handed Tommy a huge German Stein which must have held the best part of half a gallon.

Tommy looked in wonder from the bucket in Porky's fist to his round florid face and back again. 'I do remember you from school,' he exclaimed. 'Somebody brought in a bottle of gin their Granny'd made. You got plastered behind the girl's toilets and ripped off the back wall. You'd have been expelled if your old man hadn't been a captain and your mother a major.'

'Hello, Tom,' said Porky with the same affable smile, 'nice to see you again. Still stealing pennies out of telephone boxes?'

'Oh my God,' Jack wailed, looking at the clutch of beer glasses in Tommy's fist. 'Here go the bar profits before we start.'

Tommy laughed as he filled the containers. He had the feeling that it was going to be a good night. Putting a few bottles on a tray for the rest of the band, he said 'you have to put it down against your overheads.' he said, then, returning to the stage called in his best barman's voice. 'There we are my lucky lads; Charrington's best. We'll keep filling them as long as you keep playing.

Do you want a drink Phy...Geraldine?'

'Thank you for your concern and good manners,' she squeaked. 'I wondered if there was any gentleman here who'd ask. Thank you for asking, but no thank you. I've made my own arrangements.' Her skirt divided up the side and she drew back the shimmering material to reveal her long slim leg sheathed in silver silk stockings. Tucked behind the fluffy little suspenders which hung from lace covered white satin drawers was a silver flask. Daintily she unscrewed the top and took a snort.

'Phyllis,' Tommy said breathlessly, 'do me a favour, if you want another drink when you're singing, go to the ladies. If you do that when the room's full of blokes on the beer, there'll be a bloody riot.'

'I told you to call me Geraldine,' Phyllis snapped angrily.

'All right bloody Geraldine, all I'm saying is if you do that again, George will have to kill half the bloody audience.'

Phyllis thought she was being flattered, but wasn't sure. She let out a shrill laugh, just to let Tommy know that she didn't care either way and went off to talk to Hughie. She wanted to reminded him of the passages where she wanted him to play particularly soft to let the dancers hear the best bits of her songs.

The rattle of the main doors echoed through the near empty hall. Everyone looked up and the faintest buzz of conversation died into a deadly silence. At the far end of the hall from the stage, Moses held the door curtain to one side and ushered in his sister.

'My God's what's that?' Tommy demanded through gritted teeth in a hoarse stage whisper which echoed around the room. 'It's Boris Karloff and his monster.' He recognised him as one of the Jews from the Rainham Marshes, but hadn't, until this moment, tied the threads together

'Moses,' Jack exclaimed, 'what are you doing dressed up like that?'

Moses laughed and flung the threadbare cloak he was wearing back over his shoulder with an expansive gesture. 'Jack, my comrade, you must learn to relax some times. This is a dance. I thought I'd dress as Valentino. I thought it would be very proletarian. Do you remember my sister?'

Jack was dumb struck, his jaw worked, but no sound came out. He paid no attention to Miriam, nor noticed that she was carrying a music case under her arm. How could Moses do this to him, in looking a fool himself, it made Jack look one as well; in front of everybody.

Tommy saw the look of horror on his brother's face and watched as Jack fled into the kitchen. He realised that this was the Moses who Jack never stopped talking about; the revolutionary; the hero of the people; the one Tommy would never be as good as. He smiled a self-satisfied smile, the man was a clown. Just wait until George Harris's name cropped up again in conversation and Jack tried to sneer.

'Hello, I'm Tommy Sutton,' he said, offering his hand. 'I've heard a lot about you.'

'I too have heard about you,' Moses replied warily, taking Tommy's hand unenthusiastically. What he had heard about Tommy Sutton was not good.

'Beer?' Tommy asked proffering a half full jam jar.

'I will buy one later, thank you.'

'Please yourself.' Tommy paused and hung his head to one side reflectively. 'Have you ever been to a dance before?'

'No,' Moses reply was quiet, restrained. The two men recognised each other as enemies and were sizing up their opposition. 'I have never had the inclination or the time. Do you feel I have missed a valuable experience?'

'It's where the masses are, Moses, it's where you've got to go if you want to lead them to the promised land.'

Hughie caught Moses's name in the quiet, quarrelling exchange. 'You're not the Moses that's supposed to be bringing me a piano player, are you?'

He smiled, 'Yes, I'm that Moses. I told Jack I'd get you a pianist. I'd like you to meet my sister Miriam, she plays the piano, she works for nothing and she's a Party member too.'

'You are that Moses.' Hughie looked at Miriam in horror and slapped his forehead in disgust. 'Don't tell me;

this isn't the piano player?'

Moses's expression assured him that she was.

With a sigh he asked, 'Well doll can you play Quicksteps? Foxtrots? Rag Time?'

Miriam was so embarrassed that she couldn't speak, she grimaced in terror and shook her head.

'Can you play any dance music?'

Again she shook her head.

'God help us,' Hughie cried out in fury, 'a singer who can't sing; a piano player who can't play. Thank God you got the beer in.'

Poor Miriam, who was twisting her scarf nervously in her hand as she entered, now tried to tear it in half at the same time as smothering her face in it to hide her discomfort. She hadn't understood Jack's reasons for retreating out of the hall without even acknowledging her. She was just grateful that he had so that he didn't witness her humiliation. 'I told you we shouldn't have come.' she wailed quietly. 'Take me home please Moses, take me home.'

Moses gripped his sister's arm tightly and marched her the length of the hall, her tiny chattering feet scurrying to keep up with his long stamping stride. He stopped in front of Hughie, so tall that even though the saxophonist was on the stage, they were nearly eye to eye. 'Comrade,' he said, catching Hughie's lapel to stop him pulling away. 'You perhaps missed what I said at the door. This is my sister Miriam. She is a musician; she can play Chopin, Tchaikovsky and Mendelssohn. When the Party requires she can also play Quicksteps, Foxtrots and Ragged Time.'

Hughie could see the anger burning in, what were normally, soft watery eyes and backed away from the argument. 'No offence meant lady, but do you mind if we move the piano to the back of the stage? You know, just for the balance of the band.'

By the time the Town Hall clock struck nine, it was obvious that the dance was going to be a success. There was a good crowd in and the beer was disappearing fast. Jack had started pushing the teas and orange juice and Tommy was watering the barrels as much as he dare; to eke it out a little longer. The band was hot and playing a storm. Even Miriam, happy in the shadows, was pounding out the foreign rhythms right on the beat. Phyllis had taken a couple of swigs from her flask while on stage and could do no wrong as far as the men were concerned.

Both Jack and Tommy kept themselves busy sending a constant flow of drink out through the hatch and did not stint themselves in getting their share. But, for both of them, the dance had little pleasure. Neither Peggy, who should have been there or Katherine Hartwell who might have been, had turned up.

Jack returned from his umpteenth trip around the hall gathering up glasses and jars, searching the crowd for Peggy and was unloading his tray into the sink when there was a flurry of activity in the back yard and George Harris slid in through the back door.

Chapter 14

Dear Alice

Good news, Sue's got herself a nice young man from the groceries department at the Co-op where she works. She says they're going to get engaged at Christmas. I told her, what's the hurry. God knows she's not seventeen yet, but you of all people know what girls are like these days.

You remember the trouble I told you about at the Rabinovitz's house two weeks ago when young Moses didn't turn up for the Shabbat meal and it turns out that he and two boys from Edmonton have gone to Spain to fight in the war there. Well it seems that Jack's woman, the nurse, might have gone too. If it's true I can't say that I'm sorry. Jack was getting far too involved with her and I was told that she was no better than she should be. It would have ended in tears one way or the other. He is devastated, but I think it's probably for the best. He can find a nice girl, closer to his own age and think of settling down.

Tommy, on the other hand is on cloud nine. He's found himself just as unsuitable a girl, the daughter of Old Man Hartwell. That's the same one as Tom was working for when he had his accident and got laid off. I really gave Tommy a piece of my mind when I heard, but he wouldn't listen, then he never does. I thought his dad would go through the roof when he found out, but it just shows you there's no telling with men. It was him that came in one evening and asked was it true that our Tommy was going out with Katherine Hartwell. I had to say that it was, he just grunted, tapped out his pipe and went out the back to look at his garden.

It would be nice if he could be so easy going with young Jack. The two of them can't be in the same room without rowing about politics and one of them storming out. I'm really worried about our Jack, he's going to get himself in trouble before too long if he's not careful. I can only hope that woman going away will make things better, she's always egging him on to go to this demonstration or that rally.

It's funny, the change round in things. It's Tommy who's always at work, doing all the overtime that's going trying to make some money to waste on this girl who's got a hundred times as much as him any way and Jack who's always missing work. But there's no telling any of them.

Your loving sister

Aggie

'Glad you could make it George,' Tommy said shaking his hand in greeting and looking over his shoulder to see if he were alone. Jack gave a nod and a grunt as he began to rinse out the glassware and then turned away. He didn't bother to ask him for his ticket.

'What time did you start?' George asked, walking over to the serving hatch to watch the heaving dancers in the semi gloom of the hall beyond.

'We opened the doors about half past seven' Tommy replied. 'It didn't get going 'til gone eight.'

'Right, I've been here since eight.' said George. 'If anybody asks, I've been out in the kitchen with you. Any questions?'

'No George, anybody special who might be asking?' Tommy enquired.

'Nobody for you to worry about.' He glanced over to where Jack was washing up, his back set towards them. 'You got any problems with that, Jack?'

'No problems George, you've been with us all evening.' Jack tossed him a cloth, 'Want to dry a few glasses, just for authenticity?'

George hurled it hard back into Jack's face. 'Don't try to be funny with me, Jack, you know I ain't got no sense of humour. Now give us a drink. How's Phyllis going?'

'Like a million dollars George.' said Tommy, 'The crowd love her.'

'Yeh, she's a doll. What's the best one she's sung?'

'Oh they're all as good as each other George,' said Jack.

'Mississippi Rose was good,' said Tommy, 'tell her that was a show stopper.'

'And don't call her Phyllis.,' Jack added.

George was walking across the kitchen to join his crowd in the hall, but he paused at the door. He glanced back over his shoulder and snarled, 'don't think I don't know you're taking the micky, Jack. Your lucky tonight; I'm in a good mood, but remember, next time you try it, I might not be so cheerful.

After George had slipped his huge padded shoulders through the door and out among the dancers, Tommy turned angrily on his brother. 'You shouldn't push him Jack; you know he can be a hard man.'

'He doesn't frighten me.'

'Then you're a bigger fool than I took you for. He bloody frightens me.' Jack hadn't seen what he had seen when he shook hands with George. His right wrist was smeared with blood. And there was no cut on his arm that Tommy could see.

George's arrival at the dance was the signal for the serious business of putting the working week behind them. He was bound to be so outrageous that they could let their hair down and really enjoy themselves without anyone taking notice of them. The little clumps of girls dancing together suddenly became a crowd.

As if responding to the lift in the mood, there was a flurry of people at the door, trying to get in, arguing about George having their tickets. No one on the door was going to buy that so they argued about numbers, money, but finally bought tickets to come in. Most of them joined George where he had commandeered a section of the floor right in front of the band. Throwing themselves into the extravagant gyrations popular in America, they tried to keep in time with Phyllis's singing.

'Drink, George?' Tommy asked as he elbowed his way through the crowd, looking to see if Katherine had arrived yet.

'No thanks Tom,' George said with a big wink, 'I can just imagine what you and you're Jack is selling so I'm making me own arrangements, know what I mean.'

Tommy nodded 'wise move,' he said and turned away, Katherine still hadn't arrived. George caught his sleeve, before he could go and pulled him close. 'It looks like you might be on for that little earner. No promises, mind you.'

'Great,' Tommy called out with a big smile, but if Katherine didn't come then he wasn't going to take

George's money.

George raised his finger to his lips. Tommy understood, he nodded. 'See you later,' he smiled. 'I might get a snort of what you're drinking, it's bound to be better than what we've got.'

'Well at least somebody's happy,' Jack moaned as he returned from another sortie into the crowd to see if Peggy had arrived, only to return with another tray of empties. 'I suppose you've seen that Katherine's here.'

'No, where?' Tommy demanded exultantly. He reached out of the hatch and almost bodily dragged Acky through the opening. 'and I don't know why you're so miserable,' he said with a wink and a nod, indicating that Jack should look behind him.

'Peggy,' Jack shouted and, as quickly as Tommy dashed out into the hall, he raced across to the back door of the kitchen, to embrace her.

She let all the anxiety flow out of him through his lips and tight holding arms before attempting to talk. 'I'm sorry I'm late, but they brought in on old man just as I was finishing. He was more dead than alive. I think he was foreign and he couldn't talk much, but we think he said he'd fallen through his own shop window. I think he'd been beaten up really. It might have been the local fascists thinking he was for the left, though he was an Italian. You might know him, he came from round your way. Said he was a barber.

'Mr. Ferruciano?'

'Might have been, it was something like that.'

'Poor old Mr. Ferruciano, I wonder who did that.' He muses. 'I used to get my hair cut there sometimes when I was a kid. When we could afford it. Tommy still goes there, I think. He'll be upset.'

'A word in the ear of the wise,' George whispered casually from the side of his mouth as Tommy was collecting cups and jars from the edge of the stage. 'I sent one of my mates out to get a few more bottles of booze. When he come back, he said that there are some blokes hanging around outside. Now it ain't none of my business, except I'm a bit aggrieved when somebody else thinks they can use muscle on my patch. I thought I'd tip you the wink'.

'Thanks George, we don't want no more accidents tonight do we?'

'Accident?' George queried, not understanding what Tommy was getting at.

'I hear old Joe Ferruciano fell over in his shop and banged his head so bad he finished up in hospital.'

'Did he?' George asked coldly, 'well it just shows what a very careless old git he was, but that ain't none of your business. Now, do you want to know about these blokes hanging around outside or not?'

'Tell me.'

'My mate reckons that there's three of four, look like the Pitfield Street boys; looks like they're waiting for one of their flying squads to turn up from Chelsea. I'm told that they've got a few scores to settle round here, including one with your brother.'

'Right,' Tommy muttered, fighting back his feelings of anger for the beating of the old Italian barber. He knew the old man had double crossed Reggie Green and had probably got what he deserved. On the other hand, he'd known the old man for a long time and liked the old rogue. He'd let the lads read the dirty magazines he kept under a cushion for the older men. He would sell them a French Letter without any questions and there would have been no chance for him to tell his side.

Tommy tried to close his mind to kind thoughts of his barber; he knew that if he took George's money, then he would earn it by doing something similar. At the moment, he wanted that money very badly, but there was a chill on his soul. 'Thanks for the warning mate.' he said without any warmth. 'If it gets a bit hectic later, are you in or out?'

George shrugged and smiled depreciatingly. 'Sorry Tom, you'll have to count me out of this one. Nothing personal; business; you know.'

Tommy knew. Now that George did his little bit of

stewarding for the Charles Hartwell, he didn't want to take sides, it was unprofessional. 'OK George, but if you're staying out of it, do me a favour and make sure all your mates do too. We don't want no trouble in the hall'.

'Peggy love,' Jack shouted into her ear. 'Get some of the girls to look after things for a while. Our Tommy says we've got trouble with some of the Pitfield Mob outside. A few of us lads is going to sort it out, away from the hall so there ain't no damage.'

A quiet ripple ran through the crowd around the dance floor. The music didn't flag, the number of dancers didn't seem to grow less, but here and there little knots of men had their heads together and others were pulled out of the crowd to join them.

The crash of a brick exploding through a window was no more than a slap on the cymbal off the beat. It was only the group standing in that corner and who were showered with broken glass who realised that anything had happened. Almost unnoticed Tommy hurried three or four blokes out of the front entrance into the night and Acky led some more out of the back.

'Bugger,' Jack cursed angrily, 'we're gonna have to pay for that window.' Turning to the group who were going out the back door with him, he snapped, 'come on, hurry up, before they break anything else.'

'Be careful,' Peggy commanded. 'I don't want to have to stitch you up again.'

Duggie Winterton gave Jack a wink as he pushed past him into the night. Jack hesitated at the door, looking at Peggy intently. For the first time since they had met, he thought that she sounded as if she cared about him rather than the cause. With a laugh of joy, he called and blew her a kiss. 'I'll be all right, don't worry.' To emphasise the point, he picked up a big soup ladle from the draining board and whirled it round his head like a club. As he left, he said 'don't tell Moses what's happening and if he finds out, keep him in here. You know what he's like. He can't fight for toffee and I don't want to have to worry about him too.' He blew Peggy another kiss and with a great grin, rushed out after the others.

Over the next half hour they began to filter back into the hall and re-join the dancing. There had been no trouble. As soon as the Tottenham boys had funnelled out of the hall, in three times the numbers of the Fascists, the Pitfield boys had decided not to wait for their flying squad and disappeared off into the night.

After they had heard the clatter of Fascist boots running off down the silent street, Jack and Tommy stood at the back gate for a few minutes to enjoy a quiet cigarette and just make sure that they didn't come sneaking back.

'I was just thinking,' said Tommy as he dropped his cigarette butt onto the floor and ground it into the pavement, 'you can never be sure about these bloody Blackshirts, I reckon they might still be hanging around somewhere.'

'No chance,' Jack snorted, 'as soon as they saw us, they did a bunk. They won't stop running until they get to Hoxton.'

Tommy pursed his lips doubtfully, 'no, no,' he muttered, 'you can't trust the bastards, they could still be hanging about, round the corner, waiting to ambush any one on coming out of here. I don't think I'd want Kit to go home on her own. Remember what happened to that bloke Moses's sister.'

Jack fingered the scar on his cheek reflectively. He could see the way his brother's mind was working 'Yeh, you could be right,' he admitted with a quiet smile, 'evil bastards, the Pitfield boys. I'd better walk Peggy back to the hospital. But won't Katherine go home with crowd she came with?'

Tommy smiled as well, 'not necessarily. I heard George saying that the blokes were going on somewhere later, strictly men only, so I reckon she'll need a lift.'

As soon as they were back in the hall, Tommy wandered up to the little group of women abandoned at the edge of the crowd to test out his theory. 'I understand, you're a bit stranded.'

'Yes,' said Katherine fiercely.

'That might be a bit of a problem. What with those Blackshirts hanging about outside and you coming out of a Commie dance.' he pulled his face into a grimace. 'You know how it is, all cats are grey in the dark. You start walking the streets on your own and you might be in trouble.'

'Oh God, what are we going to do?' demanded a rather plain girl with glasses. 'I knew we shouldn't have come.'

'Well, talk to me nicely, Sally and I might be able to help,' Tommy smiled, 'I might be able give you a lift. Where do you live?'

'Sally and Patricia live in Palmers Green, I live in Winchmore Hill and Sue lives in Enfield.'

'No problem, but it will only have to be one at a time, I've only got the bike.'

'I've seen the way you drive,' Katherine snarled. 'Don't think I'm getting on that thing, I'd rather walk.'

'Ah, well,' sighed Tommy, not moving away, 'I'm afraid that's the other option if you don't fancy the crossbar of Acky's push bike. You heard what happened to Moses's sister.'

'Can't you get us a taxi,', the girl called Sue demanded.

Tommy shook his head sadly and drew a long breath through his teeth. 'No, you don't get cabs coming down here at this time of night. You've seen for yourselves that it can be a bit rough in this neighbourhood.'

'Is there a phone here,' Patty asked. 'I'll phone my father, he'll come and get us.'

Again Tommy shook his head and tried to look sad. 'No, there's no phone around here. I should think the nearest'll be up in the High Road.'

'OK,' said Katherine in exasperation, 'now that all the other have gone and deserted us, it looks like we've no choice. Which one of us do you want to take first?'

'I'll take you, that's the easiest.'

'How do you know it's the easiest, you don't know where we live?' Pat demanded

'Yes, I do, you told me. That's why I know that Kit's the easiest,' Tommy said smoothly. 'Come on,' he said to prevent any more arguments.

Katherine followed Tommy into the kitchen where he collected his cap and goggles off a chair. She realised that there was no reason why she should be taken first, but she had had enough of this place and wanted to go home, so didn't argue.

'I'm taking Kit home,' he said to Jack who was trying to count jam jars and work out how many had been broken.

'What about the others?' Jack demanded nodding towards the little knot of women standing dejectedly in the middle of the hall.

'Don't worry about them, I'll be back for them in a minute,' he said and gave his brother a big wink. 'Come on Kit, my bike's in the back yard.'

As Katherine followed Tommy through the kitchen, Jack moved to half obstruct the door. Katherine stopped and eyed him warily, not knowing whether to expect another tirade of abuse.

Jack nervously shifted his weight from one foot to the other for a moment and, studiously avoiding her eye, muttered, 'good night Katherine, thanks for coming.'

She realised that she was being given an apology and smiled. 'Don't mention it, it was a good evening. I hope you made plenty of money.'

It was Jack's turn smile and Katherine realised for the first time how much the brothers looked alike. 'We made nearly fifteen quid,' he said proudly.

'Very good, that'll pay for Moses Rabinovitz's train fare.'

'Pardon?' Jack queried

'Moses's train fare. Didn't you know he's gone to Spain?' she asked in a surprised voice as if it were common knowledge. 'He left half way through the evening. I found his sister crying in the ladies earlier. He'd just told her. She wasn't supposed to tell anyone, but she was very upset and it sort of slipped out.

Chapter 15

Tottenham Herald

TOTTENHAM SENDS AID TO SPAIN

An ambulance, mainly bought with donations from workmen in North and East London left for the war zone in Spain on Monday. Among the nurses accompanying the vehicle was Miss M. Watkins from Edmonton.

Out in the night, the big Triumph's engine burst into a deep roar and called her. Katherine saw how white Jack's face had suddenly gone. She gave him a sad little smile, trying to say that she was sorry for so casually breaking the news which had obviously upset him so much. She touched him gently on the arm, before slipping out into the night.

'Come on then, if you're coming,' Tommy said with a casualness he didn't feel. Plans were racing round in his head about how he could turn this trip to his best advantage. It was a shame her skirt was so full; it would have been exiting if she had had to pull it up to sit astride and ride pillion.

She expected him to show off by driving away at full speed, instead, as soon as he reached the main road, he turned down the power and coasted to a halt, kicked down the stand and ran off across the road.

'What the hell are you playing at?' Katherine demanded as he returned, 'I thought you were supposed to be taking me home.'

Tommy grinned. 'I just remembered that there is a taxi rank at Seven Sisters and I've asked one of the blokes to go down to the hall, pick up the girls and take them home. Before she could protest, he swung his leg across the tank and kicked the bike into life.

Katherine snuggled tight into his back, thrilled by the power under her. 'How fast does this machine go?' she shouted into his ear.

'Fast enough.'

'Show me,' Katherine challenged him.

'OK,' Tommy said. He twisted the peak of his cap round to the back and pulled down his goggles. 'Hang on tight.' He shouted into the rushing air. As the big machine heeled over to take the bend out of Broad Lane, the feel of Katherine's arm tight around his waist and her body pulled tight against his to protect herself from the wind, gave Tommy a sense of awareness of his own body, like jumping into an icy stream. His skin blistered into goose bumps and his hair stood on end. In exhilaration, he wanted to wind back the throttle and make the motor bike fly up the High Road, but that would have meant that it would all be over far too quickly and so he let the clock settle back to a steady seventy.

Cardinal Avenue was a wide, tree lined road on a slow incline, with big, semi-detached houses along both side. As they roared up the road, Katherine banged on his shoulder, to indicate the one where she lived. Tommy's plans all involved silence and privacy, so he raced to the top of the hill, cut his engine, turned in the road and then coasted back to Katherine's house.

He had not worked out what to say to Katherine before he said goodbye and so, risking everything, he caught her arm, swung her round and kissed her. Katherine obviously had made plans of her own. She didn't resist, but fell away slightly from the thrust of his body, into the shadow of the high laurel hedge that separated the garden from the pavement. She kissed him back as hard as he was kissing her and even as she moved his hand from the front of her blouse to a safer location on her back, her other hand was holding him tight against her.

A measureless time passed before their faces disengaged for more than a moment to take breath. It was as dark as a pit in the sheltered corner, not a glimmer of gas light penetrated the waxy wall, but each knew that the eyes of the other burned with a dangerous fever.

'I think I'd better go in,' Katherine whispered in a voice as deep and dark as treacle. 'It's getting cold.' She felt the nod of Tommy's head brushing against her hair. It was the pounding of her heart, throbbing through his fingertips which made him remember that his hand was once more held hard against her breast. The last strand of reason whispered that he couldn't have what he most desired. It was getting so hot that he had to speak or burst. 'I've got the money to go to Paris,' he whispered hoarsely. 'Enough for both of us.'

As he spoke, he committed himself. Up until that

moment, he had been convinced that he wouldn't take George's money. Whatever it was would have been too dangerous, too unpleasant, but the smell of her perfume assured him that he would commit murder to be with her, if he had too.

'How, where?' Katherine demanded, but the excitement in her voice showed that she didn't really care either. All she wanted was the chance to be with Tommy, alone in a romantic foreign city.

Tommy halted her questions with a kiss. And at last said, 'when can I see you next?'

'I don't know, soon'

'Tomorrow.' Tommy muttered, the word was a question, command, plea, all rolled into one.

'If you want. Where?'

Tommy shook his head. He couldn't think. It couldn't be at his place or here. The only idea which came to him was the tea stall on the Edmonton boundary where Jack sometimes met his girl.

'OK' she agreed not being able to think more clearly herself. 'About half past six?'

'I'll be there.'

He drew his lips across hers one last time as he moved towards the road.

She didn't move. With eyes closed, she listened to the motor cycle's stand click up, heard the hiss of its tyres as it ghosted away down the road. Then heard the roar like distant thunder as Tommy kicked it into gear and powered away into the night, this time going at a hundred miles an hour.

Oh my God, she demanded of herself, *what have I done?* Tommy Sutton was fun to be with, but he wasn't the sort of man for her to fall in love with.

***

At the end of the dance, when nearly everyone else had gone, Peggy was still picking up cups and glasses along the edge of the stage. 'I reckon that the Fascists might still be hanging around outside,' Jack said loudly, as he piled chairs back into a corner. 'I don't think its a good idea for you to walk home on your own.'

Miriam thought he was talking to her, her heart leapt for joy and she spilled her music back over the piano. Looking up at the noise, Jack saw her expression and thought that it was fear. Seeing his friend putting on his coat and walking towards the door, he ran after him. 'Acky, mate,' he called 'You walking any one home?' he asked, sure that he wasn't.

Acky shrugged reflectively, ' I thought I was, but her friend suddenly said she 'ad an 'ead ache, so my girl took her home. You know how it is.'

Jack smiled understandingly and gave his mate a friendly punch on the shoulder. 'Yes, I know how it is. Better luck next time. You wouldn't do us a favour would you?'

'What is it?' Acky demanded resignedly, he knew he was going to be given the rough end of some stick or other and accepted, like he always did.

'Well.'

As Miriam pretended to sort her music for the third time, she secretly watched Jack and his friend, from under her long dark lashes. They stood head to head, at the other end of the hall. They didn't look her way, but she knew that they were talking about her and the blonde woman. Reason told her that Jack would take the blonde woman home and she would get the chubby boy with glasses, but her heart was racing and her imagination walked hand in hand with Jack up the cobbled hill. She had never been that way since that night she was attacked.

'Oh God let him ask,' she silently prayed, as the two men walked down the hall towards her. She desperately thought of some suitable sacrifice she could offer the Almighty to support her prayer. 'I will give up the Party,' she thought, but immediately dismissed that as being sufficient, God knew how little she thought of the Party, it was too unreal, too much for dreamers like Moses. She had only joined to please her brother, who she loved and because there was the chance of seeing Jack Sutton who she loved more. 'God, let him walk me home and I will play trumpet in the YCL parade band.

A voice in her head said, 'Miriam Rabinovitz, you do not play trumpet'. She argued aloud, 'please God, I will learn.'

'Miriam,' Jack said, 'I'm not sure where Moses has got to, but it's obvious that you can't walk home on your own.'

They both knew where Moses had gone, and knew that other knew as well, but no one admitted it. It might be dangerous and would certainly cause embarrassment. 'Don't worry about it,' she said, 'it's all right, I can get a cab,' dreaming that he would not hear of it and insist on taking her.

'Oh, good, that's settled.' Totally unaware of the pain he was causing, Jack turned to Acky and said, 'You only need to walk her to the cab rank then.

***

Walking hand in hand through the midnight streets of North London, Jack's exuberance at what everyone said was a triumph, made him dance in and out of the gutter like a schoolboy. He sang snatches of every revolutionary song he knew and Peggy joined in when he couldn't remember the words.

Every few minutes, he would swing round to face her. 'We took well over thirteen pounds, tonight,' he gloated. 'We'll clear ten pounds' profit, easy.'

Peggy squeezed his hand and laughed at his boyish enthusiasm. 'You're beginning to sound like a capitalist lackey,' she chuckled.

'I know my dear,' he shrugged up his shoulders and put on a strong Jewish accent, 'Mr. Rabinovitz would be proud of me. It was a shame Ted didn't turn up to receive the money.'

'He only said that he might come, you know, if he could get away. We'll give him the money next time we go down to Kings Cross.'

She moved to one side as she talked. looking to release his hand as they approached the almond tree growing on the pavement, but Jack wouldn't let go. He caught its trunk in the crook of his arm and let his momentum swing him round to face Peggy. Like key and lock, their eyes engaged and the message in their minds silenced their chattering.

For an instant they released their handhold to pass the tree. As Jack caught hers up again, he pulled her arm up behind his back. Their lips searched out each other and the unspoken hunger of the last hour began to feast. In her passion, Peggy bit his lip hard and it began to bleed, he didn't notice. He pulled her tighter to him so that the heat of her body burned him through two heavy top coats. Forcing her mouth open with his tongue, he made it a hostage to her desire.

It was the delicious thrill of his hand sneaking between the buttons of her blouse to press hand against her bodice that brought Peggy back to reality. She unwillingly dragged her mouth away from his and half turned to remove the giddy feel of his hand from her breast. 'Jack,' she muttered, 'no. We're in the middle of the High Road. Anyone might see us.'

'Who cares,' he moaned, 'Peggy, I love you.'

'You'll care if you mother ever finds out. She'll make your life hell and I'll care if Matron hears about it.'

'She couldn't make it more hellish than it is not being with you. You're not in uniform, but if it bothers you, let's find somewhere more quiet and dark.'

Jack felt the shake of head. 'I've got to go home. I'm on duty at seven.'

'No,' Jack protested, 'no, I won't let you.' Tears of frustration ran down his face. 'Please Peggy don't go.'

The stiffness went out of her muscles and she slumped forward to let her weight rest onto him. Jack's heart raced as if they had already made love. He had won.

He didn't know how or where, but he felt her give in and he knew that he would make love to her again.

'Can you climb?' she asked quietly.

'Yes,' he said hoarsely. There wasn't a fence, a wall, tree, ladder, mountain that would have kept him from her tonight.

'There's a window. It's in one of the kitchens of the nurse's home. I'm told that one or two of the girls get their boyfriends in at night. They say it's not easy, a man broke his leg once and you would be arrested if...'

'I can climb.' He interrupted and caught her face between his hands and turned it up towards his. He kissed her deeply and when he finally surfaced for air, said. 'I can bloody fly.'

'Right,' said Peggy, 'now concentrate on what I'm telling you. This is the first time I've ever done this and if we get caught, it's not just you who's for it. I'll lose my job.'

'I won't get caught.'

'Ah,' Peggy muttered, waving him back distractedly. She was acting like a fool. She knew it, she knew she should either take him into the park and satisfy him in the dark or send him home, but she didn't listen to herself.

She knew that she was about to treat him very badly. Also there was no knowing when she might have the opportunity to enjoy his firm young body again. In fact, there was no knowing when she might enjoy any young man again. Desire overcame reason. Pointing up at the blackened brick of the nurse's home, she said 'Second floor, end window, that's the kitchen. I don't know how you do it, but I've been told that you can climb up to it. When things are quiet, I'll open the window and flick the light as a signal.' she kissed him a brief good night. 'Now do as I say. Don't you dare try anything until you see my signal. It might take a while for things to be quiet and safe.'

'I promise.'

From his hiding place in the shadows, Jack watched Peggy trot in through the main gate with a curious mixture of regret and anticipation. She gave a big smile and a wave to the man in the gate house, but never glanced back towards him. An ambulance came swinging round the corner of the hospital block making her skip out of the road onto the grass verge. Its headlights cut out into the night, momentarily dispersing Jack's hiding place. As it turned up towards the High Road, the driver turned on his bell, to race away into the night.

The light and noise forced Jack to retreat further from the hospital entrance. He backed away into the thick blackness of the park, which lay on the other side of street. Squeezing through broken railings and stumbling through flower beds, he found a place under a big cedar tree from where he could watch the window in complete secrecy.

He hadn't realised how tense he was until he was able to stand still. He became aware of his hands shaking and there was sweat running down his forehead into his eyes. He felt a desperate need for a cigarette and tapped his pockets to locate his smokes. Then he remembered the stories his father and uncle used to tell about the trenches and the danger of lighting cigarettes at night. Each of them would outdo the other with a list of friends killed by snipers. Jack left the packet where it was. He didn't want to attract any unwanted attention and he might not have to wait long.

The idea of smoking was obviously playing on his mind, he thought. He had the smell of cigarette smoke in his nostrils. For an instant he closed his eyes and imagined a fresh fat Woodbine between his lips. Opening his eyes, he saw the scarlet trail of a burning cigarette end arcing away into the night.

'What the bloody Hell' he exclaimed and jumped away from the tree. Leaning on the other side of tree trunk was another man. 'Who're you? What do y' want?' Jack demanded.

The shadowy figure chuckled. 'The same as you, I'll bet. I'm waiting for that bloody light to go on.'

'Oh,' said Jack, lamely. 'been 'ere long?'

'No, not long,' said the man. 'Only about half an hour.'

'Half an hour,' Jack repeated in horror. He'd only been

waiting five minutes and he was going crazy with desire. 'How much longer is it going to be?'

'Who knows,' said the man resignedly. 'there've been times I've stood here all night. Just be grateful it isn't raining.'

'You're joking,' said Jack, knowing that he wasn't. 'I've got time for a fag then'

'Probably, you can never tell, we might be over the wall in two minutes, on the other hand. But I'll have one too while your packet's open.'

Jack didn't protest, he drew two cigarettes out of his packet, handed one to his mysterious companion and leant forward so that the man could light them both from his lighter. Together drew deeply on the glowing cigarettes masked deep within their hands. 'Oh shit,' the man complained bitterly, coughing on his lung full of smoke. He flicked the unsmoked cigarette out after his previous dog end. The light in the second floor kitchen window had flickered on and off, beckoning them to bed. 'Come on lad, it's just like the bleedin' Somme.'

'What do you mean?' Jack demanded, not understanding.

'Over the top. Follow me and I'll show you the way. Keep your head down and don't you dare make a bloody noise. There's a bloody ward sister sleeps on the first floor. If you wake her, I'll bloody kill you.'

'If I wake her, I'll bloody kill myself.' Jack muttered grimly, feeling the ache of desire. 'Come on.'

Jack was first across the road, but his anonymous ally ran at an angle, to a point where a telephone pole and a GPO switching box stood against the hospital wall. With practised ease, the man sprang up onto the box, as if it were a vaulting horse, and pulled himself onto the parapet. The area between the high boundary wall and the side of the nurse's home was a bottomless pit. It could have been full of a million unseen dangers, like dustbins or glass. The stranger didn't hesitate, face to the bricks and with toes scraping the wall to control the drop, he lowered himself into the blackness.

With his heart pounding like a loco pulling up to the Lea level, Jack followed the man down into the coal black area. An arm across his chest stopped him stepping forward. 'Keep close to the wall,' the man hissed in his ear. A short drain pipe led up onto a flat roof. His eyes were becoming accustomed to the dark and he could vaguely see a stabbing finger, visible again in the dull light of the street lights indicated the window of the ward sister. Like the shadows of bats, the two men flitted across the roof to a second drain pipe which climbed close to the briefly illuminated kitchen window,

Claiming precedence, the man from the park gripped the iron pipe. He was just about to climb when a thought struck him. 'You working tomorrow?' he queried.

'No,' Jack said in surprise, 'why?'

'I am God damn it.' The man whispered the curse. 'If you don't get kicked out before it gets light, there's a ladder and a bucket in the cupboard at the bottom of the stairs. No one will ask any questions if you're carrying them about. Leave 'em behind the gatehouse on your way out and put the rest of that packet of fags in the bucket. Some one will put 'em back later. Now wait until I get clear until you start to climb, this old drain pipe ain't that strong. Good luck.'

'Salud,' Jack muttered back and clenched his fist behind his new friend's back. This was not the time to test his politics, but he needed the assurance of all his beliefs, to face what awaited him at the top of the drain pipe.

The man climbed with practised ease and in a few moments Jack saw his legs. silhouetted against the sky as he slid in through the window. Jack almost ran up the wall, like a lamp lighter, and dived through into the kitchen with such force that he skidded across the polished lino floor on his face.

Peggy was sitting on the table with her legs crossed and he finished up at her feet. 'I didn't realise I was waiting for Charlie Chaplin,' she laughed. Jack leapt to his feet and waddled across the room and back in the characteristic walk. Tipping an imaginary hat, he bent forward to kiss her.

She allowed him a quick peck on the cheek before catching his hand and pulling him to the door. There was no need to warn him to be quiet. She peeped out into the corridor. It was empty. Like mice, they scurried across to her door and it was only when that was secured with a chair under the handle that she let him kiss her properly.

Peggy was on duty at seven and had to be out by half past six. She didn't dare leave Jack in bed, there was no knowing who would wander in to borrow this or that, but it was too early for him to start wandering about the hospital. When she was ready, she made him dress and be ready to go. She kissed him and left with instructions that he is not to move until she popped back later and if he heard anyone in the corridor, he was to hide in the cupboard.

The cupboard door opened and Peggy looked down at him sitting on the floor. 'Very good,' she laughed 'Even I didn't know you were here. 'What have you been doing with yourself?'

He didn't tell her that to while away the time he had been reading the papers on her desk. They obviously belonged in the half open drawer with the key sticking out. In her desire she had forgotten to lock them away. It contained a copy of a letter she had written to King Street about him and Moses, about Frank, about all of them. If Peggy had been able to do any wrong in Jack's mind, he would have been angry and hurt, but in his euphoric state all his brain registered was the fact that she cared for him. Unfortunately, he still had the letter that said all this and had to thrust it inside his jacket when somebody rattled the door knob. There was no chance to put it back before he was dragged silently out of the room and pushed onto the stairs and he didn't dare tell her that he'd been snooping. He never had a chance to find out what she thought when she found that the letter was missing. Perhaps she never knew it was gone or that it was him who took it; perhaps she didn't care or perhaps she never forgave him.

Chapter 16

Dear Tommy

I'm afraid the trip to Paris is off, poor Sue is ill again and nobody wants to go without her. It's probably just as well don't you think. Seen in the cold light of day, it's likely that the whole thing would have been a disaster and an expensive one too.

See you soon
Love
Kitty

'Jimmy; Jimmy Keefe,' Tommy called out to the young lad who had just turned into Wilmott Street to deliver his morning newspapers.

'Whatcha want?' the boy demanded, stuffing a stolen comic into his paper sack.

'Want to earn yourself a tanner?' Tommy asked, fishing in his pocket and pulling out a shiny coin out to add an edge to the request.

'Might do,' Jimmy replied non-committedly. 'What do I 'ave to do?'

'Go down the brewery and see Mr. Bowler. Tell him I ain't I coming in today. Tell him I'm sick.'

'A tanner, just for doing that?' Jimmy Keefe was a boy of the world. Running a message like that was only worth a penny at best.

Tommy saw the suspicion in his eyes and recognised his mistake. He caught the boy by the arm and pulled him closer. 'It's a penny for going' he hissed, 'and five pence for keeping your mouth shut.' His grip on the boy's arm tightened until Jimmy complained and then he it tightened again. 'If you blab to anyone or even think about not bothering to go, I shall break you bloody arm. You savvy?'

'Savvy,' Jimmy nodded his understanding. He knew Tommy was a good friend of George Harris and that he was beginning to get a bit of a reputation on his own behalf down the street. Jimmy knew not to cross Tommy Sutton.

Tom didn't feel very hard when, following the directions George had given him, he caught a bus from Seven Sisters, up towards the City. His stomach was a knot of iron and he had to fight to stop constantly turning around. He had that feeling that every eye was on him, that everyone was watching, certain that he was up to no good.

Railway arches aren't that hard to find, once you've found the railway. He walked south along the narrow cobbled road tight against the brick viaduct. He crossed about three streets when he saw the battered fence with the half obliterated sign for Danny Walker's scrap yard.

Dragging the heavy gate open about a foot, he began to squeeze through.

A huge dog, the same colour as the floor of the greasy yard, flung itself at him, teeth barred and baying for his blood. Several lengths of frayed rope and rusty chain, uncertainly joined together, unravelled and checked its leap inches from any bit to bite. The dog crashed down onto its side, but was up again in an instant, trying to reach the intruder with its savage teeth.

Tommy was trapped. He needed to go on, but another step forward and the dog would have him.

'Whatcha want?' A bald little man with a bit of a hump on his back and so smeared with dirt and oil as to be the same colour as the dog, appeared from behind a tattered tarpaulin. The man was holding an iron bar like a club. As he advanced into the light, he pulled the canvas sheet, marked all over with LNER logos and which was acting as a garage door, carefully behind him to conceal anything which lay beyond.

'I'm looking for Danny Walker. Chalky White sent me.' Tommy pitched his voice low, so that the world wouldn't know his business, but loud enough to get the dog called off.

'Go on, get out of it,' the man yelled. He hurled the bar. Tommy winced and turned his head. The iron bar clattered into the pile of scrap iron and, with a yelp of pain, the dog disappeared back into its lair beneath the jumbled heap of metal.

Tommy moved cautiously into the yard, not taking his eyes off the last length of chain, which still looped out from the dog's collar. Taking a moment to regain his composure and make sure the dog wouldn't come back, he pulled out a cigarette and lit it. He hated dogs, and that was one more reason to hate pub landlords. They all had the biggest and meanest hounds patrolling behind their bars waiting to tear up an unwary drayman.

As there was no movement from under the scrap iron, he became bolder.

'What have you got for us?' he demanded, letting his fag hang from his lip as he spoke, like Edward G Robinson did in the best gangster movies. He thrust his hands deep into his pockets. He wanted to put on a bit of a swagger, to show that the dog hadn't really frightened him, but the cobbled yard was so greasy that he had to drag one hand free to catch hold of a of rusty bedstead to stop himself falling.

The little man gave a gummy smile and nodded an indication that Tommy was to follow him back behind the canvas curtain and under the railway arch. Inside the dark, dirty garage, he pulled a second tarpaulin off what might have been another pile of scrap. Under it was a black limousine which sparkled like a jewel amongst the rubbish all around.

'Oh,' said Tommy feigning disappointment, 'a Dagenham dustbin, I thought it might be something a bit better.'

Danny brushed the roof with his sleeve as if brushing away dust, only to leave an oily smear. 'Naw,' he protested. 'this is the business. This is a Ford 18, there's a V8 under there. He patted the bonnet. That's 30 horse power. I tell you, it goes like a bleedin' express train. It'll do anything Chalky wants and do it quick.'

As Walker cleared the tarpaulin away and moved a few cans to allow the car to move, he glanced at Tommy. 'Want it filled up?' he queried.

'Yes, of course,' Tommy. 'I don't want to have to find a garage on the way to the job.'

'Petrol, comes extra,' Walker sneered.

'Yeh, yeh, I know,' said Tommy, reaching for his back pocket and pulled out the brown envelope Chalky had given him. 'Fill it up.'

It was the little things that were getting to Tommy. He saw the old mechanic pull a cloth out of his pocket to undo the petrol cap and not leave any fingerprints.

'The keys are in the ignition,' Walker said and then wiped the steering wheel and door handle with the oily rag.

Tommy nodded. He didn't trust himself to speak, his

stomach was in a knot and his eyes were burning. The reality of what he was doing dawned on Tommy in a rush. 'I need a slash'.

The mechanic laughed. He'd seen a lot of young tearaways on their first job over the years and knew how Tommy was feeling. He nodded over to a corner of the garage, 'use one of those cans over there.'

When Tommy came back, buttoning up his fly, the mechanic smiled his toothless smile and handed him an old pair of gloves. 'Here you are son, you might want to borrow these.'

Climbing into the driver's seat and starting the engine made him feel better. 'Chocks away,' he joked, like a young fighter pilot about to make his first mission against the Bosch.

'You just take it easy, lad,' the mechanic said without a smile. He checked the street and opened the gate to allow Tommy out. 'It may be a Ford, but I'll bet you ain't never driven nothing like this before. It'll go like the clappers, but it's a bit heavy on the steering and don't trust the brakes.'

Chalky White, Wally Cook and George, were already at the Swan when Tommy whistled a warning and walked in through the back door. As he glanced around the bar, nothing seemed to have moved since he was there last. All the same people seemed to be in exactly the same place. As he entered, the noise died for an instant. Eyes twitched towards him and then away before the conversation came flooding back with a slightly increased volume, just to prove that there was no danger, but no-one was taking any notice.

George and Wally were leaning against the bar, drinking on their own. Chalky White was sitting by himself at a table in a corner. He looked at his watch as Tommy arrived and indicated by the merest inclination of his head, that he should join him.

Tommy took the hint. He drew a chair from the next table and sat down.

'Everything OK?' Chalky demanded.

'Yeh,' Tommy said. He glanced towards George at the bar, expecting him to join them, but George just smiled to show he'd seen him and carried on talking.

'What's the car like?' Chalky asked.

'It's OK,' Tommy repeated and then, because Chalky seemed to want more, gave him a full report of all Danny Walker had said.

Chalky nodded, 'It'll have to do. What about petrol?'

'I filled it up when I collected it.'

Chalky scratched out a line on the list on the table in front of him. 'Where's the car now?' he asked.

'I've tucked it out of sight round the back. Where I usually park the lorry when I'm making deliveries. No one can see it from the street.'

'Good lad,' he said and looked at his watch again. 'We'll go in about half an hour. Give ourselves a bit of time just in case the traffic's bad.' For a minute he stared at Tommy. 'We'll have to do something about you' he said. Before Tommy could ask what he meant, he stood up and beckoned Tom to follow. Chalky took a Trilby and muffler off the hook on the back of the door and without a word, put the hat on his head and knotted the scarf around his neck. He pulled them up around Tommy's face and then stood back. 'That's better,' he muttered, and walked back to his table.

Old Eli Hobson, a tough man in his time, now demoted to one of Reggie Green's runners, walked back into the bar from a trip to the Gents and saw Tommy wearing his clothes. ''Ere, that's me hat. get your thieving mitts off.'

Tommy blushed, but held his ground. 'It's all right Eli. I'm just borrowing it for a bit. It looks like rain. You can have it back tonight.'

Eli felt the tension in the air as well. He glanced around and saw George Harris, Chalky White and Wally Cook watching him. He'd heard that there was some sort of job going off today and backed away. 'Oh, that's all right then,' he muttered grudgingly. 'Make sure you let me have 'em back.'

Once out of the back door, Chalky stopped and let

the knot of men close up to him. 'Remember,' he hissed to avoid any chance of being overheard, 'this is going to be a quick job, in and out, no trouble, no violence. As soon as we're done, Tom'll drop us at Liverpool Street and then go and lose the car in the City. I'll take the loot and fence it. We'll meet here the day after tomorrow, about eight, to divi up. If you've got any questions, ask 'em now. In five minutes it's going to be too late.'

No-one said anything.

'Right, over the top.' Chalky said grimly and there was no doubt that he was remembering the days when someone else blew the whistle and gave the order to go. At least he could reassure himself that today, no matter what happened, no-one was going to get killed.

The traffic was quite reasonable for a Friday and Tommy was making good time. He wasn't rushing, but a couple of times before they had reached Stoke Newington, Chalky glanced at his watch and told him to slow down.

Where the old man came from, Tommy didn't have a clue, but suddenly, there he was in the road ahead of him. He slammed on the brakes; they didn't bite. He swung the wheel, clouted the kerb, mounted the pavement and scraped a lamp post before regaining the road, leaving the old man waving his stick, behind them.

'You bloody fool,' Chalky yelled, 'watch where you're going. Do you want to ruin everything?'

'You fucking idiot,' George snarled in support, 'I'll break your neck.'

'It wasn't my fault.' Tommy yelled back, shock having removed any sense of fear. 'You chose the bloody car; you could have got one with brakes that work.'

'You shouldn't be needing the sodding brakes yet,' Chalky raged back. 'Watch what you're doing, you're not taking some tart for a ride.'

'It's all right Chalky, we missed the old geezer,' Wally said, in a conciliatory voice, glancing back out of the rear window.

Chalky allowed himself to be pacified and set about

calming everybody else down. 'Right lad, remember what I said. Watch where you're going and don't attract any more attention.'

Tommy let the memory of the old man and of Chalky's unreasonable outburst blank off thoughts of the coming raid from the forefront of his mind, so, it was almost a surprise when they rolled up to the kerb in front of a nondescript building in Hatton Garden and he was ordered to stop. He might have taken it for a Peabody Buildings block if it weren't for the bars on the windows and the discrete little brass plates by the doors.

Wally got out first, Chalky and George quickly followed him. Wally led the way up to the steps by one of the doors, looked around and then stopped and fished in his pocket for a cigarette. Without a glance at him, the other two strode purposefully up the steps and into the building.

Tommy pulled the brim of his hat a little lower over his eyes and blipped the engine gently to make sure it didn't stall. He wasn't nervous anymore. He was like a runner on his mark, waiting for the starting gun.

The roar of a gun made him jerk his foot of the clutch, the car kangarooed forward a few yards before he brought it under control, but still with the engine running. Chalky and George came racing out of the building, flying down the steps, Chalky holding a black leather bag, George holding a smoking revolver. Wally was way ahead of them, running across the pavement screaming 'go, go, go,' before he had even thrown himself into the front passenger seat. Chalky dived into the back and repeated Wally's hysterical instructions.

George stopped in his flight, turned back towards the door and fired two more shots.

'Get this fucking motor out of here.' Chalky yelled.

Tommy hesitated just long enough for George to leap for the car, before burning away, the back door still flying open.

Chalky grabbed George, but not to stop him falling out, he had him by the throat. 'You fucking lunatic,' Chalky screamed totally mad, himself. 'I told you no violence, no guns. You're a fucking madman.'

Tommy had no time to bother about what was happening behind him. The traffic lights at Farringdon Road were red and there were cars across the junction, but there was space to skid through. He hit the gap at speed forcing a taxi cab to veer out of the way. They ignored the torrent of abuse hurled after them. The road ahead was jammed with traffic. 'Turn right here,' Chalky commanded.

Jack spun the wheel and skidded round into Turnmill Street. 'Oh, shit' he cried as the steering wheel continued to spin on uselessly without the front wheels responding. The Ford mounted the pavement and ground its way along the wall by the road side, at speed. There was a crash, a roar and a cascade of sparks before the car stopped, wedged between a tree and the wall.

An unoffending Express Dairy delivery horse, which had been browsing on some shoots around the base of the cherry tree, reared in terror and bolted, scattering bottles of milk in its wake.

George was catapulted out of the still open passenger door into the road where he lay still. Wally was flung up against the windscreen and broke it. Chalky crashed over the top of Tommy's seat and finished up in a crumpled heap where Wally's feet had been a few minutes before. As he flew through the air, he was like a meteor with a sparkling train, glittering after him.

For a few seconds the only sounds were the hissing of steam from the radiator and the galloping of horse's hooves as it disappeared towards Smithfields. Then George twitched, groaned and like a rising giant, pulled himself to his feet. He gazed at the wrecked car and the bodies of his mates draped around it, then the clatter of his shoes running on the cobbles in the now silent street was like hail stones on a tin roof.

Yelling with pain and clutching his arm tight to his chest, Wally kicked open his door and took to his heels after George.

Tommy had been knocked unconscious and the first thing he became aware of was Chalky scrabbling on the floor picking up handfuls of diamond jewellery. The realisation of all that had happened swept over him in a wave of horror. In a panic he threw open his door and jumped out. The car angled up the wall between him and his fleeing comrades. He leapt up onto the wing and then onto the bonnet. He hesitated before jumping down on the other side. From his lofty perch he could see over the wall to his right and watched an underground train pulling into the station below him.

Tommy looked down the street. George had already disappeared and Wally had reached the corner. All around him windows were opening and heads appearing, people were cascading out of doorways and alleys, all coming to see the car crash. He looked behind him and the first pursuer was running round the corner, shouting and waving his hands wildly. 'Get out of there Chalky, while you still can,' Tommy shouted and then, taking his courage in both hands, climbed up onto the wall and ran a few yard along the top, further towards the station. Then, hanging on to the top, he dropped down onto a steel girder on the railway side. Like the Great Blondini, he walked three or four paces out into space, before crouching down. Gripping the girder which had once been part of the roof, he swung down onto the end of the platform.

Only one man seemed to notice, he turned in amazement as another passenger dropped from the sky, but then, remembering his place in the carriage was at risk, thrust his way between the closing doors. Tom shot his foot out into the shrinking gap, making the doors shoot open once more, so that he could leap in after him.

For an age, the train just stood there, doors gaping open inviting the police to come streaming onto the platform and drag him back from safety.

'Mind the doors,' a voice called down the still empty platform. Then there was a clatter of boots on the stairs. One last, desperate, passenger hurled himself across the platform in a desperate effort not to miss this train. But the doors closed and the train jerked into motion, pulling slowly out of the station.

The outside world disappeared as the train ran into the tunnel. Tommy started as his own reflection suddenly stared back at him from the window. His hair was standing up straight in shock. His white face was marked by a red wheel running across his forehead crowning a steadily growing lump. Hanging from one of the heavy buttons of his overcoat was a beautiful diamond bracelet.

Chapter 17

Dear Jack

There is a lorry load of stuff at the warehouse at Lloyd Baker Street which needs to be delivered to Southampton Docks by Sunday lunch time at the latest to be put aboard the SS Athens Queen which is sailing on the Monday morning tide. Can you organise a driver to get it down there on Saturday? There will be a group of comrades ready to unload the truck when you arrive. Just phone Southampton 754 to say when you're going to arrive.

I may not be about for a week or two, I have to go to Glasgow and may have to go to Spain to sort some things out.

Salut

Ted

God, Jack moaned to the empty scullery. It was marvellous for Ted to think he could trust him to organise a delivery, but where the hell was he going to get a driver at this short notice. For a fleeting moment, he thought of doing it himself, but he knew, realistically, that his driving skills weren't likely to get him much further than the Marylebone Road. Mentally he beat himself over the head for all the missed chances he had had to drive. Every Thursday, on his round, Tommy's brewery lorry was parked outside the Four Feathers for an hour while Tom drank his lunch. He could easily have had a go up and down the road. Instead he had wasted the chance and they had played stupid jokes on each other.

Despite beating himself for his failures as a good Communist should, he still had to smile. On one occasion he had smeared butter all over the lorry's windscreen. Tom had come in that evening spitting cotton and threatening murder. It had taken him an hour to clean the glass enough to see out. Jack had denied it was him, but Tom knew it was, he had found a Co-op butter wrapper in the gutter. He got his own back. Tom and young Cyril had picked up his float and lifted it, milk and all, into an old lady's garden. He had had to unload it, pull it out on its end and reload it again. It had taken him ages.

For a mad moment Jack thought of young Cyril Tupper as a candidate. He'd been with Tommy long enough now to pick up some driving skill. Then he remembered what a thick head Cyril was, his mum still had to tie his shoes, and so he went back to racking his brain for a realistic choice.

After half an hour he gave up, everybody he knew who could drive was either working, busy or had gone to Spain. Peggy could have done it, he thought. The memory of his love dragged him away his present reality. He hadn't heard a word from her or about her since she left. It was inconceivable that she didn't miss him as much as he missed her. The feel of her body, the scent of her hair, the thrill of making love. People said that there was hardly any post getting back from Spain. He hadn't even heard from Moses.

The memory of Moses Rabinovitz brought a flash of inspiration. Miriam, his sister, she could drive. So she'd never driven a lorry, but it wasn't much different from the great big Austin her father had and she had driven that.

He glanced out of the window as if to confirm that it was already dark. It was Shabbat already. He shoved his head around the door from the scullery where he was working with his papers spread out on top of the copper to see what the time was. The clock on the mantelpiece said that it was five to seven. The Rabinovitz 's would be well into their shabbat meal. If he was going to get any chance to speak to Miriam, he would have to be at the house by nine.

'Seven o'clock' he mused aloud. If Tommy was coming home this evening, he would have been in by now. So he must have gone somewhere straight from work and that would mean that he wouldn't be in until late. It would take at least an hour and a half to walk up to Stamford Hill and back. Tommy's bike was parked temptingly in the front and the spare keys were on the hook. Tommy would kill him if he found out, but what the eye didn't see! He would be back by half past eight; nine o'clock at the latest and Tommy need never know.

A quarter of an hour later, he pulled up in front of the Rabinovitz house. How he had grown up since the night they brought the guns back. He leaped purposefully up the steps and confidently knocked at he door, his lies already fully formed in his mind.

Mr Rabinovitz came to the door, 'What do you vont?' he demanded, 'isn't it Shabbat already.'

'Hello Mr Rabinovitz,' Jack replied, snatching off his cap 'I don't know if you remember me. I'm a friend of Moses.'

'The old man moved a little to one side to allow the light from the hall to fall on the top step. 'I do remember you,' he said. 'You are the milkman, Mrs Sutton's boy; the one with the sister who has no carpet.'

Obviously other ears were listening. There was a rustle

of silk behind Mr Rabinovitz and his wife came hurrying out and to Jack's relief, Miriam was in the shadows beyond her.

'Has he come with news of my little bubeleh?' Mrs Rabinovitz demanded and then she screamed. 'It's bad news, I know it. My darling boy is dead, I know it. Oi veh, Oi veh, oi veh.'

'Have you news?' Miriam demanded. She smiled broadly as she pushed past her mother. She wasn't thinking about her no good brother but his handsome friend who had come to see her.

'No,' he said, 'I'm sorry I haven't. I came to see if you had any. You know Moses left without saying a word. I suppose he was under instructions from headquarters not to say anything about leaving. I'm told the police try to stop volunteers and so they have to slip out of the country secretly.

Perhaps I shouldn't have come. It's just that there have been a couple of big battles recently and I was worried.'

'Battles,' Mrs Rabinovitz shrieked waving her arms wildly in the air. 'I knew it, he is wounded. He can't write, my poor boy, the klutz why did he have to put his head in this noose for nobodies and foreign nobodies at that.'

Jack made direct eye contact with Miriam. 'I don't know if he's wounded or not, but they say the soldiers are very short of food. I have a job to send some food to Spain, but I can't find a driver.'

A little smile flicked at the corner of Miriam's mouth. She knew this Jack for the pig he was, selfish, conceited, so, so certain that he was right and prepared to use anyone for his needs, but she loved him more than life. 'I can drive,' she said. 'I will take your food where it has to go.'

'You can't do any such thing,' her father protested, 'you're a woman, a girl, a child. Anyway, it's shabbat.'

'Of course she can,' Mrs Rabinovitz argued. 'Can you live with yourself? With your only son lying wounded and starving to death on the battle field? Vait a minute.' and she rushed off.

'It will wait until the end of shabbat?' Miriam asked softly.

Jack nodded and quietly stabbed her to the heart. 'I wouldn't have asked you, but I can't think of anyone else. I will be at Manor House station at dark tomorrow. Be there as soon as you can.' He turned to go.

'Vait, vait,' cried Mrs Rabinovitz as she came rushing up the stairs from the basement. 'Take this with you.' She thrust a basket with a box of Matzos bread, some jars of pickled herrings, jam, gerfilte fish, 'Give this to my Moses, it's Kosher. He's starving for the reason that is that he doesn't have his mother's cooking. This will be something.'

Jack couldn't meet her eye. He took the basket and left.

It was a damp, mucky evening with an each way bet that if it didn't rain, there would be fog. It was difficult to be sure on such an evening when night had actually fallen and the Sabbath ended. The street lights were on when Miriam arrived, but there was still a hint of silver above the western clouds. Jack realised that she had obviously been very liberal with the idea of the end of Shabbat.

But, it was nearly five o'clock and dark when they arrived at Lloyd Baker Street. Only the girl who ran the office was left in the building. She was waiting patiently for them to arrive so that she could go home for a well-earned bath and a meal. The lorry, loaded down until its springs creaked, was parked at the road side ready to go. 'Here you are,' she said with an American drawl. 'Here are the keys, the tank's full of gas and there's a map on the seat.'

'A lorry,' Miriam shrieked in horror. 'You schlemiel. You know I can't drive a lorry.' she yelled at Jack. 'You put me through all this just so that I can't drive a lorry for you. She held her head in her hands and shook it violently.

'Gee, I'm sorry,' the girl said obviously embarrassed. 'Jack said...' she glanced at him standing behind her. 'I guess he was thinking about somebody else.'

Miriam turned and looked hard at him. 'Yes, I guess he was,' she snarled and picked up the little bag she had smuggled out of the house. 'Where can I change?'

'In the office, I guess,' the girl replied

'I hope you're a good guesser.' Miriam snarled. She knew it wasn't this girl's fault, but she felt so humiliated by it all that she had to strike out at somebody.

She was back in a few minutes, now dressed in slacks, a jumper and head scarf. She snatched the ignition keys out of the American's hand as she walked back out onto the pavement. She was so angry that she forgot not to limp in front of him. 'So, where are we going?'

'Southampton.'

Miriam slapped her forehead. 'Southampton, Oi vie. I had better phone my mother and tell her that her little kilyike is going to be late. No, a better idea. You tell her.'

'I'm not going to phone her,' Jack protested.

'Not you, Klutz! Her.' The American girl opened her mouth to argue. 'You'd better,' Miriam hissed, 'or someone had. If not, you'll have the police of the world looking for me. And if you've any sense, and I doubt it because what would you be doing here, I would wait until we've gone, before you phone and then do not expect to be home early.'

She climbed up into the cab and started the engine. Sliding open the window she said, 'when you speak to my mother, tell her...' she hesitated, what could she tell her mother that wasn't going to send her into a fit of the vapours. 'Tell her Shalom Aleichem and that you're not to tell her anything.'

The journey began very frostily. There wasn't much traffic, but each stop and start was a kangaroo ride and Miriam stared fixedly ahead, terrified that at any minute either the police would stop them or she would run into a tree. Jack glanced sideways at her from time to time. Her face was even whiter than usual, her black eyes staring out like a mad woman's. With her hair pulled back under the head scarf, her nose seemed gigantic. 'God, she's ugly', he thought bitterly, and sourly added in his mind, 'I wouldn't want to be married to her.'

Apart from an occasional direction given from the map, Jack said nothing, he thought it wiser. He could feel the anger oozing out of her body and pushing him to one side. It wasn't until they were clear of London when she seemed to have finally mastered the lorry and it was a straight road that he felt that he could relax. He looked at her and to his amazement he saw that she was crying. Tears were streaming down her face and her tight little chest was silently shaking.

'Are you all right?' he asked in alarm.

'Fool, do I look as if I'm all right. You think that perhaps I'm crying with happiness?' She sobbed.

'What's the matter?' Jack demanded, totally amazed and unable to understand what could be the trouble.

'Nothing's the matter. There is no problem. Leave me alone,' she sobbed and then after a few seconds silenced wailed. 'I'm cold, I'm hungry and I'm thirsty.'

Jack didn't know what to say.

Silent sobbing wracked her little frame. The only thing that he could think to do was to reach out and put her hand on her thigh to try and reassure her.

'Oh Jack,' The sobbing was no longer silent, his little kindness of touching her for the first time since they had met was too much. 'I'm frightened and,' she paused, 'and I need the lavatory very badly.'

He dared to squeeze her leg encouragingly. 'There doesn't seem to be many houses by the road,' he said peering into the darkness beyond his door window. 'Do you want to stop and go behind a bush?'

Miriam smiled weakly, but shook her head.

'Well hang on then, we're on the main road to the South Coast, we're bound to pass somewhere soon. We'll stop there.'

About ten minutes later, as they were driving over the Hog's Back, Jack spotted lights at the road side up ahead. 'There's a place coming up on the right,' he called. As they grew closer and he could see more of *Dave's Café* he hesitated. 'It doesn't look too....' he stopped as a word to describe the tatty shed escaped him.

'It looks a dump,' Miriam agreed, and then, as she swung

the wheel to take them across into the pot holed car park, added, 'it's still better than a bush. Just.'

Dave, in a grease stained shirt and grimy black apron, didn't bother to remove his cigarette as he said. 'We're just closing.'

'Oh come on,' Jack protested, 'we only want a cup of tea and a bite to eat.'

'I ain't cooking,' he announced flatly. 'You'll have to put up with bread and scrape. Are you American? '

'No, I'm bursting, 'Miriam snapped.

'No, I thought you weren't English. You don't get many English girls driving lorries now a-days. Used to get a lot during the war.'

'She needs the lavatory,' Jack explained.

'Oh, why didn't she say. It's out the back,' Dave indicated with a jerk of his thumb the blackness at the rear of the building.

Her need was too great to argue. Miriam turned and hurried towards the door.

'Oi,' Dave called. 'If you're foreign you probably won't mind, but the English girls don't like our khasi much. Come to think of it, the blokes don't think a lot of it.'

Jack looked horrified, he meant to appeal to the man's sense of working class solidarity and call him 'Brother', but his outrage reached his tongue before his tact and it came out, 'bugger. You can't ask her to go out there, she's a lady.'

'It's all right,' Miriam protest, too desperate to care, she turned and hurried towards the door.

' 'ang on a minute, 'Dave protested, 'You're in such a bloody rush, you'll probably fall down the bloody 'ole. I don't want to have to come and pull you out. You'd better use my one in the back.' Dave stood aside to let Miriam charge past him into the rear of the café.

Jack stood uneasily in front of the counter and glanced around. It was easy to believe that Dave was just closing. The cafe was a right dump. It looked as if it had been closing for years. There was no-one else in the place, though all six tables were food stained and grubby, the ash trays were full and a couple of places still sported empty, egg and sauce stained plates.

There were two or three limp lengths of paper chains and a couple of Christmas decorations hung from the dirty ceiling in respect to the season, but there was no way of telling if they were for this year or were a few tatters left from last.

'What cha want?' Dave demanded.

'I'd better wait till she comes back,' Jack muttered, he could see more problems on the horizon and didn't want to make Miriam angrier than she already was.

Dave repeated his question when Miriam finally returned from the rear of the café, looking very much more relaxed. 'What cha want?'

Miriam glanced up at the blackboard with the menu scrawled across it. 'What's in your 'sossidges'?' she asked, mocking the spelling.

'How the hell should I know,' Dave replied, Miriam's humour passing him by, 'they're sausages, what do you normally get in them?'

'Pork,' Miriam said dryly.

Dave raised an eyebrow in understanding, he had already marked that her nose didn't make her one of nature's beauties. 'You don't fancy a bacon sarni then?'

Miriam ignored him. 'What's Spam?' she asked.

'Pork luncheon meat,' Dave replied without the hint of a smile.

A woman's voice shouted from the back room, 'the sausages is beef.'

'I'll have sausages and beans please,' Miriam replied

'Chips?'

'What's the fat?'

'Beef dripping,' came the voice from the rear.

'Chips, black tea, two slices without butter,' Miriam ordered.

'You don't need to worry about our butter, luv, it aint never seen the inside of a cow.' A woman, also with a cigarette end hanging from her mouth came to the inter connecting door behind the counter wiping her hands on a sodden tea towel. She was thin faced, olive skinned, dark eyed and grubby. She could have had Jewish blood herself.

Miriam smiled and the woman nodded, then disappeared back into the kitchen. Dave turned to sort out Jack's order.

'Are you cooking?' Jack asked, still not sure of the situation.

Dave curled his lip at the stupidity of the question. 'What cha want?'

'Egg, bacon, sausage and chips please,' Jack replied, mentally adding up the prices on the board and measuring the total against what he thought he had in his pocket, 'and a tea.'

'Where you going?' Dave asked when he brought the teas across.

'We've got a load of food for Spain,' Jack said proudly. 'There's a ship sailing on tomorrows morning tide for Barcelona.'

Dave sniffed. 'I didn't think you were carrying circus animals,' he said.

Miriam turned to look at their lorry, just visible on the forecourt in the dull light from the café window. It was covered in slogan's 'Aid for Spain' Food Ships for Freedom' Long Live the Popular Front' and liberally daubed with hammers and sickles. 'The last place we stopped, they thought we were a mobile library,' Miriam replied in her own droll way.

'Yeh,' admitted Dave, 'I can see how they might.'

Jack glanced at the two of them, neither was smiling, but he had a feeling that they were joking with each other in a way he wasn't very good at, but he was grateful that the tension had eased.

It was almost with regret when he said, 'I suppose we'd better be getting on.' He surreptitiously pulled his money out of his pocket and counted it under the table. Then, turning to Dave, he asked, 'how much do we owe you?'

'I told you when you came in, that I ain't cooking, now bugger off and leave me alone.'

Jack didn't understand the answer and instantly bristled. Miriam touched his arm to calm him and stepped up to the counter. 'Look at that,' she snapped, 'your counter's filthy.'

'Where?' he roared and when he looked down to where she was pointing, she kissed him on the top of his head. 'Thanks Dave. I don't suppose you have a phone?'

'Don't push your luck, you' he growled and then added, 'there's one in the next village, you can't miss it. You'll be in Southampton in a couple of hours.' he sniffed, which was his way of laughing. 'I saw you come into the car park earlier. In your case, tell them an hour and a half.'

She skipped to the door. For the first time since they had left London, she was happy. She felt that everything was going to be all right.

'Oi,' Mrs Dave shouted, re appearing from the back room. 'You forgot something.' She was carrying a big cardboard box full of tins, boxes and jars of food. 'Put that in the back with the rest.'

Before they could thank him Dave growled, 'now bugger off. And don't come back, you're too bloody expensive.'

Miriam blew him another kiss and Jack gave a clenched fist salute and went out into the night.

The fact that the lorry's heater wasn't working, no longer seemed important. She was so aware of his thigh pressing against hers and the light touch of his hand on her knee, that she pressed closer and smiled.

He smiled back thinking that perhaps she wasn't so bad looking and that it was nice to have her tight body close to his. He started to whistle and she picked up the tune and began to sing. She had a nice voice. The rolling miles of the A38 raced under their wheels and it was with a sense of regret that they approached Southampton and began to search the road side for signs pointing to the docks.

It was nearly ten o'clock when they pulled up by the dock's main gate. Miriam turned off the engine and they both looked about. The dark damp streets were silent and deserted until a long whistle shattered the quiet of the night. A comrade had been keeping watch from an upstairs window of a nearby house. The arrival of the distinctive lorry was the signal and a scurry of people from houses and alley ways produced a small crowd within minutes.

A young, freckled faced youth wearing his cap at a rakish angle opened the passenger door and gave a clenched fist salute and shouted 'No Pasaran'.

Jack responded in kind, but Miriam gave a shrug of her shoulders and opened the palms of her hands. 'So where do you want, I should put it?'

'Leave it here Comrade,' the young lad said, 'me and the comrades will sort it out.'

'And what about us?' Miriam demanded.

'Don't worry comrade, it's all sorted.' The youth wouldn't let Miriam's brusque way with strangers upset him. 'Comrade Sid, here,' he pulled another youth forward to present to the heroes from London. They had heard that the driver's brother was in Spain. 'Sid will take you to Old Mother Driscoll's house. She's got a spare room. She knows you're coming and all about you. And here.' He gave Jack a folded piece of paper, 'Here's a chitty for the fish and chip shop a couple of streets away. Once you've dropped your stuff at Mrs Driscoll's, Sid'll show you where it is. You can have a good night's sleep. We'll unload this stuff and make sure it gets aboard. You'll find the lorry outside the house in the morning. OK?'

'OK,' Jack agreed. 'Do I have to pay Mrs. Driscoll?'

'Don't be daft,' the youth laughed, but his look showed that he was almost offended. As Sid led them away, the youth called after them. 'And don't worry about the petrol, the tank'll be full.' He pulled up the ends of a length of rubber hose hanging around his neck and gave them a big wink.

Mrs. Driscoll was a dumpy woman, about sixty, florid faced and friendly. She had obviously been waiting up for them because she had her hair net on and was wearing her dressing gown and slippers. Once, she used to own the little shop on the corner while her husband worked as an electrician in the docks. He had been a fiery little man, shop steward and Party activist. Because of the recession, strikes and black listing, he didn't practice his trade very often during his life, but he worked for his wife and did little private jobs around the town. When he died in a ship fire and she retired, she was left quite comfortable. She bought the little terraced house she had been born in and in which her mother had lived all her married life.

Her husband had been in the habit of making up a bed for all the waifs and strays of the world in the front parlour and she had rather carried on the tradition. 'There you are my dears,' she said with a big beaming smile as she through open the front room door. 'They phoned down from London to tell us to expect you. I've lit the fire and I expect the young lady would like a bath so I've put some water on to heat.' The old woman's eye had summed up the situation in an instant, handsome young man: not so pretty girl, but a nice figure: no wedding ring. She didn't really agree with the Party's ideas on 'free love', but it wasn't her business and she always supposed that if you were going to make a revolution, you had to start somewhere. 'I'm going to bed now, but you come and go as you please. I will see you in the morning.'

The comrade who had met them at the dock gate had underestimated the distance to the Fish and Chip shop which would give a free dinner to workers from the Popular Front. It seemed like miles and Sid abandoned Jack half way back to Mrs Driscoll's house. It was nearly an hour before he pushed the house door open and went into their bedroom.

'Don't you ever knock,' Miriam shouted and bath water splashed a she grabbed for a flannel to cover her nakedness.

'Why should I knock,' Jack snapped back, equally irritated, 'it's my room too.' He looked at her in the tin bath in front of the fire. She had been laid back luxuriating in the warm water and dreaming of her love, with her eyes tight shut as he entered. In the flickering orange light, her young slim body gleamed seductively and Jack saw her in way he never had before.

'You are perhaps thinking that I should sit here naked all night?' she demanded. It was stalemate. She attempted to hold the tiny square of cloth strategically over her body, but she couldn't move.

'You'd hear no complaints from me,' he muttered, thinking how smooth and silky her pale skin was.

'Well, you'll hear plenty of complaints from me. Either come in or get out. Either way, shut the door, there's a wind straight from Iceland blowing up the passage.'

Jack stepped in and closed the door behind him. In the flickering light of the fire, Miriam's wet body glowed like copper. Her black hair hung free down her back, the ends dangling in the water. It was like a frozen avalanche of anthracite. Even her sharp features were softened by the firelight so that she looked like a Red Indian princess from a Tom Mix film he had once seen.

'I'll put the fish and chips on the trivet by the fire, to keep them hot until you're ready,' he said. He purposely walked behind her. but the space between the bed and the end of the tin bath was narrow and he brushed against her back and felt the satin smoothness of her skin. Looking down over her shoulder, he could see her naked breasts. They were small, firm cones, crested with dark little nipples. They were a far cry from Peggy's full white bosom, he thought, but then added the mental caveat that they were very pretty and he wouldn't turn away from an opportunity to stroke them if the chance came.

A steaming kettle sat on the brass stand where he went to put the fish and chips and he had to move it to put the newspaper bundle in its place. 'Do you want more hot water?' he asked.

He made no pretence of looking away, but stood towering over her, gazing steadily at her.

As she looked up at him, silhouetted against the fire, his face was hidden in shadows. All she could see were his eyes, sparkling. He wasn't afraid of the situation. She frowned. She recognised the danger she was in. He was experienced with women and she knew that he would not hesitate to take advantage of her. She had only to say the right word. Not one of her clever cutting remarks. A kind word, a word of friendship, a word of love and he would swoop down and carry her away like she always dreamed.

'No thanks,' she said softly, her voice sounding husky in her own ears. 'I'd better get out now or the food will get cold. Would you pass me the towel please?'

As he held it out to her without looking away, she pulled herself up out of the water and stood facing him, arms by her side.

Their eyes met. Hers said that she was his, if he wanted her. His said that, at this moment, she was the most beautiful woman he had ever seen and there was no thought in his head of any other.

Taking a step forward, he brought the towel up, like a curtain between them. He draped it over her shoulders and pinned it to her back. With little force, he pulled her towards him. She had to step out of the bath or fall.

Oblivious of the water streaming off her to soak the fireside rug, she let him hold her tight against him. At first he made a pretence of drying her, but quickly his hands were below the towel, stroking her back and slipping down over her buttocks. It was only the pressure of their bodies which kept the towel between them. Her hands were inside his jacket, pulling his shirt from the waist band of his trousers so that she could experience the feel of his body. Hard muscled, hot and hairy, it was new country to her. She had never touched a man's chest before. The feel of it, the scent, made her head spin. Thrusting her face up for air, she met his coming down to deny her breath.

He kissed her and she kissed him back without fear of rejection and the towel fell away.

Chapter 18

My Dearest, Dearest, Dearest Jack.

I have pondered over how to start this letter for many hours. I settled on the above, because, to me, you are the dearest and now, after all we have been through together, I feel that we belong to each other.

Sunday morning was the strangest few hours of my life. It was not that I felt that I had died and gone to Heaven, rather that I had awoken from a coma to find myself alive.

The heady pleasure of being with you, made me shrink from the moment when I would not be with you any more. Our parting as such sweet friends was as the turning off of a light. You were walking away and I was too numb to speak; too desolate to ask when we will see each other next.

It is difficult to contact me privately at my home. God knows, it difficult to do anything privately in that house, but I have a friend, Ester Markovitz, from school, an independent woman who can be our go-between. She lives at flat 5 Connaught Buildings Goldsmith's Row, Hackney and you can contact me through her.

See me soon and write to me sooner.

Love Miriam
XXX

Jack turned into Wilmott Street with his head down and his hands thrust deep into his trouser pockets. It was both a defence against the drizzling rain and his worries. He had had a lot on his mind before the run to Southampton, but the night with Miriam had piled problem on top of problem. He hadn't thought about anything happening between them. Now that it had, he told himself, that she was a Party member, free to do what she liked with her body, just the same as he was, without any commitment. At the same time, he couldn't forget that she was the sister of a friend. He knew how he would feel if the same thing had happened to Sue.

If he had known that there was only one room, one bed, he would have slept in the lorry. It must have been that he was missing Peggy very badly. He just hoped that Miriam didn't get the wrong idea. It was all very inconvenient.

'Everything all right at your house, Jack?'

The sound of Mrs. Shaunessey's voice at his shoulder made him look up. She was leaning on her front gate, and though she had spoken to him, she wasn't looking his way. Despite the weather, she was in her housecoat with just an old Mac over her head. Mabel Potter was also at her gate, arm's folded and silently wet. They were both looking down the road.

He followed their gaze and saw a police car parked outside his gate.

'I've no idea what's happening,' Jack muttered, 'I'll go and find out.' He attempted to be casual, but made no effort to walk on.

He had been told by the recruiter, that Special Branch had spies everywhere. Someone must have informed on them, someone must have said that he and Acky were about to go to Spain and the police were looking for him. Jack knew that Baldwin and the fascists in his government had invoked the Foreign Enlistment Act in an attempt to stop the workers going to the aid of the Republic. *Well they won't stop me*, Jack growled to himself.

Jack glanced around and saw that no one was looking at him. The whole street was out watching his mother talking to two men. One, in uniform, was standing on their front path with his back to the gate, the other, in plain clothes, had his foot on the doorstep and was pressing to go inside.

They both had their back to the street, but it would have been too suspicious for him to turn around and walk away. To buy himself a few moments to think, he dropped to his knees and pretended to tie his shoe lace.

Mrs Shaunessey and Mrs Potter had lost interest in him, they leant further forward to see better, as the plain clothes policeman went into the house. Quietly Jack backed away a few steps and then crossed the road. With a last glance around to ensure that he was unobserved, he slipped through the half open gate into Ackfield's coal yard.

In the deserted yard, the need for control left him, he raced to the back door and wrenched it open.

Mr. Ackfield was having a wash in the scullery sink, 'Acky in?' Jack demanded and without waiting for a reply rushed through to the front room from where he could watch in secret.

Acky was already at the window, holding the curtain back slightly, like a nosey old lady. 'they're after me,' Jack blurted out. 'I'm going to have to hide out somewhere until we go.'

Acky gave him a disbelieving glance, he was used to his friend's dramatics. 'They haven't been over here.' he said.

'Ah,' Jack, was abashed, he'd forgotten for the moment that Acky was going to Spain as well. 'Perhaps they'll come here next. When they find I'm not in. We'd both better scarper.'

'They're coming out,' Acky reported, not moving away from his peep hole. Jack moved close to his shoulder to catch a glimpse of what was happening and to see if the policemen were coming across the road.

He could see his mother had reappeared in the doorway, silent and white faced. The plain clothed policeman, stepped past her back onto the path. He snapped his notebook shut right under her nose to further intimidate her and then followed the uniformed policeman to the road. The constable went round to the driving seat and the detective climbed in the passenger side. He wound down his window and said something to his mother that Jack couldn't catch. Then they drove off.

'So they didn't want us,' Acky said dryly, but Jack ignored him, he flung open Acky's front door and sprinted across the road, leaping the gate and squeezing into the hall before his mother had finished shutting the door.

'What did the police want?' he demanded breathlessly. 'Were they asking about me and Acky?'

His mother was in tears. She pulled up the hem of her apron to dry her eyes and shook her head. When she could finally speak she said, in anguish, 'they're looking for our Tommy. They want to talk to him. They say he's in big trouble. They said there is a warrant out for his arrest and kept asking me where he was?'

'What did you tell them?' Jack demanded, catching his mother quite roughly by the shoulders.

She began to cry again. 'I didn't tell them anything,' she sobbed, 'I don't know anything. I don't know where he is.'

'Did they say what sort of trouble?' Jack demanded.

Mrs Sutton shook her head. 'They asked me when I saw him last and I said when he went off to work on Friday. The sergeant said that he didn't go to work on Friday, they've checked. Oh Jack, do you know what this is about? Have you seen him.'

Jack shook his head. He hadn't seen his brother since Friday either. He didn't know what he'd been up to, but he'd been told that he went down the White Swan a lot and hung out with Reggie Green's betting gang. He remembered the YCL dance; he had seen Tommy and George Harris cooking up something in the corner and had wondered then what they were up to. 'Did they ask anything else?'

'They asked me if I knew an Eli Hobson. I said I'd never heard of him. They showed me an old hat and asked me if I'd ever seen it before. I said no. I told them Tommy wore a cap and that it was hanging on the kitchen door. They asked what pubs Tommy drank in and who he mixed with. I said he used the Gillespie and mixed with the crowd in there. Did I do right Jack?' she half sobbed. 'I didn't mention the White Swan and the crowd down there, but they asked me if I knew George Harris.

I said every one down the street knew him. I said his sister lived at number 32. He said they had already been in there, but there was nobody about. As they were driving off, the sergeant said that they would be back and that if Tommy was sensible, he'd give himself up.'

His mother began to cry again. 'Oh, Jack, what's Tommy been up to. What's his dad going to say when he finds out?'

Jack shook his head. He didn't know either, but he knew his father would go through the roof when he found out that Tommy was in trouble with the police. It had taken all his mother's powers of persuasion to stop Jack from being banned from the house when he had been arrested after the Fascist rally at Edmonton.

'Jack, love, go down to the White Swan and see what you can find out,' his mother pleaded.

Jack shuffled uncomfortably. He had been told by the recruiter, not to do anything that might draw attention to himself. To stay out of trouble until he slipped out of the country. 'Please, for me.' She had her hands clasped together and was leaning forward as though she was about to drop onto her knees. 'You can use Tommy's bike, I'm sure he wouldn't mind.'

It was a certain indication of how worried his mother to suggest that he use his brother's motor bike. She would normally shout at him if she saw him anywhere near it.

He couldn't resist her. 'All right,' he said grudgingly, 'I'll go down there now. I won't go on the bike though. I don't want to draw attention to myself. We'd be in more trouble if the police stopped me.'

Mrs Sutton, beamed. 'Don't go on your own though. It's very rough down there. I've heard some terrible stories about the place. I wouldn't ask, but…' she could finish and burst out crying again.

When Jack went back to Acky's house to tell him what had happened and ask him to go down to Northumberland Park with him, Acky protested that he was just about to have his dinner. 'I don't like the idea of going down to the Swan,' he complained. 'I've heard that it's a rough old place and I certainly don' fancy going there on an empty stomach. Have some something to eat and we can think what's best to do.'

Jack suddenly remembered that he hadn't had anything to eat since he left Southampton, at dawn that morning, and didn't need too much persuasion to join him.

As Jack wiped his plate with a piece of bread, he thought about what Acky had said. He didn't fancy going down to the Swan either. 'Perhaps we should try the Gillespie, first,' he said. 'We could see if George has been in there.'

Acky nodded enthusiastically. 'We could ask Phyllis if she's seen him.'

Eddie Bainbridge was working in the backyard when they arrived and they climbed up the fence to talk to him. He said that he hadn't seen George Harris or Tommy for more than a week. Which was a shame because George owed him some money. He also said that Phyllis was in Nottingham, she was rehearsing for a part in the chorus for a pantomime, and wasn't seeing George at the moment.'

As they dropped back into the alley and brushed themselves down, their eyes met. There was nothing for it, they would have to go to the Swan.

It was getting dark when they got off the bus at Northumberland Park. Spurs had been playing away, the second eleven pulled a small crowd and they had long gone home. It was very quiet. The only person they could see in the street was a man using one of the few gas lights that was working to read the sport's pages of his newspaper. He looked as if he were waiting for opening time. He didn't even glance up as they walked past him, but once they were a few yards beyond, he folded it up and slipped it into his pocket. He didn't move, just watched the two men until they reached the saloon bar door, before taking the newspaper out again and reading on.

The door was open and as they walked in, the atmosphere in the smoke filled Saloon bar was silently hostile. Every eye was on the door as they walked through. 'Oh God, we're going to get razored here, if we're not careful,' Acky muttered as they walked in. 'Have you got any money?'

Jack nodded, 'I've got half a crown. What do you want to drink?'

'Whatever you're having,' Acky replied. His glasses had misted up as they walked into the steamy room and, nervously, he took them off to clean them.

'Two halves of Mild,' Jack said to the man behind the bar who was studiously ignoring them, as he polished a beer glass. The man glanced at them suspiciously then, without stopping his housekeeping, looked over their shoulders. Jack glanced around at the group sitting at the tables behind them, but missed any sign that they had met the barman's eye. 'We ain't open yet.' He grunted.

'We're looking for' Acky began to say. Before he had time to finish, a dark, thick set man with heavily Brylcreamed hair, stood up, stepped behind him and spun him round.

'A nosey parker eh?' he snarled. 'I hate nosey parkers.' The man took Acky's glasses, dropped them to the floor and stepped on them, 'you ain't looking for nothing now. If I was you, I'd get out before you get more than you came looking for.' The man was smiling, pleased by the quickness of his wit as he played with words.

Jack stepped between them, but looked to the group in the corner. 'I'm Jack Sutton,' he said, 'Tommy Sutton's brother. We've had the Law round our house. Me mother's going crazy. I said I'd come down here and try and find out what's going on.'

The man who had broken Acky's glasses, looked to the group for instructions. A thin faced man with a camel hair coat draped over his shoulders in the same way that George Harris had worn his, stood up. His iron grey hair was smooth and his whole appearance polished. He wore a flower in his button hole and carried a pair of kid leather gloves. 'There isn't anything going on here. We are a group of associates discussing our private social arrangements. And, as you can see, as it is out of the licensing hours, we are drinking tea. That is why Mr. Murphy, our worthy landlord, declines to serve you. It's more than his licence is worth.

'Are you Reggie Green?' Jack demanded. Despite the fact that it wasn't proletarian, that Reggie Green was a capitalist jackal, an exploiter of the workers, he couldn't keep the note of awe out of his voice. This was the man that even George Harris was frightened of and his brother only mentioned him when he wanted to impress.

The man held up his manicured hand to silence any questions. 'I know your brother, a likeable lad. I don't like to hear he's in trouble. What's he been up to?'

'We don't know. The police wouldn't say. They said that there's a warrant out for him. They said they wanted to talk to him about a serious matter. They asked loads of question. Wanted to know if my mother knew some names.'

'Names?' Reggie Green queried.

'George Harris, Eli Hobson.'

'Did they mention me?' Reggie Green asked sharply

Jack shook his head, 'my mother didn't say so.'

'Well, lad, I don't know where your brother is, but I've been told that he has had a bit of bad luck and needs to stay well away from the police. If you see do him, tell him that anyone can have bad luck. Tell him that I am not displeased with him, that I do not consider the accident to be his fault, but tell him, most strongly, that he needs to get away from here for a considerable time and he is not to come anywhere near me or my associates, or this place.' Reggie Green paused then his voice became hard edged when he began again. 'On the other hand, if you should see George Harris, tell him to stay away from me as well, because I am very displeased with Mr. Harris. Very, very displeased.'

Jacked nodded and turned to go.

'A moment,' Reggie Green said and reached inside his jacket to pull out his wallet. 'Your friend here suffered because of my associate's suspicious nature.' He stuffed a five pound note into Acky's top pocket. 'That should buy you another pair of glasses.'

Acky bristled and opened his mouth to protest about the way he had been treated, but Reggie Green held up a finger. 'Just look around you lad. This is not a good time to argue.'

Acky looked around and saw the sense of the remark. He turned for the door. 'Come on Jack,' he said, but as they were about to leave stopped. 'I wouldn't want to be in your debt Mr. Green, so I thought I better warn you that there're a bloke up the road from here who's watching this place.'

'Reggie Green smiled, a thin wolfish smile, without any humour in it, 'no lad,' he whispered, 'he's watching out for this place. Now on your way and I shall be quite happy never to see you again.'

Out in the dark damp, cold of the street, Acky shivered. 'I reckon that your Tommy is in big trouble between that lot and the police. I'm sure we'll be better off in Spain than round here for the next few weeks. It's a shame your Tommy's not coming with us.'

All that Jack dared tell his parents about his conversation with Reggie Green was that no one knew what trouble Tommy was in. Whatever it was, George Harris was also involved and it was very serious and no one was saying where he was. As Jack told his story, his mother cried and his father chewed on the stem of his pipe, too anxious to be angry.

Jack couldn't sleep that night. As he lay in his bed, he was unable to forget his brother's empty bed on the other side of the room. He was wondering where Tommy was at that moment. He just hoped that he was safe. There were rumours beginning to ripple up and down the street which linked Tommy with the jewel robbery in London, which had been in the national newspapers after it happened on Friday. He could hear his parent's restlessness in the next room, the creaking of their bed as one or other tossed sleeplessly and the occasional soft buzz of conversation. Another worry to add to that of his brother was his concern about his mother. He could see how she was distraught about Tommy. How would she cope when he slipped away quietly into the night without a word?

He was lying in bed half awake, half dreaming about going to Spain, letting his fears of the unknown, his thoughts of danger and death swirl around in the dark silence of his room when he heard strange chattering sound. At first he thought it was the sound of machine guns that he had been dreaming about. Then it came again. He was awake now and placed the sound at the window.

Someone was throwing stones at it. Instinctively he knew that it was Tommy. Without putting the light on, he leapt silently out of bed and ran to the window. Opening it, he peered out into the foggy darkness. At first he couldn't see anything, then he picked up a movement by the corner of the lavatory. Tommy waved his hand, white in the darkness and Jack could just about pick out the figure standing in the shadows.

Jack pointed to the back door, grabbed his trousers off the bottom of the bed and listened. The rest of the house had drifted off into an uneasy silence. He pulled his trousers on and, as he used to as a boy, climbed down the banisters to avoid the creaking stairs.

The back door wasn't locked. Jack opened it and his brother slid in with the wisps of mist from the night. Unable to speak, Jack grabbed Tommy and hugged him tight. He felt his brother shaking in his arms and heard his teeth shattering. Jack became aware of water soaking through his own shirt. 'God's teeth, Tommy,' He gasped, 'you're wet through and freezing. Get your clothes off and get closer to the fire, I'll stoke it up.'

While the fire struggled back into life, Jack put the kettle on and took his overcoat off the back of the door to wrap around his brother's shoulders. Jack left Tommy to stuff food down his throat and get a few sips of tea inside him before he attempted conversation.

'What's happening Tom?' Jack asked quietly.

Tommy shook his head in despair. 'I'm in big trouble Jack and I don't know what to do.'

'I know; the police have been here asking for you. Mum's nearly out of her mind with worry. I went down to the White Swan to see if I could find anything out.'

'What did they say down at the Swan? Who did you speak to?'

'I went down with Acky last evening. We spoke to Reggie Green. He said that you were to stay away from him. He said you should get away from here and stay away.'

'Did he say anything else? Was anybody hurt?'

'No, nobody got hurt, not yet. Reggie Green said that he understood how mistakes happen and how he's not angry with you, but he's furious with George Harris. As I was talking to him, I was looking at his eyes, I reckon he'll have George killed if he finds him.'

'Not if I find him first,' Tommy growled. 'Everything was going fine when George pulls out this gun and starts shooting. Chalky had said *no guns*. I was there when he said it and we all agreed. There was no reason. We had to get away real quick and something broke on the car. We all scattered and I got away on the tube. I'm hiding out on one of the sunken barges on the canal.

It's so cold down there, Jack. I couldn't stand it anymore. I came here. I can't think where else to go.'

'Well you can't stay here,' Jack said emphatically, 'the cops said that they'll be back and they're keeping an eye on Milly's house to see if George turns up there.' He didn't add the fact that his father wouldn't allow it either.

Tommy could follow his thoughts. 'What do Mum and

Dad know?'

'They've heard the rumours too. Dad knows it's true, but won't talk about it. Mum refuses to believe it.'

'Do you think I should give myself up?' Tommy asked miserably. 'First offence and I was just the driver They might give me a lighter sentence.'

Jack laughed hollowly. His brief brushes with the law hadn't given any faith in its mercy. 'The only chance you've got of a lighter sentence is to turn King's evidence.'

'I couldn't do that.' Tommy protested.

'Then my advice is stay out of their hands as long as you can. You are looking at twenty years' hard labour for armed robbery at least.'

'Thanks,' Tommy muttered, 'so what am I going to do?'

'Well Acky had an idea. I'm not supposed to tell anybody this; you know for security reasons. But me, Acky, Skinny Skinner and Fred Clarke are going to Spain. We're joining the International Brigade. We're just waiting our instructions to go. It's likely to be within the next few days. Stan Wilson, the recruiter said that if we knew any more working class lads who wanted to fight the fascists we should let him know. I know you're hardly the leader of the anti-fascists in this street, but what the hell, another soldier is another soldier and I get the feeling they don't ask too many questions about volunteers.'

'Bloody hell,' Tommy muttered, shaking his head. 'You think I'm mad, I'd have to be to think of hiding out in the middle of a bloody war.'

'You got any better ideas?' Jack demanded irritably. Didn't Tommy realise the risks he and Acky were taking on his behalf?

Tommy shook his head again, but sadly. 'I don't see that I've any options.' He laughed 'I never saw myself as volunteer, particularly for the Reds. My chance to become a Gunner, I suppose. It's just that it's a long way from Highbury.'

'Right,' said Jack, 'just one thing. If you being with us, puts our going at risk, then you're on your own. Deal?'

'Deal,' Tommy agreed.

'That's settled then. I'll have to tell Acky, but Skinny's as dim as a Toc H lamp, we can spin him a line and he won't suspect a thing, Fred's never heard of you and Stan Wilson knows I've got a brother anyway, but that's all.' Jack chewed his bottom lip for a moment. 'And I think I've got a place where you can hide out in the meantime.'

'Where?'

'I don't suppose you remember, but a few months ago I went up to Broxbourne with the YCL and camped by the Lee.'

'How am I going to get to Broxbourne, its bloody miles.' Tommy protested. 'and I've had enough of that bloody canal.'

'No,' Jack protested. 'when I went up to Broxbourne, I didn't have a bike, so I pinched Loopy Lou's. I put it back after and they never knew. His mother keeps it in the old coach house at the bottom of the garden. When I put the bike back I was nosey and had a quick shuffty. It's so full up with rubbish that you can hardly get in there and the door was nearly rusted solid even then. But, where it backs onto the railway embankment, there's a little window. You can get to it easy at night without any one seeing. Take our spade with you and you'll be able to force it open. Right inside is the stairs to the old hay loft and that's empty. You can hide up there. It's not going to be warm, but it'll be dry and, more important, it'll be safe.'

'O.K.' Tommy agreed, 'Get me some food and some dry clothes and I'll get out of here.'

Jack shook his head. 'We don't dare go upstairs, someone will hear, but Mum's done some washing recently and there's a few of your things in the scullery, you can take my coat. I'll try and get some other stuff together tomorrow. I'll bring some milk, butter and cheese back off the round. I can get through the back of Acky's yard, but you'd better go round by the bridge tonight. With as much food as he thought his mother wouldn't miss and some clothes tied up in an old blanket, Jack pushed his brother back out into the night.

He'd hardly shut the door on him when Jack heard the stairs creak and a moment later his mother came in. 'I thought I heard the back door going,' she murmured distractedly. 'I thought Tommy might have come back.'

'No. it's just me Mum, I couldn't sleep. I've just been out the back for a cigarette. I'm just going back to bed now. Best you do the same or we'll have Dad and Sue down as well. He turned his mother round and pushed her into the passage. He didn't want her to see the puddle of water in front of the hearth.

Chapter 19

Dear Jack

I have been hearing some very disturbing rumours from my brother Charles, in which Tommy's name has been mentioned. There is a long history of me being told things by my brother with the express intention of his upsetting me and I have learned to treat everything his says with scepticism.

Unfortunately, I have not been able to contact Tommy through any of our mutual acquaintances or at the places where we might normally meet. Nor have I been able to speak to his close friend, George Harris.

I am very concerned and wondered if there was any chance that you could pass a message to your brother to contact me.

Because of the sensitivity of the situation, Charles's unreliability in these sorts of matters and my parent's strong disapproval of my meeting Tommy or yourself, it would not be a good idea to try to contact me here.

Tommy and I have been in the habit of meeting at the tea stall on the Tottenham boundary.

It is discrete. I shall be there on Wednesday evening at seven o'clock, if you or he could meet me there and tell me any news, I should be extremely grateful.

Yours sincerely

Katherine Hartwell

The night was cloudy. There was a drizzle in the air, but it wasn't strong enough to wash away the last of the fog and as Tommy slid away into the night, a wet blanket shielded him from any watchers. Instinct took him to the little shed in the corner of the yard where his father's spade always hung. Silently, he took it down and shut the shed door. It was by the feel of his feet on the concrete path that he managed to find the back gate. The back alley behind their house was so dark that, even though Tommy had played there all his life, he had to feel his way along the fences until he reached the turn out into Wilmott Street.

The soft glow of the gaslights in the road made life easier, but now he would have preferred the pitch black again, to shield him from any prying eyes as he crossed to the other side. He listened and there was no sound. He looked and could see no movement anywhere and so he ran quickly and quietly up to the corner. Pressing himself against the flank wall of the grocer's shop, he inched forward until he could peep around into the main road.

It was like all the times they had played cowboys and indians along the street, but this time Tommy felt he was playing for his life. There was a lone car just coming under the Railway Bridge and Tommy drew back to flatten himself into Mr. Contaninounou's side doorway. From the deepest shadow he could find, he watched the lights of the old Morris pass by.

In a desperate effort to control his fear, he counted to ten and then to ten again before moving once more. He slid himself up to the corner and out into the main road. There was no traffic now and not a light shone in any of the flats above the shops around him.

Like a fox, close in against the darkened shop fronts, he ran the fifty yards to the fence alongside the railway embankment. It was still broken, as it had always been when he played there as a kid. Gratefully he dived through into the welcome inky black beyond. In the distance he could see that the station lights were on, waiting for the next up train to Liverpool Street, but the station backed onto the houses at the other end of Wilmott Street, and their yellow glow didn't disturb the shadows where Tommy crouched.

He rested for a few moments to get his bearings and let his eyes acclimatize to the re imposed blackness. Above him, the never sleeping eye of the signal box was blinkered by the parapet of the bridge and the signal man couldn't see his patch of ground, even in daylight. There was the ruby light of the stop signal on the up line, directly above his head, but that threw even less light than the distant station.

Tommy knew that Loopy Lou Botterell's house flanked the bottom of Contaninounou's yard and the two shops between it and the railway. He could just make out the line of the roofs of the houses in Wilmott Street, darker against the black night sky. He could see nothing of their back walls or fences, nor of the shrubs and bushes that filled the abyss between them and the rails on top of the embankment. He thought that the signal column was roughly level with the fence between the two sets of back gardens and used that as his marker.

Tommy crawled as quietly as he could over the rough ballast and through the damp, dragging branches accepting the pain to hands and knees from the stones and the scratches of Hawthorn twigs and brambles.

It seemed an age until he reached the back wall of the old coach house at the bottom of Loopy Lou's garden. They had been built at the same time as the big Victorian shops in Seven Sister's Road for tradesmen who would run a horse and carriage. There had been a horse there when Mrs. Botterell was a girl.

Still operating by feel, he ran his hand over the rough brickwork in wide spans seeking the window. He couldn't find it and he felt the taste of panic, burning like bile in his mouth. 'Don't panic, you fool,' he muttered to himself and the sound of his own voice in the silence frightened him into clear thought. *Is it the right wall?* he wondered. He thought carefully about the layout of the houses, of how far he'd come along the embankment and knew that it had to be the right one. He remembered the far off days when the gang had played their dangerous games on the railway lines; climbing on trucks waiting at the signals; cutting pennies in half under their wheels; stealing fog detonators off the rails. He conjured the old coach house in his mind and seemed to see the window high up and to the right. Stretching his left arm as far as he could, he found the corner of the building. He had come a little further than he thought. Moving back, he swept the brickwork with his hand again and there, about the level of his head, he found the window.

It was the matter of a moment to feel out the hinges and slot the blade of the spade into the opposite side. He wasn't prepared for how little effort was needed to break the window catch. With a crack like a rifle shot, it flew open. The force was such that one of the panes of glass shattered and fell like tinkling rain.

Horrified at the noise he had made, Tommy shrank back into the shadows and waited for the capture that must surely follow. After a few minutes, his pounding heart began to slow and there was still no sound of movement anywhere in the world. He let a few minutes more pass, just to be sure. At last he stood up again, felt for the open window and pushed the spade in ahead of him. There was no sound of it falling to the floor. The opening was too narrow for his shoulders, but he felt that it was taller than broad so, as he pulled himself up, he twisted and slid into the inner darkness.

Outside, Tommy had thought that the world couldn't have been any blacker and yet, inside the old coach house, it was as though he had gone blind. As he edged himself forward, he moved something that rumbled unsteadily under him. He froze and lay for minutes unable to move while his heart thumped wildly.

From the outside, behind him, he heard the bells from the signal box talking to its companions along the line. He had lived and played alongside these tracks all his life and knew its language. A train was coming and the up signal was red. It would have to stop. That would be his chance to gain sanctuary without being heard.

The slowing, deep puff of the approaching engine, the squealing of iron wheels, the rattle of colliding trucks gave Tommy his signal to move. As soon as the engine vented the steam from its cylinders, he swam forward through the pile of unidentifiable rubbish. His waving arms felt the underside of the rough wooden stair, which led up into the old hayloft and, before the train was fully stationary, he was safe in the newest black void.

Tommy had no idea what was around him, what there was to knock over, fall through or otherwise endanger him. He had no option but to lie down under the blanket, pull his coat tightly about him and wait for the dawn.

He was so cold and miserably uncomfortable that he was certain that he wouldn't sleep, but the next thing he knew was that there was a bird singing and thin wisps of light were creeping up the stairs and under a few misplaced slates.

Every movement after opening his eyelids was agony as if his joints had set solid and he had to break his limbs to move them. The best he could do was to roll onto his back. From where he lay, he could see the underside of the roof festooned with black lace spiders' webs. Tendrils of ivy were pushing in from the plant, which swamped the outside. It was old and dilapidated, but at least it looked as if it would keep the worst of the weather out.

With a renewed surge of hope, he pushed himself up into a sitting position. It was infinitely better than the sunken barge. He was dry, fairly safe, he had some food and soon Jack would bring him news about his escape plan.

A pain jabbed into his side and he saw that he was sitting on the pocket of his coat. With a humourless laugh, he dragged the diamond bracelet out. Even in the poor light of the hay loft it still managed to tease him with its sparkle. It must have been worth a couple of hundred pounds, but to him, it had no more value than the rest of the junk around him. 'Fucking hell,' he moaned. What a wreck he'd made of his life and, in fury, he threw the jewel across the room into the darkest corner and began to cry.

As the light grew stronger so did his hunger. He stood up and began to move around. Investigating his hidey-hole while munching on a doorstep corned beef sandwich. It didn't take long to complete his investigation of the upper floor. The bare wooden floor was dirty and dropping stained. It was five paces from eaves to eaves and fifteen paces from front to back. The hayloft door at the front had a few cracks in it through which he could see the back of the Botterell house and a postage stamp of the street beyond. The house still had its curtains drawn and the little bit of Wilmott Street visible to him, was empty. The Ivy on the left side of the building was so thick, he could see nothing through the slates on that side, but on the other he could catch a glimpse of Mrs. Smith's washing hanging limp in the grey dawn. In the gaps between Frank Smith's shirts and his wife's knickers, he could see into Ackfield's yard. The horse and cart had already left upon its round.

He finished his sandwich and his wander round. The sound of his feet on the bare boards seemed to echo through the coach house and so he was forced to sit still. Sitting with his back against the wall, there was nothing to do but think. He realised that he had brought nothing with him to drink. The thought that he had nothing to drink, made him thirsty. He began to worry about how long it would be until Jack came and would he be able to survive. He told himself that he was being stupid, people lived days without water and he tried to thrust his thirst to the back of his mind.

That idea was replaced with the realization of how bored he was with nothing to do; nothing to see and that played on his mind even more. His watch had not survived the day on the sunken barge, its hands were fixed grimly at ten to four and no amount of winding or shaking could make them move,

By the afternoon, he needed a cigarette far more than he needed a drink. He would have been grateful to hear any sound of movement below him, even if it had been the police. By the evening he was thinking he couldn't stand it anymore, the thought of cigarettes, water, food, drummed in his mind like the worst kind of hangover. If it got any worse, he felt that he would have to give himself up.

It got worse, but he only gave up struggling. He slumped in the corner with his head on his knees and sank into semi-conscious despair.

It was dark when the sound of movement disturbed him and made him take notice again. He had no idea where he was or what the time might be. The pain, as he moved brought reality flooding back. He froze. His mind tumbled ideas of flight, fight or remaining silent in a chaotic sequence. All his despair of the previous day was forgotten. He knew that he didn't want to go to prison for the rest of his life.

There was another rattle of something falling in the coach house below him. Tommy moved to crawl silently toward the dark end of the loft where the hay hatch was. He tried to remember if it locked on the inside.

The low whisper of his name stopped his desperate imagining and his heart leapt with joy when he heard his brother's voice. 'Where the bloody hell have you been?' he whispered back.

'What do you mean, 'where the bloody hell have I been?' I'll tell you where the bloody hell I've been. I've been on a sodding bus to Turnpike Lane: I caught the tube to Manor House, the night tram to St. Anne's Road and I walked from there carrying this sodding suitcase. It took me hours and I've got to go to work in the morning.'

'What on earth did you go all that way for?' Tommy demanded after Jack had described his great loop of a journey.

'To make sure no one followed me, that why. The street is still crawling with coppers, that's why.' Jack muttered in tired exasperation. 'and there's a bloke up on the station platform watching our house and Milly's house, twenty-four hours a day and every now and then, just when you're not expecting it, the patrol Bobbie walks down the street or a patrol car drives through. It's a nightmare. First I had to hide the case from Mum. I had to get out the back way without her seeing, I had to dodge the copper on the station, hide under the bridge until the bus came.'

'All right, all right,' Tommy said trying to placate his brother's anger, 'keep your voice down. You don't want no one to hear you shouting the odds. Did you bring me anything to drink? I'm dying of thirst.'

'I bought you a couple of pints of milk,' Jack replied, 'some bread, butter, cheese. Mum baked a cake.'

'Does Mum and Dad know where I am?' Tommy demanded in horror.

Jack gave a short laugh. 'Our dad's a lot shrewder than we give him credit. He missed my coat straight away and his spade, but he didn't say a word. He told Mum to bake a cake. She wanted to know why she should bake a cake at the beginning of the week and he said not to ask any questions. If we don't ask any questions, then we don't know nothing and we don't have to lie if anyone asks.'

Tommy laughed, his dad was a strange old bird. 'Did you bring me any fags' he asked getting back to pressing realities.

Jack tossed him a packet of Woodbines and some matches. 'and I bought you a couple of papers. The Worker and a copy of the Mirror that someone left in the canteen this morning.'

'Anything about me in them?' Tommy asked anxiously.

Jack laughed again, but this time with more humour. 'You've never made the Worker and you're yesterday's news for the rest, You won't even get a mention in the Herald this week.'

'Thank God for that,' Tommy gave a heartfelt sigh. 'I can do with being the forgotten man.'

'The police haven't forgotten you,' Jack reminded him.

'No,' Tommy admitted. 'Have you heard any more

about us going to Spain?'

'I've not had a date when we're to go,' Jack admitted, 'but I've seen Stan Wilson and had your name put on the list.

Tommy twitched nervously

'Don't worry,' Jack muttered, 'The Party make dammed sure that the police don't ever get to see that list. Now I'd better go. The Party says that I've got to make everything look as close to normal as I can, so no one guesses what's going on. I've got to go to work in the morning. I'll be back after it gets dark, if I can.'

Jack quickly finished unpacking the case he was carrying, a few more clothes, some more food, a few candles and a blanket. At the bottom of the steps, he stopped. 'I don't suppose you know where Dad's spade is,' he whispered.

'No' Tommy hissed his reply. Down there amongst the junk somewhere.'

After a few moments pause, Jack muttered. 'I can't see it. I'll have to leave it.' There was a rattle as he crawled across the top of the layer of old boxes, suit cases and the rest. 'Be careful,' he cautioned in parting, before climbing down the stairs across the rubbish and out of the window.

Tommy stood at the head of steps and listened to the sounds of his brother disappearing into the night. There was a final whispered warning, from outside. 'And block up this window so it doesn't show that someone's broke in. I'll cover up the broken glass.'

Tommy pushed the remains of an old cardboard box in the broken window and some carpet behind so it looked as if the rubbish was piled right to the back. Only then did he relax a little. He pulled a cigarette out of the pack, lit it, carefully shielding the match behind a cupped hand. As he listened to the scrabbling feet climbing the railway embankment, he felt a deep sadness, but his brother's visit had restored his morale. While he puffed on his Woodbine, he thought what he could do to make his hiding place more comfortable.

He concluded that there was nothing he could do in the dark. He drank a pint of milk. Ate some bread and cheese, relieved himself into a can, wrapped the blanket around his shoulders and tried to make himself comfortable in a corner.

He slept easier than the night before. Woke refreshed and, while he had a leisurely breakfast and peered out of his various peep holes to see what was going on in the little bits of the world that he could see, planned tasks to pass away the day.

While it was light, he went down into coach house to see what he could find. First of all, he moved a few things near the window and propped up others to make it easier for Jack to get in without making a noise. While he was doing this, he found his Dad's spade and another piece of carpet and some sacks, which he took upstairs to make a mattress. A kitchen chair with a broken back made a reasonable table and an empty biscuit tin which had been used to store Christmas Decorations would be a good place to put a candle and shield the light. When his stomach told him it was lunch time he settled down to read the papers and have another cigarette. He was close to his old optimistic self again, feeling that this would only be for a day or two, then he could get out of the country. He didn't have to go to Spain. He could duck out, as soon as they got to France. He could get to a port and might be able to work his passage on a ship to South Africa or Australia.

As it grew dark, Tommy lit a candle in the protective cradle of the tin box. It wasn't enough to read by, but the soft flickering light staved off the worst of the dark thoughts that the night brought. As he watched the flickering flame eat into the wax, he mused on the idea of constructing himself a clock to mark the passing of the night. He knew that there was an up train about every twenty minutes. If he measured the candle as the next train pulled out of the station and then measured it again when a second train came, he could take some nails from the tin on the shelf downstairs and stick them down a candle shaft. He would be able to work out roughly when it was midnight. He had reconciled himself to hours of waiting until Jack thought it safe enough to come, but before the wax melted half an inch, there was movement below him.

His first reaction was that it was too early for Jack; that it had to be the police, but it was too quiet, too cautious. Could it be some kid breaking in to pinch something; somebody else who wanted to borrow Loopy's bike?

Jack whispered his name from the bottom of the steps. For the first time Tommy realised that he had been holding his breath and breathed again.

'You're early,' Tommy said as Jack's head appeared above the floor level. 'Is it safe?'

'There's no pleasing you,' Jack muttered, 'but I think it's safe. The copper on the platform has gone and Mum says that they've not seen a police car all day. It looks like they've stopped looking for you round here.

I had to come early because I haven't got much time. Skinny Wheeler met me out on the round during the day. He's had a message that we've got to go up to London tomorrow morning and get our instructions.'

'You mean?' Tommy demanded, not believing what he had been told.

Jack grinned broadly at his brother, 'Tommy we're on our way.' He dropped the small cloth bag he was carrying. 'I've brought you some more food for tonight and there's a jar of water, a razor and some soap. I suggest you use them now while the water's still warm. We'll have to go up to London by bus and you'll have to look reasonable not to draw attention to us.'

'Thanks,' Tommy said gruffly. He wanted to give Jack a big hug, but only allowed himself to shake his hand to show the heart felt sense of relief that this hiding was soon going to be over. To hide his embarrassment, he took the sack and began to empty it. 'Where are you off to?' he asked casually.

Jack hesitated for a moment. Tommy saw the guilty look in his brother's eyes and smiled. 'You're not off to enjoy yourself are you, one last fling before you go off to war?'

'No,' Jack protested indignantly. 'If you must know, I've got to go and see your woman.'

'My woman?' Tommy repeated with a puzzled expression. 'I don't have a woman.'

'Well that's as may be, she seems to think that she's your woman and I'm going to have to see her, to stop her asking embarrassing questions in the wrong place.'

'Who are you talking about?' Tommy demanded and then a thought occurred to him. 'You're not talking about Kit, Katherine Hartwell are you?'

'Who did you think?' Jack demanded. 'She sent me a letter, said she'd heard that you were in trouble and wanted to talk to me and find out if it's true. I've got to meet her at the tea stall at the Boundary at seven. I've got to go, she could ruin everything if she goes to the police and draws attention to me.

'What's the time now?' Tommy demanded as he unwrapped his shaving kit.

'About half past six, that's why I've got to go.'

'I'm going,' Tommy said quietly.

'Don't be daft,' Jack snapped, 'You're a wanted man, you can't go wandering around Tottenham, just to meet some woman. Someone will see you.'

'It's dark,' Tommy said in a tone which would allow no argument, 'and you're not so worried about me wandering around London tomorrow in broad daylight.'

'I meant that it's a risk you don't have to take.' Jack protested. He was not prepared to have his brother's love life wreck his plans to serve the cause. 'I can see her and tell her all she needs to know.'

Tommy gave a hollow laugh. 'Little brother, we're off to fight a war. There's a fair change neither of us will return, so why are you talking to me about risk. You've had your chance to say your goodbyes; this is mine. I'm going and that's an end to it.

'Look,' Jack said realising that there was no point in arguing. 'If you go, you go, but if you get caught, you're on your own. I'm off and I'm not waiting for you. Comprende?'

Tommy nodded.

They had been told that they must tell no one that they were leaving, but he was sure that if Peggy had still been here, he would have had to see her before he left. He didn't have her strength of will. 'OK, but be quick, don't hang about.'

***

Tommy bought himself a cup of tea from the little wooden trailer which lived half in Tottenham, half in Edmonton serving the bus drivers and conductors who started and finished their routes there. He loaded it with sugar and stood in the oil lamps glow long enough to enjoy its sweet fire. It was less than a week since he had the last one, but it seemed a lifetime. He smiled at his own profligacy, then, he had stubbed his cigarette out in the half finished cup, now he savoured the tea like nectar and drained it to the dregs. Like life, warmth seeped into his stomach and through his fingers into his whole body.

There would be tea in heaven, he told himself and then, with a wry smile, hoped that there would also be tea in hell, because without doubt, that was where he was headed. More sombrely, he tucked himself into his normal shadowy corner to wait and wonder if Katherine would arrive before the tea was cold.

Katherine might have been anxious to know about him, but not to the point where she could be on time. She wouldn't want to have to talk to the bus conductors and drivers or endure their admiring stares. The fact that she was late, that she hadn't changed was, in a way, reassuring. There were still a few landmarks in his ruined world. He loved Katherine Hartwell desperately; had ruined his life for her and she still didn't give a damn for anyone but herself. What a fool he was, but it couldn't be changed now.

Katherine must have been a little worried, because

the cup was still warm in his hands when he saw her car draw into the kerb a little further down the road. Tommy knew she would be scanning the shadows around the tea stall, trying to see if Jack was there. He swayed forward into slightly stronger light and raised his hand, a white signal in the night.

He didn't know whether to be angry at her antics or not. She slid out of her car on the passenger side, pulled her pretty little hat down over her eyes and ruffled her collar further up around her face. Like the best spies on the pictures, she lit a cigarette while she surreptitiously looked around. And all the time, she was standing under a street lamp, in front of a lighted shop window. She might have been on stage.

Tommy looked around anxiously, but no one even spared her a glance. He decided not to be angry. It was all a game to people like her. They didn't really understand crime. She thought George Harris was some sort of Robin Hood, a working class hero and that Tommy was exciting. Fear was as foreign to her as hunger or hard work. Like a child, she lived in a nursery rhyme world, and you couldn't be angry with children for long.

Keeping up the pretence, Katherine walked up to the counter without a glance in his direction ordered a tea, spoke pleasantly to Joe, nodded and smiled at the other customers before sidling across to where Tommy stood, watching her.

'Well, Well,' he laughed as he moved a little out of his shadow, 'if it's not Greta Garbo. Fancy meeting you here. Can I get you a drink?'

'Tommy,' she gasped, 'What are you doing here? I didn't think, I mean I didn't know…'

'That's right, you never think, but you always think you know.'

She stared at him. He sounded different, grown up, not the boy she was used to twisting around her little finger. She sensed that this was a man at bay and that he was dangerous.

'You're a fool coming out like this and I'm a fool to meet you.' She said.

Tommy stroked her cheek affectionately and ignored it, when she angrily snatched her head away. 'No,' he protested, 'you're nobody's fool. You're probably the smartest person I know, but…'

He hesitated, trying to think of a way of explaining to her, what was happening.

'But, me old china.' He dropped into the strong cockney accent of the Public Bar. 'Yours truly has been a right berk. When your skirt says she wants to fly and you're boracic, you have to get the bees from somewhere. I tried to whip it and now it all gone up the chimney. I'm like to do bird for the rest of me puff.'

'Don't talk to me like that,' she snapped angrily, but tears were beginning to run down her cheeks. 'I hate it when you do. You know I don't understand.'

He leaned forward and briefly kissed her on the lips. 'Exactly,' he said. 'Like our Jack says, different worlds.'

Now she was angry too. She brushed away her tears with the cuff of her coat. 'You don't have to talk like that. You're laughing at me. I'm not stupid, you know.'

'Kit,' he bit back. It was all going to end here and perhaps the best way was to go out on a blazing row. 'You are so stupid that you don't even know what stupid is. Stupid is to be our Jack and build your life around a Party which doesn't care that much about you.' He snapped his fingers under her nose. 'That's stupid, but not nearly as stupid as falling in love with a girl who has an education, a car, a family, a social position. A good education and is so, so clever, but doesn't realise not everyone's got what she takes for granted. Now that really is stupid.'

'You selfish, arrogant…' In her fury she fought for word which would hurt. 'I don't ever want to see you again.'

'That's fine by me,' Tommy shouted back and turned away. He stopped in his tracks and thrust his hand into his pocket. 'You might as well have this. It was going to be our ticket to Paris. I'm going on me own now and somebody else is paying the fare. I'm not going to need it.' He threw the diamond bracelet at her and walked away.

Chapter 20

Dear Mum and Dad

By the time you get this letter, me, Tommy and Acky will be out of the country and heading for Spain. A small group of us have been planning to go for some time now. We were told that we would have to leave in secret because we are breaking the law by going to the aid of the legitimate government of Spain and so I could not tell you earlier. Because of all the recent trouble, it seemed a good idea that we took Tommy with us. He should be safe from that sort of trouble at least, while we're here.

I will write to you again, soon and let you know where we are exactly so that you can write back. Try not to worry.

Your loving son Jack

'Jesus Christ, would you look at this.' The amazed cry brought them tumbling out of the darkness of the shepherd's hut into a foreign world. The light dazzled them and every one of them flung up an arm to shield his eyes from the sun.

The small knot of Spaniards clustered outside the door laughed. It was always like this when the foreigners arrived. They supposed that the sun never shone in the lands of the north where they came from or that it was so damp and dirty that their world was always shrouded in fog.

Tommy whistled at the view and Jack said, 'it's like looking through...' He couldn't finish the statement because it was like looking through nothing. It was so bright and clear that it seemed that there was no air between them and the distant hills on the other side of the wide valley.

'Would you look at that,' Skinny demanded. They turned back to where he was pointing and saw the Pyrenees. Their snow cover peaks were so high that they stuck up through the sky. 'Tell me we didn't climb over them, not in the dark?' He cried in horror.

'It was a good job we did climb them at night,' said a Liverpudlian voice from amongst the groups, 'I wouldn't have even tried it if I'd seen the bloody things first. The highest thing I've ever been on is the top deck of a Blackpool tram. I never even fancied going up the tower. We must be fucking mad.'

Everyone laughed and for the joy of being there, hugged each other. A little bow legged French man, supporting himself on a stick, pushed his way into the middle of the small group of celebrating Englishmen. He looked very serious. Giving an exaggerated clenched fist salute, he proceeded to grab Jack, then Tommy and then Acky by the shoulders and dragged each forward in turn so that he could kiss their cheeks. Of the rattle of his words, they could only pick out the necklace of 'merci's' dotted through it.

'Don't mention it,' Jack grinned back. The man had left Perpignan as drunk as a Lord and had fallen off the path about a quarter of hour after they climbed out of the lorry on the French side. The guide only spoke Spanish. He indicated to the group as they clustered around the injured man, that the Frenchman had damaged his leg and they would have to leave him. The Brits wouldn't hear of it. Between them, they had carried him over the mountains into Spain.

Still laughing from the pure joy of being there, Jack pointed to himself and said in a slow, loud voice 'milk man,' he then tapped Tommy and said 'brewer's dray man,' then Acky, 'coal man. We carry things all day long, we are donkeys, born to carry and you are very small.'

A second French man with a smattering of English obviously gave a rough translation of Jack's speech, because the bow legged man tried to kiss them all again. Garlic breath blunts the fraternal feelings for a comrade very quickly and all three of them held him off. The French contingent satisfied their honour with a rousing chorus of *the Internationale* and they all moved off in the direction of two steaming cauldrons set up over a fire just outside the hut.

One smelled of coffee, the other of stew. The coffee was dreadful, but drinkable, the stew was foul and greasy. It served to soften the hard bread, but, though they were ravenous, to eat it on its own, turned the English stomachs.

Having finished their breakfast, they lay around on the grass in the growing warmth of the sun, waiting for whatever was next. They had left London in the middle of winter, but here the air was full of the sound of insects: buzzing, humming, sawing. None of them noticed the slowly rising drone of engines until one of the Spanish guides suddenly sat up.

'Camion' he shouted and pointed excitedly down into the valley below. Crawling along the road, marginally ahead of its own dust cloud, was a lorry. For the moment it seemed no bigger than one of the lizards flitting across the rocks. By the time they all had struggled down from the mountain hut to the road, it was close enough to pick out the features of the driver and the guns of the guards hanging onto the top of the cab.

The lorry journey was like a switch back ride. Jack was never so glad that he had passed up on the greasy stew. He felt queasy enough without it and more than one of his comrades had to lean over the side of the lorry to say goodbye to his breakfast.

The journey to Figuerras was something out of a fairy story. The battered old train pulled half a dozen even more dog eared coaches at a walking pace through countryside so different to England that they might have been on the moon. Just for the hell of it, they would take it in turns to jump off the train and run alongside. Laughing, nut faced, peasants would slap them on the back and shout 'viva Russia,' These pale faced foreigners were all Russians to them. Then they would sing *The Internationale* and thrust flowers and oranges into their hands. This was truly the people's army, the Tottenham boys thought, their sort of army.

But by the time they fell off the back of another lorry at their destination, they were exhausted. Extracting themselves from the noisy heap, they milled around the courtyard, looking for corners out of the cold wind which had sprung up, and in a patch of warmer winter sun stood, waiting to be told what to do next.

From boyhood, they had listened to the stories of their fathers, uncles and all the other old men they knew, had told about their days in the army; of drill; of spit and polish. They knew that they had to hate the sergeants; despise the officers and dodge the column whenever they could. It only took the distance from the mountains to the fortress at Figuerras, less than a day's travelling, for the Englishmen to become used to the rag-taggle appearance of this army. History was all forgotten by the time the camion snorted its way up the hill into the castle barracks, and they were as slovenly as the rest. They hadn't seen an officer and all the sergeants and corporals were as scruffy and disorganised as the men.

As they lounged about the old fort's parade ground, a door in the rampart opened and a new reality emerged. A black man stepped into the sunlight. Jack had never seen a live black man before; he only ever seen them at the pictures. The black sergeant marched towards them, a swagger stick tucked under his arm. He had shiny boots and a clean, ironed shirt. He studied the list of names on the sheet of paper he was carrying and then looked up at the line of men huddled in the corner.

'Line up, there.' He shouted with a strong American accent and he waved his short swagger stick to show them where. It took several minutes of chaos before there was a semblance of a line, straggling, across the parade ground.

His look of disgust at the state of the motley crew in front of him was obvious. He slapped his calf with the stick in subdued fury and then stepped purposefully towards them. 'My God, Jack,' Nobby Clarke muttered from the corner of his mouth. 'What have we done?'

The volunteers sensed the storm, that was about to break on their heads and made a disorganised attempt to shuffle into a straighter line. Tommy stood near the end of the rank and closest to the doorway. He expected he would receive the blast first, but the little black man just stared at him with huge white eyes and moved on. The only sounds as he moved down the line was the squeaking of his stiff, baggy corduroy trousers, his boots marking a slow, measured tread and the swagger stick slapping his thigh in rhythm.

At the end of the line, the sergeant spun round to face back the way he had come. He fired a steam of angry French at them. In the corner of his eye, Jack could see the little Frenchman they had carried into Spain struggling to stand straight. He winced at the tirade. Then it was the English speakers turn. 'You are, without doubt, the worst looking bunch of bums I've ever seen.' He shouted in his broad New York drawl. 'It shows you how desperate this man's army is for volunteers, that you have been accepted. Well it's my misfortune to try to turn you into soldiers.

You've all seen your commissar and none of you took the chance he gave you to go home. You might regret that decision, but it's too late now.'

Jack recognised the Frenchman who had translated for them at the border as he stepped forward to protest. Jack caught something about 'egalite' in his response.

The black sergeant walked with a slow, measured tread, until he was level with the man standing out of line. He looked at him for a moment, in silence, then thrust his face to within inches of the Frenchman's. He screamed a tumble of invective at the top of his voice.

The poor man winced as if a bomb had just fallen from the clear blue sky and exploded in front of him. He was driven back into his place by the verbal onslaught. He stood white faced and shaking and no one else made a sound.

'As I said, you've had your last chance to back out. Now file through that door and sign your names. You are now enrolled in the Army of the Spanish Republic. You are subject to military discipline. Any dissent will be treated as mutiny. Step out of line and I'll have you shot. Questions?'

Jack was horrified. What had he done? He demanded of himself. In the utter silence that followed the question, Jack remembered the journey to London where they met Robson, the Party's chief recruiter, in a poky little office off Charing Cross Road. While they were lined up in front of him, Acky had upset Robson. Acky had told him what he did for a living and Robson had called him petit bourgoise and said that a self-employed coal man wouldn't be popular with all the miners who were going to Spain. Acky had snapped back, that he worked for his father and was probably paid less than the miners were. It didn't matter if you were hacking it out of the ground or carrying up some front path and pouring it into a bunker, it still weighed as heavy and was just as dirty.

Robson wasn't amused. He snarled that Acky had better keep a tighter rein on his tongue in Spain. Speak to an officer like that and even though it was a people's army, he'd still find himself in the slammer or worse. They had thought that Robson was just a bully, bloated with the power to choose, now they realised that he had told them nothing but the truth.

At the time, it had seemed very unfair to Jack. Acky was a good comrade and didn't need to be picked on. He thought that Robson's judgement was very suspect because Tommy passed his eye without a murmur. Even though he had tried to tidy himself up, Tommy still looked so dishevelled, unshaven and down at heel that his working class credentials weren't even questioned. He wasn't even asked if he was a Trade Union man.

'You leave Friday.' Robson announced at the end of the interviews implying that they had all been accepted. 'I needn't tell you that Baldwin and his Fascist Lackeys will stop at nothing to prevent aid getting to the Spanish people. If anyone suspects that you are going to join the English Brigade, you will be stopped and your families will be harassed by the police. Talk to no one about this. Tell no one, not even your wife or mother, what they don't know can't be held against them later.'

'You will meet at Victoria Station at ten o'clock sharp. No heavy luggage, you are going to Paris for the weekend. No one is to see you off. Wait under the clock and you will be contacted. Any questions?' He leaned forward across his desk and let his iron eyes rest on each in turn. It was clear that he didn't expect any. The four lads looked away and said nothing.

Satisfied, the gruff old soldier hauled himself to his feet, raised his clenched fist in salute 'Salud,' he shouted. They didn't know what to say, but feeling themselves dismissed they turned and shuffled towards the door. As they left, he gave them a begrudging, 'good luck.'

As the motley group built up under the clock, one of them, no different from any other, announced that he was their leader. He whispered from behind his hand, that Victoria was crawling with Special Branch, you could tell them by the Mackintoshes and good quality black shoes. As Jack surreptitiously looked around he thought that ever third man was a policeman. There were a pair of men in Macs who eyed their little group as it strode defiantly towards the ticket barrier. Their expression showed that they knew exactly who the boys were and where they were going. They saw little groups like this quite often. They hadn't been able to stop any one yet and so they had become bored with the exercise. It was more to show willing rather than any genuine interest that made one of the plain clothed policemen break off his conversation and to step in front the of the straggling group. Right in front of Skinny.

'Where are you going lad?' the special branch man demanded. He was a head and shoulders taller than Skinny and twice as wide, cutting out all sight of the comrade who had taken command.

Skinny's jaw worked for a moment, but nothing came out, then he managed to squeak, 'We're going to Paris. For the weekend,' hastily adding. 'We've got tickets,' at the same time as he rooted through his pocket, trying desperately to find the one he'd been given.

Despite their instructions to keep going, the whole group stopped and watched. Acky felt himself glued to the floor and had forgotten how to move his legs. Jack glanced at his brother. Tommy was white and his eyes were swollen with terror. Where his overcoat flapped open, there was a tell-tale dark stain in the crutch of his trousers. If any of the policemen glanced at him, they must have seen his guilt written across his face. Jack wanted to move closer to him, but was frightened that any movement might draw attention to them both. He stood as still as the rest.

Skinny was thinking that he was the one who was going to be stopped and the others would go on without him. 'I've got every right.' He tried to bluster, but he just sounded pathetic.

The policeman almost smiled and stepped back. ''course you have lad, of course you have. On your way' The last phrase was almost sad. Seeing themselves dismissed, the leader stepped out towards the barrier and the others followed. Jack heard the policeman say to his colleague, in the same sad tone, 'silly buggers.'

The policeman's words were echoing in his head when the sergeant barked at the end man in the line, three or four away from him. 'Nom?'

The man stumbled over his own name and his occupation. The sergeant snarled, sneered and frowned as he found it on the list he held. He ticked it and snapped 'infanteria'.

Nobby Clarke was the first of the English that the sergeant came to, next but one to Jack. Nobby's father had been a regular in one of the Guards Regiments before the war and had spent a bit of time as a drill instructor at Catterick. He had brought some of his spit and polish home with him after the war. Nobby came smartly to attention and shouted 'Frederick Clarke, Sergeant. Railway Porter.'

The sergeant looked up and almost smiled as he marked him down for the infantry, but with a little star by his name.

Skinny was next, he tried to be soldierly too, but it didn't work, he stumbled over his feet and his words.

'Infantry,' the Sergeant snapped, recovering his normal tone.

'But I've got flat feet,' Skinny protested. 'They said in London that I could go into the artillery.'

'Infantry' the Sergeant repeated and moved his face a little closer to Skinny's, daring him to argue any more. Skinny remained silent and in the infantry.

Jack did his best to appear military and shuffled to attention as he spoke his name.

'Trade?' the sergeant demanded.

'Milk man.'

The sergeant shouted 'infantry', made his marks and moved on.

Tommy did a very good imitation of Nobby Clarke. He snapped to attention, stared off into the far distance and shouted his name and gave the inquisitor his rank.

'Trade?'

'Motor mechanic and lorry driver,' Tommy replied.

The sergeant hesitated, his eyes fluttered, the standard pronouncement of 'infantry' hovered on his lips, his pencil wavered and then he grunted 'Autopark'.

Tommy smiled and slumped to *at ease*.

As soon as he had finished allocating the new recruits, the sergeant marched to the centre and faced them. Speaking in English first, he said. 'You are now enlisted in the army of the Spanish Republic. You have signed up to fight for the duration of the war or until the Spanish Government sees fit to release you. When you are dismissed from this parade. I will expect you to come to attention; turn to your left and salute the Spanish flag.

The salute of the International Brigade is like this.' He snapped to attention, pivoted right and brought his clenched fist to his forehead.

'You will follow the corporal to get your uniform and documents. Any questions?'

Jack wanted to know when they would get their guns. Tommy wanted to know where it said all that on any of the papers he had signed, but neither said a word.

Jack waited until the sergeant had moved on a little and was shouting at the next group of French speakers. 'You lying bastard,' he muttered out of the corner of his mouth, 'what did you say that for? You're not a bloody mechanic.'

'I reckon I'll pass for one in this Fred Karno's outfit.' Tommy muttered back. 'You never listened to what our dad said. He said stay out of the Poor Bloody Infantry. If I'm going to war, it's going to be in one of those big Russian lorries.'

His father had also said that you should never volunteer, Jack remembered. He didn't mention that, but quietly protested, 'I thought we would stick together'.

'No, I think it's better if me and Acky split up,' Tommy replied. There was the shadow of seriousness in his voice which, just for a moment, made Jack agree. By the time, the sergeant brought the new infantry recruits to order and marched them off the parade ground, he had changed his mind. Tommy, leaning against a sun lit wall at the side of the square, put his cigarette in his mouth so that he could give his brother a cheery wave and Jack realised that the Autopark was probably a better option than the infantry.

Chapter 21

Dear Mr. and Mrs Sutton

Excuse me for writing like this, but my parents and I are very concerned by the lack of information regarding the well being of my brother, Moses. It is more than six months since he went to fight in the war in Spain. Apart from a letter soon after he left and a brief post card at the turn of the year, we have had no news of him.

I have been told that both your sons have also gone to fight in Spain and I thought that you might have had news from them. If you could let me know when might be convenient, I should like to call on you to receive any information that you have.

Yours sincerely
Miriam Rabinovitz

Aggie Sutton threw open the front door in mild irritation. Why did someone always have to knock, just when she put something on the stove? 'Yes?' she demanded.

It took a moment for her to recognise the figure standing on the doorstep. Aggie had not seen Miriam since she had stopped working for the family in Stamford Hill, soon after the boys went to Spain. Sue had put her in the way of a nice little job in the Lordship Lane Co-op funeral service. The hours were longer, but it was easier to get to and the money was much better than domestic work. She stared blankly at the slim little figure wrapped in a grey shawl, which partly obscured her pale face. She looked a sad little thing, for all the world like one of those refugees from Germany that they were always showing on the cinema news reels. Despite the letter she received a few days ago, but hadn't got around to replying to yet. She hadn't really expected that Miriam Rabinovitz would come.

'Miss Miriam?' she queried, doubting her own eyes and became all flustered when she finally realised who her visitor was. 'I didn't mean, ... I mean what,' she threw up her arms in annoyance at not being able to find a proper thing to say. 'Oh, come in won't you.' Even as she spoke Aggie cringed inside as she remembered what a state the front room was in. It was littered with the contents of Sue's bottom drawer. Now that young Eddie Baxter had declared his intentions, Sue had been drawing up a list of what she had gathered and what she would need to set up house.

'I'm afraid that the front room's in a bit of a mess at the moment,' she apologised. 'If you don't mind coming through to the back for a minute while I get our Susan to tidy away her stuff so you can sit in there. She's getting married you know?'

'I didn't know,' Miriam said, trying to reassure, 'but don't worry, Mrs. Sutton, the kitchen's fine. I shan't be staying long, I'm sure.'

Aggie smiled gratefully at her, but, as she shepherded Miriam down the hall, she bellowed up the stairs. 'Sue, you come down here at once and clear your stuff out of the parlour. We've got a guest.'

Miriam and Mrs Sutton were sitting stiffly silent across the Kitchen table looking for a way to begin their conversation when Sue burst in, bristling with indignation. 'Oh,' she exclaimed when she saw who it was, the wind taken out of her sails. 'Sorry, I wasn't expecting any one to call. I'll take my stuff upstairs out of the way. I won't be a tick.'

Miriam half rose and smiled as if she were glad that the younger woman had appeared. 'Please Sue, don't bother on my account. I'm fine here, I really am.'

It was Miriam calling her *Sue* that convinced the Suttons that there was something wrong. At her house in Stamford Hill, Miriam would have always called her Susan. Both women picked up on it instantly and realised that something serious was happening. Sue shut the door behind her and took a vacant chair at the table.

As far as Aggie knew, Miriam wasn't aware of Tommy's trouble and therefore assumed the worst about Jack. 'Have you had news about our Jack?' she demanded, white faced.

'No,' Miriam protested, 'I've not had any news from him or from Moses.' She hesitated for a moment. 'I called to find out if you had. There are some bad things in the newspaper at the moment about what's happening in Spain. I've read that the British have been caught up in a big battle.'

Aggie nodded vigorously, 'Yes we've heard about that too. I've nearly been out of my mind with worry. I had forgotten about your brother being out there as well. You've not heard from him then.'

'Oh yes, we had a letter a few days ago, but all he writes about is politics. He never mentions where he is; what he is doing or about anybody who is with him.'

'We had a post card from Jack. It was written just after Christmas, but didn't arrive until a couple of weeks ago. We've had nothing else.' Sue said, getting up to fetch the postcard from behind the clock on the mantelpiece. 'It only says that they arrived safely,' she said almost apologetically when Miriam snatched it and read it hungrily.

It did. All it said was *Have arrived safely. Everyone fine. Write soon when I know more. Love Jack.* Miriam turned it over several times as if she might find something else written on it that had been overlooked.

Sue saw the look of bitter disappointment on Miriam's face. 'We've had a long letter from Tommy,' she said.

'Tommy's my eldest,' Aggie added with a tone of pride, feeling the need to defend her selfish sons from the outsider. 'They went out to Spain together. They always did everything together.'

'Miriam knows Tommy, Mum,' Sue said quietly. 'He says that he and Jack split up when they first arrived. He's with the transport corps at a place with a funny name I can never remember, Al something.

'Albacete,' Miriam said quietly. Some of Moses's early letters had been from there.

'He says that Jack and the others are with the English Battalion,' Sue continued, 'and he's not seen or heard of him since they got out there.' She proffered the envelope. Miriam didn't take it. She had her face turned away, but they both could see that she was crying.

'Oh dear,' Aggie fluttered and, unable to think what else to say, said, 'silly me, what am I thinking about. Would you like a cup of tea?'

Miriam, trying to regain her composure, sniffed that it was very kind and that she would love one. While her mother bustled about, Sue moved closer and took one of Miriam's hands. She knew her brothers better than anyone and had kept their secrets for years. 'Are you all right?' she asked quietly, knowing that she wasn't; she hadn't even mentioned the milk.

Miriam shook her head and, once more, tears began to stream down her face. A huge drop hung on the end of her nose, making her look ridiculous. She was so utterly wretched that she didn't care.

Sue brushed the tears away with her sleeve. 'You're not,' she hesitated, 'you know.'

With a howl Miriam nodded.

'Our Jack?' It was a needless question.

Aggie, standing by the stove, had caught the drift of the conversation. 'These men,' she muttered bitterly, 'if only they knew the hurt they caused.' She was thinking of her own loss, but allowed Miriam to join in her grief.

Sue had never liked Peggy; had thought her a hard-nosed bitch with a heart to match. She was certain that she wasn't right for Jack. This one, on the other hand, though no beauty, had a heart. She obviously loved her brother; perhaps nearly as much as Sue did herself and she was kind and clever. This one would do him much better. That was if he ever came back.

'I have to go to work in the morning,' Sue said without letting hold of Miriam's hand, 'but I've got the afternoon off. I was going shopping with my friend, but that can wait. I know it's Shabbat, but if you like we could go up to London. If we go to the Communist Party Head Quarters, they might be able to give us some news.'

'I'd like to go,' Miriam replied fighting harder to stop her tears. She was grateful, that Sue had made nothing of her disgraceful news. She had been afraid that Mrs Sutton might have thrown her out of the house for being *no better than she ought to be*. She suspected that her mother would tell her to go, when she found out.

It was a pleasant warm afternoon with a strong hint that winter was on the wane. The conductor put them off the bus at Leicester Square and pointed across the road to the Communist Party offices. Though Miriam was a Party member she had never been to King Street before. She looked at the glass fronted building in front of her and took a quick look into her handbag to be sure she had her membership card with her. It wasn't very inviting and looked the sort of place where she might need it.

The girls exchanged glances before braving the entrance. Secretly, neither had great expectations of their journey. The building looked like a glorified gentleman's public toilet, not the sort of place where you got good news.

Sue believed that the way that Jack must have known how his disappearance would have hurt his mother, but had put Party above family feeling, was due to the pressure the Party had put on him. They would not trade information with a mere sister. Though Sue had not spoken her fears, Miriam knew she was right. She was a member herself and understood how the Party worked. Her brother depended on her but she had been largely shut out of his political life to meet the need for secrecy.

As they walked in, a middle aged woman with grey hair tied back in a severe bun, sitting at the reception desk, looked up and eyed them suspiciously. 'Yes?' she demanded with undisguised hostility in her voice.

'My name's Sue Sutton,' Sue said.

'And I'm Miriam Rabinovitz,' Miriam butted in and waved her Party card in front of the receptionist's eyes.

If she thought that it would change the woman's attitude, she was disappointed. 'Yes?' the receptionist repeated without a flicker to soften her expression.

'Our brothers are with the International Brigade in Spain,' Sue said, thinking that must draw some sympathy for them.

'This is the Headquarters of the Communist Party of Great Britain,' the woman said sourly, speaking as if she were reading her words off a printed sheet. 'The Communist Party of Great Britain has no direct involvement with the International Brigade fighting in Spain, though we unequivocally support any stand in support of the legitimate Republican government and against international Fascism.'

Sue didn't actually stamp her foot, but her tone sharpened. 'Don't tell me that the Communists aren't involved. It was you lot that recruited them and sent them and I want to know what's happened to them. She's a member,' Sue indicated Miriam with her thumb, 'and has to do what she's told, but I'm not and I'm getting cross.' The woman's attitude was really infuriating and Sue was beginning to shout.

A door opened across the lobby and big moon faced man

looked out to find the cause of the raised voices. The receptionist looked at him expectantly. 'Take 'em round the corner,' he said in a broad northern accent and then shut his door.

'This way,' the woman said, not changing her tone in the slightest. Despite her instruction, she merely took them to the pavement outside the door. 'That Way,' she pointed up Charing Cross Road. 'Litchfield Street. At the end. No.1.' She turned on her heels and disappeared back into the building.

Their reception at the Brigade's Dependant's Aid headquarters was more friendly, but no more useful. They were offered tea. Had their details taken, lists were checked and laid out. Jack and Tommy's names were both on the first sheet laid on the table in front of them. These were some of the recent arrivals. Moses' name was on an earlier sheet. It was not encouraging to see how many names on the lists had been scored through in black pen, but at least there was some satisfaction that none of theirs had.

'Yes,' they were told 'they were all in Spain; with the British Battalion.' And 'No, they were not listed amongst the casualties' The woman interviewing them tried to be cheerful. It was wonderful that their brothers and friends had rallied to the call of the people of Spain in their fight against oppression. They and their families should be very proud, but no, she couldn't say exactly where they were at the moment.

The stony faces of Sue and Miriam indicated to the woman that any pride the families felt was swamped by their anxiety. She looked at another list and smiled. 'This is the most recent list of casualties we have, it came in a few days ago,' she said. 'It lists the wounded, missing, prisoners and...' She left the last word unsaid.

Quickly, her finger ran down the list of names, turned the page and ran on to the end. 'I'm pleased to tell you that they're not here. That has to be good news.' She did not tell them that the list had left Spain nearly two months ago and that the situation there was very confused at the moment.

'The papers say that there is a lot of fighting in the North of Spain at the moment and that the Republicans are being driven back with heavy casualties,' Miriam blurted out. She could feel the tears beginning to well up inside her, but didn't want to cry in front of strangers.

The woman from Dependant's Aid saw how upset Miriam was. She was new to this work, didn't know how to cope and was embarrassed. 'You don't want to believe all you read in the papers,' she said. 'They're all tools of big business and the Right, except for the Daily Worker, of course. You should read that to get the truth. The rest are mainly scare stories; I'm told this is a strategic withdrawal to avoid casualties. The British Battalion are based in the South; they may not even be involved.'

Miriam could not control her tears and as Sue could see that they weren't going to get any more information here than they had at Party Headquarters, she took Miriam's arm and helped her to her feet.

Grateful that the situation was being resolved, the woman sprang up from behind her table and hurried to open the door for them. 'We will let you know, if we hear anything,' she assured them as they were shepherded out onto the landing. Her words drifted down the stairs after them as they headed back to the street. 'Remember, no news is good news.'

Chapter 22

Dear Mr. and Mrs. Sutton

It is with deep regret that I must inform you that our contacts in Spain have told us that your son Cmde. Sutton has been killed in action.
    Though your sadness at this time is understandable, you will know, in times to come, that he fell in the great struggle to aid the Spanish people to resist the yoke of Fascism. His body will be laid to rest in the grateful Spanish earth where his name will never be forgotten.

Mrs. C. Haldane
Spanish Dependant's Aid Fund

The mountain road was a tunnel out of the sun. To look up burnt your eyes, but the glare off the dust road was so fierce that it hurt as much to look down. Rocky crags above the road had sucked up as much heat as they could hold and, now in the late afternoon, breathed it back onto the ragged little knots of men plodding below.

Jack trudged on in a dream, eyes half closed even though, every few minutes a stone would roll away from under his foot or a rock would stub his toe and threaten to bring him crashing down once more. He had given up all thoughts of time and distance. After hundreds of hundreds, he had stopped counting his footsteps. The dull thud, thud, thud of his sandals into the dust had a monotony that was hypnotic. It disconnected his brain from any thought of pain, thirst or fear and let it roam a thousand miles away.

On and on he traipsed, as he had all day. With no idea where he was going, no longer looking for any end, he walked like an automaton.

In his head there were constant visions of water. There was the tap in his mother's scullery running full blast into the worn stoneware sink. He sluiced the water over his sweating body. It was splashing everywhere and he knew his mother would be furious when she came home to find the floor flooded, but he let the icy water run over his body down onto the stone flagged floor. The next moment, he was by the Lea, lying naked in the shadow of a weeping willow. Peggy would leap up from beside him and dive in sending a fountain of crystal droplets up into the sky to sparkle in the sun. It didn't matter how many times Peggy dived in, it was always Miriam who surfaced. Her hair streamed out behind her like black weed in the water. With a laugh, she would toss her head and send the long tresses cart wheeling over her shoulder. A cascade of water reached out under the trees to soak him to the skin. He saw the rain washing down the gutter in Wilmott Street as he chased a match box boat and he saw the sun glinting on the reservoirs at Walthamstow as he dangled his feet alongside his fishing line.

Each stumble brought him back to the reality of Spain and nothing soothed the fire that burnt in his throat or washed away the dust which threatened to choke him.

'Avion'. The cry started somewhere far behind him, a dry ghost wind which did not stir the dust as it rustled along the road. He added his croak to the cry, giving it a push along its way. Men in front of him found sudden reserves of energy and skipped to the side of the road, others flung themselves down where they had been walking.

Jack could hear the deep rumble of aeroplanes in the sky coming from behind. He wanted to ignore them, he told himself that they wouldn't bother with a few beaten men trudging beneath an overhanging crag, they would go for the open road ahead where there would be camions and easy pickings. He couldn't afford the energy of getting back on his feet.

When they came and he heard the scream as the Stukas came tumbling out of the sky, he flung himself as flat as any man. He hugged the ground, squeezing it up through his fingers and blessed the boulders in the road which gave a hint of cover.

The road rocked and roared, noise of great explosions beat in upon his ears and desert winds full of dust and splinters of rock raged over his head.

As suddenly as they had come, they were gone. In front of him, figures, like monsters made of dust, began tearing themselves out of the ground and having reached their feet, began the mechanical stumbling on. Ten yards on from where he had taken cover, he passed a figure which had not risen with the rest. Jack didn't know if he had been hit by a bomb fragment or was just too exhausted to go on. He didn't stop to look. There was no point, either way, he could do nothing about it.

For the millionth time, his rifle strap slipped off his shoulder. Ages ago he had seen the man in front of him throw away his rifle. Jack thought that seemed a really good idea and changed his grip so that he could do the same

'Don't do it comrade. It's your best mate and we might need it in a minute.'

Jack hadn't realised that he wasn't alone, but he didn't reply, didn't turn around to see the owner of the lilting voice who could only have been three or four paces behind him. *Bollocks*, he thought, but said nothing. What did this Welshman know about best mates? Jack had just left Acky behind on the road, probably to die.

Poor old Acky, he'd been going up the hill side away from the fascists like a gazelle when a burst from a machine gun on one of the tanks went off in his direction. It probably wasn't even a bullet that caught him, just a stone chip kicked up behind him. It bled a lot, but didn't seem too bad until the second day when his knees seized up. By the third day, he could hardly walk and on the fourth day, Jack had to drag him and then carry him.

Jack had brought him as far as he could, but in the end had he had been forced to leave him. The pain for them both was too much. He had put him in the shade of a culvert running under the road, given him the last of the water and wished him luck before leaving him and heading on towards a hope of safety.

Luck? Jack ground his teeth to stop himself crying out as cracked his toe against another rock, Acky had all the luck. For him the war was over. He would be taken prisoner or even if he were shot out of hand like the polcoms' said, he wouldn't have to walk anymore and roast in Hell.

For the millionth time, his rifle strap slipped off his shoulder. For the first time, he didn't instinctively shrug it back. *What did he need a sodding rifle for anyway?* he demanded of himself *No one was going to make a stand and, anyway, he didn't have any ammunition left.* But he didn't throw it away, just changed it to his other shoulder and kept on walking.

Just when he didn't think he could go any further. It all finished. He rounded a corner of some rocks crowding in on the road and, in the shade of a clump of scrubby pines growing out of the underbrush of wild Rosemary, he found an officer sitting on a low stone wall smoking a cigarette.

'Que grupo?' the officer demanded

'English Battalion,' Jack muttered, not caring if the man understood him or not.

'Oh a limey eh. Good, there's a few of your lot come in.' the captain said in a broad American drawl. 'There's water, food, and ammunition in the trees up to your left, Report to your senior officer and get detailed for duty. We're going to make a stand here.'

'Oh, hell,' Jack muttered, another bloody battle. He'd had enough. Perhaps he wouldn't stop. He'd just keep going until he reached the sea.

'Turn off here.' The American's voice took on a hard edge as he saw that Jack was ignoring him and walking on, 'that's an order Comrade.'

It was an order backed up by a Maxim machine gun dug in behind the wall and covering the road and emphasised by the little Russian sub machine gun covering him, held by the officer's body guard. *What a beautiful little gun,* Jack thought, *like a Tommy Gun out of an American gangster picture. What a waste to give it to man like that, they might have held Belchite with a few of those out in the Aragon.*

Jack was too tired really to care. He did as he was told. He walked off the road into the field. The stumps of the vines, which had been lovingly pruned, were being trampled down by a mad melee of men and machines. If the Stukas came over now, it would be sheer bloody murder.

He didn't want to be any part of that, but looking back the way he had come, he saw that a second machine gun had been set up and the officer's bodyguard had been strengthened. No one was passing on down the road. There was going to be no more retreat for the time being and so Jack committed himself to the scrum.

'Tiene Agua?' Jack demanded of a soldier who was walking past with a sack of beans over his shoulder.

Jack had no real idea of the reply except that the gnarled free hand, waved vaguely in the direction of the

Olive grove which ran away from the vineyard, up the hill. He saw, in a desperate effort to gain whatever cover it could from the silver leaves, a small truck parked hard against a trunk of an Olive tree. The denser crowd of men milling around it were like ants around a sugar bowl was a sure invitation to any passing bomber to pour petrol on this particular nest. But needs must and so Jack pushed into the throng. He elbowed his way through the crowd to reach the tailgate of the truck where three Spaniards were alternatively filling wooden buckets with water from the tank on the back and kicking and screaming abuse at their compatriots to keep them back.

Most of the crowd seemed to be only boys, Jack no longer looked on himself as a boy. These were even younger than him and obviously new to the game of soldiering. They had thrown down their packs and rifles in untidy heaps among the vine stumps, to fight for a drink. They needed to quench the thirsts they had built up on their drive from the coast. A hard man; a man who had seen action, with the thirst from hours of marching in the sun, holding a rifle and carrying an empty canteen, had little problem in reaching the front; of commanding a bucket; of filling his canteen and then slaking his thirst.

The smell of cooking drifted through the trees, so rich that Jack could taste it. He knew that it would only be stewed donkey and beans, but he would have killed for a plate full at that moment. Even so, there was one thing he needed to do first to ensure his security in this foreign land. 'Tiente Brigada Ingles presente?' he called, exploiting his Spanish almost to the limit in an effort to find compatriots he could rely on.

'The Brits. are up the hill in the trees, on the right.' A voice replied. It was unmistakable.

'Who said that?' Jack demanded of the crowd.

'Our Jack? is that you,' was the yelled response.

'Tommy.' As if he had been resting for a week, Jack ran through the intervening clumps of people and threw himself on his brother where he stood by one of the big

Russian lorries.

Thank God, you're still alive, Tom replied as he hugged his brother tighter than he had ever hugged a woman. 'I was sure you'd have bought one in this latest shambles. Every time I see someone from your mob, lying at the side of the road, I've had to stop and see if was you.'

'You silly old sod,' Jack sobbed as he ran his fingers through his brothers hair. 'Remember me, I've got to live to marry an ugly woman.' He didn't know why he had thought of the gypsy woman's curse at that moment. It brought him up short. 'Acky copped one in his leg. I had to leave him in a culvert about an hour's walk down the road.

'Poor old Acky, he always would do anything to avoid walking.'

Jack laughed hollowly, 'Yes,' he agreed. 'He always was a lucky sod, he's probably tucked up safe and sound in one of Franco's jails by now. You got to envy him.'

Tommy sniffed. he could have been laughing. 'You're right, as I said I'm surprised that you're still alive. Mum and Dad haven't heard from you for months.'

'You've heard from them? I've not had a letter since I came here.'

'They say they write. I had a letter a couple of days ago. They forwarded a letter from Katherine. They told me to look out for you. It seems you've been a naughty boy.'

'What do you mean 'naughty boy'? Katherine who?'

'Katherine Hartwell. You probably don't remember her. You should be asking about Miriam.'

'Miriam, Miriam Rabinovitz?'

Tommy nodded. 'She's been to see Mum, trying to find out about you. It seems that you're about to become a daddy. The way that Mum describes it, it seems that it's going to be very soon. Who knows, it might already be here.' Tommy laughed. 'Poor little bastard, I just hope it doesn't have its mother's nose and its father's ears.'

'Oh shit, Tom what am I going to do?' Jack cried out.

Tommy shrugged, 'be like me and just hope that this war goes on for a long time and we both finish up like Acky, dead in a ditch.'

Where the blow came from, Jack never knew. He felt it start in the pit of his stomach. By the time it reached the end of his arm, it was travelling like a mortar shell. His fist exploded in his brother's face. Tommy staggered back, tripped over the bumper of the truck and fell, sprawling in the dust.

It was all totally confused in Jack's brain, as he moved forward even he didn't know if he was going to kick his brother's ribs in or pick him up.

He never found out. The awfully familiar sound of a rifle bolt being opened and closed made him freeze. Cautiously he turned his head towards the sound and found a little goblin of a man standing on the lorries running board with a rifle pointed at his head.

'Este bien, Miguel, me hermano' Tommy spluttered through bleeding lips and broken teeth.

Miguel obviously thought it perfectly normal for brothers to fight. He spat, took his lighted cigarette from behind his ear and drew in deeply. The rifle now pointed at the ground. Satisfied that Tommy wasn't going to die, he had lost interest in what his driver was up to. He couldn't drive and needed his Russian to stay fit and well to get him out of this devil's kitchen and back to the relative peace of the auto park.

'What the hell was that for?' Tommy demanded when he regained his feet. 'You've knocked one of me teeth out.'

'Oh I don't know Tom. You just had it coming. You've had it coming for years and you shouldn't have called my kid a bastard.'

Tommy shook his head and spat. 'Right, our kid, sorry. I was out of line. Never do it again, I promise.'

Jack nodded. For some stupid reason he was crying. And even more stupidly, Tom was crying too.

'Tom,' he wailed. 'I want to go home. I don't want

to die in this God forsaken country.'

'Oh shit,' Tommy cried and he smashed his fist into the front mudguard. It clanged like a bell. 'Come on Miguel, Arriba.'

'Where're you going Tom?' Jack hardly dared to ask as his brother swung himself up into the cab.

'I'm going to get Acky.'

'No Tom, don't, don't risk it. Let someone else go.'

Tommy jumped up onto the lorry's running board and swung the door open. 'Do you believe in magic?' he demanded looking down on his little brother.

'No,' Jack admitted, 'but I've been wrong before.'

'Haven't we all, but don't let Comrade Stalin hear you say that.' Tommy laughed. He climbed into the cab and slammed the door shut. 'I'm not letting Acky duck out of this war that easy. If we can't go home, then he doesn't go either.' The great Russian diesel engine boomed into life and Jack's shout of protest was lost in its roar.

Habit made Jack turn for his rifle and pack before beginning to chase across the field after the lorry as it turned then lurched towards the road.

'And where do you think you're going, boyo?' A dark figure emerged from amongst the gathering gloom in the Olive grove.

Jack couldn't see him clearly, but he recognised the voice. It was the sodding Welshman from the road. 'My brother's driving with the camions. I'm going back up the road with him to show him where we left comrade Ackfield.'

'Sorry comrade, you're needed here, just tell him where to look. I'm making you a section leader. I'm putting you in charge of those five Spanish lads over there.' He pointed to a small knot of boys standing self-consciously out in the open. 'get 'em under cover, keep them together and keep them alive for as long as you can.

About half an hour later, Jack heard a lone lorry out on the dark road. It was driving out of the West, racing down the dying rays of daylight, heading for the coast. The driver leant on his horn as he ran, at break neck speed, down the incline, past the vineyards and olive groves where the soldiers had made their camp.

Jack felt that he had been able to hear the throb of the engine for minutes before anyone else had lifted their head and taken notice. He crouched low against his olive tree, waiting to see if it were friend or foe. When he was sure it was safe, that the noise was on the road and not in the air, he rushed out into the open. He raised his fist in the air in salute and gave a great cheer as the silhouette of the lorry thundered past with the outline of men hanging all over it, like presents on a Christmas tree. All around him others appeared to cheer. From nowhere, from everywhere, the strains of *The Internationale* broke out and he sang like he'd never sung before.

The machine gunners covering the road, cocked their guns and waited for the order to open fire and stop the lorry. If it came, they didn't hear it over the singing and cheering, so the camion passed through.

A great weight lifted off Jack's shoulders. 'Come on you lot of silly buggers,' he said to his uncomprehending section who had followed him out into the open. He could hear the drone of aircraft again. 'Get back undercover.'

They laughed and chattered as if it were all a great big game and he were a hero, but didn't object as he pushed them back into the cover of the olive trees.

Chapter 23

The Times Correspondent July 1938
Barcelona

There was only light bombing activity last night. The authorities report that a force of Nationalist bombers was driven off. The aircraft failed to reach their target and only minor damage was caused.

'Paddy.' The C.O.'s voice came roaring down the branca. With the same effect as an artillery attack, it shattered the hot insect-humming peace of the afternoon and the men put their heads hard down against the earth. There was some sort of panic on and they didn't want to be chosen to become part of it.

Paddy Doyle rose unwillingly from his patch of shade at the side of the gully and, out of habit, stooped down as he walked towards the pile of boxes and branches from where the call came. They formed a small compound, the entrance of the shallow cave dug into the bank of the dried up stream, which was now serving as battalion H.Q.

It took a moment or two for his eyes to become accustomed to the gloom. There were no embarrassing foreigners or Party apparatchiks visiting the battalion, so he didn't feel the need to salute. Sam obviously didn't expect one. He shoved a sheet of paper into his lieutenant's hand. The ribbon on the typewriter, which had produced it, was so worn that the words were hardly legible and Paddy moved back towards the bright sunlight of the entrance to read it.

Sam saved him the effort. 'It's from Harry in London,' he said. 'It's pretty routine, but if you read between the lines, it looks like he's put some stuff for us on a ship called the Baltic Queen from Liverpool; parcels, letters and the like. I've just had a phone message from our people on the coast to say that the Captain sends his regards. I want you to go down and collect the stuff.'

'What pick them up from the Commissariat when they've been cleared?' Paddy queried. 'That'll be days yet.'

Sam rubbed his hand over his stubbly chin. 'No,' he said. 'Take a lorry and a couple of reliable lads and collect them off the dock.'

Paddy raised an eyebrow. It was a strict order that all imported material destined to the Brigade had to be vetted by Customs first. They would pass anything onto the Brigade's Central Commissariat who would distribute it to the appropriate Battalion.

'Harry doesn't say anything definite, you can't be certain who reads these things, but he wants us to see the Captain. He will release whatever he's got, to us, personally.'

Paddy raised both eyebrows. This was highly irregular.

'It's O K,' Sam blustered a little and Paddy could see that he was on the defensive. 'Harry says that it's all personal stuff. Parcels, letters for the lads with a few treats mixed in. The usual stuff, you know.' Sam hadn't really meant to try to keep his political commissar in the dark. Paddy was too sharp for that anyway. It was just that he could be very starchy when it came to regulations and he didn't like breaking them. They were the authority of the Party in military matters in Paddy's eyes.

Leaning forward, he said 'I want you to keep this under your hat, Paddy, but there's a consignment of ten thousand Woodbines with the parcels. And I want to make sure that they don't get lost along the way. With what we've got coming, this is not a time for sharing.'

Paddy nodded his understanding. He would never admit that anyone in the Spanish Republican bureaucracy was corrupt. On the other hand, there were the secret Fascists. Sometimes things got so fouled up that Paddy suspected that there were a few Franco supporters at the International Brigade headquarters. Also, ten thousand good quality English cigarettes were better currency than gold. Such a prize might even tempt their Spanish brothers in arms

Paddy took off his beret and ran his fingers through his greying hair. 'You know, Sam, I've got to go to Mataro anyway. Perhaps I'll take a section with me for a bit of leave. We can do any other little jobs that need doing while we're there.'

Sam smiled and nodded. 'You're right Paddy, the lads deserve a few hours off duty and no one can really object.'

'No,' Paddy agreed, 'not at all. We've done it

before and no-one said anything.'

'Today,' Sam said in a tone, which implied an order.

'Today,' Paddy agreed. Forgetting himself for a moment, he saluted before hurrying out.

'Jack, Ted, Roy,' Paddy barked as he strode through the elongated camp towards his shelter. 'Report to the lorry park in a quarter of an hour. Full kit and ammunition; on the double.'

There was a soft chuckle from those not chosen. These sorts of details had the habit of being dangerous.

'We're going into town' Paddy added.

Ten minutes later, the three who had been chosen for the trip, ran back down the trench, their pockets stuffed with every peseta that they could borrow. The thought of a two-day trip into town, spread broad smiles across their faces and they responded to the whistles and jeers from the rest of the Company with V signs. Two days without training; without guard duty; without route marches in the blazing sun and with a chance to visit a cantina, look at the senoritas and not have anybody try to shoot you, was close to heaven.

Roy drove with Paddy in the cab, Jack, Ted and Pablo, the interpreter, made themselves comfortable in the open back and looked at the rugged countryside with a more tolerant eye than when they had to march over it.

It was late afternoon by the time they reached the dock gates and the sun was already dipping into the mountains through which they had just come. Paddy leapt out and, with Pablo, hurried into the Dock office to get their papers stamped.

There were always delays at times like this. The customs officials argued with the dock administrators, who consulted the dock guards as to who was to stamp which form. Luckily it was getting towards the end of their shift and they were anxious to be out of the port area before the bombing started. It took less than an hour for them to be cleared onto the dockside and directed to the quay, where the Baltic Queen was tied up.

Roy drove cautiously through the flurry of activity continuing along the quayside. Despite the gathering gloom, nervous captains shouted at the Stevedores to hurry up. They wanted to steal out into the night on the midnight tide and try to miss the bombers and any lurking submarines.

As they drew level with a big Russian freighter, a docker stepped out in front of them and stopped them with an imperious hand. Out of the darkening sky, a big black shape like a huge crow hovered overhead. A crane was lifting a light tank out of the hold of the ship. It delicately placed the black metal monster on the stone wharf in front of them.

Without another sign, the docker turned his back and walked away, allowing them to drive on. They didn't speak, but watched the bustle around them with mixed emotion. It was wonderful that the Soviet Union was pumping aid into the beleaguered Republic. It gave them a fighting chance against Italian tanks and German guns, but on the other hand, there was an ominous build-up of armaments in the roads and squares they had driven through and that meant trouble.

The Baltic Queen was already battened down and ready for sea when they arrived at her mooring. 'Roy, you and Pablo stand guard by the lorry,' Paddy ordered. He wouldn't need an interpreter on board and he would rather this business was dealt with by the Brits. 'Jack and Ted, you come with me.'

A young lad was leaning on the rail at the top of the gangway as they hurried up. He was mildly curious about the three Spanish soldiers climbing up to the ship particularly as they were armed and shouted a warning. No-one on the dock could speak English so he didn't need to be polite. 'Spiks on the gang plank with guns, Captain. You'd better hide the booze.'

'And you'd better learn to watch your mouth, Sonny,' Paddy said quietly, 'it might get you into trouble.'

'Eeh, you're English,' the boy exclaimed, his jaw

dropping.

'No, I'm Irish,' Paddy snarled. 'Now, where's the Captain? He's expecting us.'

'He's checking the forward cable locker. I'll get the steward to tell him you're here.' He said and then shouted 'Chinky, some people to see the Captain, tell him, I've sent them up to his day cabin.'

Turning back to them, he pointed to an iron ladder. 'Up, there.'

Jack gave him a big wink as he walked past. It was wonderful to hear fresh English voices. There had been a bloke called Reg Tucker at the dairy, who used to do the Stoke Newington round. He came from Bootle and this broad Liverpudlian accent tugged at Jack's heart, reminding him of home.

For a moment, he thought of ducking into a dark corner and hiding until the ship sailed. He would be home in a week, delivering milk, safe and sound. Ted came up the ladder behind him, snapping at his heels, anxious to get up to the Captain's cabin. There might be goodies there, a real drink, a cup of tea with sugar, beer, English cigarettes. 'Hurry up Jack,' he called.

'If he were going to desert, then they'd all have to go together,' he thought. It was possible that Roy and Ted, even Pablo, had had enough of the war, but he'd have to shoot Paddy first. He would certainly shoot them, if they tried to leave. Paddy had always said that he was there to the end; victory or death. With a sigh, Jack hitched up his gun and hurried up onto the bridge and the Captain's day room, which lay beyond.

A young man, in his mid twenties clambered up the companionway behind them. He was smartly dressed, wearing a collar, shirt and tie and sporting a new Trilby, though his jacket and trousers were smudged with dust. They thought he must be some passenger escaping the rigours of the Republic.

'We're waiting for the captain,' Paddy said feeling that some explanation of their presence was necessary.

The young man nodded and smiled. 'Yes,' he said, 'I've been expecting you. I thought you might be here earlier. In fact, you nearly missed us. We're off in a couple of hours.'

'You're the skipper?' Paddy asked, the disbelief evident in his voice. 'You don't look like a sailor.'

A broad grin spread across the man's face. 'I've been for a run ashore,' he said. 'You've got to dress up for the ladies. They sort of expect it. After all we're not all Captain Ahab,' he said and then added, as an afterthought. 'Anyway, you wouldn't get the old timers on this run. It's far too dangerous.'

Fishing a great bunch of keys out of his pocket, he went to the locker under the map table. Opening the door, he indicated three large brown paper parcels. 'There you are lads,' he said, 'it's Christmas.'

Jack bent down and pulled the first out. 'Paddy, it's been opened,' he exclaimed and then saw the exposed contents. 'Bloody hell, it's full of fags; Woodbines.'

Paddy spun round to confront the Captain.

'I can't watch them all the time,' he said with a shrug 'and they're good enough lads. They only took enough for the voyage. Don't begrudge them, they'll have earned them before they finish this trip.'

So much for the solidarity of the workers, Paddy thought, but he knew that there was nothing he could do about the missing cigarettes. He scowled and spat on the floor to show his disgust at a crime. He thought it would rate with stealing from beggars, but he said nothing.

The Captain laughed bitterly at the eloquent gesture. 'You're wrong, mate.' He said. 'Your lot are all volunteers; you chose to come here. So did I, but these lads,' a vague inclination of his head indicated his crew. 'They go where the work is, they get almost nothing for risking their necks. You should be grateful it was only a few of the fags. They might have taken the lot.'

'If you say so,' Paddy muttered, unconvinced and he indicated the room about them with its drinks cabinet and easy chairs. 'It looks comfortable enough to me.'

'Well that shows all you know. It's bloody dangerous here, believe me, and that's why I'm not offering you any hospitality. I'm shoving off as soon as its dark and I'd advise you to do the same. Barcelona docks are not a good place to be when the Ities come calling. And they come calling every night.'

Accepting the lack of hospitality with the same bad grace as they accepted the loss of their precious cigarettes, they allowed themselves to be shepherded back down onto deck. Looking over the rail, onto the quay, they could see that the gloom was still full of shadowy figures. Paddy draped his jacket over the broken pack. Sam had been right, it was a good job they had come themselves and not relied on the usual channels. With an open package like this, flaunting its contents to the world, it was unlikely that any of the Woodbines would have made it off the dock.

With a nod to his men that they were going, he thanked the Captain curtly.

Instinctively they moved as if they were going out on patrol into no man's land. Ted walked ahead rifle at the ready. As he walked down the gangplank, his eyes roved ceaselessly through the shadows. Jack unslung his rifle from his shoulders and stepped in tight behind Paddy and watched their rear.

'Wait a minute,' the Captain called. A Lascar seaman came running up the deck towards them. The captain took a hessian sack from him, and dumped it on top of Paddy's jacket. 'It's not much,' he said, 'some tea, sugar and the like. Call it fair exchange.'

Paddy's nod had lost the stiff anger of the moments before. 'Good luck,' he said.

'And you,' replied the Captain.

With the coming of night, there was a steady flow of people hurrying out of the gate. They joined the stream and no one stopped them.

'Where are we going?' Roy demanded as he sped out towards the broad boulevard, leading away from the sea.

'I've no idea,' Paddy admitted. 'Find somewhere to park. We'll sleep in the lorry and go on to Mataro tomorrow.

'How about there?' Roy enquired, indicating a square off the main road. The light from a little pavement cantina flooded across the cobbles until the trunks of dark orange trees cut it into shreds. Inside a guitar was playing and the music spilled out into the night. 'If I put the truck under the trees, it'll be out of sight and we can have a drink and keep an eye on it at the same time.'

Paddy considered for a moment. 'OK' he said. 'You've been driving all afternoon, you deserve one. You, Ted and Pablo go and have a drink. Me and Jack'll sit in the lorry. We'll swap over in an hour.'

Jack thought that it was a crime to have to roll a cigarette from the harsh Spanish tobacco in his pouch while they were sitting on thousands of proper cigarettes, but even though there was a parcel already open and no-one would miss a few more packs, he didn't seriously think of taking one.

Jack noticed how Paddy's hands were shaking as he made his cigarette, even worse than his own. He said nothing, there was no point. He waited until Paddy had run his tongue along the edge to seal the roll before Jack flicked his lighter into life and both leaned forward to light up, out of habit, masking the light with their hands.

They never did light those cigarettes. A boy, blowing a whistle and banging a saucepan came dashing out of a narrow alley into the square, suddenly filling it with a cacophony of noise. From nowhere, the square was full of people milling about, some dashing out of houses, some dashing in. Shutters were slamming shut. Men were shouting, women screaming, children crying. Then, almost as quickly as it had begun, the noise petered out into almost quiet. The only sound was the throb, throb, throb of aircraft engines, high up and coming in from the East.

Without a word of command, Jack had jumped out of the lorry with Paddy close behind. Roy, Ted and Pablo sent their table and chairs flying across the pavement and came sprinting across the cobbles to meet in the uncertain safety under the truck.

From somewhere behind them, near to the docks there was a gigantic bang. Everything in the square, that was loose, rattled as if there were a tube train going underneath. Before things had settled and were still, there was a brilliant flash, a roar and the ground shuddered as a second bomb landed in a street beyond the cantina.

'One, two, three, four,' someone was counting. They got no further. A tall, old house on the other side of the square evaporated like a brilliant orange firework. Then there was a roar and the ground bucked, the lorry jumped about on its springs and there was a rain of masonry, glass and trees. And then, for an instant, there was silence again.

In a gradual crescendo came the crackling of burning timber and then the crying of a baby and the shrieks of a woman. Before Jack and the others had even scrambled out from their hiding place and gained their feet, the sounds were cut brutally short. They all ran frantically towards the burning house. A few feet from the door, they crashed into wall of heat that there was no getting through.

A mad man, screaming to God and his neighbours to help, tried to run into the fire. His neighbours pushed him to the ground and stood on him. There was nothing else that they or all the others who had run with them could do. In stony silence, they watched the stricken building burn. No one came out.

Without a glance at any of the others, the Brits turned away, they walked back to their parked lorry, climbed aboard and drove away into the night.

It was only a short run up the coast from Barcelona to Mataro, but it was a journey between two worlds. The Catalan capital was busy. It shrugged off the bombs, which fell every night and tried to get on with life. Trying to forget there was a war on.

Mataro was a little fishing village to the north. It hadn't quite come to terms with the birth of the Republic let alone the war. Life there was much as it had been for centuries. None of the Brigaders had been there before and didn't know their way about the town. They came in towards the centre by an eccentric route, Pablo telling Roy to turn left or right, almost as the whim took him. As The IB truck squeezed through these narrow streets, they were almost empty and there was nothing to slow them down. An occasional window opened on the excuse of shaking a broom, so some old lady inside could catch a glimpse of the activity below. In scattered patches of black shade an old man would be sitting on a chair, smoking a cheroot, feigning indifference to the traffic, watching the world go by.

Turning a corner, they moved from calm into chaos. The new street, no wider than any of the others, contained the hospital. A convoy of, about ten ambulances were drawn up on the shady side of the street. Their drivers were congregated by the lead vehicle, in a noisy cluster. Orderlies were scurrying up and down, opening doors or closing those left open by the man before.

'We're here,' Paddy announced 'Park over there'. He pointed to a place where the road widened between the corners of two buildings to form a little square with a little shade. 'Jack, pass me the open parcel. We can take them in with us for any of the English lads who are here. You and Ted stay with the lorry to guard the rest. Roy, Pablo, you come with me.

Jack passed the cigarettes through the small window at the back of the cab and Paddy wrapped them in his jacket. 'Can't I come in with you, Paddy?' Jack pleaded. It was too much to hope that either Tommy or Acky could be here, but they might be, or someone might know where they were.

Paddy understood. 'Ok,' he agreed. 'Roy, you stay with Ted. We won't be long.'

The crumbling white stucco on the walls of the hospital threw the early morning heat back into the street like the open door of a furnace, but as they walked into the gloomy entrance tunnel, it became much cooler.

There was a nurse sitting at a table in the shade.

Paddy waved his papers at her and stumbled through an explanation of their presence in broken Spanish. The nurse laughed and shook her head in incomprehension, but she was busy and waved them through. 'Ingles,' she shouted after them pointing beyond them, into the courtyard. Jack didn't know if she was directing them to some other checkpoint or telling them that there were more English in the courtyard.

If there were, it was difficult to spot them, the light was brilliant making them squint and then they could see that every shady spot was packed with the injured. The little colonnade which ran around the dusty courtyard had serried ranks of men on stretchers lined up like keys on a piano, with the black notes representing a space for the attendants to dance between them. In each patch of shade thrown by a palm or orange tree sat a little group of the walking wounded.

'Hola, Paddy; Jack, over here.' A man, sitting with his back to a palm tree, shouted and waived to attract their attention. When he realised that he had been seen, he forced himself on to his feet with the aid a walking stick and the shoulder of a companion.

'Harry,' they called, recognising Harry Piat from No.2 Company. 'How's it going?' As he walked across, Jack acknowledged the group around Harry's tree, with a nod. A couple were strangers to him, but most of them were British Battalion and though he didn't know their names, he'd seen them around.

'Not too bad, not too bad,' Harry said. 'What you doing here?'

'Paddy had some business in town, so we thought we'd drop in and say hello,' said Jack. 'We brought you some fags.'

'Bloody marvellous,' a man Jack recognised from Albacete sighed, 'I'd murder me granny for a decent smoke.

'Let your granny live forever,' said Paddy with a laugh, throwing him a pack of Woodbines and then started to distribute packets to the others. Two were obviously strangers to Paddy as well and he hesitated in front of them.

'That's Kieren Otterburn,' Harry introduced him and the tone in his voice explained that they were his friends, 'He's Mac-Paps, lucky bugger got his foot blown off at Brunette. And the other one,' he nodded to the man who was as black as the shade, 'That's Otis Phillips, he's a Yank. Got one in the head at Belchite.

Paddy tossed each of them a packet. He had six or seven packets left. Every eye in the courtyard was on him. He didn't have it in his heart to put them back in his pocket and so tossed them to Jack. 'Dish 'em out,' he said, 'as far as they'll go.' I just need to pop into the office.

It didn't take long to get rid of them and when he returned to the British lads, Harry had only just lit up and was still luxuriating in his first deep drag. ''We're lucky you caught us,' he said with slow satisfaction. 'A couple of hours and we'll be out of here. The gossip is we're being moved to a hospital up north, near the frontier and then we're on our way home.'

Jack snorted derisively, 'I know what I'd rather have between twenty Woodbines and a ticket home. I don't suppose anybody's come across a bloke from No. 1 Company called Acky Ackfield or an Englishman from the autopark called Tommy Sutton?'

Someone said that they knew Acky, but hadn't seen him. No one gave a sign of recognition of Tommy's name. Jack shrugged, 'The word is that they were in one of the hospitals up north, maybe the one you're going to. If you do come across them, Tommy's my brother and Acky's my mate. Tell them I'm still alive and was asking after them?'

'Certainly,' Harry said, 'but why don't you look into the office, there's an English nurse in there at the moment and she's got a list of everyone who's been through here. She might be able to tell you something.'

'Is it O K if I go and ask, Paddy?' Jack asked as the lieutenant returned.

'Yeh, but don't be too long, we're going to have to be going soon, if we want to be back by dark.'

The things in this war which frightened Jack most were mortars. You could hear the artillery, hear planes, but so often you didn't hear them fired and you couldn't hear the shells coming. There was just a sudden big bang out of nowhere.

Walking into the office was just like that. Bang! There was Peggy in the arms of a fat foreign uniform.

As he walked in, Peggy leapt away like a guilty school-girl. 'Get out,' the officer shouted in such a guttural accent that Jack hardly recognised the words. It was the uniform rather than the order, which drove Jack back out into the sun.

Jack's reaction to an order, which had been drilled into him for nearly a year, was to obey and deny reason. It was the German political commissar who made a tactical error. He followed Jack into the courtyard to emphasise his displeasure. 'Soldier's do not enter the rooms of officers without permission. You have no permission.'

From where he stood, the inside of the office was the blackest shadow and Jack could see nothing, but Peggy too, took a step forward into the half light at the threshold.

Jack frowned. She looked frightened. Suddenly he glanced down and saw that his hands were shaking again. As he looked back at her, over the head of the pompous little man, so draped in gold braid that he looked like a cinema commissionaire, he realised why she was so scared. She could see that Jack was going to kill him. Slowly deliberately, he unslung his rifle. With his finger on the trigger he flicked the butt under his arm.

Peggy screamed 'no Jack,' then buried her face in her hands. It was Paddy's restraining hand resting gently on his arm which stopped him. 'It's not worth it lad,' he said quietly and so deep was the hush which had fallen on the courtyard that the words bounced around the walls for everyone to hear.

'I shall have you shot,' The Commissar shrieked in a voice as high pitched as Peggy's. 'Mutiny,' he screamed. 'Trotskyist, Revisionist, Fascist.' As he shouted, he dragged at the holster on his patent leather belt and drew a little silver automatic pistol.

Like the sound of so many breaking twigs there was the rattle of rifle bolts. They all turned and behind them a dozen men, some sitting up on stretchers, some leaning against trees and walls with their crutches at their feet, had their guns aimed at the little group in the corner of the courtyard.

'No, comrades,' the German shouted, 'do not shoot him, the Party will deal with him as they deal with all traitors.'

'Comrade,' Paddy felt his shoulders slump. He felt very tired. This war had gone on too long and cost too much. 'Comrade,' he repeated quietly, 'I don't think it's Jack they mean to shoot.'

The thought that the common soldiers would dare to threaten him, a Party apparatchik, had not occurred to him, but a look at the men's bleak faces convinced him that Paddy was right. 'Order them to put their guns down,' he snapped, but fear cracked the words.

Paddy looked back at the cold-faced men behind him. 'They will not listen, Comrade. I think it would be wise for you to put your gun away. You couldn't do much harm with that little thing anyway.'

'You cannot tell me what to do,' The Commissar raged.

'No Comrade, I merely advise.'

The little German looked from his pistol to Jack's blazing eyes and then to the men beyond. He took the advice. 'I want you to take the names of all the men who lifted their guns against me,' he growled in a low voice, not wanting to be heard across the court, 'including this one.' He nodded contemptuously at Jack. 'I want him put in the front of the next attack. I do not want him to survive. That is an order, lieutenant.'

Jack heard. He laughed. 'Charlie Chaplin here, has ordered me to be put at the front of the next attack so I get killed,' he said loudly, so that the men behind could hear.

They laughed as well.

'Jack,' Peggy's voice was gruff with terror, 'he can do it.'

'Oh, you stupid cow.' Jack was angry again. 'It doesn't matter what this clown says. It's going to happen anyway.' He looked around at his gaunt comrades. 'We are the Quince Brigada, we are the best of the best. We are the Brigada Inglese. We're always at the bleeding front. We're always getting killed. Remember all the lads from Tottenham, well me and Skinny are the only ones left. And after this next battle?' he shrugged his shoulders.

The commissar could not resist defending his countrymen. 'The German's are the best,' he said puffing up with pride. 'We were first in Spain; we are the first in every battle.'

'Used to be,' a voice called out from the crowd with an accent which mirrored the Commissar,' Now they are all dead and we are left with cripples and fat little clowns with pop guns.'

And that was it. Paddy glanced at his watch. 'Time to go,' he muttered. 'Get these fags back to the lads. They'll be dying for a smoke.'

'Yeh, yeh,' Jack agreed. It was like the cinema. They had reached the point where they had come in, and, as if Peggy and the German commissar were just figures on the flickering silver screen, he turned away and headed for the archway, which led back onto the road. So what if Tommy or Acky had been through here? It didn't really matter. At least they would be safe out of it. And what if Peggy was kissing a Bosch commissar. He knew what she was like. He'd read her report on him and the others. What the hell, he'd think about it after the battle.

The evening was already on them as they turned off the coast road and headed back into the mountains and Roy had to squint into the sinking sun as it set the world on fire. Pablo sat in the cab as well, his feet up on the dashboard, quietly strumming his guitar and singing sad songs of the far off south, which he would never see again. Red wine did not go to his head like those of the foreigners. Anyway, what did they know of La Mancha, of hot air like molten glass, of the brave bulls and the glory of death?

In the back of the truck, Jack, Paddy and Ted were singing and drinking, drinking and singing. At first Paddy had led them through *The Internationale* and the *Song of the Fifteenth*. By the third bottle, Paddy was even further away from the Aragon than Pablo, far, far away in the north, singing of a different war and not caring that Jack and Ted didn't know the words. Here they were the enemy and could not join in.

It was the song about death on the Jarama River which brought them back to Spain. By the fifth bottle, they were all so drunk that they forgot about distant places and sad songs of death.

Hanging onto the rocking canvass of the roof, Paddy hurled the last empty bottle at the line of heavy guns crouching under the olive trees. What did he care? 'We are the Quince Brigada,' he bellowed out into the countryside.

They followed with the chorus

Viva la Quince Brigada,
rumba la rumba la rumba la.
Viva la Quince Brigada,
rumba la rumba la rumba la
que nos cubrirá de gloria
Ay Carmela! Ay Carmela!
que se ha cubierto de gloria,
Ay Carmela! Ay Carmela!
and the lorry passed on into the West.

Chapter 24

POST CARD

Dear Mr and Mrs Sutton

Just a brief note to tell you that I saw Jack yesterday as he passed through the hospital where I am working. He's not too badly hurt and hopefully he will be home with you soon.

Yours sincerely

Peggy Watkins

The common cry of 'avion' began among the Spanish machine gunners up on the hill side and was echoed among the crowd below, 'avion' 'aeroplano' 'planes'. In the babel of languages, the meaning was clear, even to the newest recruit. There was a stampede and when, a few minutes later, the three Italian Caprioni bombers flew over the vineyard, the litter of clothes and equipment was indistinguishable from the trampled vines.

The throb of their motors had hardly faded from the hot summer air, when voices up and down the hill began shouting. 'Right Lads, let's be having you. Forward. Avanti.' And then the artillery opened fire.

'Oh, sweet Jesus, I'm hit.' The words were the first sound to break the silence after the shrapnel finished raining down. Then the rifle fire started again. The sharp cracks of the fusillade merged into the sound of a hundred football rattles supporting the opposing sides. Bullets whistled and hummed like angry insects as they zipped through the shimmering air, nesting in trees or the bodies of men, or flying away to be lost forever.

Jack ran fast and low and then dived for cover like a rugby player going for the line, though it was a game he'd never played. Safe among the dusty rocks, he slowly lifted an eye above the rim of the rock he was huddled behind and saw a prone figure ahead of him. His arms and legs were moving as if he were desperately trying to crawl the ten yards which would take him out of the sun's spotlight and into the tenuous safety of a ruined wall; the memory of a building wrecked by age rather than artillery fire, but he wasn't moving.

A bullet slammed into Jack's protective boulder and a sliver of stone sliced his cheek. As he jerked his head back, bright stars of blood sprayed across the grey green leaves of the Rosemary, tingeing the lavender flowers scarlet. He didn't look up again. There were quite enough scars across his face already.

In a brief lull in the firing, Taffy's sad lilting voice called from below him on the hill side. 'Paddy, keep your head down, boyo. Lie still, you're just drawing fire,'

Jack risked a second glance. The man who was down was Paddy Doyle. He had heard the call and now lay perfectly still.

'Come on lads, let's give it one more try.' Lennie's harsh cockney grated after Taffy's sing song tones. Now that Paddy was shot, Lennie was next in line of command and took control. Their orders were to clear the Moors off the crest of the hill and secure the left flank of the main attack. If they couldn't shift the buggers off this hillside, the Nationalist sharpshooters would pour enfilading fire and cut down the Republicans on Hill 681 like grass.

Looking back over his shoulder, Jack could see the fold in the ground where Lennie was lying. He saw him push himself up out of his security, his rifle thrust forward and tautened his muscles to follow.

Even as Lennie moved there was a fusillade from the crest of the hill. It was impossible to pick out which shot cut him down, but he slumped back behind his shielding bank with his shoulder turned to sausage meat. No-one else moved. By the common consent of the comrades, the counter attack was over. They had come too far, lost too many and could do no more.

'You hit bad, Lennie?' Taffy called.

'Pretty bad,' Lennie replied between gritted teeth.

'See if you can get yourself down the hill and out of the way' Taffy's voice sounded more mournful than ever. There was the sound of rolling rocks and black oaths behind them as Lennie slid away. Then Taffy groaned, 'Oh cachu; I guess I'm in command.'

Dreading the answer, Jack called out, 'do you want to give it another go Taff.?'

'No, boyo. We're near enough the top, to make 'em keep their heads down. Leave it for a while. You never know, they might get some more men up here. There were guns moving back down the road when we came by. We could get some artillery support or they might get a machine gun set up somewhere to support us. Dig in and hold.'

'By the God I don't believe in, I love you Taffy,' Jack mouthed. They could hear the ceaseless roar of the guns from over the next hill and see the dust in the air. He knew, like they all knew, that there were no more men, no guns to spare for this little skirmish on this God forsaken hill. On their maps, none of the hills had names, this one probably didn't even have a number. Cautiously, he pulled the bayonet off the muzzle of his rifle. He used the spike to stab the ground and move thin soil, rocks, twigs, clumps of grass from under and around him and piled them in front. Inch by inch, he sank into the ground, like a flat fish settling on the sea bed, building temporary safety around himself. He broke a few branches off the shrubs growing all about, to improve his line of sight. The smell of their aromatic leaves in the hot sun was like the garden for the blind the council had built in Tottenham. That was in the middle of a cemetery too.

From the security of his own position, Taffy carried

a brief roll call. It was hard to say who was still there, among the Spanish lads, but amongst the Brits. Only Paddy and Lennie didn't answer their name.

Once he stopped digging, Jack turned his mind back to thoughts of duty. After the first salvo of shells had cut down the Spanish Lad with buck teeth, the others had very wisely gone to ground at the bottom of the hill. He had shouted at them to get up and follow him, but because he was shouting in English at the same time as diving from one scrap of cover to the next. They had decided that this was a good time not to understand.

He allowed himself a little smile. Country boys they might be, but they had a lot more sense than him. They were safe for the moment and he didn't have to worry about them.

He, on the other hand, had been charging through the scrub, hot on Paddy's heels when the last shell burst. Now, unfortunately, he had to be the furthest man up the hill who was not wounded or dead. He would have to be the spotter for the remains of the Company.

With a deep sigh of resignation, he refitted his bayonet, laid his rifle over the dusty parapet and once more, lifted his head that smallest fraction which would bring his eyes above the lip of his shallow trench.

There was a rustle among the underbrush above his head. He saw the flash of a dirty white cloak and the splash of a bright red fez. For an instant a Moorish soldier was silhouetted against the sky. He had gone before Jack could raise his rifle. 'Taffy, up to the right, they're moving down the hill,' he shouted a warning. There was a reassuring clatter of rifle bolts to show there were still enough of them left after the murderous barrage to hold the Fascists for a while.

Close and to the left, a Liverpool accent called out to the wounded man. 'They're coming, Paddy, get rid of your hat.' Looking back, Jack could see the speaker's legs sticking out from behind the trunk of an olive tree. Though he recognised the accent, he couldn't identify the voice. Parched lips and a dry throat distorted it beyond recognition. For the first time for over an hour, Jack remembered how thirsty he was. He had not eaten since they left camp before dawn and he had finished his water before this scouting patrol turned into a counter attack to dislodge the Moors.

A few yards behind him was an olive tree with a thick trunk and dense black shade, it beckoned him with a promise of cool security. He would have to break cover to reach it, but it wasn't far. He turned away to face up the hill. He wasn't going to be the first to fall back without an order. 'Throw the fucking hat away Paddy,' he shouted.

Paddy's hand crept out towards his black beret. It was his pride and joy, representing all he believed in, the Party, the Revolution and the Spring of a new age where the workers would seize all that was rightfully theirs. Jack watch the hand lie across it. It had stopped trying to move. The scouser to his left could obviously see it too. 'Paddy, it's only a fucking hat. I'll get you another one.'

It was strange that they could speak so clearly without giving anything away to the enemy. There were probably no more than a hundred or so Brits. left fighting in Spain and about a dozen of them, alive or dead, were on this bloody hill side. More than three quarters of No.1 company were Spanish now and couldn't understand English. And half of the enemy could only speak Italian or Moroccan. But what did it matter that no one could understand anyone else? Jack thought. There was no quarter asked or given in the Aragon.

Mercy was an oversight, sometimes the wounded were over run and, at the end, were gathered in with all the rest of the broken corn. If the Fascists continued their advance down the hill there would be no such oversight for a political commissar. If they saw Paddy's hat, with its tell-tale brass flashes, beside his crippled body, they would shoot him out of hand.

Paddy's hand tightened its hold and with a weak flop of his arm, the beret rolled a few yards. It was not far enough to be safe, but Paddy could do no more.

'Oh shit,' Jack muttered to himself and without giving time for second thoughts, he leapt out of his scrape, ran, ducked, dived, rolled and scrambled into the cover of the ruined wall. Everyone was so astounded that not a shot had been fired in either attack or defence and there in his grasp was Paddy Doyle's hat.

'Well done Jack lad,' Taff called, 'Now keep your bloody head down, you silly sod; them Moors know just where you are.'

Jack meant to do just as he had been told, but he could hear the bushes above him thrashing under the weight of running men. 'They're coming.' he cried,

All fear, thirst, and thoughts of safety were washed away by adrenaline. Men lifted themselves above the security of their dugouts and brought their rifles to bear. There was a split second of vulnerability for the attacking soldiers as they climbed from their defences and stood against the sky. That smallest fraction of time was too long for most of them. The men down the hill were the best, the shock troops of the revolution. They had seen more battles than they had seen years. They were still alive because they were lucky and could shoot fast and straight. Within a minute twenty Moors and thirty Spaniards lay dead or dying on the crest of the hill and all the rest were as still.

The world was frozen in molten glass. The Brigaders couldn't retreat without revealing themselves to the snipers above and on the next hillside. The Fascists could not advance without taking unacceptable casualties and the artillery, all of it in fascist hands, could not fire without hitting its own side, the front lines were so close. The sun was past its peak, but slid so slowly towards the horizon that the shadows never seemed to move.

'Water. Agua, Wasser, L'eau,' The cries came from all around, up the hill and down, but all Jack could hear were Paddy's moans and his call for water.

Jack might possibly have been able to throw a canteen to where Paddy lay, but his was dry. As he let his mind dwell on water, he remembered how his swollen tongue was sticking to the roof of his mouth and how his puffed up lips were so brittle it hurt to breath. Perhaps he wouldn't have risked his water on a man who was probably going to die anyway.

In the precarious stalemate on the hill side, the minutes dragged agonisingly into hours. The cries for water faded away as the wounded died or drifted off into a blissful unconsciousness. Even those who were whole, sank into lethargy and remembered British lakes or Irish rivers.

Little broke the deadly monotony. On one occasion a wounded fascist, suddenly sat bolt upright, his face showing amazement at waking from a dream, then all light went out as the Brigaders shot him down. On another, Taffy called out, 'Bloody hell, I'm going to have to move. I'm dug into an ant's nest and they're eating me alive. Cover me lad's.' He wasn't running away and so everybody laughed. The sound of men, lying under the shadows of machine guns, convulsed with mirth, did more to keep the fascist's heads down than heavy artillery.

Painfully slowly, the shadows lengthened, and it became cooler as the March night came on. Jack began to wake from his dreaming, to shiver and miss the sun, to think of water and of safety. He looked up to where Paddy lay, wondering if he was still alive. Suddenly, this man who lived for the cause and the Party, the man who, a few days earlier, had sat with the comrades to explain the need to destroy the church, shouted aloud, 'Oh sweet Mary, Mother of God.' There was no call on Marx or Lenin for intercession for the commissar. The cry was so loud that the flies which crawled in his mouth and drank from the fountain of blood in his side, rose up in a black cloud.

Jack thought they looked like a soul rising into the cooling air. 'Hang on Paddy'. He lied through broken lips, 'It'll soon be dark and we'll come and get you.'

The flowers were beginning to close for the night, nothing moved and no one made a sound. The flies settled back on the warm earth. On a silent order, the living checked the dead and began to slip away down the hill, past the little farm, they had left just before dawn, down to the road where the lorries had brought them. Their breath hung in the air, like memories, as they limped away into the night. The moon came up to light their way into exile and they left Paddy lying out there among all their hopes and dreams. It was too dangerous to try to bury him there and no-one had the strength to spare to carry down a dead man

Not much more than twelve hours later, when Jack was charging up another hill, the lights went out for him. One moment he was scrabbling to get behind an olive tree, the next, he was on a train.

He woke up with that awful certainty that he had slept beyond his stop. He couldn't remember where he was going. He could be in Cambridge, out in the wilds of Essex or Hertfordshire, he could be anywhere. It was the movement that brought him back to Spain, this train didn't roar along like any English train. It jolted and juddered, swayed and wobbled through the night. And the smell. At first it smelled like a lavatory and then it stank like a hospital. He was lying down and, oh, there was such a pain in his head and shoulder.

The pain made him groan and the noise brought movement, just behind him, just out of his vision, but it hurt too much to try to move and see. For an instant he thought he was on Stamford Hill and had just been razored by the Blackshirts

'Are you all right?' a woman's voice asked quietly.

'Bloody hell,' he whimpered, 'I've been shot in the head. I'm blind.'

'It's the blackout, don't worry. Your head's all right,' the woman said, 'A bit of concussion, that's all. Your leg's a bit of a mess though, you were hit by shrapnel. The doctors stitched it up and splinted it. It should be OK, though you'll limp for a while.'

He reached down under the blanket to make sure the woman wasn't lying to him. Even though he couldn't feel it, his leg was still there.

'Where am I?' he asked

'You're on the ambulance train being evacuated back to the coast.'

'Who are you?'

'I'm nurse Duncan.'

'Am I going to live?'

It was nice to be able to give good news and there was a chuckle in her voice as she said. 'Oh, yes, you'll live.'

'And will I be going home?'

He felt her hand ruffle his hair, 'Yes,' she said, 'you'll be going home.'

'Thank God for that,' he muttered and surrendered to sleep.

Chapter 25

CENSORED BY P.O. BARCELONA

Dear Dad

I'm writing to you at Auntie Sue's because I've got bad news and you'll know best how to tell mum. Tommy was always her favourite and she's not going to take my news well.

The war's been quite hot here and this is the first chance I've had to write. I saw Tommy a few weeks ago and he told me that you never got any of the letters I wrote. I'm sorry because they were good letters, full of hope and the expectation of victory. I don't know how to write this letter, but its important that I try.

When I saw him he was **XXXXXXXXXXXXXXXX** *and he went back down the road to rescue Acky. I'm told he picked him and a bunch of wounded men out by* **XXXXXXXXXXXX** *and was taking them back to* **XXXXXXXXXXXXXXXXXXXX**. *I'm told that he didn't make it. A group of our lads who were* **XXXXXXXXXXXXXXXXXXX** *on that bit of the road say that they were bombed by the German fascist bastards. They say that Tommy was killed and* **XXX XXXXXXX** *buried him near* the river. They say they took his papers and personal possessions and handed them over to one of the American commissars.

I suppose it might be that I'm telling you something you already know. You might already have had official notification. You'll think me very hard when I say I've not shed a single tear for our Tom and you'll know how much I loved him, but life's cheap out here and who can say who will still be alive at the end of the day. There's not much hope left

xxxxxxxxxxxxxxxxxxxxxxxxxxxxxxx
xxxxxxxxxxxxxxxxxxxxxxxxxxxxxxx
xxxxxxxxxxxxxxxxxxxxxxxxxxxxxxx
xxxxxxxxxxxxxxxxxxxxxxxxxxxxxxx
xxxxxxxxxxxxxxxxxxxxxxxxxxxxxxx
xxxxxxxxxxxxxxxxxxxxxxxxxxxxxxx
xxxxxxxxxxxxxxxxxxxxxxxxxxxxxxx
xxxxxxxxxxxxxxxxxxxxxxxxxxxxxxx
xxxxxxxxxxxxxxxxxxxxxxxxxxxxxxx
xxxxxx

There is always hope, we hear stories of lads being reported dead and buried and they turn up so we must cross our fingers. If he's dead then at least you can tell Len. Ackfield that I hear that Acky is still alive. You don't have to tell him that he's supposed to be in a bad way. They say he's in a hospital away in the mountains in the North so

I doubt if I'll get the chance to see him **xxxxxx xxxxxxxxxxxxxxxxxxxxxxxxxxxx xxxxxxxxxxxxxxxxxxxxxxxxxxxx xxxxxxxxxxxxxxxxxxxxxxxxxxxx xxxxxxxxxxxxxxxxxxxxxxxxxxxx xxxxxxxxxxxxxxxxxxxxxxxxxxxx xxxxxxxxxxxxxxxxxxxxxxxxxxxx xxxxxxxxxxxxxxxxxxxxxxxxxxxx xxxxxxxxxxxxxxxxxxxxx** *You never know, you might see him before I do.*

Love Jack.

Tommy lay in the corridor of the train, rocked by its steady rhythm, he was content to drift between waking and sleep. It was one of those warm nights that late autumn occasionally throws up to confuse gardens and gardeners. The windows were open a notch on the leather strap and the smell of coal smoke drifted through the carriage. Almost out of his dreams, a woman apologised as she stepped over the stretcher. It was a young voice and he opened his eyes to look at her ankles and as much of her legs as he could see. The pain of moving tore a groan from his throat. He relaxed, he didn't need to see, she was sure to be pretty. It was enough to be able to understand all the voices which surrounded him.

'Is the poor man all right?' the woman asked nervously, 'I wouldn't normally disturb you, but you are right outside our compartment and blocking the corridor and I need to reach.... you know.'

'He'll do, probably.' The comrade from the Spanish Dependants Aid Committee had collected his little clutch of sick and lame in Perpignon about thirty hours ago. He hadn't slept much since and was too tired to be polite or informative.

Tommy heard the woman's high heels tap on the wooden floor a couple of time and then stop. There was a moment's hesitation and the woman asked in a fluttery, fearful voice. 'Are you really Communists? Are you the ones who were fighting in Spain?'

'Comrade,' the Aid worker's voice was loud, hard and brittle, but he was too exhausted to seriously battle with this latest class enemy. Was it worth pointing out that, by demanding first class travel, she denied all working men the comfort that was their due. 'Don't worry about us,' he growled, 'we've got our place on the floor so we've decided not to start the revolution until tomorrow. In any case, I'm sure the guard will sit with you if you feel in danger.'

'I didn't mean to.... I just.....I'm sorry. '

Tommy could hear the embarrassment in the girl's

voice and the hurried steps, which took her into the comforting privacy of the lavatory. 'I'll bet you're not married,' Tommy whispered hesitantly. 'You really have no idea how to handle women.'

'What d' you mean,' the man protested, surprised that the comrade was awake. 'I've been married twenty years. I've got four kids.'

'Then you've lost the knack mate. Wait till she comes back and I'll show you how it's done.'

The poor girl must have been wracked with embarrassment and lingered in the toilet far longer than nature could require, but eventually must have decided that she couldn't stay there for the rest of the journey to Victoria. The bolt on the lavatory door clicked open like a rifle being cocked. Tommy let out a long low groan which was only half put on and, opening his eyes, focused on the plump young girl with a mass of permed brown curls. Her face was frozen with white horror as she gazed at him. She looked as though she thought he was going to die.

'Excuse me miss,' Tommy said as firmly as he could, 'you wouldn't have a cigarette for a poor wounded soldier would you?'

'Er, no,' the poor girl stuttered, 'I'm afraid I don't smoke.' she hesitated. 'One of my friends does, I'm sure she'll have a cigarette. I'll get you one.'

'You're a gem miss,' Tommy whispered, 'a jewel. You couldn't get one for my mate too, could you? He didn't mean to be rude just now. We were bombed in Madrid and '. He closed his eyes as if shutting out a horrible vision, then opened them again and smiled. 'You know how it is.'

'Of course,' she said, 'I understand,' and scurried off.

'What do you mean telling her all that rubbish for. I've never been to Spain, you know that. And you was wounded on the Aragon not in Madrid.'

'And I was wounded in the arse, but I'm not going to tell her that. Gor blimey mate, haven't you worked it out yet, most of the people in this country have only just heard of Spain. She's never hear of the Aragon or Tortosa del Ebro. Anyway she feels better now that she thinks you're shell shocked rather than down right rude. What's your name?

'George, George Harvey, why comrade?'

'Come on George, I'm off duty and I'm too tired to be called Comrade, just call me....' Tommy let the words die away. After a pause he said, 'Don't worry George, we'll get our fags, trust me.'

Tommy heard the sound of a carriage door sliding open and the now familiar sound of the woman's heels clicking across the floor. 'I've found you some cigarettes, my friend had a new packet, Gold Leaf, I hope they're all right.'

'Miss,' Tommy whispered, 'if an angel had come down from heaven, she would have been carrying Gold Leaf. You couldn't have brought me anything better. You wouldn't care to light one for me, would you?'

'I'll try,' the young woman twittered, 'But I'm not very good at it.' She knew what was expected of her, at the cinema she'd seen Merle Oberon lighting cigarettes for wounded soldiers coming back from the First World War. After a couple of attempts she struck a match, lit the cigarette in her mouth and transferred it to the wounded man's. The pleasure that he gained, was disconcerting for her. His eyes, which had been flickering open, closed tight, he drew in the smoke and let it out with a sigh which was almost sexual. She blushed and involuntarily pulled at her skirt which had ridden up to her thigh as she crouched beside him. 'I'd better go,' she whispered.

Tommy couldn't move his arms. As he spluttered in an attempt to talk and keep her close, the cigarette fell out of his mouth and began to burn his neck. The girl gave a little shriek of horror and snatched it up.

'Don't worry,' Tommy said trying to calm and reassure her, 'it's all right miss, it's all right, it didn't hurt me, honest.' He paused, 'if you don't mind me asking miss, what's your name?'

'Emsley, Patricia Emsley,' she replied

Tommy coughed, 'Miss Emsley, Patricia, if I don't make it to Victoria, I just want you to know that you're the sweetest, kindest, prettiest girl I've ever met. I shall be happy that it is your face I shall carry with me to the grave.'

'Oh,' she wailed. she caught hold of his hand and held it tight against her breast. 'Don't say that, please don't say that. Don't die. I don't know how I could cope if you died.'

George Harvey reached across Tommy's body and prised his hands out of her grip. 'Leave him with me miss; I'll look after him and make sure he doesn't die. You get back to your friends; better that way.'

What did you do that for?' Tommy demanded furiously, after George had shepherded the girl back to her compartment. 'I was in there.'

'You bastard! You were frightening the kid to death.'

Tommy laughed, 'you're a good bloke George, but you don't understand women. And even you have to admit that she was an angel. And did you see what I saw. I could see right up her skirt, I could see stocking tops, George. I can't think of the last time I saw a woman in stockings.'

'I understand women better than you think. I've got a lass of just fifteen and I've seen blokes like you hanging around her already with their tongues out like barber's strops.

'From what I could see, I'll tell you that that one was a lot older than fifteen,' Tommy said with a chuckle, 'and she wasn't that scared.'

'And if she wasn't scared, she should have been.' George muttered, 'I sometimes think that all young lads should be lying in a ditch in Spain. You'd cause a lot less trouble.

'George, George, I'm a hero of the working class, I've been fighting the Fascist hordes. Uncle Joe wrote to us all and promised us our reward.'

'If that there was my girl,' George whispered 'I'd

smash your bloody teeth in, hero of the proletariat or not. I'm not good on theory, but you sound more like a bloody Trotskyist to me. Here, smoke your fag and hope it don't kill you before we get to Victoria.' George slipped the cigarette back between Tommy's lips. Content with the soft full flavour of an English cigarette, Tommy gave up trying to goad his protector and settled down to enjoy it.

'I saw your medical notes when the nurses put you onto the train, Bill.' George said, also made mellow by the expensive smoke, he normally rolled his own. 'They said that there was a chance you weren't going to make it and I should keep a close eye on you, but I think you're going to be OK. Is there going to be someone to meet you at the station?

Calling him 'Bill' brought Tommy back to the reality he had been hiding from. He was alive and out of Spain, but, as the gypsy had said Tommy Sutton was dead and buried among the willow trees on the banks of the river Ebro. For the first time he thought about who was going to be waiting for him at the station, Tom Sutton, Len Ackfield, the police?

Thinking about it was too much of an effort, and there was nothing he could do about it now. The episode with the girl had tired him beyond thinking, he would sleep and perhaps it would sort itself out.

What with the train being late into Dieppe, the delay in getting the wounded on and off the boat and the suspicion of the Customs officers and Special Branch at Newhaven, the boat train was running nearly an hour late as it steamed into Victoria Station and it was gone eleven o'clock at night.

The smoke and steam from the last train to somewhere or other, waiting to leave and a smoky little shunting engine, busy shifting carriages, had already shrouded the sparse yellow lights in fog when the Boat Train pulled in. The big express turned the inside of the station into a pea souper. The scattering of people waiting on the platform were enveloped in the incoming cloud and lost to view. Easing itself up to the buffers, the engine gave a final gasp of steam.

Before the train had stopped, carriage doors were slamming open. Day trippers to France, returning holidaymakers from the seaside and travellers to the coast began to spill out before the final squeal of the brakes brought it to rest. They rushed to try to make up lost time. The swirl of bodies, as much as the light breeze, stirred the smoke and sent it drifting away from the platform. A sparse crowd of still, silent, waiting people emerged like grey ghosts out of the mist.

The travellers all rushed towards the barrier searching for their tickets. The whining children, overtired after too long a day, were dragged down the platform, by parents at the end of their tether. The last drunken lads, winding their way home from a weekend of high adventure in Paris sang their way to the barrier, not noticing the anxious faced sentinels who stood like rocks along their path. The flurry of people lasted for a minute or two and then the platform was still. Towards the back of the train a small group of broken men and a few helpers began to crawl from their carriage.

'Excuse me,' Tom Sutton addressed a woman in a khaki shirt and corduroy trousers. 'Are you with the lads coming back from Spain?'

Her dark eyes, set deep in a tired, sunburnt face, looked at him and his companion suspiciously. The two middle aged men had the thin worried faces of people growing old in relentless toil, their long dark overcoats were well worn and their battered caps suggested that they were workers. But she was not totally convinced, she had done this trip so many times that she knew the sharks that swam in the wake of the International Brigade hunting for Communists or newspaper copy. She swept an imaginary wisp of hair from her face with the back of her hand and looked from Tom Sutton to Len Ackfield hovering apologetically, at his shoulder. He didn't look like a fascist and was too dirty to be a policeman though he might have been a journalist.

'I 'ad a letter,' Len stuttered. 'It said my boy was going to be on the Boat Train tonight. My neighbour bought me down on his motor bike.'

'What's his name?'

'Ackfield, Bill William Ackfield,'

Convinced, the woman looked at the list of names she had written on a scrunched up piece of paper. She was close to the end of her strength too, her hands were shaking and she was obviously finding it difficult to read in the smoky gloom of the station. 'Yes,' she said at last, 'He's one of the lads on a stretcher.' her hand waved towards a heap of people knotted up in the gloom further on down the platform.

They were not easy to make out as individuals, but slightly apart from the group was a man on crutches, trying to light a cigarette with his remaining hand. At his feet a man without legs sat hunched up in despair, his white bandaged head resting on his hands. 'Is he OK?' Len. demanded anxiously. He accepted that it was a stupid question. He'd been in France and men of his generation knew that soldiers on stretchers were never OK. If you could walk then you walked, if you'd got no legs, but were going to live then you sat on your stumps. What he wanted to know was if his son was going to live, but didn't know how to ask the question. It had always been the way with officers and nurses, they never understood the question, they spoke a different language and were too embarrassed by it all to try to explain to people like him and Tom.

This middle age nurse was no different, she wiped the haggard despair from her face and painted on a smile. 'Oh, yes,' she said, 'he'll been fine, I'm sure.'

'If I get a cab, can I take him home?'

The woman shook her head, in the weak light Len noticed that she was probably no more than thirty, but was quite grey. 'Sorry,' she said retreating into the defences of the medical profession, 'the doctor says that he's to go to the Middlesex Hospital for observation. We're waiting for the ambulances to come back and collected them.'

'Can I go with him?' Len asked anxiously.

'Oh, yes, I'm sure that will be all right. You can help carry the stretcher.' she hesitated for a minute and then looked at Tom. 'In fact,' she said,' We're really shorthanded here and you can both help. Your friend can make himself useful too, instead of standing about like a lump. Go down and see that woman standing by the porter's trolley. Her name's Mary and she'll find you a job to do.' Having dismissed Tom Sutton, she turned back to Len.

'Miss,' he protested, 'You shouldn't a spoke to him like that. He's got two boys in Spain. He heard a couple weeks ago that one of 'em's dead. It's bad enough when one of your mate's get it, but when it's one of your own, it's right hard.'

The nursed turned to watch the man walking away into the smoke. 'I'm sorry,' she muttered. 'I didn't know.' It seemed very inadequate, but she was too tired to do anything about it now. 'If you wait with your son, perhaps you can help carry him out to the ambulance. they won't let us bring them inside the barrier.'

Len. Ackfield knew there was something wrong before he even reached the man on the platform wrapped in a single red blanket. The body held itself wrong, it was too long, too dark. He felt the scream of pain turn his stomach and come out like vomit, it bounced amongst the girders of the roof echoing the whistle of a train departing from a distant platform.

The waiters in the night half turned away and looked at the man sideways, thinking that they understood his pain. Then busied themselves with little jobs so that they didn't crowd in on his grief.

Tommy woke with a jump from his troubled doze, the sound had become the shriek of Stukas falling out of the sky when there was nowhere to hide. He saw Len Ackfield standing over him, white faced and all the creases etched with coal dust. He looked like a drawing of a dead man.

'I'm sorry Mr. Ackfield,' he whispered. 'I'm very sorry.' He tried to sit up and, thank God, the pain in his leg took him away from all reality.

It was the jerky movement of the ambulance running over cobbles which brought Tommy round. He had a surge of panic in that split second when he woke and thought that he was driving and had fallen asleep at the wheel. He sat up with a cry and flung out his arms to grab the steering wheel and curse Miguel for not keeping him awake. Slowly he subsided onto his stretcher as the brilliant white of the inside of the ambulance flooded his mind. He closed his eyes, but could not blot out the sight of Len Ackfield sitting beside him with tears streaming down his cheeks.

'I'm sorry about this Mr. Ackfield,' Tommy said without opening his eyes again, 'I didn't plan this to happen, but it was the only way I could get out of Spain.'

'Is Bill?' Len nearly choked on his Adam's apple as he framed the word, 'dead?'

Tommy nodded his head slowly.

'Are you sure?'

Tommy nodded again and then to fill the abyss of silence said, 'yes, I'm sure.

We got shot up in the Aragon. I don't know where we are now, but that must have been the middle of March. I had met our Jack in a field near a place called Gandesa. I just bumped into him getting ready for a battle. He said that he'd had to leave Acky by the road a few miles back. He'd been shot in the leg and he couldn't carry him any further. I took my lorry and went and got him. We'd almost made it back to the river when the last patrol of Italian bombers, of the day came out of the sunset behind us. They began to shoot up the road. We left the lorry and ran for it, I dragged Acky into a ditch.

Bastard Itie, couldn't hit a barn. He missed the bloody camion by a mile and put his sodding bombs in the ditch. There were the best part of thirty blokes in that ditch. Most of them were dead or dying when some of Lister's men from the Fifth Regiment turned up.

The silence that followed was so heavy Tommy felt

it pressing down on his broken ribs. To break the silence, he asked quietly, 'have you told my dad?'

Len shook his head. 'Didn't get the chance, he was helping somewhere else down the platform. They're running the ambulances in a shuttle, taking the worse first, they wouldn't wait and I couldn't see him when we left.' He shook his head again. It was all too much for the suddenly old man and he didn't know what to do or say and he lapsed back into the long silence.

There wasn't much traffic about at that time of night and the ambulance driver built up a good speed through Hyde Park and up towards Marble Arch. In respect to the sleep of the rich and famous, he turned off his bell. In the relative quiet of the rocking vehicle, Tommy said, 'I didn't mean any of this Len, you must believe me. I tried my best to save Acky's life. It just didn't work out. He was cold and I put my jacket round him when I picked him up. It can get bloody cold there at night, even in March. It had all my papers in it. They must have thought he was me. We'd left his gear in the cab. They buried him thinking it was me. Took me to hospital thinking I was him. I was out of it for weeks. When I finally worked out what was happening, it was clear I wasn't going back to the war. They didn't want me in Spain anymore and they were sending me home. I know this is madness, but I thought it might just be a way of staying out of prison.'

'It was you in that robbery then?' Len asked.

Tommy said nothing. He fished in the breast pocket of his shirt for the packet of Gold Leaf he half remembered George Harper putting there. He pulled out a cigarette and put it in his mouth.

Taking the hint, Len Ackfield pulled out his lighter and thumbed it into flame. Having lit Tommy's cigarette, he blew out the flame. For a moment it seemed that he had forgotten what they were talking about and his mind had gone off at a tangent. Looking at the lighter nestling in the palm of his hand, he said 'Do you know I've had this lighter for more than twenty years. Your Dad's got one too. There was a bloke in our outfit who used to make them out of spent Vicker's cartridges and swap 'em for fags.'

Without Tommy offering, he helped himself to one of the Gold Leaf and lit it. He drew the smoke in with deep satisfaction. 'I killed a man once,' he said completely out of nowhere. There was a long, long pause. Tommy didn't speak. Len had his eyes closed. 'His name was McKay, Sergeant McKay. He was a bastard. Everybody hated him. We went over the top on the Somme and we got plastered. I was pinned down in shell hole about five yards from our own trench, my mate Billy Watson never even made it that far. I could see him hanging down over the trench wall and next to him Bloody McKay was laying about this young lad with the butt of his rifle trying to make him go forward. I was never going to get back into our trench if McKay was alive, so I shot him.

He was an unlucky bastard. I must have been the worst shot in our platoon and I blew his bloody head off.'

Tommy said nothing. When Len looked up to see his reaction, he saw that his eyes were shut too. The cigarette had fallen out of his mouth and was smouldering on the blanket under his head being used as a pillow. Len rubbed out the smoking fabric and stubbed out the Gold Leaf, putting the stub behind Tommy's ear for later.

'I know how it is lad, needs must.' He hadn't noticed that the ambulance had stopped and when the back door banged open, Len jumped as if he'd been shot. Two porters in white coats stood outside.

Come on mate, let's get you upstairs,' one of them said to the unconscious figure and then turning to Len, added, 'we'll look after him now, guvnor. Best thing for you is to come back in the morning.

Len nodded and jumped down on to the deserted and silent forcourt. As they pulled the stretcher out, Len touched the still figure lightly on the shoulder. 'Good luck, son,' he whispered and then, reaching into his pocket pulled out the lighter and shoved it into Tommy's shirt pocket. 'you'll be dying for a fag later.'

Chapter 26

Dear Jack,

Thank you for your letter. It is good to know that you are well now that you have returned from your travels. You cannot know how delighted I was to receive your post card, it is such a boost to our moral to know that we prisoners, languishing in foreign gaols are not forgotten. Even our milkman remembers us.

Life is hard here, but bearable and it has improved since the British Consul spared a little of his precious time to visit we poor unfortunates.

Rumours abound of release and repatriation. We believe some of our fellows have already left. Though we are told nothing, by our captors, I live in hope that I shall soon be home. Remember me to my family and friends.

Some prisoners receive packages from home via the auspices of the Red Cross. If you get the chance, you could try to send some little luxuries like soap, tobacco, food and anything to read. I'm sure my friends will want to send the earth, but it would be better if it were a few trifles sent by you.

I will write again, if I have the opportunity and you must do the same. Tell anyone who knows me, not to worry. Pray that I shall be with you soon.

Your affectionate friend

Michael

The Stukas were coming. Jack could hear the dull throb of the engines just beyond the mountain ridge. In terror he began to run. He ran as fast as he could, but the loose stones just slipped out from under his feet and he couldn't make any ground. He fell, scrabbling amongst the dust, struggling to pull himself forward and upwards, to run to safety. Looking back under his shoulder he saw that the fascists had already rounded up the prisoners on the road and now were begin to fan out across the hill side, to hunt down the fugitives.

Then the German aircraft crested the hill behind him and the explosion of noise beat him back to his knees. The scream of the dive-bombers made him want to cover his ears, but he needed his hands to pull himself up through the scrub.

Acky went down. He wouldn't get up. No matter how much Jack shouted at him, he wouldn't move. Jack wanted to help. He knew that if he didn't, Acky wouldn't make it, but he was certain that if he didn't reach the ridge he was going to die. In terror, he thrust himself back to his feet, threw away his rifle and began to run.

He heard the scream of first bomb, even worse than the sound of the bomber, which had launched it as it screamed down through the air. It crashed down beside him. It threw him into the air. His arms and legs thrashed wildly and as has he struggled in the clinging undergrowth, he could hear the scream of the second bomb coming.

And then the brilliant Spanish sun went out. It was dark, the clinging bushes had softened into blankets and he was lying on his back, half out of bed, where he had fallen.

He was awake, but the screaming went on, high pitched all around him. He scrabbled for his rifle.

'You were having a bad dream.' Miriam's frightened little voice came out of the darkness and drew back the veil of the night. He could now make her out sitting straight backed, silhouetted against the slightly lightly square of the curtains. Buried in her black shape he could see the white blob of her breast and the baby's face. It was the baby that was screaming.

'You frightened her.'

Jack struggled to his feet and then slumped back onto the edge of the bed. Rubbing his hand across his face he felt the sweat running down in cold rivers. He realised that his shirt, his whole body was soaked and the bed around was a battlefield. 'Sorry,' he whispered, 'a nightmare. Didn't mean to wake you.'

He watched the silhouetted head nod its understanding. 'I did not know it was to be such a bad one,' she said 'I would have taken her down stairs. She's a good baby, but she was frightened.'

It was his turn to nod his understanding. Miriam persuaded the baby back on to her breast. The screams were muffled into sobs, to snuffles, to silence. Minutes of the blessed calm followed only slightly ruffled by the soft sound of Miriam crying.

'Don't cry,' Jack said gruffly. He had never been able to cope with women crying. Now it reminded him of the silence after the bombing raids. A silence full of women crying for lost homes, lost children, lost men.

'It must have been very bad,' she whispered, saying anything in the fight to control her tears.

Not knowing what else to do, he walked to the window, drew back the curtain to look at the back garden in the iron grey of the earliest morning. 'Yes,' he muttered lowly,' it was very bad, very bad.'

Looking at the wrecked bed, Jack couldn't tell if she had slept in it as well, but he remembered that she hadn't been home when he finally went to bed the night before. 'Did I wake you too? He asked.

'No, no,' she protested. 'I was very late in. They cut the night buses. I had to wait for ages. You were very restless so I slept in the chair.'

'Did, you get much sleep?'

'I'm lucky,' she lied,' I don't need much sleep. I'll have a nap later.

The baby will sleep now. She is very good, she is really, it's just that you frightened her.' She repeated. Again the long, long silence and then, 'Your mother's been very kind, letting me stay here.' There was another pause, a long one. 'You won't send us away, will you?' Jack heard the quiet fear in her voice and he realised that she was living her nightmare. It had to be an awful lot worse than Stukas.

'No,' he said, 'if any one goes, it will be me.'

Miriam twisted her head away and scrunched up her eyes as if he had raised his fist. He didn't mean to hurt her, all he was trying to say was that he didn't know what was happening. He had only just got back from a year of war. How could he know?

For the first time since he entered the house, he reached out and touched her. Softly, on her neck, she winced and involuntarily drew her head away.

Too tired to do more, Jack stepped back from any argument. 'What do you call her?' he asked, indicating the baby.

'We call her Grace, Gracie. Your father says that she's got lungs like Gracie Fields and...' She stopped in mid-sentence. 'No,' she said, 'she has no name, it is only proper that her father should name her.'

'Grace is all right with me,' he said quietly. 'Grace is a nice name.'

As if to give his blessing along with a name, he touched her lightly on the cheek with the back of his finger. So soft, he thought.

The baby ignored him, content in her mother's arms, and he withdrew his hand.

'You can't really see them now,' he said quietly, leaving his hand hanging in space between them, 'but I had two cuts on my hand for ages where I smashed our Tom in the mouth for calling her a bastard.'

Miriam would have staggered at the word, as if he had hit her in the face if she had heard it, but she was asleep and heard nothing. Looking down in the quarter light, he saw an old woman, thin, lined, worn and ugly. He shook his head wearily. There were so many things to say, to do, to sort out. He should tell somebody that he sent Tommy to hell with broken teeth, that he didn't want a wife and child, that he didn't know what he was going to do, but he was too tired himself to do anything about it now. Though he was exhausted, he was too awake to try to sleep.

Taking a blanket from the bed, he folded it and draped it across Miriam's knees. Then he placed the pillow behind her head. The house was in complete silence. If he went downstairs, it would break the spell and bring the world to life. He didn't want that. He didn't want to have to think or to act. All he wanted was to hide up here in the dark until the world went away.

Standing at the window, he looked out into the darkness. Someone was already up in one of the houses over the back and the light from the scullery window was a star in the early morning mist. He had been born in this house and it was a view he had grown up with. It was not a jot different from the last time he looked out. He shook his head to try to clear his thoughts. That had been over a year ago. Now, this was the foreign land, no olive trees, no oranges, no clicking buzzing insects, no warmth, no one out there wanting to kill him, no brother, no friends, no love, nothing left to believe in.

Behind him in the deeper dark, the baby began to burble. She was bored and was trying to make up her mind whether to sleep or cry. She thought she would try crying to see what happened and gave a couple of half-hearted bleats.

The last time Jack had heard a baby cry was in Barcelona, in the burning house. It had been a long wail of terror, cut short. No one had come out of that house. He didn't think he could stand the noise of a baby crying, but if he went downstairs, the sound would only follow him and draw the family with it.

Tentatively, he picked the baby out of its mother's lose grasp. Miriam hardly stirred. Little Grace looked up at him, suspiciously, but stopped her cries. He was amazed. She was so tiny, so light, like one of his sister's dolls. But she was beautiful, with a round open face and even wider, brown eyes; eyes, like her mother.

She didn't smile at him, but there was no fear in those eyes. *Well, and what sort of man are you?* she wondered and, knowing that she couldn't believe anything he told her, yawned, shoved her fist into her mouth and went to sleep.

It was Jack who began to cry. Suddenly, he had to get out of that room. His body shook silently as he forced himself into his clothes. By the time he reached the top of the stairs, the tears streamed down his face and he was sobbing.

Grace stirred in his arms, but she was used to tears, her mother often cried. She was warm and dry, tightly held and not hungry. She snuggled down and continued to sleep.

Mr. and Mrs. Sutton had lain awake in the room next door since their son's nightmare had echoed through the house. When they heard him on the stairs, Aggie moved to get up. Tom's retraining hand held her back. 'Not yet,' he whispered, 'not yet.'

'But he needs me,' she pleaded and tried to rise.

His hand across her chest pinned her to their bed. He had come back from the trenches to a world at peace. He knew what it was like to be a stranger in a strange place.

Jack didn't know where he was going and without conscious remembrance, he passed through the scullery and out into the garden. The cold, damp air checked him. He paused to make himself a cigarette. It was only as he patted his pockets, he realised that he still had his daughter in his arms.

He couldn't face going back in the house and so tucked her under his jacket. Yesterday or the day before or the day before that he had still been in Spain. The CO had made them stand their watches to the very end, even the one's with walking sticks. Now, with a baby rather than a rifle, he rolled a cigarette one handedly and watched to see that no one came near. Instinctively, he turned his face into the corner so that the flare of his lighter couldn't be seen.

Up on the railway line, empty trucks bumped together

and clattered as a train strained against the signal, anxious to be on its way. It was too like the sound of machine gun fire for Jack and he pulled himself tighter against the wall.

Just awake enough to avoid being put on a charge when the officer did his rounds, Jack stood guard. He watched, but saw nothing. He was unaware of the extinguished cigarette or the darkest grey of early dawn lightening into dismal day.

It was the baby grunting and straining against the crook of his arm and the sudden smell as she filled her nappy that brought him back from the Aragon. A new form of fear gripped him. How to cope with a baby awake, in discomfort and working itself up to cry. He did something he had not done in a year. He abandoned his post and fled indoors. Miriam would have to wake up and deal with this.

His mother was standing at the head of the stairs, an apparition in a long white night dress and a hair net. She stopped him in mid bound with a single finger raised to her lips. Having stopped him, she wafted him silently back down and steered him into the kitchen. 'Your father will be up soon,' Aggie said. He's working now. He's got a nice little job with the Council at the depot. We'll let Miriam sleep in for a while. God knows, she doesn't often get the chance.

Turning her attention to her granddaughter, she chattered to her quietly, 'and we'll get you comfortable shall we my duck?' She stripped the dirty nappy off the baby and left her kicking on the kitchen table while she looked for a flannel.

Jack retreated to the scullery doorway to watch the chuckling scrap reaching for the ceiling. 'Who's a good girl then?' Aggie purred to little Gracie, seemingly ignoring her son, 'You're Granny's best girl aren't you? You're Mummy's best girl too. You sleep well, you feed well, you're no trouble.'

Grace gurgled her agreement

Aggie smiled, 'you're a happy little thing too. And she's going to need you to be, so you'll have to be good and don't you dare forget that your Granny and Granddad love you too, because you're our precious as well.'

When she finally pinned the clean nappy and straightened up, she glanced towards the scullery and saw that Jack had silently slipped away. 'You're going to need all the love you can get, my lovely. There's big trouble coming,' she whispered, planted a kiss on Grace's forehead.

It was mid-morning when Miriam came, dishevelled, into the kitchen. She protested that she shouldn't have been allowed to lie in bed for so long. There was so much to do. She talked to Aggie, but she was watching Jack from the corner of her eye.

Aggie replied that she needn't worry and that she deserved it and that she had a disturbed night and Gracie had been as good as gold. She had her back to Jack who was sitting at the table, but the stiffness of her back, showed that she too was anxious about what her son would say and do.'

'There's tea in the pot, if you want one,' Jack said quietly.

Miriam nodded over enthusiastically

'I'm sorry that I disturbed you.' He said.

Miriam waved her hand to dismiss any apology 'I'm sorry the baby woke you up. She doesn't usually wake up in the night except for her feed. It was just that your shouting frightened her. I'm sorry.'

Her plaintive words were fringed with tears. 'I wanted it to be so good when you came back. I wanted to be here to welcome you, but we didn't know when you were coming. And the band played a Barmitzvah last night. I had to go. I was the one who organised it and it paid well and we needed the money.'

'I'm sorry too.' He said 'but it wasn't important.' and with a quick glance at his mother to make sure that he didn't offend her, he reached out and touched Miriam's hand. 'I was thinking that I should go and see Acky in hospital tonight, if that all right.'

Miriam looked at Mrs Sutton with an expression of concern, but said nothing. Aggie snatched up some dirty washing and hurried it out into the scullery where he could hear her crying. Inside his head, he wrote Acky off. They didn't need to say, but it was certain he wasn't going to make it. He shrugged. What did it matter. It was just one more friend who had died. There really were too many to worry about. He cleared Acky out of his mind and went on to think of other things.

'I'm sorry about last night, it was a bad dream,' Jack explained, 'the worst I've ever had. There were some bad nights in Spain, but never like that. It was loads of things, all mixed up together. I suppose it must be something to do with being safe again, but it's a good job I had the dream. It made me remember things that I'd forgotten'

He didn't want to talk about the fighting and the pain. He didn't think she would understand. Why should she, he didn't really understand it himself, but he had to try to explain. 'I was at a place called Calaciette. We were ambushed by the Italians. Number One Company, my company, was at the front and we marched straight past the Italian column. We thought they were Russian tanks. Then all hell broke loose behind us and somebody shouted the order to scatter. I was running up the hillside at the side of the road, to escape. Acky was right behind me. Suddenly he swore like a gypsy and went sprawling. He'd been hit in the knee.

I stopped for an instant and looked back. Over my shoulder, I could see blokes from the Brigade being rounded up in the valley below. I pulled Acky to his feet and we made the cover of the trees.

All that was true, that was how it happened, but then my dream sucked in air raids, artillery barrages, burning buildings and death from all sorts of places. That's what made it a nightmare.'

It was Miriam's turn to reach out and touch his hand. 'You don't need to talk about it, if it hurts, but I know the place, or I know the name. It is where the men say that Moses was killed.'

Jack snatched his hand away 'Moses,' he croaked, aghast. 'Moses. I'd forgotten all about him. I'm sorry, I didn't know he was dead too.'

'It seems so long ago and so much has happened that I sometimes forget myself. At first he was just posted as missing, but as the weeks turned into months, there was no word about him. He's not turned up anywhere. We hoped he was a prisoner, but they say he isn't. Now we are told that he is dead. My friend says that my parents have taken it very badly. I was banned from the house when it was obvious that I was pregnant. You can understand it. That brought great shame on them. They really couldn't do anything else. Not without losing their standing at the synagogue. Your family have been very kind to me and Gracie.

Jack nodded abstractedly. For a moment he could look out from his own despair and could see another problem. He couldn't do anything about himself, but he had this picture in his mind, which would make things better for Miriam. 'It's odd,' he said. 'In that nightmare, I saw Moses, I remember. I was up on the hill. As I grabbed Acky by his collar, I looked down into the valley. I wanted to see where the Ities were, so I knew which way to run. It was only a glance, but I saw a lot of the lads standing in a huddle on the road with their hands in the air. You could see Moses in the middle of them. He's so tall that you couldn't miss him. He had his hands up too. He had surrendered. I know they shot a couple of the prisoners. I saw their names when I was up in Ripoll, but Moses's name wasn't there.' Jack held onto the vision and a certainty grew in him. 'Moses is a prisoner.' He said quietly, 'I'm sure of it.'

Miriam shook her head wearily. 'No,' she said, 'Sue and I have been to Lichfield Street two or three times, but there was no word about him. His name wasn't on any list. I even wrote to my MP. He told me that Moses was missing believed killed. Later Dependant's Aid told us that he was dead.' She began to cry again. 'I didn't know if you were alive. Moses was my only hope of getting back into my parent's home again. Despite all they said, my parents worshipped their first born, he would have had the fatted calf prepared on his returned and he would not have gone in without me.'

'I tell you, he's alive,' Jack said stubbornly. 'I saw him.'

Miriam wanted to say yes, she wanted to say yes to anything he said, but she couldn't in this. 'No, my love. It was a dream. He is dead like all the others, unless he escaped and is in hiding somewhere.'

Jack laughed bitterly. 'We're talking about your brother here. Moses couldn't escape out of a paper bag. He was a hopeless soldier. He couldn't hide behind a tree properly even when they were shooting at him.'

Miriam couldn't argue any more. She hugged the baby tight and rocked her gently.

'Don't worry,' Jack muttered, 'I'll get you back in to that house.' He picked up his walking stick. 'I have to go out.'

Miriam was crying openly now. 'I don't understand.' She said. 'I don't want you to go. I don't want you to leave me. It's been horrible here without you.'

'You can come with me if you want. I have to go and see your parents.'

Miriam's face hardened. 'They won't see me and I don't want to see them. They threw me out. If your mother hadn't taken me in, I don't know what I would have done. I don't ever want to see them again; we could have both finished up in the river for all they cared.'

Jack sighed; it was time to start putting things right. 'We have to go. I 'm sure your brother is still alive.'

'If they take me back, will you leave me there?' Miriam asked with a dead voice.

Jack said nothing, but in the scullery, Aggie did something she had not done since she was a little girl, she pulled her hands up into her face and prayed.

Jack knocked on the door. He heard slow footsteps in the dark hall beyond. The door opened and for a moment he saw Mr. Rabinovitz's moon face, but as soon as he was recognised it was slammed back in his face.

Jack knocked again. There was no reply, but he assaulted the silence by thumping on the door as hard as he could with his walking stick and then his fist. He hit it so hard that it shook in its frame.

'Go away,' a voice whispered from just behind the woodwork.

'No, I need to speak to you, Mr. Rabinovitz,' Jack replied.

'I have no need to speak to you. Go away or I will call the police.'

'You do need to speak to me, Mr. Rabinovitz, believe me. I can give you back your children.'

'I have no children. They are dead, all of them dead. Did you see the Chanakah lights burning in this house? No? No there is no reason to light the candles here. All we are left with are the bitter herbs. There is no one left to light the Chanukiah.'

'Mr. Rabinovitz,' Jack spoke with a cold calm, which said that he was going to be listened to and was not going to go away. 'None of your children are dead. Open the door and let me in and I will give them all back to you.'

'Liar,' Mr. Rabinovitz whispered, but there was a little rustle of words from further back in the house. The door opened a fraction and Jack could see the old man's eye at the crack. 'I know you. You are the Sutton's boy, the milkman, a curse on the day they first carried you up these steps. A curse on you and on your family.'

Jack allowed himself a half smile. He had told himself that whatever happened, whatever was said, he would not get angry, but the old man's words stung with their unfairness. 'Too late with your curses old man. It's already been spoken.' He lifted his walking stick as a sign, 'and I lost my brother in Spain.'

'Your brother and my son. You were there perhaps. Perhaps you are here to tell me how he died. Perhaps you bring me his dying words, a message for his mother. Perhaps you bring his things? The letter said that they were lost with his body on the battle field.'

'Mr. Rabinovitz, I don't think Moses is dead.' Jack persisted

'Oi Vie,' the old man moaned and his wife standing somewhere in the dark behind him echoed the wail. 'We have letters. They say he died in a place called Argon.'

'Aragon,' Jack echoed, 'yes, I know the place, I was there, but I saw him and he was alive.'

The door softly closed and the intense mutter of voices from the passage beyond. After minutes of debate, the door reopened a fraction. 'What do you want?' Mr. Rabinovitz asked.

'I want to come in,' Jack replied.

Mr. Rabinovitz looked past him, down the steps, to the pale figure standing on the pavement with a bundle in her arms. 'If you have brought her with you, I take it that you will not come in on your own?'

'No,' Jack agreed, 'I'll not leave them in the street.'

The door slid silently shut once more.

Miriam couldn't bear the waiting. She had to know if she was being brought back home, to be abandoned again. Knowing her parent as well as she did, she realised that they would not give in for their own sakes. Surreptitiously she slid her hand under Gracie's shawl and pinched her fat leg. The Baby gave a great yell, loud enough to make all the neighbour's curtains twitch.

'Israel, the neighbours,' came Mrs. Rabinovitz's low wail from the hall. 'Bring them in, bring them in and hide them in the cellar. Lord, can no more shame fall on this your house?'

The door opened and Mr. Rabinovicz used it as a shield against them. From the darkest depths of the hall where the stairs went down into the basement, Mrs. Rabinovitz spoke darkly. 'So Mister miracle man, give me back my son.'

'Have you got the list of the prisoners of war?' Jack asked.

'He is not there.' There was a bitterness in Mrs. Rabinovitz's voice that was quite foreign to the normally amiable woman. 'A million times have I read and a million and one times he is not there.'

Miriam shivered. It was a side of her mother, she had never seen before. Until this moment, she had believed that if she could get inside her parent's house, she could work on them until she was forgiven. This woman, with her voice like a cemetery wind, was not going to forgive the daughter without the return of her beloved son.

'The list,' Jack insisted. Mr. Rabinovitz fetched it from his desk and handed it to him. 'May I?' Jack asked, indicating the gas light on the wall.

The old man nodded his unwilling agreement. He did not want these people in his house, but if they were there, he did not want to look upon them.

Jack pulled the toggle so that the gas flame flared and the mantle burst into light. He read through the names and he knew most of them. He could put faces to names, but there was no Moses. 'I know he's alive,' he whispered, rubbing his face defensively. 'I saw him captured.' He read the list again and then again, even more slowly. On the last page, he let out a great sigh. 'Got you.'

'Let me see, let me see,' cried Miriam and she moved more quickly than either of her parents. Despite the encumbrance of the baby, she snatched the list from his hand and held it close to the light. 'Where, where?' she cried, her black eyes full of fear. 'They'll not have me back without him.'

Jack smiled. Somehow he felt more in control of the world than he had for almost a year. He allowed himself a gentle stroke of her hair. 'Look at the addresses on that page.

Miriam did as she were told, reading each in turn. Half way down the page she saw a Michael Walker of Abercrombie Buildings Cable Street. 'She stabbed it with her finger. 'That's where we took the rifle,' she said and, remembering her parents, instantly changed it to 'where we took the package.' She turned to her mother with a nervous smile. 'No-one lives there, Mama, they are workshops. We took a parcel there for Moses, once.'

Turning back to Jack, she caught his arm and shook him.

'So who is this Michael Walker?'

'There was no Michael Walker in the Battalion. It's Moses,' Jack laughed, 'It Moses, I'm sure. We always called him Michael in Spain. No one called him Moses.

'And Walker?'

Jack shrugged. 'I don't know, but you don't take a Jewish name into a fascist prison. Hookey Walker was our Quartermaster. It was probably the first name that came into his head.'

Mr. Rabinovitz shook his head not daring to believe. 'I will write to this Walker and we will see.'

Jack shook his head. 'That wouldn't be a good idea. If the Fascists found out that he was Jewish, it would put his life in danger. It would be better if I wrote.'

'So what is so wrong with his being Jewish,' Mrs. Rabinovitz demanded. 'Can't a father write to his son, even.'

Jack shot a searching glance at her husband.

He shrugged, 'What sort of question is that? Ask your Mother or your Uncle Rubin. God bless their memory. Let the goy write and we will put the world on hold.'

'So, while we wait, can I extend the common decencies to this baby. I'm sure I can find some Chicken broth in the kitchen. I would offer as much to a beggar.'

'She is no beggar,' Miriam snapped 'and neither is her mother. Her name is Grace, she is three months old and she drinks milk.'

Mrs Rabinovitz raised her eyes to heaven, *oi vei, Grace, what sort of name was that?* but she was not going to argue. 'Milk schmilk,' she commented. 'I'm sure I will find her something, even in a poor kitchen like mine.'

Miriam let her mother take the baby out of her arms and bustle it out of the room.

'Will she be all right?' Jack asked anxiously.

'Which?' Miriam asked, 'Gracie or my mother?' She smiled bitterly. 'They will both cry, but it will change nothing, if you cannot deliver the Prodigal Son.'

'And when I deliver him, what then?'

She looked at him intently, 'I don't know. I will be allowed back into the fold by the back door, I expect, if I want it.'

'Do you want it,' Jack asked quietly.

'Beggars can't be choosers,'

'You said it yourself, there are no beggars here. Don't play word games with me. This is important. Tell me what you want.'

Miriam drew herself up to her full five foot six and looked him squarely in the face. 'I want you. I've always wanted you, it's all I've ever wanted. I don't care what the terms are, I just want to be with you.' She laughed at her own daring effrontery, but she never let go with her eyes. She had just laid her soul bare on the Persian carpet before him knowing that he might easily trample on it.

'Are you sure,' Jack demanded. 'I've got no prospects, no nothing.'

Miriam began to cry, but the tears trickled down past a smile. 'Jack Sutton,' she whispered, 'you are such a fool. You do not understand how much I love you. I don't want anything else. I don't expect you to marry me. Just put me in your pocket and take me with you.'

There was an explosion of bombazine as Mrs Rabinovitz burst back into the room. 'What foolishness is this,' she shouted. 'Of course he must marry you. So he's no great catch, I could have asked for a nice Yiddisher boy, God I do not ask for much, I would have settled for a not very nice Yiddisher boy.' With her free hand she grabbed her daughter by the shoulders and shook her. 'This is not the time to be choosy. Remember you are no great catch either, even though your father has his own business. This is the best we're going to get. Be grateful woman, at least he produces pretty children.'

The big grandfather clock, which stood in the hall, chimed the hour. Miriam took a deep breath, then took her baby from her mother's arm. 'We have to go,' she said.

'Go?' Mrs Rabinovitz demanded. 'Go? What is this go? You have only just come, so why are you talking about going already?'

'Mama, remember me. I am the waif, the stray, I have no one. I have rent to pay, food to buy. Do you think that this is the Promised Land and there is Manna from heaven? I have to go to work'

'What is this no-one? You have re found your family, we will not let you or the little one starve.'

Miriam smiled and met her mother's eyes with a look which said that she had, until this moment. 'No,' she said. 'I must get Gracie settled before I go out. I have piano lessons to give. It does not do to be late.' Without waiting to see the result of her speech she opened the front door and left.

The old lady raced after her. 'When will I see you again?' she demanded. To hell with the neighbours.

'I may come tomorrow, if I have time,' she replied. Jack followed her out into the gathering gloom of the evening. She had just reached the pavement when her father pushed past her mother's bulk to stand on the steps above. 'Mimi.' He called plaintively and his hand delved in his pocket.'

'Don't you dare try to give me money,' she said angrily.

Mr Rabinovitz had his house keys in his hand. He threw them down to Jack. 'You and my daughter are welcome in my house at any time you can make it.'

Chapter 27

CONDOLENCES CARD

Dear Mr and Mrs Sutton

Having only just heard the news, I would like to offer my deepest condolences on the death of your son. No one can know how sad it made me to hear the awful news. I apologise for the delay in writing to you, but I have had not been in touch with Tom or any of our mutual acquaintances for some time. I had no sure word of him until I read the tragic obituary in the Herald.

Yours sincerely
Katherine Hartwell

It was gone midnight when Len Ackfield walked out of Seven Sisters Station. It was a clear, bright night, mild for the time of year and almost quiet. The few people left about were wandering idly home, enjoying the reprieve from the usual winter's blast. Len walked as slowly, but he had no idea what the weather was, nor where he was going or what he was going to do.

Somehow he found himself on his own front path, at his own front door with the key in his hand. The street was quiet, but his house was silent, it was black and empty, totally uninviting. He didn't want to go in. He knew that on the kitchen table were all the mementoes of his son's life, his first shoe, photographs, school reports waiting for them to laugh at together.

Looking around, he saw the faint light through the glass panel in the Sutton's hall door. They were obviously still up. He could imagine them sitting, in wretched silence, in the back kitchen, mourning the death of their son.

There was a soft chattering of the knocker on the front door as if the caller didn't really want anyone to hear them. In the silence, both Aggie and Tom heard the noise and exchanged despairing glances. They didn't want to talk to anyone, not even each other. Bill Ackfield's return had brought back all the memories of their Tom. The soldiers who arrived that night were the last apart from the prisoners and there were no more coming back. It was the last tattered threat of hope breaking which took their hearts with it.

With a deep sigh Tom pulled himself out of his chair. If one of their neighbours was knocking at this hour, it had to be important and had to be dealt with.

He opened the door and saw a figure standing in the gloom half way down the path. It took him a moment or two to recognise Len Ackfield. He looked strangely pale in the poor light, ghost like. 'Len,' he said when he recognised his friend. 'You back from the hospital?' He was slightly surprised, remembering how he'd left him, Old Tom hadn't expected to see Len again that night. 'How's Bill?' he asked. It sounded totally (?), but he couldn't think what else to say.

'He's dead,' Len gulped out.

Tom staggered back a pace as if he'd been hit. 'Oh, no,' he groaned. 'Not you too.' Now it was easy. He lunged forward and caught Len around his shoulders and pulled him closed, letting him in on his own grief. 'Come through into the kitchen, Aggie's just making a pot of tea.'

'It's Len,' Tom Sutton said walking ahead of him into the kitchen and announcing what he'd been told. Trying to avoid the pain of his old friend telling the news again. 'He's just back from the hospital. Bill didn't make it.'

Aggie turned her red rimmed eyes towards him and smiled a thin smile of understanding.

'He's been dead for months,' Len whispered in an emotionless monotone.

'What?' Tom demanded, thinking that he hadn't heard right.

'It wasn't my Bill that came back tonight,' Len muttered.

'No,' Tom protested. That wasn't fair, it wasn't right, but he knew the cock ups that armies could make. He'd been posted missing himself once when he'd been on leave in Paris. 'Who was the bloke at the station then? Some poor sod whose people don't know he's home?'

'It's your Tommy.'

The old brown teapot hit the floor a second before Aggie who fell in a dead faint.

***

It was dark when Jack and Miriam finally got back to Wilmott Street. The baby was now griping. She was wet and hungry. She wanted to have done with the day and go to bed. Miriam felt very much the same, she had had enough of worrying and being on her best behaviour

Jack didn't try to persuade her not too, but he was restless. He couldn't settle. He felt that everyone was on edge. They seemed to spend all evening walking on egg shells, bursting with feelings. Wanting to scream, but all the time being nice to each other. They leant over backwards to be considerate, but spent the whole time avoiding each other's eye and admitting how they felt.

Jack felt so out of touch with the world that he would almost rather have been under the blazing sun with Stukas falling out of the sky. He paced from the scullery to the front door and back again. He opened books but could not read, opened cupboards and did not want to eat or drink 'Have you got enough milk for the baby,' he asked. 'I could easy wander up to the depot and get a couple of pints.'

'No, no,' his mother protested. 'You stay in with us. You could do with an early night as well. We've got plenty of milk. They obviously thought a lot of you at the yard, because they normally drop a couple of pints in during the week, sometimes a bit of butter or cheese. You should go down the yard when Mr O'Halaran is about, he's manager now. I'm sure he'd give you your old job back.'

'Yeh, yeh,' Jack muttered in a voice that meant that he probably wouldn't. After a few minutes more pacing, he said, 'I think I'll go up to town and see Acky in the hospital. I've been putting it off, but its something I ought to do. After all, due to me...' The sentence drifted off into guilty silence.

Jack felt the tense atmosphere suddenly tighten. His mother was behind him, but he knew she stiffened and that her silence was her choking on a scream. He looked for his father's eyes. They were going past him and were full of pity at the sight behind him.

'Jack,' he said in a voice hoarse with emotion. Then, not able to face the confrontation, reached for his tobacco jar on the mantelpiece. 'I need to have a word.'

'Later, Dad. When I get back, eh?' Which was Jack saying 'no'. He couldn't face anymore hassle. He only really wanted to get out of the house and away from them all.

Tom banged his empty pipe against the hearth, took a pinch of Old Holborn and stuffed it into the bowl. Without looking at his son, he said 'No lad, it needs to be now. In the garden, eh?'

It was funny how the garden had always been a sort of neutral territory. Whenever there was a telling off for someone or bad news to be given, it was always in the garden. And it was always his father who did it, but there never was any question who had pointed the finger.

Jack knew that none of this was his father's fault and it was probable that he had been put up to it by his mother, but the thought that he was going to get a lecture on the benefits of Socialism over Communism was too much. He didn't need to be reminded that the family were against him going to Spain and that they were right because it had all ended in tears and that it was all his fault.

Out in the crystal darkness, Jack struck first. 'Dad' he said, 'a lot of water has passed under the bridge since we last stood out here. It's probably not occurred to you, but not only am I the eldest son, but I'm also a grown man. I don't need you telling me what it was like on the Somme. I've been there, I've seen it. And, unlike you, I was on the losing side.'

Tom said nothing. That old briar pipe was both a sword and a shield for the old man. When he was angry, he would wave it around or poke the stem hard into your chest to make sure that you hadn't missed the point he was making. Now it was a defence to hide behind for a minute while he worked out what to say. He just puffed and puffed at trying to light it securely. His dark eyes were visible through the night and they were fixed on Jack. 'I said a lot of hard things before you went. I take them back.'

Jack snorted, he was not going to be bought off having a row as easy as that. 'Yes you did. And it cost us a lot of blood to show people like you, what was what.'

The old man nodded and side stepped the argument. 'A lot has changed here too, while you've been gone. The Shaunessy's have gone back to Ireland, Old Mrs Grimble died and there was a fire a number twenty-two and its empty now. I'm working. I've got a job as maintenance man for Edmonton Council. It's not exciting, but it's regular and reasonably paid.'

'Wow, m'dad working,' Jack sneered, 'I'm surprised that didn't make the papers in Spain.'

Tom didn't seem to hear. 'We heard about your lot,' he said. 'About the British Battalion being pulled out of the line and that you were all coming home. All that were still alive. About ten days before you came back, Len had a letter saying that Bill was in a small group of badly wounded were coming into Victoria. I went down there with him and got roped in carry one of the wounded blokes to an ambulance. I never saw Len after we split up on the platform, but he came back here later that night. He told us that Bill was dead. Had been for months. Then he told us that it was our Tommy who had come home on the train. It seems that Bill had Tommy's jacket on when they were bombed. Most of them in the lorry were dead, those that weren't were dying or badly injured. They were just putting names to corpses. Tom got one of the names that was left over.'

Jack was astounded. His dad couldn't be saying what it sounded like. He'd known for months that Tommy was dead. He'd been with people who knew, who had been saying 'sorry about your brother'. 'I don't understand,' he muttered.

'Tommy's alive.'

'I don't believe it.'

Old Tom put his hand on his son's shoulder. 'He's alive, but it's good that you don't believe me.' He said, 'and you're right. That's the way it's got to be. As far as the world is concerned, Tommy is dead. He's lying quietly in a Spanish field somewhere. And Acky is home, badly hurt, but home.

'I don't understand.' Jack muttered again and then corrected himself. 'I do understand.' So many things were falling into place that he was now only surprised that he hadn't expected it. 'What I don't understand is how you think you,…we…can get away with it.'

'Len is a good old stick and he's got no one left, he'll go along with it. What has he got to lose apart from doing a few years inside for aiding and abetting a fugitive. He said that Tommy can stay at his place as long as he needs.'

'He can't come back to Wilmot Street,' Jack protested, 'everybody knows him here. He'll be arrested as soon as he puts his face outside the door.'

Old Tom shrugged. 'we can't think of anything else. This will have to do until we can. It'll be weeks before he leaves hospital, months before he can walk.'

'Your mad,' Jack muttered, shaking his head as if to clear it from a muddle of thoughts. 'You're all mad. You can't try and pass our Tom off as Acky and think no one will notice. For one thing, he's nearly a foot taller; he's probably two stone lighter; his hair's a different colour and Acky wears….wore glasses.'

His father puffed reflectively on his pipe for a while, assessing what Jack had said and then said. 'You may be right, but from what Len says, he doesn't look like his Bill, but he doesn't look like our Tommy either. He's had one of his legs smashed, that, and the way he stoops when he drags himself off to the lavatory, makes him look a lot shorter. He's as skinny as a rake. There's no way he could lift a beer cask now.' He hesitated and then added 'or a sack of coal. His hair's grey and we can always get him some glasses. He lost the others in Spain after all. None of the police have seen either of them. He'll be all right for a while unless someone down the street talks.'

Jack shook his head in despair and tried to think of a saner alternative. 'Couldn't he go and stay with Auntie Alice. Apart from the family, nobody would know him there?'

And why would your Auntie Alice give Acky a home. She's only ever met him two or three times.'

'Who would know?' Jack demanded.

'You'd be surprised, lad. Something else that didn't make the newspapers in Spain. The police picked up one of the gang who robbed the jewellers in Hatton Garden. One was a bloke called Wally Cook. They found him living rough on one of the derelict barges on the Cut a couple of weeks after you went to Spain. He came from Edmonton, Lorenko Road. I'd never heard him, but some people up the Gillespie knew of him.

'Yes, I knew a Wally Cook; vaguely.' Jack murmured, 'Lived next to a family who were in the Party,' Jack said. 'Mean little man, but hard as nails. There are a lot of them like that in Little Russia.'

'Well, your Wally Cook wasn't so hard. They say that the police lent on him. Said that they thought that he fired the gun. They threatened to charge him with attempted murder. That scared him, he turned King's evidence and sang like a bird as they say on the pictures. He named the rest of the gang, including our Tommy, and told them all he knew. He said that the leader of the gang was a bloke called Chalky White. It seems that he came from Liverpool and the police up there found him, a few months back. He's got form as long as your arm, breaking and entering, robbery, demanding money with menaces, grievous bodily harm. He worked for Reggie Green from time to time. Now he's doing thirty years' hard labour on Dartmoor for armed robbery while Cook's doing ten in Parkhurst.' Tom snorted at the thought and then added. 'At least Cook's doing it in solitary. He can't mix with the other prisoners He's been knifed once and he's been thrown down the stairs'.

Jack had to laugh at his father's easy use of criminal slang. 'You know a lot about what's going on.'

'Yes,' he said grimly, 'I've spent a lot of time helping the police with their enquiries. Your mother, your sister, we've all been taken in for questioning and I was held overnight. Everybody down the streets been questioned. They even took Mrs Botterell and Loopy in for a while. They were not gentle, I can tell you, but everybody down the street said they knew nothing.

We said we didn't know what he'd done or where he was. When they asked about you, we told them that you and Bill had gone to Spain. We didn't think it would do any harm. I think they must have carried out some enquiries and found out that's where Tommy was too. It seems that there was no extradition treaty with Republican Spain.

When the notification came through of his death. I took the letter into the police station down the High Road. I thought it might stop them bothering your mother. They didn't seem surprised. They admitted that was where they thought he was. They really didn't seem that bothered, Tommy was just the driver. They closed the file on him while I was there. We've not been bothered since.

They're still looking for George Harris though. When I went down to the station with the letter from the Dependant's Aid Organisation, I was in a bit of a state. Tommy having been killed and everything. One of the inspectors spoke to me as I was leaving. I knew him slightly; his eldest brother had been in the Diehards with me in the war. He said he was sorry about our Tommy. Even though he was a villain, it was a shame it had to end like that and I could be proud of him. He said that he hoped you made it all right. He also said that if I heard anything about George, I should say. He was in no doubt that George fired the gun. He said that he was an evil bastard, a maniac and if he wasn't caught, he was going to kill somebody. He didn't want it to be one of his lads.'

'My, God, what a ... a...mess.' He was trying to swear, but found that he couldn't in front of his father. He knew the old man wouldn't box his ears now, but he still couldn't do it. 'Whichever way you look at it, it's loss, defeat and ruin. We'd all be better off dead.

Old Tom puffed at his pipe for a minute and then said quietly, 'Just because you lost a war, doesn't mean you were wrong, you were just fighting someone bigger than you. Just like when you fought the Blackshirts, up Stamford Hill. As I see it, you've come out this better than most of them. You've come up smelling of roses. Minor wounds, good wife, pretty daughter, rich father in law, the world's at your feet if you want it.'

Jack said nothing.

'On the other hand,' his dad continued. 'Learn from your mistakes lad. A year ago, you told me there was another war coming and I said, *rubbish*. I believe you now. You're a trained soldier; you'll be fit again and without a major injury when it comes. If you're not careful, you'll be called up right at the very beginning and find yourself fighting Germans this time and they are hard buggers. In my experience, the first ones in were the ones that get killed first.' He put his hand on his son's shoulder and shook him like he had when Jack was a boy and his father wanted to make sure he was listening. 'Take my advice for once, don't go back to the milk round and don't let Miriam's dad talk you into taking a job in his factory. The world runs quite sweetly without milk being delivered and new trousers in wartime. Get yourself a reserved occupation. Sign up for one of these new government training schemes for lathe operators. A job making the guns is what you want; let someone else shoot them. That should keep you safe.'

Jack laughed and gave his father a play punch in the chest. 'Well, I must be getting old. I'll think about what you say.'

Still laughing, he pulled the crumpled old black beret out of his pocket. He put it on and pulled the front down like a cap. With a mock salute, he limped off down the garden path. He stopped at the gate. He was in the real world again. Looking up and down the street, he had no idea which way he was going. The scene was so familiar; if he closed his eyes there wasn't a smell he didn't recognise or a sound he couldn't identify. Opening them again, everything was exactly the same as the night he slipped away, except that he didn't feel that he belonged there anymore.

His gate was in shadow, half way between two lamp posts, but up the road, on the other side, there was a lamp post outside the Botterell's house. During the day the kids had tied a rope to the ladder bar fixed an old chair leg and the other end, so by running like crazy and then leaping astride it was converted into a chair-o-plane and they could fly like at the fairground. Now it was dark and they had gone for their tea, Loopy Lou had scampered down his path, to try. He was heavier, uncoordinated and less brave than any of them, but he skipped and jumped and occasionally made a low semi-circle around the iron post.

There were more people down the station end of Wilmott Street and so he planned to sidle past Loopy Lou on his side of the road. He was so intense in his play, that he might not see him. Jack wanted a cigarette, but it would wait.

Loopy saw him almost immediately he stepped through the gate. Almost on hands and knees he disentangled himself from the rope and waddled across to Jack's side.

He glanced nervously back to his own front door; he wasn't supposed to cross the road, but his mother wasn't looking. 'Jack, Jack, Jack,' he beamed and clapped his hands in joy. 'Mother told me you were back.' Safe on the pavement, he stopped and looked hard. 'It is you Jack, isn't it?' His moon face crumpled into a frown. 'You look very…' he didn't have the word he needed and tried again. 'You look very not like Jack.'

'It's all right Louis, it is me.' He moved further into the lamp light to reassure him. Looking down at himself, he realised why Loopy had got so confused. He looked so different from the boy of a year ago. He was thin, his mahogany brown short hair was bleached by the sun. And in looking, he realised that he was still in uniform, or what passed for a uniform in the Brigada Inglese. Worn espadrilles, bald, stained corduroy trousers and a brown cotton shirt, no wonder he was so cold. Even in Spain doing night guard at this time of year, he had worn a great coat.

'Mother told me that Tommy wasn't coming back and Acky was badly hurt. She was very sad. She cried. She does not cry a lot. She says that you are very brave. She says that I have to be brave. She says that there will be fighting here. I'm going to be a soldier. Can I be a soldier with you?'

Jack looked at the Mongol boy. *Why not?* he thought; he remembered the five boys he's left at the bottom of Hill 481. He was sure if Loopy had stepped up to the mark the sergeant at Figueras would have shouted Infantera and given him a gun. Sadly, he admitted, 'not with me Louis, not with me. I'm finished; I've had all the fighting knocked out of me.'

Tears welled up in Loopy's eyes. 'I shall have to be a soldier on my own them. I have to look after Mother. She says that the Germans don't like people like her. She says that they don't like people like me either. I'm not very clever and I can't run. Can I have your gun? I will look after you as well as Mother and me.'

'I don't have a gun anymore. I had to leave it in a heap in the town square, like rubbish.' Again he laughed, it had been rubbish, inferior Soviet Russian rubbish, but he had loved that gun. As the Welshman had said, it was his friend and he had just abandoned it.

Loopy was becoming increasingly agitated; he moved restlessly from one foot to the other. 'What am I going to do Jack? I can't be a soldier without a gun and a uniform. How will I keep mother and me safe? Who will look after you? Who will look after your lady? Who will look after little Gracie? She is very pretty. She held my finger and smiled. I'll need a uniform. Can I have your uniform Jack?'

If he could, Jack would have given it to Louis, but they were the only clothes he had now that would fit him. Reluctantly, he took off his hat, shook, stroked it and placed it on Loopy's head. 'That' all the uniform I have left and that wasn't mine.' It was ridiculously small above the cherubic face, it looked like a yarmulke. He smiled, but wasn't sure that Paddy would have understood and approved.

'I have a better idea,' he said and took the beret back. He reached in his pocket and pulled out his lighter. 'A soldier has to learn many things,' he said. 'You will have to learn to smoke cigarettes, because soldiers all smoke.' He put the lighter in Loopy's podgy hand. 'and this will be your friend. It will bring you comfort, bring you light and keep you warm. Keep it safe. You can give it back when you finish being a soldier.'

With a chortle of joy, Loopy rushed off to show his mother. Jack replaced the beret on his head, but this time he wore it as Paddy had, raised at the front with the brass flashes showing.

Jack turned back towards home and walking past Loopy's lamp post, took the chair leg and flung it as hard as he could. It flew away and round and round and round, tying itself in a tight snake against green fluted iron post until the wood clanged against the base. He didn't stop to watch it slowly unwind. He had things to do, people to see; a wife and daughter to get and to get to know.

'God bless the gypsy,' he told himself. None of this was her fault; it hadn't been a curse, she was only telling it as it was going to be. Only one last thing to get it done and finished.

With a straight back and a sharp step, he marched back up the street and began singing,

> Viva la Quince Brigada,
> rumba la rumba la rumba la.
> Viva la Quince Brigada,
> rumba la rumba la rumba la
> Ay Carmela! Ay Carmela!